Praise for National Bestselling Author L.A. Chandlar's

Art Deco Mystery series

"Engaging, vivid, and intriguing, this historical mystery is
not only a fascinating behind-the-scenes of Fiorello La Guardia's
New York, but an action-packed adventure with quirky
characters, snappy dialogue, a hint of romance—and starring
one of the pluckiest, most entertaining heroines ever."
—Hank Phillippi Ryan, national bestselling author of *Trust Me*, on
The Gold Pawn

"Chandlar does a good job of evoking the period."
—*Publishers Weekly* on *The Silver Gun*

"*The Silver Gun* has humor, excitement, mystery, danger, romance,
lots of great characters, and more! I highly recommend *The Silver
Gun*, especially to those who live, work, or vacation in the
Big Apple, and to cozy readers who like their mystery mixed
with history." —*Jane Reads*, 5 stars

"[*The Silver Gun*] was just phenomenal . . . I absolutely loved
this book and HIGHLY recommend it to anyone who is a
mystery lover." —*Valerie's Musings*, 5 stars

Also by L. A. Chandlar

The Silver Gun

Published by Kensington Publishing Corporation

THE GOLD PAWN

L.A. CHANDLAR

KENSINGTON BOOKS
www.kensingtonbooks.com

KENSINGTON BOOKS are published by

Kensington Publishing Corp.
119 West 40th Street
New York, NY 10018

All Kensington titles, imprints, and distributed lines are available at special quantity discounts for bulk purchases for sales promotion, premiums, fund-raising, educational, or institutional use.

Special book excerpts or customized printings can also be created to fit specific needs. For details, write or phone the office of the Kensington Sales Manager: Kensington Publishing Corp., 119 West 40th Street, New York, NY 10018. Attn. Sales Department. Phone: 1-800-221-2647.

Kensington and the K logo Reg. U.S. Pat. & TM Off.

eISBN-13: 978-1-4967-1344-5
eISBN-10: 1-4967-1344-3
First Kensington Electronic Edition: October 2018

ISBN-13: 978-1-4967-1343-8
ISBN-10: 1-4967-1343-5
First Kensington Trade Paperback Printing: October 2018

10 9 8 7 6 5 4 3 2 1

Printed in the United States of America

To Jack and Logan
My inspiration to live, laugh, and love well

"This, as I take it, was because all human beings, as we meet them, are commingled out of good and evil . . ."

The cloaked figure waited in the thick, dank fog rolling in from the river. Halos of light circled the streetlamps. The cold was clutching, reaching through to the bones. The figure grasped the silver gun, feeling its strength, its purpose almost pulsating through the fingers.

The timing was right. It was just like that moment of destiny when the gun fell from the Queensboro Bridge. Two items. One in each hand. Both meant death. But to the holder, they meant victory. More than that, though. They meant a future. They meant ruling the dynasty. *His* dynasty.

Up ahead, a primal scream tore through the air. A snarl of a smile stretched across the face hidden in the dark hood. A door slammed.

A man came stumbling out of a staunch, old building. A small piece of paper fell from his fingertips, alighting on the ground like a delicate butterfly.

The man looked up and spotted the hooded figure. Instead of seeming afraid of the strange apparition coming toward him through the fog, he looked like the sight strengthened him. He straightened up, gathered himself, and slowly sauntered over. His confidence, which had been eclipsed by whatever that little piece of paper held, slowly returned to him with every step.

The silver gun came out of the folds of the cloak and fired, seemingly of its own volition. It had a purpose to fulfill, after all. The man's face registered genuine surprise, then, finally, a ripple of fear trekked its way across his arrogant features. The shot fell him to his knees, and then he slowly sank to the ground.

The shadowy vision crept over, whispered a few choice words, then emptied the gun into him. At last, the final piece. It always was a hell of a calling card. The gold pawn was placed with reverent care, right on top of the blood-soaked chest.

As the cloaked figure crept back into Manhattan, an eerie whistle wound through the air as the fog closed in like the curtain at the end of a play.

CHAPTER 1

The images twirled and flashed like they always did. Red mittens, a blue scarf, my laughing parents. This time the dream skipped over the detailed parts that were the most fear-filled, as if my subconscious had much work to do and needed to get down to business.

I strolled along the front yard of my childhood home. The petunias, the little fountain, my purple maple tree . . . filled me with an old and familiar sadness. I walked in the front door and the stairs leading up to my father's library were before me. I touched the railing, caressing its smooth, cool banister as I stepped up and up. Leading to what? I opened the door to my father's personal sanctuary. Thousands of books lined the shelves, the dark green walls and oak furniture radiated masculine comfort. My eyes shifted to a wall safe, my hand clutched a cold key, and I slowly drew near. I wanted to reach out and stop my own hand, but I couldn't. It was imperative that I open it.

I reached for the handle, turned the key, and within were three things: the lethal silver gun with the red scroll on the handle, a gold chess piece, and lastly . . . I jumped back, surprised at what I was seeing and more than a little nervous. I gathered myself to take a closer look. It was a photograph of a ghostly gray hand languidly pointing to the right.

My eyes fluttered open, my heart thumping in my chest. The curtains slightly ruffled from a soft morning breeze, making little hushes against the windowpane. My eyes ran over the pleasing, smoky blue walls of my room, the comfy white and blue down quilt over my bed, the white chair in the corner by the window, the dark brown dresser with the glass knobs . . . and Ripley. I started abruptly as his earnest furry face was only a few inches from my own, staring at me with his very concerned and furrowed German shepherd brow. His hot breath puffed indignantly into my face. Not exactly a pleasing scent to wake up to.

I laughed, "Hey, boy! What are you doing up here so early?"

He muttered a deep, "Roaw." Suddenly I heard a bellowing human storm coming from downstairs and I knew why Ripley had come up here. I was late for work, damn it! And you can't keep the mayor of New York City waiting. Especially if that mayor happens to be Fiorello La Guardia, close family friend, boss, and world renowned bellower.

I bounded out of bed, threw on my favorite deep blue-green dress suit with three-quarter-length sleeves, brushed my dark brown hair, and pinned into place a pillbox hat. I brushed on some mascara and eyeliner, and threw on a coat of light pink lipstick.

I raced down the stairs in record time, smelling the heavenly aroma of breakfast. Scrambled eggs, bacon, biscuits, and steaming hot black tea.

"Good morning, Fio!" I said as I sailed past him to my breakfast plate. He ate as fast as he did everything else—faster than the Duesenberg J with its 320 horsepower and cranberry red paint job. Fio never gave me much time before we headed to work, so I followed suit and ate quickly.

"Good morning, Laney Lane, my girl!"

"Grrrrrr," I replied. This was our customary morning ritual. And I went by Lane. Just Lane. He knew that.

Aunt Evelyn greeted me with an amused smile. "Good morning, dear. Sleep well?"

"Mm . . ." I said uncertainly. "Pretty well. Had another dream. Can't quite figure out what it means yet."

Mr. Kirkland entered the dining room. His tall, slightly stooped frame with craggy good looks reminded me of a deep-sea fisherman yet he incongruously laid a fresh plate of homemade biscuits down at the table. He'd been Aunt Evelyn's close friend for years. But well before I came to live with her thirteen years ago after my parents died, he had been established as her housekeeper and butler. He was the antithesis of a butler. He was swarthy and was a casual sort of man versus a stiff and polished servant. But it worked for them. I smiled up at his deeply lined face with the halo of gray, longish hair.

I occasionally amused myself as I inquired about the possibility of deeper emotions between Evelyn and Kirkland and then would sit back to enjoy the great show of colors play out on one or both of their blushing faces as they avoided my questions.

I hadn't been listening to anyone as I thoroughly enjoyed my breakfast, but suddenly got the feeling I should have been paying attention. I sensed a certain tension in the air. As Fio paused to take a quick breath, I broke into the discussion with my usual subtle and graceful ease. "So! What are you talking about?"

Mr. Kirkland gave me a wry look as he patted Ripley, who was standing guard next to his chair. Fio shook his head. "I'll fill you in on the way to work. We have to get going. We have work to do!"

With that daily exclamation, I knew my breakfast had officially drawn to a close. I took one last drink of my tea, swooped up my large handbag with my ever-present notebook and office essentials, said a quick good-bye to everyone, and hustled out the door.

Today Fio had his car. "Hi, Ray!" I exclaimed to Fio's driver. He was a wary fellow and continually on the lookout as the mayor's driver and self-proclaimed bodyguard. Unless there were dire circumstances making security an even higher priority than usual, Fio didn't employ detectives or official bodyguards. Instead, his main idea to "save the city money" was to have the New York Fire Department install two compartments in his car. For pistols. One for him and one for Ray, both of whom had gun permits. Fio fought in the Great War, was a bomber pilot actually, so he was no stranger to guns. At heart, he was a gun-slinging cowboy and knight in shining armor. He was practical and efficient to the extreme. And yet, he was also a big romantic. Art was deeply rooted in his heart. He felt that music and beauty were essential to the city. It was more than just adornment, it was like the heartbeat of the people. Without it, it wouldn't be life. He often stopped in to the High School of Music and Art that he opened earlier in the year to check on his dream school and the dreams of the students and staff.

I looked over at Fio, already working hard at his desk that he had installed in his car. Fiorello was five-foot-two-inches tall but radiated energy and power that made you think he was well over six feet (not to mention he had staggering talents in the yelling and temper departments that added to that impression). He was fearless, taking on the gangsters as well as the corrupt political institutions. Such as Tammany Hall, who had a stranglehold on the Democratic Party and who backed former mayor Jimmy Walker.

I was just graduating high school the final year of that crazy era. *What a time!* If you looked at any other decade, you wouldn't see so much change as you did in the Twenties. Even our clothing showed it. After the Great War ended in 1918, we all reveled in modern life. It felt fresh and new. We were done with long skirts, big hats, waist-length hair, old and trapped ways of thinking and living. We longed for change after those aching years of trench warfare—you could feel it in the air. Just like we wanted to get the men home and out of that mud, we mirrored that same desire for change in radical new ways. Skyscrapers were built, formal dinner parties went out and cocktail parties came in (in secret, of course, because Prohibition also came in), and women finally got the vote. I can't even begin to express all the cheers and tears from Aunt Evelyn and her friends who had helped lead that cause for so long. She had been blessed with a family that made sure she could be a woman of independent means. But so many friends of hers had been trapped in all kinds of terrible situations from their lack of equality. Her fiery eyes held a fierce look of determination upon that victory. It took my breath away.

Just then, our car passed the Chrysler Building with its Art Deco doors and famous triangular windows at the top. I loved that building like an old friend, even though it was only five years old. Art Deco was the most beautiful and inspiring art form for me. It had sharp geometric angles that mingled with natural elements like leaves and flowers. Even the elevator doors of the Chrysler Building were a work of art. *How symbolic.* How did all that beauty come out of the horrors of the war? And then there was the Depression we were just beginning to get out of . . . Whenever I looked at the Chrysler Building, I would always think of just what this era meant to us all. Where we'd come from.

Fio finished arranging his accoutrements in the car and began barking out orders and duties for me to add to my never-ending list in my notebook. I began scribbling furiously as he shot through the day's schedule.

Finally, as the onslaught of information ebbed and he took a deep breath, I broke in. "So, what were you all talking about at breakfast? Is there something going on?" I tried to sound light, like I had just wanted an inconsequential piece of information. But Fio, as always, could see right through my feigned subtlety.

"God, Lane. I'm sorry," he said, adjusting his fedora to a slightly more rakish angle. "I should have said something sooner. Finn is fine. It's not about him," he said in a big hurry, flapping an arm dismissively, trying to dispel the anxiety that was probably written all over my face.

I exhaled and said with a much happier and curious tone, "So what's up? What's going on then?"

"Well, we're not sure. It's not in the papers yet, but it will be by the end of the day. Mr. Hambro—do you remember him? He's an old friend of mine since before the war. I've known Ted and his family for years."

I nodded my head as I recalled the tall bank president, with the charming look of a dignified professor masking a witty rascal beneath. When he and Fio had coffee or drinks, they would often put their heads together in solemn, urgent conversation with the air of dealing with *important states of affair*, then let out an ear-splitting peal of laughter that made it absolutely obvious they'd actually been sharing an uproariously funny joke—probably dirty. Where Fio was rotund and short, Hambro was skinny and tall. Where Fio was black-haired, clean-shaven, and almost always favored a hat, Hambro had smoky gray-and-white hair, a rich goatee, and went against convention going hatless much of the time. But that was on the outside. On the inside, they were very similar men and shared a deep bond of friendship.

"Sure, what about him?" I asked.

He took another deep breath and tilted his hat up in a baffled gesture. "He's completely vanished."

CHAPTER 2

We arrived at City Hall, Fio having filled me in on Mr. Hambro's disappearance as we climbed the steps. He had been at work in the afternoon with nothing exceptional happening in any way. But by the end of the workday, his desk was empty and he never showed up at home nor anywhere else. His wife had no idea what had become of him. The Manhattan Trust Bank didn't seem to have any issues going on that could have caused him to leave of his own accord, which was a pretty frequent occurrence these days. Since the devastating crash seven years ago, businessmen from all spheres had found themselves in hopeless positions and many just walked away and disappeared . . . or they took the permanent way out. At some of the major hotels, it became a dark joke that when a businessman went to the front desk to book a room, he was regularly asked, "To sleep or leap?"

That just didn't seem like Mr. Hambro. Mrs. Hambro had notified the police and they were following up, but there really wasn't anything substantial to go on. On top of worrying about the man himself, word was leaking out that he had disappeared and there were legitimate concerns that the investors at his bank would start to get nervous and pull their money. Too many people had seen things like this happen before.

Fio asked me to go along with him to see Mrs. Hambro. I agreed and we made plans to pay her a visit in the late afternoon.

I got into the office, dropped off my things, and headed to the coffee room as I was mulling over the items we had discussed in the car. I waved to Val as she sat at her desk typing at a furious pace. She raised her honey-brown head and gave a big smile in greeting, not missing a beat on the typewriter.

In the coffee room, I came across someone else.

"Morning, Lane," said Roxy as she put out the stub of her cigarette.

"Morning, Roxy," I returned. Roxy and I had a tricky past, but the truce we struck continued in peace. She recently cut her glorious white blond hair into a short, trendy do, with glossy waves hugging her cute little head. And I have to say, I didn't think it was possible, but the shorter hairdo accentuated her perfectly curvy figure. Today she had on a tight (as always) light blue sweater highlighting her favorite assets.

I exhaled wistfully, "You look great, Roxy. I love your new haircut."

She smiled. "Thanks, Lane."

We had both learned a lot of surprising things about each other. Things that we had never spoken of, but we held a mutual understanding that there was much beneath the surface to us both and a grudging respect had emerged.

Just as I was about to ask her if she had any plans this weekend, in swept Ralph, the office chatterbox and flirt. His dark curly hair had also been cut recently, so the lock that used to fall over his eyes was a little too short for his taste and he self-consciously pulled at it all day long, willing it to grow back. His forehead had a network of creases and his looks weren't traditionally handsome, but he had a wide, contagious grin. Roxy locked eyes with me, a wicked gleam in her eye and a smirk to her lips. I nodded once.

Ralph started in at top speed, "Hey, gals! How's it going? Did you hear about the new band playing at the Orchard Club tonight?"

Roxy quickly started to say, "Yeah, we were think—"

"You should come!" he interrupted, speaking so fast it was hard to keep up. "It's gonna be great, they're playing all the good stuff and they redid the inside of the club, so it should be the cat's pajamas. How about you, Lane?"

Ready to cram in as many words as I could, I only got as far as, "Sounds gr—"

"Fantastic! Bring your friends. I told Val about it, how about Dorothy from accounting? You should bring her, too, she's really cute. Okay! I gotta run. See you girls later!" He raced out of the coffee room, completing a backhanded throw of his napkin into the garbage can.

"Damn. Thought I had you," I said as I handed Roxy her dollar. "You win. You got out four words. I only got out one and a half."

"Thanks!" she said with a knowing grin, tucking her winnings of our ongoing bet into her ample cleavage. I'd be lucky to hide a dime.

"I'll work on it. I'll get my dollar back next time."

"You got it, Lane." We clinked our coffee cups sealing the deal and she chuckled as she walked out.

The rest of the morning carried on as usual, Val and I deciding to have lunch outside in the park even though it was brisk. We bought a couple of sandwiches and Coca-Colas, and walked to a little table. There were several other brave souls outside, too. Even though it was about fifty degrees, there were several of us eating in the park. We could feel the inevitability of winter coming, so we just had to get in another lunch outdoors.

My fingers made circles on the metal table, feeling the texture of smooth holes in the cold surface. The earthy scent of fallen leaves surrounded us along with the cheerful murmuring from the other lunchers as we soaked up the sunshine on our faces while enduring the stiff fall breeze.

"Are we still on for tonight, to go to the club Ralph was telling us about?" I asked Val.

"Sounds great. I think Pete and some of his buddies are going," she said.

She and Pete were an on-again, off-again couple. They were both very tall, which was a treat for Val. Val was almost six feet tall, which made it difficult to wear the fun shoes she loved and yet still be able to look up at a date.

Val had delightful, sparkling green eyes and they held a look of mischief today.

I narrowed my eyes and said, "What are you up to, Val?"

"Well . . . I had something funny happen today. I've been dying

to tell you about it," she said with a sardonic smile, her freckles
making her pretty face seem more mischievous than she actually
was. I think her share of mischief fell on me. She continued as I
leaned in closer. "You know how you have that fantasy of falling
and then suddenly a handsome stranger appears out of nowhere and
catches you?"

"Val!" I whined exasperatedly. "You said you wouldn't speak of
that again!" I said in mock anger.

She laughed. I rolled my eyes. It's true, I had fantasized about
that. I watched a lot of movies and read a lot of novels. Obviously.

"Let me tell ya, Lane. It's not *nearly* as romantic as you might
think."

"*What?*"

"Shhhh. Stop yelling," she chided. "I was walking through Penn
Station and you know how beautiful that hall is . . ."

"Mm hmm," I said, nodding as I took a bite of my chicken salad
sandwich. I loved that hall, it's just about as wonderful as Grand
Central.

"Well, I got right to the dead center of the hall, was looking up at
the ceiling . . . and tripped. On the completely smooth floor, mind
you. And it was one of those long, laborious trips where your body
tries desperately to keep itself upright, but you manage to just keep
tripping and running on and on," she said, about to snort.

"It felt like I'd been falling for *hours* and I was making noises
like, 'Whoa! Woo! Whooooaa!' And then finally, as my body gave
up the fight and I was almost horizontal, about to hit the pavement,
someone caught me," she said as she raised her eyebrows in meaningful emphasis.

"*Really?*" I squeaked.

She nodded. "Mm hmm."

"Who was it? It wasn't Pete, was it?"

She shook her head.

"Who?"

She shrugged her shoulders. "Some tall stranger. Thank God he
was tall, otherwise I would have taken him out."

"Well . . . What happened? Did he say anything? Did you say
anything?"

She laughed. "Well, I was a little embarrassed and after he set me upright again I was speechless. I could feel myself blushing from my toes to my hair. I think I stuttered something stupid like, 'Uh, thanks.' He just looked at me, adjusted his hat that I had knocked askew, and smiled. He had these amazing, dark blue eyes. He just said, 'Anytime.' Then walked away."

I had stopped eating and was looking at her with a great, skeptical lift to my eyebrow. "Hmph."

"Hmph?" she echoed.

"Yyyyyeah. Right. *Not* romantic at all."

She blushed again and I just shook my head. She had all the luck. We ate amicably for a few minutes. As Val took a long swig of Coke, I felt her eyes on me.

"Have you heard from Finn?"

I shook my head. "No, nothing since he sent word that he arrived safe 'n' sound a couple of weeks ago."

It seemed inadequate to call Finn my boyfriend. We were more than that. We'd shared intense passionate moments, telling each other things we had never shared with another person. We both had complicated pasts that seemed to draw us closer.

It's funny how the little moments became the important memories, the ones that came back to mind frequently and with a special kind of poignancy. I kept thinking about the day right before he left when we had taken a long walk through Central Park and were making our way back to my house. I had asked him if he'd help me start taking down some of the patio furnishings that weren't winter-worthy. The afternoon temperature had dropped suddenly, and I started to button up my coat when we were still several blocks away from home. My fingers had gotten so cold and numb, I was fumbling with the buttons.

Finn noticed and pulled me over to the side. He looked down at my blue fingers and said, "Here . . ." He gently took my stiff fingers into his warm, toasty hands. It felt heavenly. I looked up at his dark brown hair and the jawline that I knew like the back of my hand. His gray-green eyes smiled with kindness and the crinkles at the corners made me automatically smile back. He brought my hands up to his lips and kissed them. "Better?" he asked in his delicious part-British and part-Irish accent.

"Yes, much." Then he slowly and carefully buttoned the remaining two buttons on my coat, both of us intensely aware of our closeness.

Finn was a detective in the NYPD. For the past couple of years, Fiorello had worked with him to infiltrate the remaining Tammany guys to see if there were any leftover troublemakers. Finn had ended up working deep undercover with two dangerous criminals: Donagan Connell and the horrifying Daley Joseph. Daley did not survive the battle, Donagan was in Sing Sing. About two weeks ago Finn was sent on an urgent errand to Europe. Most of it had been coordinated by Fiorello, but Finn had been assigned directly from FDR. As in President Roosevelt. Not exactly an assignment you could say no to.

Europe was a mess. The Great War was supposed to be the war to end all wars, but it was looking more and more every day like that might not be the case. *God, I hope not.* Adolf Hitler of Germany veritably ran over the Treaty of Versailles last March when he started to bring his thirty thousand troops into the demilitarized zone of the Rhineland. But Europe was so utterly devastated and war-weary, they kept appeasing him. I'd never forget that day and the ferocity with which Mr. Kirkland reacted. He blew his top and I was shocked to see this normally placid and in-control man viciously throw a kitchen chair across the room when the news came on the radio. He yelled in a Fio-worthy rant that "if France just showed the least bit of resistance, bloody hell, the Germans would have hightailed it!" Of course, that rage was sprinkled with profanity that would make a sailor blush. But I couldn't blame his seething anger. He had lived through the Great War.

Just a little over two years ago Germany's president Hindenburg died. Hitler, then chancellor, fashioned a complete takeover in the German government beginning with proclaiming himself Führer, a combination of president and chancellor. He'd already killed off his opposition with a purge of all anti-Nazi leaders on what was called the Night of the Long Knives, suspended civil rights, instituted the reprehensible Nuremburg Laws, and executed a military draft complete with a new air force called the Luftwaffe. Some people thought he might be able to turn Germany around. Fio hated him. Immediately. He got a lot of flak for speaking out against him. But I was with Fio. Hitler scared me. There was a lot of hatred and fear behind those eyes and screaming speeches. As if he had not a lack of a moral compass, but a twisted one.

To be fair, I could understand France. They had the heaviest losses in the war. America lost about one hundred thousand men and women in the war, a horrible number. France? They lost around almost a million and a half, England one million. Total losses from the war? Somewhere between twenty to twenty-five million people. It was unimaginable. An entire generation of men completely wiped out. *No one* was ready to jump into that again. The horrors of the never-ending, muddy, rat-filled, poison-gassed, trench warfare only ended about seventeen years ago. No one had recovered yet.

And that was the melee that Finn had been sent into. I didn't exactly know what Finn's assignment would entail, but I knew that it involved trying to find out if there was a greater threat than what we expected from an old crime syndicate that had recently surfaced called the Red Scroll Network.

Valerie and I had been eating in companionable silence as I pondered Finn's whereabouts. Val nodded, having come to a conclusion about our weekend plan. "Well, let's go out tonight. It'll do you good. And how about your Michigan trip? Are you ready to go Monday?"

I nodded enthusiastically. "Mm hm. I'm arriving the night before Aunt Evelyn and Mr. Kirkland get there. They want to be all together when we see the Rochester house, but the timing just didn't work out and they'll be a day late. I'm fine with that, I like traveling alone and we'll still be together to drive out to Rochester."

"Plus, you can check out some shopping in Detroit! I hear it's pretty great. Did Roarke fill you in on some of his favorite places?"

"Yep, and I'm really excited. A little nervous, too. I'm both looking forward to and dreading seeing the house," I said with a wary smile.

Val nodded. "I'm sure you are. It's a mixed bag of emotions, isn't it? Wish I could go with you. Maybe next time."

A cloud scuttled across the weak ray of sunlight that we had been enjoying. The temperature immediately lowered a few degrees. I took a bite of my sandwich and looked at the brown leaves being tossed about by a flirty breeze, a pensive mood washing over me. I was looking forward to seeing my childhood home. I hadn't been back since my parents died. *Were murdered.* That was still hard to admit. Val was right, it certainly was a mixed bag of both sweet memories and tragic ones. I suddenly wished Valerie could come with me. I wasn't afraid of being alone, but I felt a shiver of apprehension.

I took a sip of my Coke, mulling over the way it would feel to walk into that house. A strange, cold feeling crept up and over my shoulder. Like a shadow. Or that thing that makes you want to run up the basement stairs after you shut off the light.

CHAPTER 3

Valerie and I returned to the office, and then Fio and I left for Mrs. Hambro's house in posh Gramercy Park. It was a lovely area with townhouses framing a darling little gated park. It was quiet, expensive, and highly desirable to live there. We walked up a set of marble stairs to a large, rounded black front door and rang the bell.

Fio had been giving me instructions the entire time we drove over, but now he was quiet, bobbing up and down on his toes. When he did that he was either excited (like when he was at a fire helping out his firemen) or he was anxious and lost in thought.

A butler came to the door and Fio greeted him with a familiar slap to his back, calling him Robbins. Then Robbins, who wasn't too thrilled about the hearty back slap, ushered us back to the formal living room with a weirdly condescending, rod-stuffed-up-his-ass kind of gait.

The house was old with marvelous woodwork everywhere. The walls in the wonderful living room were done in several tones of rose with cream accents. It was obviously designed by a woman, but still a place where a man would be comfortable. Rich textures and fabrics made the room warm and inviting.

The woman standing at the mantel of the large fireplace had, at first glance, an austere demeanor with a rigid posture and tightly clamped lips. But then I caught a gleam in her eye that belied some humor amidst that businesslike manner.

Fio went directly over to her and took up her hand. "Dear Cynthia, how are you?"

She took a contemplative breath and exhaled, saying earnestly, "I don't know, Fio. So many things could have happened and yet there is a conspicuous lack of evidence. It's frustrating in the extreme, not to mention I'm deeply worried about him. What are we going to do?"

I liked her directness and her ability to be honest and yet not dramatic. Her golden blond hair was graying in attractive streaks and her eyes were singularly blue. The kind where you can see the cornflower blue even from a distance.

Mrs. Hambro and Fio chatted quietly, giving me a moment to look around. There were no photos of children or grandchildren, but a few pleasing pictures of her and her husband. Beautiful pieces of artwork livened up the walls, and there was an impressive smattering of books on the tables that looked like they were there actually for reading, not just looks. They were mostly the classics like Austen, Dickens, Brontë, but I also noticed the extremely large romance novel that came out recently, *Gone with the Wind*. I smiled wryly. I was currently reading it myself and was eternally exasperated with Scarlett's staggering blindness to Rhett Butler's love and her driven, utterly pointless attraction to the hapless Ashley. I tore myself away from Scarlett's plight and continued my mental inventory of the room.

"Cynthia, this is my aide and good friend of the family, Lane Sanders. Lane is quite talented at helping me see subtleties and things I might overlook. I asked her to help us, perhaps she'll spot something you and I might miss since we are both so close to the situation. Plus, I have a feeling you'll just enjoy each other."

"Pleased to meet you, Mrs. Hambro. I'm so sorry it's under these circumstances," I said as I shook her offered hand. We looked each other directly in the eyes, both us of sizing up the other. I liked her.

"So, may I ask you some questions about Mr. Hambro?" I asked her, my eyes not flinching from her poignant, blue stare.

Her eyes crinkled at the corners as she smiled just a bit. "Of course. I would appreciate any help you can give me. I . . . I realize that this could look rather . . . as if Mr. Hambro . . ."

It was painful to watch her hash through what the lurid possibilities of her husband's disappearance could look like to the outside world.

"Mrs. Hambro," I carefully cut in, "I know the police have to follow every possibility. But Fio and I know Mr. Hambro and there isn't *anything* in him nor any evidence that makes us suspect he's involved in something illegal or immoral."

Her shoulders unclenched for the first time since we arrived.

I decided to add with a smirk, "Although, Fio's and his sense of humor leave a lot to be desired . . ."

"Hey!" said an indignant Fio.

All her ladylike reserve flew out the window and she laughed with a loud, "Ha! You could say that again!"

After the ice had clearly been broken, we all sat down on her comfortable sofas and had a cup of tea. Robbins came in and brought us a plate of lemon sugar cookies and then proceeded to hover. He at last gave up as none of us was about to begin talking until he left the room.

"Fio tells me that Mr. Hambro went to work, he was there most of the day, left at some point between four and six o'clock, and he's not been heard from since. Is that right?" I asked. Fio had me go ahead and take the lead in asking some questions. He believed everyone needs an editor, an outside perspective to see the holes. I excelled at watching people, reading their nonverbal communication, and getting them to relax and talk. I enjoyed the sudden thrill of being a detective.

"Right," said Mrs. Hambro.

"How about anything going on at the bank, anything out of the ordinary lately?"

"No, nothing that I can think of," she said openly.

"And, family-wise, anything unusual at all? Even if it wasn't something bad, just anything that comes to mind that was different from usual routines and habits?"

She put a hand to her chin in contemplation. "Hmm . . . a change to habits . . . Now that I think about it, around two months ago Ted started having an early morning meeting every Wednesday. He said it was just a business meeting, but he'd never had it before and he'd leave the house by five. Whatever it was, he never said a word about it. He never acted nervous or apprehensive, but he'd definitely deflect my casual questions."

"Wait a minute," said Fio. "Wasn't it a Wednesday the day he went missing?"

Her face paled a little. "Actually, yes. You're right," she said.

"Okay," I said. "Is there anyone at all who might know where he was going? Or who he was meeting?"

We all thought about it for a moment while chewing our cookies, then slowly one by one, we all looked up at one another with someone in mind. Mrs. Hambro said, "Let's talk to Robbins." Fio and I nodded our mutual agreement.

We contemplated tactics and at first, we thought that perhaps a subtle approach might work best. But given Robbins's dour personality, we all doubted that subtlety would work. We agreed upon a full-force attack. Mrs. Hambro called him in on the pretense of asking his help with the tea things. Fio was first to pounce.

"Robbins, when Mr. Hambro had his Wednesday meetings at five in the morning, did you know where he was going?"

"Yes, Robbins," piped in Mrs. Hambro. "Did Mr. Hambro ever say anything to you at all, even in passing, about where he was going, what he was doing, or why?"

And I landed the final blow, appealing to his sense of duty. "Because, Robbins, we all know that a man of your responsibility rarely does *not* know the exact goings-on in the house. And . . ." I paused, really getting in the groove of the detective drama, which drew a cocked eyebrow from Fio. "Lastly, if you do not say everything you can to help with this inquiry, you could be accountable for obstructing a police investigation." I was making this part up, but I figured a healthy dose of bluster couldn't hurt.

"Ah, Lane? You can take it down a notch," said Fio.

"Oh, ah, certainly. It just got a bit exciting." Fio was about to roll his eyes, but then he caught the look on Robbins's face.

Robbins had become drawn and pasty, his eyes darting from side to side. Beyond a doubt, he knew something and it was costing him greatly.

Mrs. Hambro caught the expression racing across his face and was absolutely livid. She stepped closer to him with a firm foot, pursed her lips, and pointed her finger at him like a mother telling her son if he knew what was good for him, he'd *better* not lie. "Robbins, you tell me *every single thing. Right now,*" she said in a low, quiet, menacing voice.

He was flabbergasted at the strength of her words; it was likely he'd never heard her use that tone of voice.

"Yes, ma'am," he said with a shaky voice completely devoid of all his usual imperiousness. He backed up a few unsteady steps and landed awkwardly in a chair.

"Robbins, why don't you start at the beginning," I said more gently. "I understand these early morning meetings began about two months ago. Tell us everything you've noticed or heard on any of those Wednesdays, even the smallest detail could be important. So . . . around the beginning of September or so . . . ?" I prompted.

He cleared his throat, then inhaled deeply like he was bracing himself, and unfolded the details that he had witnessed.

"All right, for the first few meetings there was nothing out of the ordinary about it other than the very early hour. Mr. Hambro would get up, dress, eat something quickly in the kitchen, and be out the door. Mr. Hambro always walks everywhere and he likes to take public transportation, even when he has meetings down on Wall Street, and that was the first odd thing that I noticed. Around the middle of September, he walked out the door and I happened to come by the side window. He had walked to the right, down to the corner . . . and I saw him get in the backseat of a car that must have been waiting for him."

"What kind of car was it?" piped in Fiorello.

"Oh, it was a large black sedan, dark windows, quite nondescript. I couldn't see anyone in the car as I was too far away."

"All right, what else did you notice?" I asked.

"Then maybe a couple of weeks later I saw him carry a rucksack out with him, which was highly unusual as he only ever carried his briefcase. I went up to his room, and as I'm familiar with all of his clothing, I'm Mr. Hambro's valet as well, I saw that he had taken a set of his casual clothes with him. There was a pair of wool pants and a flannel work shirt and an old, scuffed pair of work boots that he used when going shooting or playing with the dogs at his brother's home in Long Island. After that, a few other items also seemed to disappear, too. An odd sweater or pair of pants, a shabby hat . . .''

Mrs. Hambro looked like it wasn't adding up at all in her mind. "That is so odd, Robbins," she said. "I mean, what could he have been doing?"

"I have no idea, madam, but the last thing I saw that was out of the ordinary, was one day a week ago. I think it was Monday. I was here to see him gather the mail that had come that afternoon. Something had been posted to him in a red envelope that looked like an invitation to one of the many parties you both attend. He selected that out of the pile, slashing it open so quickly that he got a bad paper cut. As he read it, he stumbled once and dropped the note. I went over to help him, but he had caught himself on the foyer table. And when I bent down to get the note for him, he looked up at me with wild eyes and said fiercely, 'Don't touch it!'"

"What did you do after that, Robbins?" asked Mrs. Hambro curiously.

"Well . . . I went back to work," he offered guiltily. But you could hardly blame the man, servants were taught to mind their own business, and ones who didn't were never at a job for long. Mrs. Hambro looked mutinous nonetheless.

Fio caught the look on her face and intercepted her. "Ah, Cynthia . . ." he said as he shook his head slightly. With a crestfallen look, she sat back into the sofa.

"Is there anything else at all that you can think of, or anything that the other household staff may have mentioned to you?" I asked, hoping to prod his memory once more. He shook his head miserably.

To sum it up, we had a disappearance, sudden mysterious visits with an anonymous person in a car, and a striking red envelope that delivered a terrifying message. This was quickly becoming a most interesting case.

CHAPTER 4

Back at the office, we dove back into the day's routine. About an hour later, I was typing up some notes. Now, I had seen a lot in my line of work. My boss keeps us all on our toes. In fact, the press camped out across from City Hall, waiting for a good scoop, and Fio never disappointed. But this day, I looked up from my desk and jerked out of my chair, practically falling over because I couldn't believe my eyes.

A short, five-foot-two-inch *tiger* was trying to get through the door. I saw a top hat hit the floor and heard the loud screeching of a delighted Fiorello as he wrestled a full-size tiger skin into the office. He made it through the doorway passing right by me with a wake of office staff gawking at him. He hummed a little ditty as he went through to his office, looked around finding the perfect angle, and spread out the skin with the massive head facing toward the door with a menacing greeting.

"Hmm hmm hmm," he hummed. "That about does it. Lane!" he barked out.

I'd been leaning up against the doorframe, my ankles crossed, arms folded across my chest, shaking my head. "What are you doing, Fio?"

He smiled his bright, La Guardia grin at me and waggled his brows. "Do you get it?"

I looked down at the tiger. "Oh, good grief. It's the Tammany Tiger."

"Oh yeah," he said, rubbing his hands together with a sneer of delight.

The Tammany mascot was the tiger. This was most decidedly a jab at Tammany, a declaration of Fiorello's victory in ousting the corruption.

"That's not going too far, is it, Fio?" I asked, trying hard to stifle a laugh.

"Nope! I never go too far."

That was laughably debatable. I walked over toward his desk. I looked forward to witnessing all the surprised office guests over the next few hours. I sat down and asked, "So Fio, have you heard of any kind of red envelope being delivered to other people like the one Mr. Hambro received? It seems like red continues to be a color that surfaces when any trouble arises. . . ."

He nodded, putting his elbows on the desk, clasping his hands together. "I personally haven't heard of any red envelopes, but I wonder if they are indeed a link to the Red Scroll Network. Let's get with Kirkland and see if he's heard of them. I'll wire Finn about it, too, make sure he knows what's going on. I can't imagine Hambro being involved with that group in any way, but it's too coincidental to dismiss outright."

I sat back, crossing my legs. I started thinking about the people behind the latest threat against the city and Fio and how we'd thwarted their efforts. "Well, we know Donagan is in Sing Sing. Eliza is probably on the loose and that rumor of a new *über* gangster in town is a possibility to consider. But again, they might not be involved at all. This could be something totally isolated." I wanted to sound hopeful. But it was an odd string of events: a red envelope, a disappearance, mysterious meetings . . . "It feels like someone's playing games. This isn't a typical crime."

He nodded again. "I agree. It's very odd, Lane, very odd indeed. Let's keep our eyes open. All right! We've got work to do!" he said as he clapped his hands.

"Gotcha, boss! Let me know if you hear from Finn, okay?"

He looked at me over the rim of his glasses. "Of course, Lane. You got it. And don't trip over the tiger. He's even bigger than I'd hoped!"

* * *

That night, the Orchard Club was a lot of fun. I had a Bad Romance. The drink. I found Roarke, my close friend and sleuthing partner, and we got a chance to catch up while we danced. He looked fantastic in his signature wide-striped suit and black tie. He always cut a dashing figure. He smiled, full dimples, and said, "You look great, Lane! Hey, I hear you're heading to Michigan on Monday. Are you excited?"

He twirled me and then brought me back in. "Yeah! I am. I think I am."

He looked at me closely and then said, "I can imagine that might be a daunting and complicated trip. Exciting, but surreal, right?"

"Exactly."

"Hey, make sure to pop into the barber shop and say hi to my friends. They helped a lot when I needed some information about those gangster ties from Detroit."

"Will do!" He filled me in on some of his favorite places in Detroit and new friends in Rochester. It helped. It made it more real and concrete instead of just a ten-year-old's memory.

"Oh! And while I'm gone, can you keep an eye on Fio?" I asked.

"Of course. Is the Little Flower getting himself into more trouble?" he asked. His fervor for investigative reporting knew no bounds. His eyes immediately glistened with interest; it was his passion. The hunt for a good story was powerful. I filled him in on some of the details he hadn't heard yet about Hambro and the red envelope.

"And just wait until you see Fio's new office décor." I grinned and shook my head.

"Hmm," he said skeptically. "That should be interesting."

"Oh yeah."

"Will Fiorello let Finn know about the red envelope? I think he should know about that. Feels like it could be connected to our last case."

I gave him a satisfied smile. Roarke was the only one to join me in calling our last big intrigue a *case*. He was a great sleuthing partner. Except for getting me into trouble. But I could take care of myself. Pretty much.

"Yes, and I'll write him about it, too."

I started to mentally toss around the new developments with Hambro and the red envelope. When the silver gun of my nightmares recently resurfaced in the hands of some local criminals, it seemed as if old ghosts and villains were returning. Perhaps the red envelope and subsequent disappearance of Hambro was a notice of their arrival. To top it all off, we'd been warned that a new *über* gangster was in town with ties to this revived syndicate. That particular person was thought to have swapped out a body at a crime scene, to throw us off the scent of the real victim. Or, as we expected, throw the scent off the fact that the victim, Eliza, was still alive. Whoever this new gangster was in town, he—or she—was powerful enough to have disguised himself as medical staff, find a similar body in another morgue, and exchange it.

We needed more information. My parents had ties with that network back in the war. If these new developments were linked to the underground crime organization, the Red Scroll Network, then maybe my trip to Michigan would not only reveal more about my parents and their untimely deaths, but perhaps I might find information on this syndicate that began before I was born.

"Ooh, you're far away," said Roarke.

I laughed. "Sorry. I'm just thinking through the case."

"Are you going to do any sleuthing back in Michigan?" he asked with a wistful look in his eyes.

"Most definitely."

"Hmmm. Keep me posted and let me know if you need anything. Boy, I wish I could go, too. But I have some major deadlines," he said, shaking his head.

"That's okay, I really need to do this on my own. It's been a long time coming. I just haven't been up for . . . facing all that, you know?"

"I know. It's a lot. But if there's anyone who can face it head on, and find some clues to the mystery to boot . . . it's you. Come on. Let's go get a drink."

We joined Valerie and some other friends at the bar. By the time I finished my drink, I had mentally wrapped up my week and was ready for my trip to Detroit and Rochester. My capable friends would hold the fort here, Fio and I would get word to Finn about this new development of the red envelope, the police would dig into Hambro's disappearance, and I'd start a new journey to fill in the holes from my past. And maybe, just maybe, it would shed some light on this new case developing in New York.

CHAPTER 5

Finn sat at the café table, his hands clasped around a bowl of café au lait that was sending out ribbons of steam into the chilly air. Up ahead he could make out the form of the giant that watched over London with a lordly eye. Big Ben. He'd never tire of it, despite his rather antsy feelings about being back in his hometown, after many years away. A lifetime away. Finn had a lot of ghosts to face here.

But what was really troubling, making him uneasy and wakeful even in the middle of the foggy London nights, was not the ghosts of his own past, but Lane's. He'd sensed for a while that her path was taking her somewhere that would join her past and her present very soon. Her parents had been murdered when she was only ten years old, and the same event that killed them could have easily killed her as well. Lane always made cracks about her past being like a predictable beginning to an adventure story. She'd scoff at books and movies where nothing seemed to happen to a central figure unless one or both of their parents died. However, beneath that veneer of humor, he read anxiety. And deep-rooted pain. She had a family who not only took her in, but loved her and gave her a great life. But you can't just skip over a tragic beginning. He, of all people, knew that well. The beginning of that painful history happened back in Michigan, back in her hometown where she was planning on visiting soon.

And he was stuck here. Damp, cold London. Full of old memories and old pain. Except for one person whom he was delighted to get to spend time with. And she'd love Lane. They would become fast friends; of this he was absolutely certain.

Finn reclined in his chair as he lit a cigarette and watched a line of jostling, laughing students walking home from their day at school in their navy jackets, red ties, and plaid skirts for the girls. One of the boys leaped up and grabbed a high branch showing off to the other lads. He smiled inwardly, wondering what exactly made boys constantly jump and leap to see how high they could smack the sign, the tree branch, the awning . . . They all did it.

The thought of grabbing onto the tree branch made him think of the time this fall that he and Lane had helped Mr. Kirkland take down the more delicate lights and chandeliers from their enchanting patio to prepare for the winter. He'd never imagined such a place. It was just a simple, rather tight backyard just off their townhouse, surrounded by other townhouses like a rugby scrum. Kirkland had flowers all over the place plus several pieces of comfortable outdoor furniture. But the ingenious thing was the maple tree that he had kept pruned to form a natural canopy. They'd strung lights, small chandeliers and lanterns, all mismatched in friendly randomness on the branches of the tree to create a place that seemed straight out of a fairy tale, yet not silly or frivolous. It was a welcoming place that seemed alive when the breeze would dance with the glowing lights.

Finn had been bringing up some boxes from the basement for those lights that couldn't handle a New York winter. He walked outside to find Lane dangling from a branch, one hand holding her up, the other holding a lantern she'd just unhooked. The ladder had been sent sprawling from an errant kick.

"Need a little help?" he had asked with a grin as he'd run over to her.

"That'd be great," she croaked while she tried to maintain her grip on both the branch and the lantern.

He took hold of her around the waist, supporting her torso while she carefully got her balance and a better grip on the lantern. Then he lowered her down, taking more time than strictly necessary, enjoying her nearness, the scent of her perfume, her soft curves up against him.

After he had set her down, she uprighted the ladder and then started to climb back up. The ladder looked as if it had either endured the Great War itself or was approximately 265 years old. Just as he had been about to tell her to be careful on that fourth step, which looked particularly dubious, it cracked as she stepped fully on it. As she'd tried to right herself, her body twisted, and she reached out to find support. He dove over and grabbed her, saving her from hitting her head on the pavement, just inches away.

It had been a perfect moment. They were nose to nose, her body pressed up against his.

"You did that on purpose," he whispered to her.

"Maybe," she whispered as her eyes flickered down to his lips.

He kissed her. The taste and feel of her had been delicious and hard to bear all at once. She made him physically ache just thinking about her. He was too far away. He dragged hard on his cigarette, shaking his head to clear his mind, which had been so absorbed. Back in New York.

All right, he declared to himself as he put out his cigarette definitively. He had a job to do. The quicker he made his contact and found the answers to his questions, the quicker he could go home.

CHAPTER 6

Before I caught my train to Michigan, I had an appointment to keep. I walked just a couple of blocks, to a little luncheonette and soda shop. I spotted up ahead a slight, lithe form with dirty blond hair leaning up against the wall outside of the soda shop.

"Hi, Morgan," I said.

"Hi, Lane!" she greeted. "I think I might order marshmallow today!"

I followed her inside and we headed to our usual table. We had rescued Morgan from a horrible predicament a while ago. She had been part of a group of street urchins for . . . well, I didn't know how long. We'd hoped that she'd like to stay in a home for girls that Aunt Evelyn and several of her friends including the first lady, Eleanor Roosevelt, had set up. But it didn't take. Although grateful, Morgan found that her street life was something she couldn't leave and she disappeared. In the short time that I had gotten to know her, I knew Morgan loved ice cream and had fallen in love with this soda shop. I had walked around here quite often, trying to find her. I finally did one day, and we set up a weekly ice cream appointment.

After she gobbled down the grilled ham and cheese that I made her order first, she was at last making her way through chocolate ice cream topped with marshmallow goo. I asked her about something I had been pondering. "Morgan, you're young, but you've lived on your own for so long it's like you're older than you really are."

"You can say that again," she muttered.

"Why didn't you like living with the girls?"

"Oh, they were all right," she said while putting a strand of her hair behind her ear in a surprisingly feminine gesture. "In fact, better than all right. But . . . I don't know." Her blond hair was lighter than when we first found her. We had given her a thorough bath and she came out gleaming and her hair was much fairer once the dirt had been removed. She hated it. I looked at her, thought about the life she lived, the things she lived through . . . I had an inkling as to why she left the girls' place.

"Morgan, you might have heard from someone else, but my parents died when I was ten."

"And that makes you an expert on me?" she said with a defiant upturn of her chin.

"Not at all," I said calmly. "Just telling a story. When I came to live here with Aunt Evelyn, it was good, but awkward, too. Not because she wasn't great, she's wonderful. You know . . ." Morgan allowed herself a little smile as she thought about Aunt Evelyn.

"But, well, let's just say that I was angry. Really angry that my parents had died. And part of me felt like they betrayed me." Morgan stopped shoveling in her ice cream and only her eyes shifted to look at me directly.

"It's now thirteen years later, and it might not seem like it on the outside, but sometimes it's a little hard for me to let people get close. When they get close, they have power over me. Because it would hurt a lot if they decided to leave or were taken from me."

"But, Lane, you have a lot of close friends," she said with an earnest tilt to her head.

"Yeah, it's not quite the word I'm looking for. It's not that I have a hard time making friends, but it's the independence I like. I don't want to *have* to depend on them."

She exhaled with a puff.

"So now, I'm still learning, believe me. But I know I have to fight it. I mean, I'd still rather do things on my own, but after a while I learned that it was worth it to take the risk. To trust." I put down my cup of coffee. "Anyway, thanks for having an ice cream breakfast with me. Want to meet up again next week after my trip?"

Morgan licked her lips, considering me carefully with a sidelong glance, then said, "Yeah. That would be great."

I smiled. "See ya later, Morgan."

The past week full of travel preparations, a rousing night of dancing with Val and our office buddies, a quick ice cream with Morgan, then hurrying to the train that I almost missed due to traffic . . . All of it led up to this moment.

I was finally sitting in the middle of the hopping, glittering Statler Hotel in Detroit . . . a long way from home. Alone.

My table was for two, but currently I was a party of one, waiting for a Miss Tabitha Baxter to come and meet me. She was the daughter of the couple who were taking care of my childhood . . . *home* . . . in Rochester, a little town an hour or two outside of Detroit. I still tripped over that word. *Home.* It felt far away and isolated, like a distant relative whom I was seeing for the first time and feeling uncertain if she would receive me with open and friendly arms, or a chilly formality.

I felt enveloped in a heavy coat of nervousness, like the new kid at school. Nervous about everything. About seeing the place where I was raised until I was ten years old, about meeting people who would remember me but whom I might not remember, about seeing the lake where my parents perished, about discovering more bits and pieces to their mysterious and troubling past . . . And then there was Finn.

I missed him. Still no word from him, but I had sent my own letter off to a discreet London address that he had given me. I hoped he'd get it. And he'd certainly get Fio's telegram; at least he'd be aware of the red envelope situation and Hambro.

I just wanted to hear how he was doing. I knew that a trip to Europe could bring painful memories back to Finn. He had been born in Ireland and that seemed to be the happiest time of his childhood. But once the family moved to England, his brother, Sean, became twisted and was the cause of deep pain and betrayal. And there was one person there in England who worried me: Gwen, Sean's wife. Finn had tried to warn her about his devious brother, he'd had feelings for Gwen at one point. And, well, let's just say that I was highly annoyed to be even the slightest bit concerned about her, but there it was.

As I sipped a glass of chianti, the thought of a strange recurring dream last night suddenly came rushing back to me. My own past had a lot of holes to it. Often, my dreams were my subconscious giving me details and memories of my life when I was ready for them. Well-known bits of my dreams had vanished recently as I had figured out their own separate mysteries. Like the lady in the green hat who flitted in and out of dreams for years, Daphne Franco. In real life, she'd loomed over me trying to finish me off after the incident at the lake that had taken the lives of my parents. Once I figured out her significance, not to mention she was safely locked away in a mental institution on Welfare Island, she was thankfully no longer part of my dreams. The main element that remained was that silver gun with the red scrollwork on the handle. And just lately, two new pieces fell into my recurring dreams: a shining gold chess piece—a pawn—and a picture of a ghostly gray hand pointing off to the right. It was puzzling, to say the least. Not to mention, I was terrified of two things: spiders and ghosts. *Perfect.* I at long last got rid of the diabolical lady in the green hat only to be replaced by a ghost hand. *Fabulous.*

I finished my wine and looked at my watch; Tabitha was now twenty minutes late. New Yorkers were regularly fifteen minutes late, but this wasn't New York. I thought I'd ask the barkeep if there was a message for me. I walked over and he rang up the front desk. Sure enough, Tabitha had just called to apologize and to say that she couldn't meet tonight because their car broke down. She'd be here tomorrow morning at ten to collect me, Mr. Kirkland, and Aunt Evelyn.

I thought about ordering another glass and what I was going to do now that my evening plans had changed. Now I wished Aunt Evelyn had been able to come right away, or Mr. Kirkland, but they would be arriving tomorrow. Which I would normally be quite fine with, I enjoy roaming around new places on my own; Detroit had some interesting sights and shopping that I was excited to see. But I had done a good amount of that already, and tonight of all nights! With all the teeming emotions of seeing my childhood home, I really could have used some company, if only for the distraction.

I felt someone sit down next to me at the bar, then a friendly little nudge with his elbow.

"Tucker! What are you doing here?" I exclaimed with genuine pleasure, enjoying the familiarity of his easy smile and open face.

"I'm here on business, Lane. I'm staying right here at the Statler and happened to walk by the bar and saw you. What are *you* doing here?"

"Oh, I'm visiting my family home in Rochester. I haven't been back since I was a kid. It's about time I got some things in order."

"Well, do you have dinner plans?" he asked.

"Actually, no. They've just fallen through."

"I was planning on going to Carl's Chop House for a steak. Care to join me?"

Tucker and I went on a couple of dates before things with Finn solidified. It was a little awkward for a while, but over the past weeks as we ran into each other from time to time, our smiles became easier again.

"A steak sounds fabulous. I'm starving!"

He chuckled, "All right then! Let's go!" He gave me his arm as I hopped down from the stool.

We walked out the hotel and Tucker strode over to the valet stand. "I think we'll drive, Lane. It's only about a mile away, but . . . I really like the car I got for this trip." He smiled like a little boy who got to play with his favorite toy. I was just about to tease him about it, when a gorgeous vision drove up to the curb. A cream-color 1936 Cadillac Series 60 convertible. With a cognac-brown leather interior. I had a thing for beautiful cars. Tucker had to come to retrieve me because I was stuck in place, staring at the car. It was a warmer night than it had been the last week, so the lovely, lovely top was down.

With a chuckle, he took my elbow and led me over to the passenger side. I said in an awed tone, "I was going to make fun of you for looking like an eager little boy, but . . . Oh, my God, I love this car." I needed to learn how to drive if only to be able to drive this marvelous machine.

We drove around a bit, to enjoy the sparkling sights. We drove past some of the wonderful stores that I had visited earlier: Himel-hoch's, D. J. Healy's, and B. Siegel. I loved the Hudson's that I reached by trolley car and the big clock by the corner of Kern's where friends rendezvoused for lunch and shopping. Detroit was a hustling hub of business, a city of firsts, biggests, and bests. You wanted the largest or first manufacturing plant of pretty much any kind? You built it here. From all that production and innovation, the city had its own style, its own kind of pace.

We arrived at the large brass doors of Carl's, the valet took the keys from Tucker, and we swooped in to glittering lights and the delicious scent of steak. It was a great place. Ah, take that back. Try amazing, spectacular, and enormous. With dark wood ceilings, crisp white tablecloths, candles, and red leather circular booths lining the walls. It took me by surprise as I'd been expecting more of a steak house tavern with casual elegance like my favorite, Keen's, in New York. This was not just a steak house, it was an event. It must've been able to hold a thousand people.

"Oh my gosh," I breathed out as I took in all the sights.

Tucker squeezed my arm and looked down into my eyes. He said, "Breathtaking, isn't it?"

"You could say that again," I said. There were many places like this in New York, but I didn't get the chance to frequent them. Let's just say that my income didn't allow for places *quite* like this.

I was just about to make *are you sure about this?* noises, but Tucker intercepted those thoughts and ushered me quickly in. "Come on, I have a reservation. I'll just make sure it's changed to two."

When we got to the golden podium where the host was waiting, Tucker went up to him and said something quietly in his ear. The host nodded and looked over at me with a gracious smile, saying "Right this way . . ."

Our table was a cozy circular booth in the corner.

Tucker said, "You look gobsmacked, Lane."

"Yes. Between your car and this place? Yes, I am," I said as I closed my gaping mouth.

"I'm really glad I ran into you. This was looking like it was going to be a boring trip full of monotonous meetings. Nice to run into a friend," he said.

"Yes, I can say the same thing. Not so much the boring bit, but it was definitely nice to see a familiar face tonight."

He looked intently at me for a moment, putting his fist to his chin in a thoughtful gesture. "You look unusually . . . hmm . . . tentative. It's an emotion I've never seen on you."

I thought about that and replied, "I'm excited for my trip here, but there are a lot of unknowns. Not sure how I feel about it all, you know?"

"Unknowns?"

"Well, I was born here, in Rochester. But when I was ten, my parents died in an *accident* . . ." I wasn't prepared to delve into the fact that they had been murdered. Not exactly scintillating dinner conversation. ". . . and I haven't been back since." I looked around nonchalantly, taking the awkwardly large menu in my hands and trying hard to seem at ease but failing miserably.

He nodded, still looking at me intently, probably trying to read between the lines. Thank God he did. "Well, how about this . . . Let's have some fun, and you can forget some of your worries for just a couple of hours. Sound good?" he asked, with a kind smile and eyebrows raised askance.

I exhaled gratefully, "Sounds really good, Tucker. Thanks."

We both looked at the monumental menus and ordered T-bone steaks with mushrooms, the house tomato salad, and mammoth baked potatoes. Apparently, *everything* was large in this place.

"Do you want a glass of wine? Or a sidecar? I love those. Hilty Dilties are good, but the name leaves something to be desired. . . ." Tucker asked me as he looked at the wine menu.

I bit my lip and looked at him with a wrinkled nose. "Actually, I'd really like a beer," I said with a sheepish grimace.

He let out a bark of a laugh. "You never cease to surprise me, Lane."

Beer was seen as more of a man's drink. And definitely not the usual beverage at such a classy establishment. But beer went *so well* with a good steak.

I lowered my voice and asked, "Do you think it's not ladylike enough for this place?" Things were finally changing for women now in 1936, but . . .

"The hell with that!" he laughed. "If we want a beer, we'll get a beer! Besides, steak is *so good* with beer."

"Exactly."

The servers didn't blink at our request for a beer. They brought them out in frosty, oversize wineglasses, which worked out perfectly. The delicious food mixed with friendly service took the edge off the snootiness that you might expect in a place of this caliber. The evening couldn't have been a better reintroduction to Detroit. The colors, the glitter, the laughter, and the good conversation.

During dinner, Tucker and I talked about current news, the excitement of fall and winter events coming up, but especially our enjoyment of the fact that President Roosevelt had just been re-elected. Soon we'd be gearing up for Fiorello's own election campaign. The steak was to die for, cooked to perfection. We both had a coffee after dinner and sat with that relaxed and content feeling from a wonderful meal and easy company.

"So, how's your job going, Tucker?"

"Oh, pretty well. I have some new clients and some new responsibilities that are much more interesting than just paper pushing." I believed that. There was something different about his demeanor. He had a job in finance, a very reliable and dependable type of person. But there was something slightly tougher about his face, a little more worldly these days, like the job captured his imagination and passion.

"Say, Lane," he said, cutting into my thoughts. "The band is playing. Do you want to dance?"

I hesitated, knowing that he and I had shared some nice dances as well as some nice kisses a while ago, but now . . .

He read my face and said with a smile, "Don't worry, Lane. I know you're dating someone. Just a dance for fun. Come on," he said with an engaging smile.

I laughed. "Sounds great."

I took his offered hand and we headed out to the dance floor. The band was playing a pretty lively number by Bing Crosby. It was fun to see all the colors of dresses against the crisp black suits. To hear the large band with all their brass instruments, the crooning lead singer, and the chatting, frolicking, fun crowd. My deep purple dress swished and swayed around my knees as we danced. I had been saving up and I was wearing a new pair of black high heels that had a ruffled bow of purple on the peekaboo toe. They were glorious.

The song ended and a slightly slower song began. Tucker brought me a bit closer and concentrated on my eyes for a minute, like he was looking for something. His strawberry blond hair shone in the lights and just the tiniest bit of stubble was growing in as the night hours approached. He blinked a couple times like you do when you realize you've been staring, then asked, "So Lane, how long will you be here?"

"Oh, not for long. Just under a week. But maybe this spring or summer I'll be back for a while longer. I have to start looking through some of my parents' belongings and whatnot. I'm a little nervous about it, actually."

"Yes," he said, "that has to be a strange feeling. I bet you . . ." But he didn't get to finish his sentence. I followed his distracted gaze. A couple of big guys at the edge of the crowd had their eyes on us and it looked like they were about to push their way through the people on the dance floor.

"Ah, Lane? I think we should get going. There was some bad business between my firm and the company those two big guys . . . eh . . . represent. I'd rather not get into it here. Do you mind?"

I didn't like the looks of the two burly men with scowling faces. They started coming toward us.

CHAPTER 7

Tucker took my hand, firmly leading the way as we wound through the crowd in the opposite direction. I tried not to look back; I felt the nervous spark that went up my spine and fluttered in my stomach when I played hide and seek or a game of chase with the pursuer right on my heels. I saw the leering grin of one of the guys in a mirror we passed so I picked up the pace. Tucker held my hand tightly and at the last second, he pulled a dark red velvet curtain aside and we slipped into a small closet of sorts. The crisp line of his exquisite suit and the strong muscles of his arm were silhouetted against the bright light that lit up the red curtain.

I whispered, hardly making a sound, "Can you see anything?"

"Shhhh," he said softly. "Back up." His arm pushed against me, and we took small steps backward, just a few inches. I looked around for anything we could hide behind, but it was a small closet full of coats. Just then a footstep came directly outside the curtain and we heard the guys talking to each other, but I could only make out a few words. My heart raced and Tucker's arm automatically came around my shoulders and pulled me close. Then we heard the distinctive sound of clipped steps, going away from the curtain.

Tucker exhaled. He looked down at me; we were pressed up against each other and our faces were a little too close. I smelled his expensive cologne and felt his heart beating fast. "I think they said they lost us. And don't worry, they're not the sharpest knives in the drawer, Lane."

I chuckled and pulled away. "Do you think it's all clear?" I asked softly.

"Yeah, but let me check." Tucker went to the side of the curtain and pulled it open a fraction of an inch. "They just went out the door. All clear," he said in a louder voice.

"Well, now. Don't you offer a gal an interesting night!" I said. Sheesh. It was just like being with Roarke. Almost.

He pulled the curtain fully open and his appealing smile lit up. "Oh, most definitely."

Tucker had already paid the bill, so we did a big circle of the place, picked up our coats at coat check, and left the building.

When we got outside he said, "Sorry about all that, Lane. It kind of cut our night short."

"Oh, don't worry. It was a great evening. Besides, I'm getting a little tired."

When we arrived back at the lobby of the hotel, he gave his delicious car back to the valet. "Thanks again, Tucker. I had a lot of fun. It was nice running into you," I said.

"You too, Lane. I hope your visit goes really well. Take care and I guess maybe I'll see you back in New York."

"Thanks. Good night, Tucker."

He looked at me for one second longer, took my hand, and kissed it quickly. I turned around and headed up to my room, walking up the wide, deep red stairway. Now that I was nearing my bed, I realized just how dog tired I really was. It was a godsend running into Tucker even though the evening had a surprisingly mysterious tone to it at the end. *Well, I'm quite familiar with mystery*, I thought with a wry smile. Regardless, it felt good to start out my time here with a friend.

The next morning, I awoke refreshed and feeling more light-hearted than I had in weeks. It was probably the beer and good steak. I quickly dressed in a pair of casual trousers, since I was going out to the country, and a light pink sweater. I was practically giddy at the expectation of meeting Tabitha and getting to see the house.

I ran down all the main stairs of the hotel instead of taking the rickety elevator. I sat down at a café table and had a quick breakfast of toast, jam, and coffee. I was waiting by the front door as I glimpsed the familiar forms of two dear people walking toward me in animated discussion.

Aunt Evelyn's busy pace was making her head bob up and down and Mr. Kirkland's tall form was loping along beside her. Aunt Evelyn was talking a mile a minute, making huge gestures and even from a distance I could see Mr. Kirkland nodding and smiling at her banter. Her black slightly gray-streaked hair that happened to be the indicator of her mood was in a neat and tidy updo. They caught my eye and I waved, standing on tiptoe. I ended up running over to them the last several yards. I gave Aunt Evelyn a huge hug and Mr. Kirkland just about lifted me off my feet as he squashed the air out of me.

"How was your trip?" I croaked.

"Great, smooth as could be. My visit to my cousin went very well." It was a cousin on her father's side, and I didn't know her, but Aunt Evelyn felt the need to go and help her get things in order as her husband had just passed away. Aunt Evelyn's generous heart couldn't say no to such a deep need, and her love of organization couldn't resist either.

But before we could talk more at length, a large and well-used sedan pulled up to the front of the hotel and out jumped a round-faced, lovely girl of about seventeen. She waved at us.

"Hello, Tabitha dear!" exclaimed Aunt Evelyn. She gave her a quick hug and Mr. Kirkland shook her hand vigorously. "This, Tabitha, is Lane Sanders. I hear you had car trouble last night?"

"Hi, Lane, nice to meet you," she said quickly while we shook hands. She seemed nice, but she wouldn't make eye contact with me and I caught myself bobbing and weaving trying to get into her line of vision.

Her black curls of hair bounced around her face as she busied herself with the luggage. She cut in before I could reply, "Yeah, the car broke down, but Dad fixed it pretty quick. Just not quick enough to make it last night."

Aunt Evelyn turned to me. "Yes, Lane, I hope you made out all right on your own last night."

"I did! I actually had a great night. You wouldn't believe it, but I ran into Tucker."

Her eyebrows shot up and her face tilted down, saying without words, *Really, isn't that interesting.*

"He happened to be here on business. I have to say, it was nice running into a familiar face. And you should have seen his car! It was divine," I said with a sigh.

Mr. Kirkland looked skeptical, but said, "Well, that's *nice* you weren't alone . . . I guess . . ."

Tabitha, evidently all business, cut in again, "So, are you all ready to go? Here, you can put the bags in the trunk." She had run around to the back and opened the trunk, tossing our things in with a hurried effort, like she was trying to get back to Rochester as quick as she could. After our bags were situated, we all loaded into the car. We let Mr. Kirkland and his long legs get into the front seat with Tabitha, while Aunt Evelyn and I sat in the back.

The three of them talked and chatted amiably, but I lost myself in the view out the window. I loved looking at the city as we drove through it, past the steadfast General Motors Building, only eclipsed in size by the Penobscot Building. Past the golden roof of the Fisher Building and Michigan Central Station built by the same architect as my own beloved Grand Central of New York City. And then as we left the city limits, the houses and roadways sprawled out like spokes on a giant wheel. Farther and farther away, the houses gained more space between them. We'd occasionally drive through little towns here and there as we got into the country. I hadn't been out of New York City in quite a while, so the sheer space and the fact that you could see the horizon everywhere you looked was surprising. It was a funny feeling. I felt like I had breathing space and the sky seemed so huge, but at the same time I felt a little lost. A little exposed.

With that notion, the worry started creeping in again, making me want to look over my shoulder as if someone was following me. I wasn't sure what would be waiting for me. I used to love looking at my parents' photo album for hours on end. But after they died, it often felt like I was looking at their story from the outside. And I so desperately wanted to feel like I was part of that story.

After our last case, where I learned more about them and about their past, I had begun to feel like their story was mine, too. But as we drove farther from the city and the passing miles made me feel more and more vulnerable, doubt began to creep in again. My parents were involved in intelligence in the war, not just the simple bookstore owners I had thought they were. They worked with Mr. Kirkland on occasion, but some of the details of their activities were a bit sketchy since they worked undercover with the Red Scroll syndicate. There were rumors of stolen art that never surfaced and it made me wonder if they'd had a hand in it. I only knew them as bookstore owners, so there was a lot I didn't understand about them. I loved my parents and I know they loved me. But did I trust them?

Whether she noticed my silence or if something else gave it away, Aunt Evelyn reached over and held my hand.

We finally came to a sign that said WELCOME TO ROCHES-TER. It was a small town, with a smattering of stores and a few restaurants lining the street. Main Street. As we slowly went through town my eyes devoured all the stores, wondering if things would look familiar or if the town had changed as much as I had after all these years.

"Oh look! There's D & C's Dime Store!" I yelled excitedly. I spotted the jewelry store, a couple of barber shops including Baldy Benson's, the C. W. Case Hardware Store, the Wilcox & LeBlond Pool Hall, the Avon Theater, which looked like it showed films and had live shows as well, Zimmerman's Shoe Store, Brown & Dungerow's Tavern, and what I remembered most was the small opera house with large, semicircular windows on the front. A trolley car rattled down the street as I spotted Knapp's Dairy Bar. And *Knapp's* was the place I hoped hadn't changed one iota. They had chocolate malts like no one else's. I could practically taste the malt as we drove by.

We turned left onto Pine Street. We went up a few streets, turned left again. I rubbed my sweaty palms up and down my knees, and . . . there it was.

I reached over and squeezed Aunt Evelyn's hand. The Tudor-style brown-bricked house that at once was foreign and strange, yet familiar like an old friend. My house. It had a large triangular peak in the front, slanting down almost reminiscent of an Austrian chalet; then the living room was to the left of the triangle with its mullioned windows. The front door was curved at the top with a rectangular window to the side, which made me miss Ripley. There was the enormous pine tree to the left of the house that made the perfect hideout beneath its long-reaching, fragrant branches. And then to the right, the tree. *My tree.* It was there; it really was still there. The purple maple tree with the big branch reaching out to the left. Even in mid-November, a few of the deep purple leaves remained. Like they had been waiting for me.

Before the car came to a complete stop, I leaped out to Mr. Kirkland's laughter. I ran around the back of the car and over to the tree. A few paces away, I stopped. It was bigger than I remembered, of course. It surely had grown over thirteen years, just as I had. Some of the branches were a little lower to the ground, like elementary school desks that seem to shrink in size over the years. I walked over to the familiar branch that I used to climb the tree a thousand times. I closed my eyes, reached out my right hand, and grasped the cool bark. I moved my hand slowly to the right and I felt the knots that were like handholds, right where I knew they'd be. I instantly pulled myself up onto the branch like a gymnast. I inched over to the trunk and I knew right where those branches were to be, like my own personal ladder. My legs carried me up and up, and then I stopped and leaned back. Since many leaves had fallen to the ground creating a great carpet of dark purple and red, I had a clear view of everything around and I drank it in.

A funny little ache appeared in the back of my throat and stung my eyes, like a need to cry, but also like it wasn't the right timing and something was holding me back. Just a little while ago, I'd had a vivid dream of this very view. A deep and familiar memory from childhood. Something I relived and reviewed daily, many times.

I looked around, not in a dream world, but the real world. My forehead furrowed in consternation as I realized with a coldness of heart that things were missing. The view was incomplete. There was something important that was deeply lacking. A breeze whipped the hair about my face. I felt a penetrating coolness that had nothing to do with that breeze slowly creep in through those well-worn tracks of doubt and anxiety. In some kind of decision, I took a deep breath and clenched my jaw.

I looked around one last time. A darkness blossomed in my spirit at the same moment a fast-moving cloud came across the sun. It brought a sudden, cold shadow over the lawn. Over me. I looked at the red brick planter. But it was a blank canvas of brown dirt, the bright petunias of the summer were long gone. The black fountain was empty. The clear, tinkling water didn't happily splash around in the shell-like basin. At the bottom of the tree, my dad wasn't there, shaking his head and laughing. The corner kitchen window . . . My mother wasn't standing there. It was vacant and lonely.

I closed my eyes slowly, tightly, then after a long moment of resignation, opened them again with a snap. I gathered myself mentally and I erected in my mind and around my heart, piece by substantial and angry piece, a very large, thick, impenetrable wall. It was powerful, like a living and breathing object, keeping out whatever I wished—whomever I wished. It was a dangerous thing, but I embraced it.

CHAPTER 8

"A change had come over me."

I slowly, methodically climbed down the tree plastering a small, toothless, mirthless smile on my face. I got down and turned to a cheery Mr. Kirkland and Aunt Evelyn.

"How was your climb?" asked Aunt Evelyn.

"Fine."

"Oh, I remember hearing many stories of you up there. Your mom would go on and on about it. She loved seeing you up there," continued Aunt Evelyn. I blinked.

There was a long silence and Mr. Kirkland said, "Uhhh . . . Would you like to go in the house, Lane?"

"Sure. Of course. Let's go."

He darted a wary glance at Aunt Evelyn.

Tabitha tilted her head to the side, her black curls glistening, and said, "Well, I should be going now. My parents invited you over for lunch. In about half an hour, just come by."

"Okay, Tabitha, thanks so much," said Aunt Evelyn.

Silence.

I took a deep breath. "All right, let's go check out everything."

Mr. Kirkland and Aunt Evelyn exchanged more dubious glances and I smiled a closed-mouth smile that held no warmth inside or out, and forged ahead. I went in the front door and walked quickly through the familiar kitchen, the living room, the dining room.

I said without equivocation or elaboration, "I think I'd like to wait until next time to go upstairs."

They nodded at me without saying a word.

I continued in a firm voice, "And after lunch I'm going back to Detroit. Then I'm going home."

Aunt Evelyn started to say, "But honey—"

But as my eyes flashed to her, Mr. Kirkland put his hand on her arm and interrupted, "It's all right, Lane. You do that. We can wrap up a few things here by ourselves and we can all head back to New York early. I'm sure I can switch our tickets to tomorrow or the day after. Sound good?"

I nodded curtly and told them I'd take a walk and meet them at the Baxters' in a while.

I went out the door and turned to the right. I had to move, I had to use up the weird energy that was coursing through my confused body. I used the time to even more securely shore up my wall that protected my mind and my heart. And kept things out. There was something not only defensive about that angry wall, but it was on the offensive, it was aggressive.

After a while, I went back to Tabitha's and met her gracious parents. Can't remember what we ate, but my humor returned a bit and I could see Aunt Evelyn sigh with relief. She just didn't realize that was part of my offensive strategy, too. I didn't want anyone to breach my wall, and humor would distract them and keep them out.

Tabitha's parents were surprised at our early departure, but we were able to catch a ride with a neighbor who needed to go to the city anyway, so Tabitha didn't have to drive us all the way out there again.

On the way back I avoided Aunt Evelyn by taking the passenger seat of the car, next to the driver. I made a constant stream of small talk with him the whole way back to Detroit. I don't recall one minute of that trip. I made excuses to Aunt Evelyn and Mr. Kirkland and had dinner on my own that night. They didn't push. I wasn't very hungry and just grabbed a sandwich from a cart and read some novel or other long into the night, submerging myself in another world.

The next day came and went in the same fashion. I walked around, shopped, said little, ate little, felt little. Finally, the day to go home to New York rolled in and, thank God, Mr. Kirkland had been able to get earlier tickets. It was like I couldn't stand one more second of the place.

We took the Detroiter, which would get us into Buffalo in less than four hours, and I pretended not to see the growing concern on Mr. Kirkland's and Aunt Evelyn's faces. Luckily, with every state we traversed through, I could feel a physical dismantling of my wall. With every *click clack* of the train, it was like a construction worker was taking down another layer of bricks, laying them aside. Within reach, but aside. I gradually felt more like myself, my shoulders unclenching, the pit in my stomach lessening.

By the time we pulled into Buffalo to switch trains, it was pretty much like it had never happened. Almost.

We got into New York late that night and I went up to my room with as few words as possible. I walked into my blue and white refuge and took a huge breath of relief. I turned on the light on my nightstand. My eyes were drawn to my bookshelves and a gold glint of the slender volume I'd read a few months ago caught my eye. Its words had been coming unbidden to my mind a few times these past days. I walked right to it, put my finger into the top of the binding, and delicately drew it toward me.

The navy-blue leather with its swirls of gold was lovely. In fact, the binding was a work of art. There was great beauty, but then something left me agitated as I took a closer look at it. Like an intentional angle that threw off the otherwise perfect symmetry. Very similar to that compelling feeling of building up a wall around my mind and heart in Michigan, there was part of me that loved this book. And part of me that hated it. But for now, I just needed it. I stroked the brilliant cover, held it tightly, and walked to my side of the bed. I disrobed and eased myself into the warmth and comfort of the soft sheets. I began to read.

CHAPTER 9

*"I knew myself, at the first breath of this new life,
to be more wicked . . . and the thought in that
moment braced and delighted me like wine."*

The next day I surprised everyone by going in to work. I wasn't due back for another week. But as this time of year was always busy, hardly anyone batted an eye. I dove right in as if I hadn't even taken a trip.

Valerie and I decided to have lunch together and even though I took great efforts to avoid questions from Aunt Evelyn, I found it easier to think about unloading some thoughts with Val. I left a little early, deciding to meet her at the diner, as she was finishing up a project. I took my purse and as I walked down the steps of City Hall to take a stroll in the park across the street, I firmly grasped the book I started to read last night like a strange talisman.

Val and I ate at our favorite place. I wasn't myself yet. But I felt lighter, happier. I was back in my city, no longer feeling so lost and vulnerable. I soaked up the energy that coursed around me, enjoyed the fresh and festive city air, the regular routine of our greasy diner. It was good to be home.

As I took a bite of my hamburger, Val looked at me from her side of the booth and said with her hands on her hips, "All right, girly, spit it out. You're home early from a trip you've been dying to take for years, you haven't talked much all day, and your face is full of all sorts of emotions. I can't even begin to guess what you're thinking." She paused, and then taking her hands off her hips, she said softly, "Are you okay, Lane?"

I swallowed, considered for a moment, and then said, "*That* is a good question, Val. It was the strangest visit, the most unusual reaction I could have ever guessed that I would have. I'm . . . a bit baffled."

I unpacked the trip. The night of being lonely and running into Tucker, the long drive out to Rochester, the climb up my tree, and finally to the moment I put up that damn wall and abruptly decided I was done with Rochester for the time being.

She asked, "Have you talked about it with Aunt Evelyn?"

"No. I haven't wanted to. You're the only one. I can't figure it out. That feeling when I was in the tree, looking around at what I'd lost, was like something alive and tangible. It was powerful, Val. And it was in response to being by that house again, and maybe there's a part of me that knows Kirkland and Evelyn are tied to it or something. I don't know. But the good thing is, on the train ride home I could feel myself coming back," I said with a self-deprecating smile.

"Gosh, Lane, I'm sorry. You know, though, with all you've been through it's not that shocking that it wasn't easy. That's an awful lot to take in. Give yourself some time. And one thing I'm absolutely sure about—don't get mad—I don't think that wall was healthy. When people start barring themselves from the people they love, nothing good comes of it. I saw it firsthand when my father started shutting us all out when his business failed."

I nodded as I knew she was right. Val had lived with a father who all but walked out on her mother and her young siblings. He was still around, but only bodily. He checked out in '29 and never came back. Valerie, her mother, and her oldest brother worked to take care of the family. Val constantly sent money home to them and we'd often send food, clothing, and even extra money for groceries whenever we could since Val was like an extension of our own family.

Thinking it through, I said, "I know. You're right. I even knew that when I was in the tree, thinking about everything. But I've never felt anything like it, ever. It was like, in order to survive, I had to clamp down for a while. I'm sure it's not a big deal. I guess it's just a lot to figure out all at once. I do need to talk about it with Evelyn and Kirkland. I know they're worried. But in the meantime . . ." I said, changing the subject. "What's the scoop with everything here? Anything interesting happen the last few days?"

She looked at me with her chin in her hand. I could tell she wasn't too happy about the whole thing, that my reaction had been surprising to her despite the fact that she logically understood how difficult it was for me to get my mind wrapped around it all.

"Well, all right. You can change the subject. For now . . ." she said.

I smiled and she continued as I began eating again. "Mr. Hambro is still missing, nothing too new in the papers, but I can tell that people are getting nervous. They're thinking that maybe there was some bad business and he disappeared of his own volition."

"That's not good," I said, fully knowing the consequences of a panicky public. But just then a familiar face pulled up a chair.

"Hey, Roarke!" I exclaimed, standing to give him a hug.

"Sorry to interrupt, gals. How are you? I thought you were supposed to be out of town. Didn't you go to Michigan, Lane?"

"Well . . . I did, but I came back early."

He raised his eyebrows.

"Yeah, I know. I'm surprised, too," I said grudgingly. "I actually got all the way out to the house in Rochester. But I'd had enough. I walked in the door, saw the kitchen and living room, and left to take a walk. I went back to Detroit and Mr. Kirkland changed our tickets to come back early."

Roarke had been ready to banter, but I could tell he was genuinely surprised at this turn of events. He had the same scrutinizing look as Val, as he tried to read every inch of my face. Reading between the lines of what I had said, seeking information behind my eyes. I let him look. I had no idea what was behind there.

"Okay, Lane. You know, if you ever want to go back and you need a friend, I'd be happy to go with you."

"Thanks, Roarke. I'll let you know. I know I'll go back at some point, I just needed some space and some time to deal with it, I guess." It was still perplexing to me, so it was hard to put words to what I was feeling. I thought I'd quickly change the subject yet again. "Hey, Roarke, any new leads with the Hambro case?"

"I hear the public is getting jittery that Hambro's disappearance could be a symptom of a banking problem, which isn't surprising. There are so many stories like that these days. I do have a lead, Lane. He can shed some light on whether or not this *is* a banking issue."

"What kind of lead, Roarke?" Val asked.

"Well, I have this buddy." I started sniggering. Roarke had buddies, informants, snitches, pals, and *eyes* everywhere. I loved to tease him about it. "Zip it, Lane. And he's a junior manager at Hambro's bank. I set up a meeting at the park. It's odd because he was a little twitchy about meeting at all. So we thought we'd meet at Bethesda Terrace, nice and open and full of people. Do either of you want to come? Might make him feel more at ease, like a few friends going for a leisurely stroll." He tried to sound persuasive, knowing full well that he and I had gotten in plenty of trouble on similar sleuthing sprees in the recent past. But this one didn't sound dangerous.

Which, on second thought, sounded a lot like Famous Last Words right up there with *It couldn't hurt, It can't be that bad,* and *What's the worst that could happen?*

CHAPTER 10

"Hence the mask and the avoidance of his friends."

After work, we arranged to meet at 72nd Street and Fifth Avenue. The air was cool, but the sun was warm on our faces. Central Park was covered in a velvety soft brown coating of autumn. Here and there were bursts of red, yellow, and orange, but most of the leaves had fallen, creating a brown carpet of crispy leaves and the unmistakable earthy scents of fall.

We walked along in amicable silence for quite a while. I couldn't walk through Central Park without thinking of Finn. *I hope he comes home soon.*

I could tell Roarke wanted to ask me more about Michigan, but other than Val, I wasn't ready to talk about it. I was moody and swinging back and forth between feeling better, and then suddenly grouchy and annoyed.

To get him on another track, I started peppering him with questions about his latest articles, if he had any trips coming up ... things I knew he loved to talk about. I knew full well my investigative reporter friend wouldn't be put off the scent completely, but he was willing to go off the trail for a while. He talked of a new, promising company that was just starting out: Zippo lighters. I thought it was a weird name. He also talked about some new gangsters that were in-fighting and the first edition of a new magazine called *Life* coming out November twenty-third that featured a cover photo from a *female* photojournalist; a huge step forward for women in the workforce.

We were walking toward the Poets' Walk and as we neared this favorite part of the park, we both inhaled deeply, enjoying the great majesty of the towering trees arching over the wide path, scattered with sculptures of famous literary heroes. The band shell came up on our right that would bring in hundreds of us on summer weekends as we'd dance outside all night long. We crossed the park road and arrived at the top of the stairs that led down to Bethesda Terrace with the centerpiece being the huge, graceful fountain. Beyond it was the waterway with rowboats and even a couple of gondolas. I thought of Tucker and last year's funny afternoon where, despite my whiny attitude about the frustrating nature of rowboats, we had enjoyed a very pleasant afternoon. I snorted out loud as I remembered him dropping his oar at a poignant moment, case in point.

"What are you snorting about?" laughed Roarke.

"Oh, just a funny time I had with Tucker Henslowe a few months ago. It was a nice afternoon."

"Tucker?" he asked. "Hmph." His laughter had instantly gone away, but I couldn't figure out why.

"Why the serious face?" I asked.

"Oh, no reason," he said, still thinking hard and looking suspicious. But then he went on to ask, "Hey, Lane, have you heard from Finn lately?"

"No. Not for a while. But I've been sending him letters that hopefully he'll get at some point. I knew I might not hear from him for a while, so I'm not worried."

He cocked an eyebrow at me.

"Yeah, I know, a big fat lie." I laughed. "But it sounded good, right? Pretty convincing?"

"Oh yeah, sure. Had me utterly convinced," he said with a roll to his eyes.

We stopped at the railing, looking down at the fountain, a few artists scattered about painting on easels, one juggler, and I could hear a trio singing a cappella in the cavernous tunnel beneath our roost where the acoustics were glorious. Roarke spotted his buddy.

"There he is, the one with the gray suit, red tie, and holding a book," he said.

"I see him. The one sitting on the edge of the fountain?"

"Yep. See anyone else suspicious or like they might like to shoot at us?" he asked.

"Nope! That's exactly what I've been looking for, though," I muttered.

"I bet."

We walked down and nonchalantly bought a couple of ice creams, strolling closer to the guy. He stood up, nervously dusted off his pants, and walked off toward the path that led over the Bow Bridge. We followed at a discreet distance.

"Aw, damn it!" I said.

"What?" exclaimed Roarke. "Did you see something?"

"No," I said irritably. "My chocolate ice cream started leaking through the cone point. I hate that."

He snorted.

"You snorted, Roarke."

"I felt I was in good company."

The guy was up ahead, just off the Bow Bridge and went to the left up to the paths that led to the Rambles, a network of lovely knotted trails through thick forest and little springs, leading eventually up to Belvedere Castle. It was a wonderful area, some places being so thickly wooded in the summertime, it was hard to believe you were smack in the middle of Manhattan. Red Tie Guy sat down on a bench by a stream with a large wall of rocks to our right.

We sat down on the other end of the bench like a couple just taking a break from a nice walk together. Roarke spoke up first. "Marty, have you heard anything at the bank that makes you think Hambro was running from something?"

Red Tie Guy (Marty, the junior bank manager) looked nervous as he pretended to read his book and started to speak out the corner of his mouth. "No—it's the strangest thing. I've been over the numbers a thousand times and the numbers are *fine*. There is nothing there. But if there's nothing there, I just don't get it."

He was a fairly nondescript guy with light brown hair, a flat nose, and on a regular day I could tell he had a friendly face. Today he looked edgy, yet he had a determined air about him, prepared and wanting to help. He liked Mr. Hambro.

"Why are you so nervous?" I blurted. If the books were on the up 'n' up, why all the twitchy behavior?

Although it was cool, his brow beaded with sweat and he wiped it with the back of his hand as he went on to say, "Well, it's like this. See, the thing that I wanted to tell you about, was that the day before Mr. Hambro disappeared, he received a letter that clearly shook him up. The only reason I noticed it, was that I happened to go in his office and the letter came in a bright red envelope. Looked like a party invitation—you don't get party invites at the bank. And when he read it, he rubbed his forehead and ran his hand through his hair, like it was bad news or something. The rest of the day he carried on as usual, but he was definitely preoccupied. The following day he came to work, nothing out of the ordinary. But at some point, he just disappeared. No one remembers seeing him leave, no one remembers anything. Roarke, do you think you can help? He's a good man."

Roarke and I exchanged knowing looks. *A second red letter.* Someone was making a point.

I admired Marty's devotion to his boss, his earnest concern written all over his face. I looked closely at him, as nonchalantly as I could, of course. He wore gold, perfectly rounded Windsor glasses and his left hand shook a little as he put his hand on his knee, trying to regroup and master his emotions. He opened his mouth, about to say something, then closed it again. It seemed like he was holding something back, like there was something on the tip of his tongue.

Roarke looked at him, his brow furrowed, his dimples hidden. He said, "Are you sure there isn't anything else? I mean, the red envelope isn't that earth-shattering to make you this anxious," he prodded.

He exhaled with a rush. "Well, I really don't know if it's part of this or not . . . but it's big. One night just a day or two before all this, maybe it had been the day he got the envelope . . . Yes! It was. It was that day. I remember now. Anyway, I was leaving later than I usually did. I was going to a concert and decided to go straight from work. I went out of the bank and stopped to have a cigarette outside. I saw Mr. Hambro leave the bank and a black sedan pulled up. He got in." His voice had gotten increasingly softer and shakier as he spoke. He finally got to the punch line. "And when he opened the car door, inside the sedan in the backseat, I saw Louie Venetti."

Ah, thus the nervous behavior. That made perfect sense.

"Oh no," I murmured.

Louie Venetti was one of the most notorious gangsters in New York City. He was powerful, could use barbaric measures if needed, was a ruthless businessman . . . and he helped me immensely on our last case. Even helped save the city from a bombing that could have killed thousands. I hated him and I liked him at the same time.

Roarke had shot me a *sheesh* look at my lame murmur. Marty nodded in wholehearted agreement. "But I'm determined," he declared. "I am going to ask a lot more questions. I want to get to the bottom of this." Before we could ask anything further, Marty looked quickly down and said, "Don't move, someone's watching us. Do something!"

So, should we not move or should we do something, I thought irritably. Roarke suddenly put his arm around me and nuzzled my neck like we were a couple. I took the cue and started making goo-goo eyes at him while leaning into him.

Marty got up and started moving away up the path to our right. I looked at the guys through the curtain of my hair to see what they were up to and they most definitely noticed his movement. There were two of them, big guys with such brawny arms that they stuck out from their sides like they had invisible rolls of newspaper under their armpits. They both wore hats, one had a mustache. And then I noticed a bulge in the back of mustache-guy's suit coat.

"The guy's got a gun, Roarke," I whispered.

"Oh shit."

CHAPTER 11

"I shall make it my business to see you are no loser."

I am such a loser. I couldn't believe I let Roarke get me into another predicament!

The two thugs were more interested in Marty than with us, but they effectively barred our exit. We quickly decided the only way to go was toward the stream. With a mutual nod in that direction, Roarke and I picked ourselves up and walked behind the bench up toward the boulders. It quickly led to a rock wall where the stream flowed down, rainbows shining in the droplets of water. It was an easy climb with good footholds—about twelve feet up—and I watched kids do it all the time. Right now, the place was deserted. The Rambles were full of New Yorkers and tourists during the weekends, but during the week it could be pretty secluded. I was glad kids weren't around just then, but I would have given a lot to have a nice big, loud bunch of tourists meander through.

Just as we got to the farthest part of the rock wall and I had started to get ready to climb up, Roarke urgently exclaimed, "Go, Lane!"

I didn't even look back; I started climbing for all I was worth, which was no easy task since I had on a skirt and high heels. Shocking, but I hadn't really planned on rock climbing when I dressed for work that day. Just as I was about to get up the final large rock, I felt a mighty heave right on my posterior that shoved me upward, shooting me up and over the top of the wall, landing on the path with a poof of dirt and plenty of swearing.

Roarke abruptly appeared like he'd levitated up the rocks, with not a speck of dirt on his clothes. He said incredulously, "Lane! What are you doing?"

I glared daggers at him, but he pulled me quickly to my feet and we started running up the path to our left, then a quick right. We kept going and going. There was just no one in the Rambles today. *Would it have killed Fio to have this area patrolled a little more frequently?* The only place I knew that the trails led to for sure would be Belvedere Castle. But we needed some assistance that had bite; a rescue party a little punchier than a handful of tourists.

While panting up the path I asked, "So what exactly happened back there?"

"Those guys had been after Marty, but it looked like they were just talking with him. Then they saw me and evidently decided to come after us."

"Huh. We seem to have that effect on a lot of people."

"You could say that again!"

"Do you think those are Louie's guys?" I asked.

"I don't recognize them, but that doesn't mean anything. I'm sure he has hundreds of people working for him. Plus, their type all look alike: big, beefy, vacant eyes, gun-happy . . ."

"Winning . . . combination," I panted, getting well and truly out of breath.

Just when I thought maybe we'd lost them, I heard some yells and running footsteps. It wasn't looking good. We had to hide somehow. There were trees all over the place, but it felt barren without the full foliage of summer. We would be exposed and vulnerable anywhere and everywhere.

I had an idea.

"Roarke, this way!" I whispered urgently, veering to the right. We ran and ran, I could still hear footsteps behind us, but I was happy to notice a lack of guns firing. The paths in the woods were knotted all together going this way and that. I just hoped I was going in the right direction. Finally, up ahead I saw it. There was a road that cut through Central Park here; the tricky part was that the road was cut deep into the ground to protect the park from noise and pollution. It was at least twelve or fifteen feet below us and the cars were zipping by dangerously fast. We'd have to lower ourselves down the smooth face of the wall, but if we could get to it before those guys saw us, we'd be hidden since only insane people would attempt climbing down something like that.

Roarke instantly knew what I had planned as soon as he saw the roadway and well . . . We were both crazy enough to try it. We ran right up to the ledge and before I could say a word, he took my arms and started lowering me down the wall onto the extremely narrow sidewalk that flanked either side of the road. We had done this same maneuver on the Queensboro Bridge recently. That time, I had been dangling hundreds of feet above the East River; now I was dangling by the side of a speeding roadway. *Ah, yes.* Moments to treasure.

Roarke let me drop the last few feet to the pavement and I landed steadily. He lowered himself down and we plastered ourselves up against the wall. We didn't hear anything so we slowly started to walk east, trying to keep as close to the wall as possible. I looked back at Roarke to smile and tell him I thought we'd lost them, but as I turned, over his shoulder I saw a mustached face in a bowler hat peering over the edge. The guy yelled a deep-throated, "There!"

Blast. We began running again and luckily the road started to curve to the right so we'd be out of gunshot range should they decide to give that a try. And finally . . . finally. I saw what I was hoping to find: the Central Park Police Station. We ran right in the entryway, startling two patrols on horseback. The horses whinnied a little, but we ran on slightly farther before we felt like we could stop. We both bent over, hands on our knees, panting and heaving with stitches in our sides. The two policemen on horseback decided to canter over to see what we were up to. I heard and saw the brown horse legs and horse hooves before I looked up to see the men. I was also looking at my poor shoes. They used to be cute little cream and brown polka-dotted shoes with a bow on the toe. The bows were both gone and the shoes were pretty much all brown now. I hated to think what the rest of me looked like. I slowly straightened up to say hello.

"Hey! Is that you, Lane?" said the officer on the left.

I looked a little closer and remembered him. Someone had recently *attempted* to snatch my purse down in the subway and as that week had been particularly trying, I'd had enough. I ran after the miscreant, tackled him to the ground, and got my damn purse back. One of the policemen who had arrived on the scene tried to ask me out. This was the guy.

His buddy on the other horse said, "That's Lane? That girl you told me about?"

Roarke was laughing.

"Hi. Scott. Right?" I asked between great gasps of air.

"Right," he said with a smile. "Uh . . . What's going on? Why do you look . . . ?"

"Like I've been rolling around in the dirt?" I supplied.

His friend guffawed and Roarke started to ineffectually swipe at the dirt on my back and rear end.

"Cut that out, Roarke. Yeah. Well, actually we could use your help."

I filled them in on what we were doing running around. Their laughing faces turned serious and they called over another couple of policemen and went out to have a look around for our two *friends*. Roarke and I sat down heavily on a bench outside and one of the men brought us some water. I took out a brush in my purse and got most of the leaves and dirt out of my hair. I looked at Roarke and it was like the guy had some magic Dirt-Away spell. Where my hair was tangled and I had scuffed and muddy shoes, not one single hair was out of place on him, and his suit coat looked impeccable.

"What?" he asked, noticing my scrutiny.

"Nothing," I said with a roll to my eyes.

By the end of the day, the police hadn't found our beefy friends, I'd had two requests for a date despite my grubby looks, and Roarke was working furiously on a new novel he'd decided to write. I looked dubiously up and down from his face to his notebook and back again. He'd told me about writing a book. But another notion hit me.

"You're writing down our escapades, aren't you?" I accused.

"Oh yeah. This is good. I couldn't make this stuff up!" he exclaimed enthusiastically. *Oh boy.*

CHAPTER 12

"Compose yourself, said I."

We straggled home to my townhouse on East 80th Street. Roarke and I were dead tired from running for our lives, climbing rock walls, and the delightful fresh air. Ripley was waiting by the side window of the red front door. Mr. Kirkland waved from the bay window in the front that had the copper top and bottom. I loved this house. Aunt Evelyn peeked out the topmost story with the curved dormers that opened up to her studio, perfect for her painting. I waved to her and we walked wearily up the steps as Mr. Kirkland opened the door.

"Lane! What have you been doing?" he asked in his gruff voice.

"I know, I don't look so great. Roarke took me for a stimulating jog through the park today."

"Hmph," was his only remark.

I patted Ripley and after Roarke greeted Mr. Kirkland, we all filed through the house to the kitchen. I went to the fridge and took out four beers. I figured Aunt Evelyn might like one, too, as she was sure to join us. And in she swept, not to miss out on what I knew she must have surmised from our vainglorious entry.

Sure enough. "You two were sleuthing again!" she accused. But the funny thing about it was, she looked amused and relieved. It hit me how hard it had been for her these past few days. I'd always confided in her, I loved her dearly . . . I still didn't know *why* I was feeling like excluding her and Mr. Kirkland.

Suddenly, in his typical way of being everywhere at once, in barged Fiorello. Ripley was delighted to have his favorite people collected together and showed it by running to each of us in turn. Fio came into the kitchen and I greeted him while retrieving one more beer from the fridge. Sensing an uneasy silence, I turned around and everyone was looking at me.

I took in a deep breath through my nose with a determined set to my mouth and proclaimed, "So, a little intervention, huh?"

Roarke laughed and a smile tugged at the corners of Mr. Kirkland's mouth.

Fio put his elbows on the kitchen counter from the stool he perched upon and cocked his head to one side. "Lane, you haven't been yourself and Evelyn and Kirkland filled me in on your quick departure from Michigan. You're entitled to your privacy, of course, sort of . . . We all just want to know if you're all right. It's very . . . er . . . extremely . . . um . . . *strange* for you to not talk about how you're feeling."

"Hmm, yes, I'm not exactly the strong silent type," I said wryly.

Roarke mumbled, "Not silent . . ." I wasn't sure if that was a compliment to the word *strong* or an insult to the word *silent*. I just looked at him until he cleared his throat and said, "Uh . . . sorry . . . do go on."

As quickly as I had felt relief at having a rollicking good sleuthing escapade with Roarke, my moodiness swung the other way suddenly and I had to fight the feeling of annoyance at being trapped. I hated a big fuss made over me and yet I knew I had been the impetus to this fuss. I also found it galling to not understand my own emotions. I loved emotion and felt deep passion for things and for people, but I was also very logical and I hated not being able to simply understand my past and how it made me feel. I reflected back to that moment of being in my favorite maple tree in what used to be my home. I very clearly remembered that intense, raw emotion that caused me to painstakingly, determinedly put up that wall.

I'd done a good job avoiding the issue and the sleuthing spree was distracting and fun, despite the danger. As usual. But I felt heat creeping up my collar and my face. I backed up a little, hating the feeling of being a bit cornered.

I wanted to be tactful and grateful. These people loved me. But

I was more annoyed than appreciative. "Well, I'm really sorry," I said in a clipped voice. "It's . . . I just don't know what to say. I still can't figure it out. I thought I was ready to go back, was looking forward to it. But when I sat up in my tree, I hated it. I did not want to be there one second longer than I had to. It was a fight, half of me longing to be there and wanting to figure things out. The other half wanting to tell it all to go to hell." I was clenching one of my fists as I tried to put it to words. Punching something sounded good. The anger was close to the surface. And strong.

Aunt Evelyn nodded. Even though I knew my reaction had been rough on her, I saw her strength written all over her steely eyes and firm jawline. It made me unclench my fists, which were ready for a fight.

I looked at Fio. He knew all too well about loss. He nodded. "Do you think you'll want to go back, Lane? Or is that a chapter that you'd rather have closed for you?"

"Oh, I definitely want to go back. I'm not sure when, but there's something I need to face. But this time, I'll know what I'm heading into."

Mr. Kirkland gave a small, closed-lipped smile. "You just say the word, Lane, and we'll get you back whenever you like."

Everyone went home after we had a little lighter time to chat about normal things. Roarke and I had also given a small overview of our jog through the park, all of us thinking through what it could mean. After everyone left, I sat in our parlor and wrote a letter to Finn. I wasn't even sure he was getting my letters. I put my pen down, stretched, and listened to the silent house.

I looked around the room and remembered my birthday in August. A night full of family and friends, good food, thoughtfulness, laughter. That evening, there'd been this sting at the unfairness of the fact that my parents couldn't be part of it all. A sting that grew dangerous roots that night and festered into *something* that reared its head while I was sitting in that maple tree. Now Finn was out of touch, across an ocean, for an undetermined amount of time. With ghosts of his past, one of whom he'd been in love with at one point. Gwen.

The room suddenly seemed very empty. And cold.

CHAPTER 13

The wind chilled Finn to the bone as one of London's famous fogs rolled in. It truly was as thick as pea soup and the gray mist blurred the gas street lamps, producing golden halos. He listened to the click of his shoes on the pavement as he crossed the bridge, just able to make out the dome of St. Paul's Cathedral in the distance. He was thinking about the things he gleaned from his meeting that afternoon, unsure of what it all meant. Finn went over the cloak and dagger conversation in his mind. . . .

The greasy, dirty, ancient face of his contact had looked back at him with shifty eyes, darting to and fro, never stopping, never resting, ever-searching for danger lurking in the shadows. Finn's usual calm started to be rubbed away as the anxiety pouring from this person started to infect him. He felt the hairs on his neck rise.

Finn tried to assure him. "Miles, we weren't followed. The people who had been chasing you have been dead and buried for years." He tried to reason with him, but reason had nothing to do with it. Primal fear had molded and shaped this keenly anxious man before him. It had been a miracle that he'd even found him.

The man's voice was a residual of what it once was, a raspy croak. "Oh . . . You can't be sure of that, Mr. Brodie. You can never be sure." His shaking hands reached out to Finn, making signs that he wanted—needed—a cigarette. Finn pulled one out of his inner coat pocket and lit it for him. The light of the match made a shocking show of warmth and otherworldliness in the midst of this clawing damp that reminded one of prisons and dungeons. The damp was so complete, so chilling, that Finn had to fight off the illogical flicker of fear running up his spine that whispered to him that he might never grasp the cozy, homey feel of a fire in the fireplace ever again. He shook his head to clear those thoughts out of his mind.

"All right, Miles, tell me what you know. I've been searching for a remnant of the old crew."

"Old crew, eh? For someone so certain that those who were after me are dead and buried, why would you have the need to find one of us?" The old man might be paranoid and anxious, but his mind still worked like a steel trap. At least sometimes.

"We have reason to believe that those in charge might have left . . . oh, let's just say, an heir or two," said Finn, searching for words to describe a notion, an idea, that he had just started to be able to put together.

"An heir . . ." the old man sputtered. "But he only had one child and that son died years ago. You can't mean Rex had more than one child?"

Rex. Finn had been waiting for him to say that name. He'd heard that name only once or twice before and knew hardly anything about the mysterious man. Rex Ruby was the leader of what became known as the Red Scroll Network, a group that organized an effort to take advantage of war-torn Europe. They systematically raped and pillaged several countries of their precious works of art, jewels, and anything of value left unsecured as the countries fought off their more visible enemies. Ruthlessly, they'd befriend wealthy citizens and promise to smuggle out their jewels, their priceless paintings and sculptures, and keep them for them in America, then help them escape and the treasure would be waiting for them to help kick-start their new lives in the New World. Then the network would just disappear with their loot and leave the trusting people without a dime, and nothing to help them against their enemies as they were rounded up and killed or taken as prisoners of war. And there was no coincidence about the red scroll on that silver gun of Lane's nightmares; this same Rex once held that lethal gun in his own hands.

"No, we're as sure as we can be that Rex only had one child, that son you mentioned. But was it possible that he had grandchildren?" asked Finn.

"Oh God," said Miles, pulling so deeply on his cigarette that Finn worried he'd burn his lips as the burning ashes made their way up the cigarette at an alarming rate. Miles's hands shook even more violently.

In fact, the embers did burn his lips and with a shocked reflex, Miles abruptly brushed the offending stub away. He was irritated from the unexpected spasm from the burn, but that momentary sharp pain seemed to clear his head. Finn watched him with fascination as emotions swept across his face.

Miles tilted his head and pursed his lips as if giving ear to advice or a deep consideration, and something altered in his haunted eyes. Resolve made a spark, albeit small, come out of those shifty eyes. He suddenly seemed more human, more aware and alive. Miles started talking faster, still with a heavy rasp like he'd grown up in the coal mines, but the cogs of his mind were really moving now.

"All right, Finn. I've wondered for years why I was left here alive. Yeah, might as well do something besides just survive. It seems hardly substantial, but right now the only lead I can give you is that Rex Ruby worked closely with an architect who did some work in New York City and a few other major cities in America. Rex loved to be in the spotlight. Well, that's not actually accurate. He didn't want a lot of attention, but he wanted a lot of credit, like . . . like . . ." Miles rubbed his dirty temple, like he was trying to coax coherent thoughts out of a mind that had just been retrieved after a long and wandering journey. "Like a god. Yeah, yeah, he was a master of manipulation and wanted to be behind everything, wanted everyone to think that he was everywhere at once and you could never, ever get away from his control." Finn nodded, taking it all in. This was the most information he'd ever gotten about the elusive and powerful Rex Ruby.

Miles went on, warming to his topic. "So, he would have monuments erected or get the architects of monuments and statues to create little signs woven into their work, like puzzles or clues. Yeah, and then he'd get his kicks out of leaving his mark everywhere; even if it was small, it mattered to him. In fact, it was even better if it wasn't very obvious and in the open. Like it was more sinister, reminding people that he was always watching, even when you weren't aware of him. He liked things like that, yeah. He liked things like that a *lot*."

He and Miles had parted, exchanging information on how to reach each other if they thought of anything else. Finn had a new ally. He instinctively liked this man who had transformed before his eyes. He still smelled awful, and his eyes remained haunted, but the man once again had a mission. Finn found him a place to stay and paid for the month. Hopefully some good meals, rest, and a roof over his head would help him become once again the man whom Finn heard about.

Finn took one last pull of his cigarette as he smiled to himself about that meeting. He heard the loud mew of a cat from between two buildings just ahead and he pulled up the collar of his coat against the growing cold. He'd have an invigorating chat about all these things with Kirkland, Evelyn, and Fio when he got back, that was for sure.

And Lane. God, he missed her. He'd received a couple of letters from her, but because of his mission he hadn't been able to get any back to her. He knew she'd understand, but he also knew she loved him enough to be worried about him, which filled him with an unexpectedly gratifying sense of being needed. Something that secured him, grounded him more than he had felt . . . well, perhaps ever.

That issue of Mr. Hambro disappearing had him concerned; that was so unlikely from a man like him. And he had dire forebodings that a mystery of this caliber would draw Lane and Roarke toward more sleuthing sprees. And he wouldn't be there to help them out if they got into a spot of trouble. He took courage in knowing that Lane could take care of herself, but he was still uneasy. She had this independent streak that made him wonder what was at the root of it. No, *independent* wasn't the right word . . . Too tame a word, for Christ's sake.

But her letters were so good to receive, like having her just a little closer. Other than Mr. Hambro, nothing out of the ordinary had been happening. She was on her way to Michigan the last he had heard from her. He wondered if she'd remember much more about her past. He hoped that she wouldn't uncover more uncertainty, but find something that would bring her some peace.

Just then, he thought about the moment that they had opened the slim black case from the safe-deposit box, left to Lane by her parents. And inside was that damn silver gun, a deadly gleam to its shiny surface, the scarlet scroll deeply carved into the handle—the gun that had haunted her dreams for years. They didn't know what to make of it. It had been a sign of malevolence in her dreams, something that she hated and feared. And now to have it inextricably linked to her mother and father was a strange turn of events to say the least. It was Rex's gun, all right, retrieved when Kirkland and Lane's father finished him off. But there had always been twin guns like an evil yin and yang. And one was missing. Eliza had dropped it over the Queensboro Bridge and it was gone.

The scroll. The thought dawned on him like someone had just slapped him across the face. He thought back to opening that package that contained the gun, and took a good look at the mental photograph of those scarlet etchings in the grip of the gun. *My God. The scroll.* His new friend Miles said that Rex enjoyed making his mark on architectural pieces of the city . . . *The Glade Arch Bridge.* On a walk through Central Park he and Lane found that exact scroll in the decorative ornament along the cement railings on both sides. A diamond shape with loops at each of the four corners, and in the middle a symmetrical cross with fleur-de-lis at each point. He had to get a telegram to her as soon as possible.

His mind went round and round about these things as he walked toward the home. The lonely door was up ahead, many windows glowing in the evening darkness. He looked forward to his grandmother's warm company. He wished he could get her into someplace better than this home, but it was clean and safe despite its lack of grandeur. And the workers loved her; that was the most important thing.

As he went up the walk, a young lady came out the door and closed it behind her with a smile on her face. He stopped dead in his tracks, and the hundreds of details flowing through his mind went wafting away into the deep fog. She looked up at him, astonished.

"Oh, my God, Finn! What are you doing here?" she exclaimed in a surprised, but friendly manner.

"Gwen."

CHAPTER 14

"These are all very strange circumstances . . .
but I think I begin to see daylight."

At work the next day, we were all occupied with an onslaught of details surrounding a new housing project that Fio developed. He had been hounding Washington and, once again, Roosevelt backed Fio's plans with some money. Roxy was typing away as fast as her considerable skills allowed, her short blond curly hair quivering in the exertion of the lightning speed of her fingers.

We hadn't hired a new secretary to fill in the void that Eliza left when we discovered her criminal activities. Turns out that without her catty friendship to distract her, Roxy got plenty of typing done with time to spare. So Fio left it at promoting Roxy and giving her a nice raise.

Fio was in the middle of a meeting that was carrying the usual loud talking and yelling that accompanied all his gatherings. He kept his business conferences going at a brisk pace by employing some unorthodox methods. Last year, I discovered that he had some maintenance guys come in and saw about an inch off the front legs of the chairs in his office. No one knew he did it except me; I had walked in on one of the guys sawing away at the legs. With the subconscious discomfort of those chairs, people didn't dillydally. And when Fio was feeling particularly ornery, he wouldn't allow me to take people's coats. So, during any given meeting, people would be overheated and perpetually tipping the slightest bit forward. *Fio, Fio, Fio.* What was I going to do with him?

After lunch, Roarke came in for a quick meeting to tell Fio about the article he wrote concerning Mr. Hambro. He walked by my desk, greeting me and then greeting Fio, who had opened the door to his office and waved him in. Fio waved at me to come in as well. I brought my own chair. I kept a small one that I could scoot in and out with ease. I made up some story about having a back problem and that this chair helped. I think Fio knew that I had found out about his enhanced office chairs, but we just kept that little secret to ourselves.

Roarke was a first-class reporter, and he wrote some articles that pushed back against Fiorello. Fio wasn't always thrilled with that, but he respected Roarke's work because of it. He asked Fio whether he thought Mrs. Hambro would be up for another interview. He'd interview Mrs. Hambro whether Fio agreed or not, but it was a polite consideration for him to ask. And Fio knew it.

Fio nodded his head contemplatively with his hands clasped together, index fingers pointing up and supporting his chin. "Indeed I do, Roarke. Mrs. Hambro is quite competent."

"Oh!" exclaimed Roarke. "I also had a chance to speak with Marty, Lane. You won't believe this, but I just met up with him and when he was talking with those two huge guys in the park, they simply had a message for him, and surprisingly not a threatening one. They told him that their boss said, and I quote, 'Not to worry about anything.' He asked them if they knew where Mr. Hambro was, but they said they didn't. It sounds like, when they caught sight of us they thought maybe we'd been after Marty ourselves, so they ran after us."

I asked him, "Did they say who their boss was?"

"No. And we're wondering if that message was a real message; that things are under control according to whoever sent the message? Or was it a message to throw us off the trail?"

"Okay, Fio, what do you think? I can fairly hear the cogs in your head turning about," I said, sitting back and crossing my legs.

"Hmmm," he said ruminatively. "Well, other than not liking that you were running away from thugs through a deserted area of the park, I think I will have to give it some more thought." And with that, he dismissed us. I was baffled. Fio likes short, efficient meetings because he can't deal with incompetence. But when there are theories and mysteries afoot, he always has something to say. I wondered what he was up to.

Late in the afternoon I received a telegram. My eyes went straight to the bottom, and it was from Finn. I read it as fast as I could, devouring it, making sure he was okay.

GO BACK TO BRIDGE STOP CONXN WITH
SCROLL AND BRIDGE STOP LOOK FOR
ANYTHING UNUSUAL STOP SEND GRAM BACK
STOP MAMBO LOVE FINN END

I laughed at the addition of *Mambo* at the end. The telegraph office must have wondered exactly what kind of message this was. I knew it was a word letting me know that he missed, just as much as I did, our dance in Little Italy. It had been to "Mambo Italiano."

I enjoyed an enticing little mental picture of him as he wrote this note, his eyes that were greenish gray in the light and almost black at night. I loved making him laugh, sharing inside jokes, enjoying the tiny moments of realizing we knew each other very well.

I shook my head, getting myself in the game again. I looked up from my daydreaming and there before me, Roxy and Val were leaning up against the doorframe, ankles crossed, faces grinning. I met their eyes, feeling sheepish. Roxy's eyebrow went up. I could feel my face turning red and then all at once, the three of us cracked up.

Val's hands went right to her hips. "All right, girly, what's the telegram about?"

"How long have you been standing there?" I asked.

Roxy said, "Long enough. It's from Finn, I take it?"

"Yep. Okay, girls, we have a mission."

They both pulled chairs up to my desk and I let them read the telegram. They looked perplexed and since they both had been deeply involved in the previous case, I decided to take them into my confidence. I filled them in on my recurring dream, the gun from my parents, and the bridge in the park that Finn had to have been talking about. I had thought about it from time to time, but so much happened after that walk of ours when I first saw it, I had been occupied with more pressing issues. Like being kidnapped and dangling off a bridge, for instance. Finn must have discovered something about it.

"What do you two think about taking a little walk through Central Park after work?"

I saw a self-conscious look flutter across Roxy's face, and a tiny smile pull at her lips, clearly happy to be invited to the sleuthing. They had brought in their coffee cups, so we saluted the park mission with a clink all around with our three mugs.

After work, we made our way to Central Park. We decided to take the bus up Madison to 79th and enter in at Cedar Hill. The park was nearing its winter mode. Just like the midsection where Roarke and I enjoyed the Rambles, some leaves were still golden and brown. The gingko fanlike leaves were their magnificent yellows and the oaks had their crispy brown coats that would remain rustling through most of the winter. But the majority of the leaves had fallen and the grass wasn't its verdant green, but a brownish green hue. Even in the growing starkness, the park held a beauty all its own. The squirrels were growing more and more fluffy and fat as they were busy gathering their acorns for the winter store. The wind blew across us and made my wool coat flutter. I was glad I had worn my dark brown, tall boots.

I was almost ready for a warm hat. I hated to smash my hair with a winter hat, but this city was all about survival. One winter day at a busy subway stop, I looked around and even though we were far down under the ground, it was a particularly cold station. Every one of us, whatever situation in life—even the women who looked like models—we all had hats on. Warm hats. Not just the cute ones we wore on a regular basis that just perch on your head leaving your hairdo untouched, but warm ones that covered our ears. I knew then and there that New Yorkers were concerned with survival and comfort and we weren't about to put up with vanity making us uncomfortable. We just bought cuter warm hats.

I talked with Valerie and Roxy about my walk with Finn that summer day and we took the same route, walking toward the bridge. We walked right to the railing where Finn had stood behind me, putting his arms on the railing, encasing me in his arms, his face next to mine. The feel of his breath on my neck had sent shivers of desire right through me.

I cleared my throat, getting down to business. "All right, we were standing here, and *here* is the scroll," I said, as I pointed to the cement square with that familiar scroll. They were both nodding, their minds clicking away, thinking about everything I had told them.

Val began, "So, Finn told you to come back here and look for anything out of the ordinary?"

I said, "Yes. We meant to research this bridge, but a lot happened right after our discovery and it went to the back burner. But clearly it can't be a coincidence that this is the same scroll as the one on that silver gun. Let's take a good look at it and see what we can find."

We all stepped closer and looked at the cement scroll. There wasn't anything on it that seemed out of place. We took a small step back and looked around. Several scrolls just like it adorned the railings on both sides. But nothing set them apart from one another when we looked at them up close.

Roxy decided to take a few more steps back, just off the bridge, getting a larger and wider perspective. "Hmmm," she murmured thoughtfully. "You know? This might be a stretch," she laughed, "but those figures that are all along the bridge that support the railing . . . Don't they kind of look like chess pieces?"

I stood straight up as my stomach dropped. Turning abruptly, I ran over next to her. I turned back to the bridge, took a deep breath, and got a good look at it. Sure enough, between the scroll pieces, the chunky spindles holding up the railings were actually figures that looked like chess pieces. Pawns, to be precise. Like the one I'd been dreaming about.

CHAPTER 15

"I see there is something seriously amiss."

"Lane, what's wrong? You look like you've seen a ghost," said Roxy, her laughter from the moment before completely gone, realizing that maybe her hypothesis wasn't a stretch at all.

"That's exactly what Finn said to me when I saw the scroll here the first time."

Val came over. "So, do those figures mean something to you, Lane?" I looked at her for a moment as I got my thoughts together. Her golden, honey-brown hair was done up in a complicated updo, and her navy blue wool coat sparkled like a soldier's uniform with the bright silver buttons. She wore a heavy wool hat. Smart girl.

I shot a look to Roxy as well. Roxy had on a hat, too, but it was a stylish little black number, in direct contrast to her white blond hair, that did nothing but adorn her cute head; her ears were red with cold.

I hesitated. I wasn't sure I could bring myself to completely reveal why this meant something to me. It sounded so . . . silly and unbelievable.

"Well . . ." I began slowly, a little nervous as to how my statement would be received. "This is the deal: I've always had dreams about my childhood. So much of it was cut short. I think my dreams are part of my subconscious remembering details, you know? I'd had memories of Eliza's mother and that silver gun for years. Well, a few months ago, a new thing entered my dreams, over and over again. It's a gold chess piece. A gold pawn. And, I'm certain, it's the exact shape of these figures on the railing."

Roxy's face had at first held a little skepticism that reminded me of her old bitchy attitude, but she caught it, blushed, and adjusted her face to a look of concern. As I talked about my childhood memories, her face absorbed it with a sadness that seeped into her baby-blue eyes, like she very much understood matters such as those.

"Gosh, Lane," said Val, "no wonder you look like you saw a ghost. Okay, we better take a really good look at this. Let's write down everything we come up with."

Roxy started counting the pawns. "There are ten pawns in each section, five sections on each side," she called out.

I called to Valerie, who had taken out her pad of paper and was jotting down the information, "There are twelve scrolls total, six on each railing on either side of the bridge."

Then I walked to the opposite side of the bridge. I carefully assessed the railings, back and forth, on each side. The floor of the bridge was tiled in a harlequin design, but nothing remarkable stood out. Then I went back to examining the railings. There was something there, something different. I looked back and forth, to the right, to the left. That was it. On just one side, the side that overlooked Cedar Hill, the ten pawns in the very middle of the bridge were different from the others. Those ten pawns, in a row, straight as soldiers, were made with a few more turns in the design and slightly wider, making them appear a little bigger and a little more regal than the rest. I told Val and Roxy this and we all crept closer to those pawns. I bent down, so that I was at eye level with them. Yes, ten larger pawns were in the center of the bridge rail.

"Wait a minute!" exclaimed Roxy, with her head bent to an awkward angle, looking at the base of the pawns, peering between them. "Do you see this?"

Val and I went over to her. "Here, right here," she said, and I took a close look at where her slim finger pointed. At the bottom, between the pawns, there was an X etched deeply in the concrete. I looked to the next one, same thing. All along, there was one X at the base of each one of the pawns, except for the last three. The last three in the line of ten were blank.

Val verbalized what we were all thinking: "Huh."

After looking around a little bit longer, we decided we found everything we could. We all walked back to my place, seeking warmth and sustenance, which were always in abundance at our home, thanks to Mr. Kirkland. We climbed the steps, tuckered out from our journey, our breath making puffs into the brisk air. Ripley was wagging his tail in the side window. Roxy, behind me, stuttered, "Uhh . . ."

I chuckled, "It's okay, Roxy, I'll have a word with security."

She responded with a chuckle that was half-laugh, half-nervous *Are you sure?*

I opened the door and patted Ripley's big head and whispered in his ear, "She's okay, big fella, you can keep your eye on her, but she's a welcome guest."

Val, who had heard my whisper, laughed. Roxy still looked a little dubious and was just about to say something. I intercepted her, saying, "Oh, and Roxy, don't call him *doggie*, he hates that. 'Ripley' will do."

"Ookkaayy," said an even more nervous Roxy. "Hi, Ripley. Uh, how are you today?"

Ripley cocked his head at a funny angle and looked at me quizzically.

I grinned and took their coats. We all headed back to the warm kitchen where the unmistakable and scrumptious smell of chicken noodle soup was brewing.

"Hi, Lane. Hello, Val and Roxy," said Mr. Kirkland with a gruff and friendly growl.

"Hi, Mr. Kirkland!" we all chimed. He laughed as we couldn't take our eyes off the humongous pot on the giant stove. "Hungry, girls? How about I dish up some soup for you? You look a bit chilled."

We all responded at the same time. "Thanks!"

"That would be great!"

"Oh, my God, yes."

Val and Roxy plopped down at the table while I poured some tea. Our faces were red with wind and cold, eyes bright, giddy about the soup. Mr. Kirkland brought us the steaming bowls and a plate of sourdough bread with a big dish of butter. *Heaven.*

"So, what have you girls been up to? Looks like you did more than just come home from work. Anything interesting?"

At that juicy question, Aunt Evelyn came sweeping in. "Interesting? Hi, girls! What have you been up to?"

I filled them in on Finn's telegram and our walk through Central Park. Mr. Kirkland's and Evelyn's attention had been fully captured and they joined us at the table, looks of deep and satisfying contemplation etched on their faces. They enjoyed a good mystery just as much as I did.

"So you saw this, during the summer?" asked Aunt Evelyn.

"Mm hm," I replied with a mouthful of noodles. I swallowed and said, "We also found that on the one side, there were ten larger pawns than all the other parts of the railing. And on seven of those pawns was an engraved *X* at the bottom. Three were left blank."

Mr. Kirkland asked, "So what made you start looking at the pawns exactly?"

I hadn't told them about my dream yet, and a wave of peevishness came over me. I knew Evelyn and Kirkland understood my dreams and memories, but Kirkland's tone implied he knew what it was about and it annoyed me that he might be keeping more secrets. But that was ridiculous. I shook my head, trying to get rid of the weird bad mood that had suddenly descended on me. "Well, you know how I've been dreaming about that silver gun for years? A little while ago, I, uh . . . started dreaming about a gold pawn." I noticed that everyone had stopped eating, but I just kept going, filling them in on the strange image of a chess piece.

Mr. Kirkland's spoon clanked to his bowl. He abruptly got up, shoving his chair backward, and ran upstairs.

"Uh-oh," I said. "That can't be good."

"Oh dear," said Aunt Evelyn.

"Evelyn!" bellowed Kirkland from upstairs. "Do you know where my rucksack is?"

"You have ten! Which one?" she yelled as she made her way to the bottom of the stairs.

"The . . . the . . . big greenish brown one!"

Aunt Evelyn muttered exasperatedly, "Oh good grief, they're all greenish brown."

At that, a memory nudged its way into my thoughts. One day a couple of months ago, Valerie and I had taken one of his rucksacks to the park and Finn ended up meeting us there . . . That was it. I ran upstairs, taking them two at a time. "I got it, Mr. Kirkland! I know what you're looking for!"

I ran to my room. I had found something at the bottom of his rucksack that day and had pocketed it, not thinking anything about it. It had looked like a child's play thing, but I had kept it in my dresser drawer. I retrieved it and ran back down, hearing Kirkland's footsteps pounding right behind mine. When we got to the kitchen, I opened my hand for everyone to see. On my palm was a black chess piece, a pawn. As I looked closer, it was unmistakable.

The thought hit Valerie and Roxy at the same time. Roxy nodded enthusiastically as Val said, "*That's* the shape of the pawns on the railing of the bridge!"

Mr. Kirkland was nodding. He looked at me and I handed him the pawn. He sat down with a sigh.

"I hadn't thought of that in over a decade," he said, looking out the patio window, although I was sure he wasn't thinking of the patio. He looked far, far away.

I said, "Sssssssoooo, what are you thinking, Mr. Kirkland?"

"Well, Lane. Here, take a good look at it."

I took it into my hand. It was heavy. I looked closer and although dirty, I could see through a bit of the grime. And then the weight of it hit me.

"Oh, my God. It's solid gold, isn't it? What's engraved on the bottom of it?"

Evelyn snatched it right out of my hand.

"Wait a minute. *This* is the pawn from your dream?" She looked closely at it, rolling it around in her hands. She got up and went to the sink. She brought down a chemical from an upper cabinet and rubbed the piece with it. In a few moments, it turned a bright shiny gold. She brought it back over and placed it in the center of the table, all our eyes completely glued to it. And directed right at me, on the base of the pawn, was a clear and deeply etched *RR*, now extremely vibrant against the gleaming gold.

All our eyes went to Mr. Kirkland.

"All right. Fine, let me think for a minute," he growled. He growled often, but I couldn't tell if the growl was indicative of him needing a minute to figure out how to explain another secret being revealed, or because he was exasperated that I found something I wasn't supposed to find. Again. I did have a knack for that. He muttered a few other choice words as he went to the fridge and pulled out some courage in the form of a beer. I heard Roxy make a noise that was like a laugh that she turned into a cough just as Kirkland's eyes darted to her.

He sat back down, now ready to take us on. "All right. The *RR*. Well . . ."

He was interrupted by a door slamming open and screechy bellowing echoing through the house. Fio was here on his almost nightly visit on the way home. Mr. Kirkland looked relieved, but I said, "Oh, no you don't. You can take a break while Fio comes in, but we'll pick it back up again, mister."

I was joking and he knew it. But there was part of me that knew there was so much more that we needed to understand to put this together. I had so many questions about my parents and everything they were involved in. I thought I knew deep down that they were good people, but I had doubts beginning to form as I discovered things like the silver gun. They had been undercover trying to infiltrate the Red Scroll Network. But when someone goes undercover, they often have to make choices for the mission that they'd never make in real life. How far were they willing to go? And how far was past the point of no return? In some circles, there were innuendos about them being involved in art theft in the war, some art that they supposedly retrieved but was never returned. Was I prepared to believe that they were just as bad as some of the people I fought against? And Kirkland worked with them; there was no way that he had evil intentions. No. It just didn't fit. There had to be more, much more, to this story.

Fio came in flapping and bellowing. When Valerie was forced to put her hands to her ears, he moderated his voice.

"Oh, hi, Valerie. Hi, Roxy," he said. He sat down and Mr. Kirkland gave him a bowl of soup.

"Well . . ." said Aunt Evelyn with a furrowed brow. "This is what's going on. . . ."

Thank heavens she filled him in quickly and with the precision and ease that only she can achieve. I didn't have it in me to do it *again*. We should have just called a council of war, as we grew accustomed to calling our meetings.

Fio's agile mind took everything in, calculating all the while, and then looked at Mr. Kirkland. "Okay, so what is this *RR* all about?"

Then the doorbell rang.

I ran to the door, yelling, "Coming, Roarke!" It *was* that time of day that our friends happened to appear on our doorstep.

I swung open the door to a bewildered Roarke. I grabbed his arm, pulling him along, telling him at breakneck speed the details. He laughed, but I knew he was listening and the gleam of investigation was in the forefront of his eyes.

Mr. Kirkland began, at last. "Finally. Well, it's Rex Ruby."

Of course it was Rex Ruby. But my heart still skipped a beat as I heard the name of the man who had been behind the Red Scroll Network. Mr. Kirkland continued after a long swig of beer. "As you know, your parents and I had been working against this network of thieves, retrieving art and returning it to the perspective countries. Not only was the art sacred to the countries, but the havoc that this ring of people wreaked was abominable. Hundreds of innocent lives taken for the sake of money. These were unscrupulous, soulless thieves and murderers, promising safety and security, only to steal the priceless, ancestral treasures and leave the people to the wolves. As hard as it is to take a life, it wasn't hard to take this guy's. When your father and I, uh, *dispatched* Rex, we found two of these pawns on him. I took one, your father took the other. After Rex was gone, the network seemed to have stopped in its tracks, so we never found out what they meant. It wasn't until Daley Joseph and Donagan Connell came around with an interest in the silver gun that we realized we might not have killed the organization when we killed Rex. It may have just gone into hibernation."

I nodded. The atmosphere that had been light and jovial with all our usual bantering was now thick and solemn.

I added, for Valerie's and Roxy's sake, "This ring of thieves was called the Red Scroll Network."

Val almost whispered, "Just like the scroll on the silver gun, right?" I nodded.

Roxy added, "And on the Glade Arch Bridge."

Mr. Kirkland continued. "Your parents and I had a long history with them. Your parents had gotten in with some of the agents of the network as they worked undercover. After a while their cover was blown, but we'd learned enough to at least be able to start tracking their movements. We followed them across Europe, taking out the perpetrators if they fought us, trying to bring them in, but not one single person surrendered no matter how hard we tried. Probably knowing that it would be far better to be killed by us than face their boss with failure. After years of searching, we at last located the leader, Rex Ruby, and we took him out. Your parents had already moved to Rochester; a place where you could blend in. Figured a small town was better than a busy city."

We were all silent for a usually boisterous group.

Fio took over at this point. "Yes, Lane, because of the interest in the silver gun, we have been wondering if Rex Ruby somehow had lasting connections with our last case and with Donagan Connell. Donagan Connell was starting a new enterprise, for sure, but we wanted to know if he was really trying to reignite the Red Scroll. It's actually why we sent Finn to Europe. With Europe in such a mess right now, President Roosevelt felt that a revived crime syndicate—especially this one—could be extraordinarily dangerous."

In an incredulous tone, I sputtered out questions fast and furious. "Wait. Lasting connections? What do you mean? You think Rex actually survived and it's been *him* that's behind all this? Is he the guy that Venetti warned me about, the mysterious new gangster whom no one knows about with a ruby ring on his pinky?" I frankly found that hard to believe.

Fiorello said, "Well, no. The evidence of Kirkland taking out the original Rex is incontrovertible. He most definitely was killed.

However . . . We know he had a son. Finn and other contacts are trying to find the whereabouts of this son. It seems there was great care taken in keeping him hidden. It's possible the son has taken on the mantle of Rex Ruby. And Kirkland, what do you know about red envelopes being delivered when Rex was in control? Because it seems that my friend Hambro received one."

Mr. Kirkland looked a little pasty. "Your friend who disappeared got a red envelope?" he quietly asked.

"Two," said Fio.

Kirkland squinted in thought. "Those red envelopes died with Rex, until now. He sent them to people, usually to terrorize them. Occasionally, he'd send one to a high-ranking employee to tell him he'd been promoted. But it was most often a death knell. He truly liked to toy with his people."

I had another thought. "Let me ask you, Mr. Kirkland. How many of these Red Scroll Network people did you take out? Not including Rex."

He ticked the numbers on his fingers. "Six. There were six of them."

Val broke in, "Lane, are you thinking of those seven marked pawns on the bridge?"

"Yeah. I was wondering if those seven *X*'s marked the players who were taken out. And I'm certain they don't involve Rex himself, he surely considered everyone else his pawns."

"That sounds right, Lane," agreed Mr. Kirkland. "But there were six, I'm sure of it, not seven."

CHAPTER 16

The diminutive elderly lady rubbed her lower back like she was trying to ease away years of arthritis. Her stooped shoulders shivered in the cold wind as she made her slow and rickety way up the gray, unwelcoming walk. The walls were tall, dreary, and menacing. The barbed wire viciously kept people in and kept other people out. She adjusted the veil on her hat and hobbled forward.

The hardened guard at the door leaned down, unsmiling, peering at her face. This particular guard had seen her every Monday over the past few weeks. He said in a gruff voice, "Morning, Mrs. Connell. Go on in. Visiting time just started." He hit an invisible button behind him in his booth.

The old lady shambled forward, her ankles wobbling, each step just a couple of inches. She muttered, "Thank you, thank you." The guard looked at the long path and wondered if she might miss the visiting hour altogether she was so slow. But every single week like clockwork, she made her laborious way here to see her son.

After what seemed like hours, she at last got to the room where he would come in. She sat gratefully down on the chair provided. It was nailed to the floor. So was the table.

Finally, Donagan was brought in. She thought he never looked like himself in here. His clothes, the cut of his hair, his face, somehow, was even different. Of course, hair stylists, makeup artists, fashion designers . . . these were all luxuries that he wasn't afforded in prison. And those pieces of character were essential to the real him. They were just as much a part of his personality as his face and his limbs.

Donagan sat down gingerly, the guards backing away a bit, giving them a modicum of privacy, but not exiting the room.

The guard on the left watched Donagan carefully. He wasn't allowed to touch his mother, they could only speak. He looked down into her homely face and smiled. The guard noted with distaste that Donagan's smile just wasn't right. *God, he's a disturbing creature,* the guard thought.

"Hi, Mother," said Donagan. "So good to see you again."

They exchanged small talk, a mother talking with her son. After a few minutes, the guard yawned and the old woman looked up into Donagan's face. "Donagan," she whispered. "I've missed you. *When?*" He smiled devilishly at her.

He held a special kind of hatred for those who put him here, in Sing Sing. His deep passions and lusts were not quenched in here, nearly suffocating him. But he would get out, and he would get his vengeance, *that* was goddamn sure. All that outrage was carefully, but expressively poured out in saying her name. "Eliza," he whispered, barely moving his lips.

Her eyes were alight with the glow of fierce devotion. Only *he* understood her bloodlust and her bitterness and anger. Only him.

Donagan stroked his chin in deliberation, pursing his lips. She noticed that his nappy halo of rust-colored hair was more coarse and irregular than he liked it to be. And the scar on his face was more accentuated, an angry red that he usually covered with makeup. She supposed that having scars in prison was a good thing, a statement. Although, she didn't think Donagan would have any unwanted attention; his very being emanated brutality. She loved that, reveled in it. He had a strong face, not exactly handsome . . . but not ugly either. It was his power that attracted her.

He suddenly grew wary of her rapidly approaching departure. He whispered, again hardly moving his lips, "Wednesday. Be ready."

Donagan stood up and the guards stepped toward him, taking his arm. He looked down and said, "Good-bye, Mother. See you soon." Eliza kept in character, her face and hands perfectly twitching the slightest bit like a very old woman with a palsy. She slowly, painfully stood up and said in a soft, aged voice, "See you soon, Donny, see you soon."

On her way out, she slowly, slowly passed the guards who had let her in; her patience to play it out to the very end was rock solid. The surly guard turned his head to the other guard at the gate. "That old lady comes here every week. Huh, I guess even the assholes have mothers," he said shaking his head, making his friend bark out a harsh laugh.

CHAPTER 17

"O, we must be careful."

My thoughts were consumed with the details that were brought to light over the last few days as I tried to concentrate on the final arrangements of two community projects coming up. I couldn't shake the feeling that I needed to get back to Michigan. I wasn't sure I was ready, but my anxiety was mounting. I needed to figure out some clues that were just out of reach of my grasping fingers. I hadn't had time in Michigan to dig through the house nor to look in that safe to which my parents had given me the key. But I knew I'd find answers there to the mystery of what my parents were really involved in; if not answers then at least more clues. And perhaps there would be a link that would help us figure out this new gangster in town, who had a proclivity for sending red envelopes, and what he might ultimately be wanting to accomplish.

I *could* find answers there in Rochester, but what else would I find? I generally thought I was a level-headed person, but there had been a visceral and emotional response evoked in me that I was unable to keep in check. It was compelling and overwhelming, like it was devouring me. And the scariest thing was that part of me wanted it to. And then . . . there were my memories that were so completely centered on that beloved house. *My house.* My home. And when I dreamed about my old home, my heart ached for the safety of my parents, for the sense of belonging that was taken from me, for a known and understood home and childhood.

As I finished the final note on my work and slapped the folder shut, Roarke came into the office. He stopped by my desk, his eyes sparkling, dimples dimpling.

"What are you up to?" I said with a searching squint at his face.

"Me? Up to something? Never!" he exclaimed with mock innocence.

There was a long silence, just grinning. "So you're not gonna spit it out, Roarke?"

"Nope!" An eye roll from me.

"Unh," I said as I smacked my forehead with my hand and leaned on my desk.

He chuckled, "I'm just stopping by to say hello. You know I enjoy our bantering ways, Lane."

"I know," I said in a long-suffering manner. "Hey, Roarke, I have an errand to do today, do you want to come with me?" My tone when I said *errand* piqued Roarke's interest as his eyes glistened with excitement.

"Wouldn't miss it!"

After work, we met up and took the train uptown, then walked over to Central Park. There was a peanut cart on the sidewalk by 70th, so we bought a bag of the hot, toasty nuts. The peanut seller had an engaging demeanor, reminding me of an eccentric circus performer who might at any moment walk across a high wire or do a backward flip. He didn't speak much English—mostly Italian. He was cheery, with a huge black mustache and bushy brows and he chattered away in his native tongue, clearly happy that we had bought something from him.

Once again we entered the park via Cedar Hill, finishing up our snack and tossing the bag in the trash can, ready to get down to business. I had taken the time between work and the park to fill Roarke in on everything. I even told him about my dream with the gold pawn and the photograph of the ghostly white hand that reminded me of one of the fortune-teller machines down in Coney Island.

". . . and I really want you to see the bridge up close. See if you notice anything else we might have missed."

He nodded smartly, always game for a good intrigue. As we came up to the bridge I pointed out the pawns, the scrolls, and the larger pawns in the middle.

Roarke was nothing if not thorough. For the longest time, he walked back and forth, looking at everything up close, then farther away. Once he even stood up on one of the railings, compelling me to scold, "Careful!"

At first I had followed suit scrutinizing the bridge, but after a while I gave up and leaned against the railing. I drew the haunting blue and gold Book out of my bag, picking up where I had left off. The volume had strangely started to carry the importance of a capital letter.

Roarke's perseverance paid off. "Wait a minute!" he yelled from below, almost into the tunnel beneath the bridge. Then he came bounding up the ramp to the top of the bridge where I was standing with my hands on my hips.

Roarke was pointing to the last of the seven larger pawns that had been marked with an *X*. "Here! Right here! There's something else marked on the bottom. I caught a glimpse of something from below. It's on the back, on the side facing out to the lawn."

We both knelt down. Because the pawns were so close together, we couldn't get our heads through to look at the other side. I took out the mirror in my compact from my purse. I held it out through the railing, scraping my knuckles on the rough cement, and there, reflected back to us was 1-22-23.

I pulled my hand carefully back through, clipped the compact shut with a snap, and sat down with my back leaning against the railing, a deep chill running right through me.

"So . . . it's a code or a combination or something?" asked Roarke.

"No. No, it's not a code," I stated with an exhale.

"What is it then?" he asked, sitting down next to me, shoulder to shoulder.

"It's a date. It's the date my parents were killed."

"*What* does *that* mean?" bellowed an outraged Fiorello. He had stopped by our place on the way home from work, conveniently at dinnertime. Marie and the kids had gone to visit her aunt for the week, so he was a bachelor this fine Tuesday night. We had roasted chicken with some of the dried rosemary from Mr. Kirkland's garden and lemon and garlic. It was tender and delicious.

Roarke stayed, too. Of course.

I was starving as usual and ate my dinner with total enjoyment, but my mind stayed focused on turning around and scrutinizing the events of this week. Evelyn had said my name and I realized all eyes were on me.

"Oh, sorry. I wasn't paying attention. Did I miss anything good?"

Aunt Evelyn replied, "We were just talking through possibilities of what all this means. I take it from your face you've been doing the same and come to the same conclusion we all have: We don't know anything yet."

Mr. Kirkland barked out a laugh.

Fio chimed in with, "Well, I think we ought to send Finn the information you found. Do you want me to send it or would you like to?"

"I can do it tomorrow on my way into work," I said as I slathered more butter on another roll, my mind already picking up where it left off when Aunt Evelyn broke into those thoughts.

I could feel Roarke looking at me. "Lane . . . You look like you're thinking about something specific."

I put my elbow on the table and pensively rested my chin in my hand. "Well, it's obviously alarming that the date of my parents' death is marked on a monument that is supposedly for the Red Scroll members. It makes me worried that they were involved in more than we thought. I don't know. It just feels like we are only seeing a small part of the story. And I can't shake the feeling that the only way to get the big picture is for me to go back to Michigan."

I expected an indignant ruckus from that statement. Fio, Kirkland, and Evelyn all exchanged glances, but I was shocked to see that they weren't the outraged mother hen glances that I fully expected.

"What?" I asked accusingly.

Mr. Kirkland said gruffly, "We figured you'd come up with that conclusion sooner or later."

Aunt Evelyn replied to my astonishment, "Lane, we know that

trip threw you for a loop. But we also know *you*, my dear. We knew you wouldn't let it keep you down."

Roarke pointed at me with the fork in his hand. "Say, Lane, Fio thought we could check up on Mrs. Hambro. See how she's doing and if she has any more tracks for us to run on. I have an appointment set up around lunchtime day after tomorrow. What do you think?"

"Sure! I'd love to see her again. Fio, this Hambro case is quite the intriguing mystery, but how are you *really*? He's your closest friend, are you okay?" Fio was a very sensitive person inside, quite contrary to his rude outbursts. But it was that sensitivity that made him fight for what was right and for the people who needed someone in their corner.

He nodded thoughtfully as he drank a big swig from his frothy beer. "Thanks, Lane. It's not easy. Half the time I'm just working this mystery through like a particularly difficult business deal and yet knowing that the more time that passes, the more likely it is that . . . that . . ."

"Yes, we know, Fio," said Evelyn sympathetically.

At this sober moment, Ripley's pointy ears caught my attention. He was out in the kitchen, just in line with my sight, and his ear tips were on the other side of the counter so that was all I could see of him.

"Uhhh . . . Mr. Kirkland?" was all I got out before the remains of the chicken carcass slipped from the counter and we heard the unmistakable clatter of dog paws that can't quite make purchase on a slippery floor, trying to make a speedy getaway.

Mr. Kirkland had read my amused face, and as he heard the thief's noises he leaped from the table in hot pursuit. Aunt Evelyn was completely unfazed as she raised a glass to us all as if Mr. Kirkland hadn't just bounded from the table cussing up a storm. She declared, "To this dear, dear family of ours. Cheers!"

The following day, before I went in to work and sent my telegram to Finn, I had an appointment to make.

"Hi, Lane!" said Morgan as she opened the door to the luncheonette for me.

"Hi, Morgan. How are you?" I asked.

"I'm good. I've been busy."

I raised a skeptical eyebrow, wondering what kept her busy. She looked up at me with the sublime look of someone who has it all together. Peaceful and assured. Well, that made one of us.

"Why the funny look, Lane?" she said, reading my perplexed and probably annoyed look.

"Well . . . My trip to Michigan was weird. I don't know. I don't want to bother you with it. It's just something I can't quite figure out."

She'd ordered a coffee—black—like a forty-year-old, and took a thoughtful sip looking for all the world like a professor about to lecture.

I put my elbows on the table, clasping my hands together and resting my chin on them. "Yes, Professor? Would you like to enlighten me?" I asked.

She completely disregarded my sarcasm. "Well, actually, yes, Lane. I think we're a lot alike. Remember when you talked to me about trusting people? How you have to take that leap?"

I nodded. "Sure. I trust my friends and family."

"Oh, I know. I can tell you trust and love them. But, like you said, you're used to working on things alone, aren't you? You see, you don't have to only trust them, you have to work with them."

"But I like working by myself. Sometimes, don't you have to work alone?"

She took a bite of her BLT and nodded. After she was done chewing, and patted her lips with a napkin, she said, "Sure. The trick is knowing how and when."

"How do you know all this, oh wise and ancient one . . . ?" I dug into my hot brownie with caramel sauce.

She smirked. "Let's just say I had a similar situation with my friend Spry—Eric, I mean—and I had a choice to make. I knew I could do this big task on my own, but if I worked with him, I had a much better chance of winning. Well . . . actually, surviving."

"A choice, huh?" *What on earth had she been involved in?* We finished our meal and I felt annoyed yet again. I loved spending time with Morgan. But why did this young street urchin seem to have one up on me? I was the one who was supposed to have it all together. I fancied myself a sort of mentor to her. I was irked that I seemed to be the mentee.

After my rather scary snack time with Morgan, I sent my telegram to Finn, as well as an airmail letter to him on my way into work. In the longer letter, I tried to work out some of my thoughts, hoping I wouldn't confuse him too much. For the telegram, I kept it short with just the pertinent details.

Writing the letter was cathartic. And it brought back more memories with Finn the last couple of months. One day in particular brought my past and my present into a humorous mishmash of my life, which was often stranger than fiction.

"What's that?" he'd asked, pointing to the wooden target on the large tree in our backyard.

I had been waiting for him to see it. It was something I had discovered about myself and my history with the help of Mr. Kirkland. More and more memories about my childhood had been coming back as of late. And a couple of months ago, Mr. Kirkland gave me a mother-of-pearl inlaid dagger for protection. It had been my father's, and when I had gotten myself in a predicament, I found that I took to it quite readily. I could balance it, knife point up, on my middle finger, then flip it over so the handle was in my grip. And boy, could I throw it. But that part, Finn hadn't discovered. Yet.

Even as a young child my parents were always teaching me little things about life and survival skills. My dad took me on several camping trips and I found I had a natural talent for archery and, well . . . handling a knife, apparently. He had me helping him start fires from before I could remember. And with that came handling a Swiss army knife and a small hatchet to break down bigger sticks and branches. And when Mr. Kirkland gave me his dagger, a lot of it came swiftly back. Like riding a bike. I liked the feel of the heavy handle, perfectly balanced with the sharp blade.

That day, Finn had looked askance at me, and then back to the heavy wooden bull's-eye that was hanging on the tree. "Have you been holding back on me?" he'd asked with an eyebrow lifted.

"Oh, it's just a target for target practice with Kirkland," I'd said, trying to sound casual.

"Uh huh. Okay, show me what you got," he'd said in his accent that comes out more exaggeratedly Irish when he's preoccupied.

"Well, we've been working on some things my parents taught me. And well, some of the skills came back."

"Like what, archery?"

"Sure. That. And . . ."

"And . . . ?" he'd asked. I had started to feel a little awkward. It's not every day that you learn someone has this . . . talent . . . that I have. I felt a little ridiculous.

He could see my awkwardness and had read it wrong. "Oh, it can't be that bad, Lane. Where's your bow and arrow? Just give it a try. Here, I'll do it first." He had located the bow and arrows that were resting in the corner and had gone ahead and gotten them, trying to assuage what he'd read in my hesitation as an embarrassing inability to do something I once could.

He'd taken the bow in his hands, drawn it back, and *twang* went the arrow and it had landed almost dead center. I was laughing. I couldn't take it anymore.

Chunk! went my knife as it hit the bull's-eye almost dead center, right next to his arrow. I had thrown it from several feet behind Finn. He turned to me with eyes wide, unable to say anything.

"I know. It's weird, huh?" I'd said, smiling and slightly bashful. Slightly. And then he'd started laughing so hard he had to sit down suddenly on the Adirondack chair that was right next to him.

When he'd finally stopped, he managed, "That was *very* sexy."

I felt myself grinning from that memory as I walked through Grand Central, from Western Union where I had sent my telegram to Finn, to the subway station. I adored the Main Concourse. It never, ever ceased to make me pause and enjoy. That soaring ceiling with glittering green constellations, the thronging crowds, the loud noise of hundreds of conversations . . . Soon we would be kicking off the Christmas season and part of the hall would be filled with a Christmas bazaar. Maybe I could find something interesting for Aunt Evelyn there.

I'd always loved Christmas. And the thought of it coming up in a month made me pause. I pulled off to the side in Grand Central, and leaned up against the wall. I looked at all the people passing by; here I was in the midst of thousands of people, yet having a moment all alone. I thought about the decades of people going to and fro in this very place. The thought of time passing made me think of how my childhood had been cut short, how I had to understand and grasp things way before my time, and I wondered if I looked older than I really was. And then the future . . . I knew I was coming to a point when questions would be answered about my parents' history; the story would be filled in where it had previously been blank. I knew that I was coming to some kind of juncture. Choices would have to be made. Practical decisions about life, but also deeper decisions.

I felt like I was walking up a tall ladder that led to a high diving board. I was just getting to the top, where I'd soon have to take that knee-wobbling walk along the narrow board to the end, ponder the cool water far below, and then . . . jump. I looked in my bag to make sure the book was there. Its words were a strange piece of solace as I patted the cover.

Christmas . . . I wonder if Finn will be home by then. I finished walking through the hall and walked down the steps to my subway platform. I turned my head in surprise as I heard my name called out from behind me.

"Hey, Tucker! Are you on your way into work?" I greeted.

"Yes, along with fifty thousand of my closest friends," he groused as someone pushed past him, knocking him off balance.

We rode the train together all the way downtown. We didn't have much time to chat as the train was packed with the morning rush hour. As we climbed up several stairways at the City Hall stop, we got caught up.

It was cold. I had my wool winter hat on along with my scarf and gloves. Of course, it can be steamy in the subway, so everything I wore had to be able to be peeled off and put back on easily, otherwise you roasted or froze alternatively—a constant issue in the city.

Our breath made white puffs in the crisp morning air and Tucker, in his dark brown hat and dashing caramel-colored overcoat, turned to me saying, "Say, how was your trip to your house in Michigan?"

"Ooooohhhhh . . ." I said with an indecisive sigh.

"That good, huh?" he quipped.

"Let's just say, it's complicated. It wasn't that great of an experience, but it's all right."

"That's a shame. Do you think you'll go back anytime soon?" He looked at me, studying and searching my face.

"I don't know," I said noncommittally. As I had been thinking of going back to Rochester the past few days, I started to get excited all over again. But then . . . there was a tiny, black, ugly crumb of something. Fear maybe?

"Hmm . . . Well, I go back there frequently, let me know if you need anything. I always stay at the Statler. You can leave a message there anytime at all. Really, Lane. Just let me know."

"Thanks, Tucker. I'll do that. All right, here I am," I said as I came to the bottom steps of City Hall. "It was good running into you. Take care!"

"You too, Lane!" he exclaimed with a wave as he made his way past me.

After a long day at work, trying to focus on my job, but having trouble doing so, I was just about to pack up and head home.

"Lane, you need to hear this," yelled Fiorello from his office. I rolled my eyes. I popped up from my desk so many times a day, sometimes my thighs hurt as if I'd been doing squats at the local gym.

"Yeah, chief?" I asked, taking a quick look back at my chair, wondering if I should bring it in. I'd hoped to have a night to relax but that looked uncertain now.

Fio was at the police radio and he was patting it like it was his pet. Then he leaped up and grabbed his hat and coat. "Just heard it on the radio, Lane. We have to go!"

"Wait! You want me to come, too?"

"Yes! Go, go, go!"

I grabbed my hat, coat, and purse, and ran out the door after my surprisingly fast boss. Outside, we found his car and driver and jumped in. Fio told him Union Square. We raced up to 14th Street and Fio leaped out of the car before Ray could even come to a complete stop, making the usually calm driver swear a rant worthy of Mr. Kirkland.

I jumped out and warily made my way to what was obviously a crime scene. Fio was almost always a first responder, his dedication to the police radio and all city drama was limitless. A few police cars had arrived, their lights flashing. A body was slumped on the ground near a park bench, as if it had slid off the bench.

"Oh God, it's not . . ." I stuttered.

"No. No, it's not Hambro, Lane," said Fiorello, easily reading my thoughts as I'm certain that had been his own fear. "But it doesn't look good," he said in a low voice.

It most certainly did not look good. Sticking straight up from the guy's back was the hilt of a knife. Just then, a little flash of light caught my eye. Next to the man on the cold ground were a little pair of circular gold glasses lying forlorn, crumpled, and crushed. Right at that moment, one of the officers turned the guy on his side, to get a look at his face.

"Oh no," I whispered.

"What, Lane?" asked Fiorello.

"That's one of the junior managers at Hambro's bank. Red Tie Guy."

"*Who?*"

"I mean Marty. Roarke knows him. He's the guy Roarke and I met in the park to see if an insider at the bank had a feel for what was going on." I looked over at the bench. "That's a lot of blood. You're right. This definitely doesn't look good."

"You don't know the half of it," uttered Fio, his face a pasty white.

"Why? What do you mean?"

"That's Hambro's bank manager?"

"Yes."

"Well, *that's* Hambro's knife."

"Oh shit."

"Oh shit," said Roarke outside the mayor's office, where the press camped out waiting for my boss to create headlines.

"I know." I had filled him in on the horrible news of Marty and the damning evidence at the scene. It was indeed Hambro's knife with his family crest nice and shiny on the hilt. Two eyewitnesses had seen two men on the bench when another person wearing a long overcoat joined them from behind and drew a gun on them. One was obviously Marty, and the other he was sitting with sounded like he belonged at the old Hooverville that used to be in Central Park, with an old torn coat, dirty hat, ratty-looking gloves, and shoes with holes in the toes.

"So, if that was Hambro's knife, one of those men must have been Mr. Hambro?" asked Roarke.

"Seems likely. There had been a big scuffle and witnesses say the guy with the gun who had come up behind them was suddenly flashing a knife around. It sounds like both the other men might've gotten stabbed in the fight. But after Marty sank to the ground, the knife sticking straight out of his back, it was pandemonium. No other useful details after that. It wasn't a theft; Marty's wallet was intact. And they know it was recent—not only because of the eyewitness accounts, but because the blood was still wet," I said, a little nauseous.

Roarke thoughtfully stroked his chin. "Yeah. It doesn't sound like a mugging gone wrong. It's actually harder to stab someone than the movies make it seem, without the knife getting caught up on a rib or a button or whatnot. And for it to be in his back, he'd been about to run away. Seems to be someone who knew what he was doing."

"Or she . . ."

"Definitely. Or she," said Roarke, nodding.

I shivered at the thought of the stabbing. To get back on track, I quickly said, "It was pretty dark out already. There were just vague descriptions of the hobo. Tall, probably white male, bearded, dark hair, and somewhere between thirty and seventy."

"Aw, jeez. Half of Manhattan fits that description," said Roarke.

"Yeah, and it also fits a general description of Hambro. And the gunman's description was even more vague, so Hambro fits that description, too."

"*One* of the two men must be him. I can't imagine him pulling a gun on someone, let alone stabbing Marty. So let's just say the hobo was Hambro, how did the other guy get his knife? I mean, why come up behind two men, draw a gun, but then use a knife?" asked Roarke.

"Well, it's quieter, or maybe he wanted to implicate someone other than himself . . . But, yeah, it doesn't make sense," I said. "The police are looking for any other evidence on Marty and at the scene."

"Okay," said Roarke. "Keep me posted. I'll get my contacts looking around."

"Thanks," I replied. "That knife is definitely Hambro's, but I just can't see him being the killer. And if he's not, we don't know where he is. It sounds like he could be injured, or worse."

Roarke nodded and then blew out a huff of air. "Lane, I hate to say it, but no matter how we feel about Hambro, the evidence is pointing to him."

I nodded. "I know. He's the number one suspect."

CHAPTER 18

*". . . a look in the eye and quality of manner that seemed
to testify to some deep-seated terror of the mind."*

Roarke and I arrived at Mrs. Hambro's home the next day and
rang the bell. Fiorello had already visited her personally to notify
her about the incident at Union Square. The police questioned
her about the knife and anything else that might shed light on Mr.
Hambro's whereabouts.

I wasn't looking forward to unearthing more unhappiness for her
as we scoured through the details. I had liked her immediately. The
doleful, stick-up-his-ass Robbins answered the door as if he'd been
lying in wait.

"Hello, Robbins," I said. "This is Mr. Roarke Channing. We
have an appointment with Mrs. Hambro."

"Yes, ma'am. Come in, please."

We were led past that beautiful rose and cream-colored parlor
that we had enjoyed the last time I was here with Fio. I practically
groaned as I longingly looked into it, wanting to enter into its cheerful, soft comfort. We went to the back of the house to Mr. Hambro's
office.

I had expected it to be dark. It seemed that most men's inner
sanctums were covered in dark, masculine colors with heavy wall-
papers and large furniture. But this office was a soft shade of wheat,
with oak beams and caramel brown pillows mixed with other tones
of neutral colors. It was very masculine, but had that same inviting atmosphere as the front room with many textures and tones. A

bright aqua caught my eye. A white earthenware bowl sat on the desk with the little blue mints that were too peppery for me, but that Mr. Hambro always carried. Sometimes, he reminded me of a grandmotherly type who kept butterscotch candies and lemon drops in her purse at all times. If Mrs. Hambro decorated these rooms herself, she had an artist's eye, that's for sure. I wanted to go around touching everything. I had to rein in my texture-hungry fingers.

Mrs. Hambro was at the desk in the middle of the large window on the back wall. She stood to greet us and we sank down into the chairs in front of the desk. The worry lines of her forehead had deepened a bit and she looked tired. It was easy to imagine that sleep could be elusive for her.

As we settled ourselves, I looked around at the many books covering the walls and the other pieces of Mr. Hambro's life that were set about with intention and care. He must have liked horses; photographs and a few horsey mementos were lying about on the shelves. The many photos of Mr. and Mrs. Hambro together on vacation in various places brought a smile to my lips as the couple looked like they were enjoying themselves immensely.

But, as I sat there admiring their delighted faces as they sat at a European bistro or in the back of an old-fashioned horse carriage and other tourist traps, there was something about those photos that was striking me as odd. I couldn't put my finger on why. The frames were all in a similar silver finish. The photographs looked like they were taken over at least a couple of decades with both Hambros looking slightly different as styles came and went. Mrs. Hambro mostly looked the same, however, quite ageless and lovely in her insouciant way.

I mentally shrugged as I crossed my legs and got right to business. "So, we know Fiorello came by with the police to get your statement and any other information that might help. We set up this appointment just to get another updated interview for Roarke's paper, but now with this new development . . ." She nodded grimly. "Roarke and I, let's just say, we like to give a helping hand where we can. The police are of course investigating, but Roarke has a lot of contacts and we want to help. And let's just face it, we're nosy."

Roarke snorted and it brought a small grin to the side of Mrs. Hambro's mouth. "Would you mind if we looked into this, too?"

She answered promptly, "Frankly, we need all the help we can get. I would definitely appreciate your assistance."

Roarke asked, "So were you aware that Mr. Hambro had that knife when he disappeared?"

She hadn't known he'd taken the knife, but these days it wasn't all that unusual for a gentleman to take along a small weapon of some sort. The rest of the conversation just went over all the details that we already knew, but wanted to confirm once again. She felt awful about Marty, but had no idea why he would be a target for anyone, let alone her husband.

"There's just no reason he'd kill Marty!" she exclaimed in frustration. "It just wouldn't be advantageous at all." She resolutely nodded her head.

She looked at me, assessing my eyes, my face. *I* could think of a reason he'd been a target. "But . . ." she prompted me.

I paused, and took a breath. "Well, Marty was the one who found Mr. Hambro with a second red envelope at work. *And* . . . he witnessed Mr. Hambro enter the vehicle of Louie Venetti."

"Louie Venetti?" she whispered breathlessly. She pensively brought her fist to her lips. I don't know what I expected, but I didn't expect this quiet reaction. No one reacts quietly to an announcement that Venetti is around. She tapped her mouth pensively with the knuckle of her thumb, and said to herself, "Venetti . . ."

But there was something else happening. Something different. She was still just as honest and open. None of the details of her story had been adjusted in any way. But that niggling thing about the photographs . . . her demeanor . . . there was something definitely different from the previous time we'd met.

I looked at her with a tilt of my head. "Mrs. Hambro, has Mr. Hambro made contact with you?"

"No," she said, not too quickly and not too slowly. She looked into my eyes. Was she trying to communicate something?

"Has anyone else contacted you?" Roarke asked.

She shook her head. "No."

But there it was again. Last time, Mrs. Hambro held an air of fear and concern, her mouth tight, her eyes wary. She was still deeply concerned, but despite her fatigue that I'd noticed earlier, and the worry lines, she was somewhat peaceful. Even with mentioning Uncle Louie and the fact that Mr. Hambro might be implicated in a murder, for cryin' out loud. *Kinda strange.* I gave her the once-over with a squint to my eye, taking in her cornflower-blue eyes and her blond hair streaked with gray framing her lovely face. Her eyes were intense, full of wit and wisdom.

"Mrs. Hambro, are you . . . ? I beg your pardon, but are you holding anything back? You seem *different* today."

She sighed, putting her elbows on the table. She looked carefully at Roarke and me in turn, considering her next words. "No. I honestly don't know what's going on. And I'm devastated about poor Marty. But I have a . . . how shall I say it? A sense of peace that I didn't have the other day. I admit Mr. Hambro is in more trouble than I could have possibly imagined, but I certainly don't believe he's a murderer. I'm worried about how he got involved in all this and that he may be hurt," she said as she shuddered. "I know this sounds silly, but a friend dropped off some chestnuts today, on my doorstep. It was such a cheery thing to do. And, you see, Mr. Hambro and I have a joke about them. He loves nuts, yet vehemently hates chestnuts. I relentlessly tease him about it because it's like he's mortally wounded that chestnuts are soft and mushy. I know it's dippy," she said, with a self-deprecating grin. "It's a typical inside joke, only funny to us. I guess receiving those chestnuts just made me feel that he was all right. I know it sounds strange, but I just feel that in my heart I would know if he had died or something. I guess I have . . . *hope.*"

We left her house after we wrapped up a few further details. I hoped this case would clear soon, as I wanted to get to know her when the circumstances weren't so strained.

Roarke and I left and walked out toward the gated and only privately owned park in the city: Gramercy Park. Even though it was cold, I wanted to take a stroll through there. Mrs. Hambro sent Robbins to open the garden gate for us, and as he did so, down the block I spotted a little cart with hot beverages being wheeled about. I thought a hot coffee or hot chocolate might warm us up a bit for our walk. I told Roarke to hold the gate open and that I'd be right back.

He smiled as he saw the cart. "Good idea, Lane."

I went back to Roarke with two cups of piping hot chocolate and he said, "Nice!" as he took the cup I held out to him. As we walked around the brown path, the artistry of the garden that would be opulent in spring and summer strolled about with us, waving hello in a sweeping branch of wisteria and a clutch of papery hydrangea. I made a mental note to come back in a greener month.

Through the clutter of the last few weeks, it was hard to believe that tomorrow was Thanksgiving. It had been such a busy, regular work week that the holiday crept up on me suddenly. Mr. Kirkland and Aunt Evelyn were having their annual Thanksgiving party at the house, including any and all friends or family that we could possibly ask. It's a day that I'd always loved. And you never knew who might show up.

"What time is everyone coming over tomorrow, Lane?" asked Roarke, mirroring my own thoughts.

"I think about three, we'll eat around five."

"I could practically drool, thinking about it," he said. I don't think I remembered Roarke ever making a meal for himself. He always ate out, so he was a devoted visitor to our place for home-cooked dinners. For Thanksgiving and Christmas Mr. Kirkland and Fio went all out. They cooked for days on end to prepare with the aromas of cranberries, brown sugar and apples, cookies, and baking bread filling our home.

"So, Lane, do you think Mrs. Hambro was telling us the truth? Do you think she knows something?" he asked.

"She seemed very earnest, and not overly so. It didn't seem like she was lying . . . But . . ."

"But what?" he asked, taking a careful sip of the hot chocolate.

"I don't know. There's something there. And I believe her, she and Mr. Hambro seem very close and she might very well sense if he was in danger or dead. But there was something more than that. She seemed relieved and even before I picked up on that, I had been looking around at his office and had the feeling that there was a clue looking right at me. There was something up with those photographs on the wall, but I can't figure out what it was."

"Was there anything out of the ordinary? Anything seemingly out of place or strange?"

"Nope, not a thing. Just a lot of photos of the both of them together over many years. And for the record, I still don't sense anything amiss about their marriage. I don't think his disappearance has anything to do with infidelity."

"Yeah. With all the red envelope business, and now this stabbing that's linked to him, it's something else. For sure."

"Exactly. Plus, they seem to be kind with each other. There's no contempt in either of them. I feel like you see that in couples who are in trouble," I said.

Finishing our stroll through the little park, we made our way to Park Avenue and started north to catch the subway at 23rd. The sound of sirens approaching fast smacked up against us in direct opposition to our peaceful retreat that we had just enjoyed. Sirens were a common noise, of course, but in the city, you distinguished the different tones of sirens. Like the insistent, tinny siren of fire engines, the beeps of the ambulances, the roar of the larger ladder trucks and police cars . . . Or *this* most alarming sound: all of the above.

Why did I have to pick these darling navy blue high heels today? I should have worn something more suited for running. I should *always* wear something more suited for running. We looked down Park Avenue and sure enough, there was a fleet of police cars, followed by fire trucks coming up fast. Looking east toward Lexington, two flumes of smoke were reaching up above the short buildings. But it wasn't a house fire. It was something different. And I didn't like the look of all the commotion.

"Come on, Lane!" yelled Roarke as he started sprinting toward the smoke.

I made it there pretty close to Roarke, holding a huge stitch in my side. When I turned that final corner, a tight, tense feeling in the air startled me as if I'd run into a wall, making me stop dead in my tracks. There was a weird, strained quiet all around even though there was a lot of commotion. Roarke stood stock still, arms out to his sides in a tense, ready-to-jump posture as we took in the scene of absolute chaos.

I struggled to make sense of it. People were running wildly on the sides of the street. In the middle of the road was a crashed delivery truck with thick black smoke and flames shooting up from the engine. Directly behind it was a police van that had smashed into it, the driver slumped at the wheel.

Right then, about six men in black suits with black masks and machine guns circled around the police van. Roarke and I dove to the ground just as the machine guns erupted in a furious storm.

When they stopped, I carefully peered up and at first I thought they had shot randomly into the crowd; there were a few bodies scattered about either injured or dead. But then I saw that their aim had been directed mostly at the back of the police van. A large masked man grabbed an ax and approached the van. With one mighty hack, he cracked the now shattered rear door and lock. Through the smoke of the fire, I saw the door raggedly swing open. Right in the opening stood a guard with his hands desperately grasping at his neck, his legs kicking out, trying to fend off the attack.

Someone behind him held the chain of handcuffs around his throat, pulling tight. The guard finally slumped, his legs coming to a standstill. The chain was pulled up and over the guard's head and he was shoved out of the van with a boot to the back.

Into the sunshine, with his rusty, nappy head held high, his large chest expanding as he breathed in a deep and satisfied breath . . . stepped Donagan Connell.

CHAPTER 19

"He meant to murder you. You had a fine escape."

Suddenly the cars all started moving at once and the men in black dissolved into the crowd, taking Donagan with them like a vile magic trick.

The cavalry arrived. But it was too late. Fiorello was distraught as his sedan pulled up, and all of us were in a tragic state of bewilderment. Casualties, possible deaths, and Donagan Connell was on the loose.

Roarke and I chipped in helping the wounded and calming the crowd; there was one fatality. Fio was livid. Donagan shouldn't have been escorted *anywhere*. He must have had someone on the inside schedule the transfer. Fio would be having some choice words with the warden and the guards at Sing Sing who were supposed to inform him of any visitors for Donagan.

Hours later, back at the office, Fio called in the warden, Mr. Lewis Lawes, and two guards. Fio had me come in, too.

I walked in, pad of paper held tightly in my sweaty and nervous hands. The warden and two guards were very pale with wide eyes. Deep sadness and seething anger was also just beneath the surface of their somber faces.

"Lane? Have a seat, I called you in so you can take notes and see if there's anything we might have missed." I forgot to bring my chair, so I had to take one of Fio's *enhanced* chairs.

"All right," Fio continued. "Let's go over it one last time."

The warden, a large and sturdy-looking man of about fifty, well known as a proponent of prison reform, began. "Well, as you know, we received the typical documentation about transferring the prisoner to the courthouse due to a trial date that had been moved up. Nothing looked out of the ordinary about it. As is the case with all transfers, I handled the vehicles personally and did not notify any of the guards about who was being transferred or exactly what day or time until that very moment. So there couldn't be a leak at my prison."

"No," said Fio, thoughtfully tapping his pen on his desk. "You're right, I think the leak is higher up. If you received falsified paperwork, it's definitely higher up. But Donagan had to get some information back and forth." He turned his eyes to the guard on the left.

"And you say there were no visitors?" Fio asked him.

"No, sir, nothing odd at all," he replied with a gulp.

Wait a minute. Fio hadn't asked about any visitors out of the ordinary or odd, he'd asked about any visitors *at all*.

"Hold on," I interjected carefully. "Did Donagan have any visitors at all? Any family or anyone?"

Fio's and the warden's eyes darted to me, then back to the guard. The guard said, "W-well . . . his little old mother came in every week. But she's ancient. It took her almost ten minutes just to walk from the guard station to the door."

Fio gripped his pen with ferocious strength, his fingers turning white, and made a strangled sound in his throat. But I caught his eye, pursed my lips, and gave a curt shake to my head. He took a breath and collected himself, containing his rage.

"All right, gentlemen, thank you for your information. And on a grave day like this, we appreciate you coming in. We will do all we can to catch the people who have done this." With that, they were dismissed. After I showed them out, I walked wearily back to Fio's office and sank down into one of his miserable chairs.

Fio looked at me unsmilingly. "So. This little old mother making weekly visits to Donagan. Who do you think orchestrated that?"

"*Pfft.* Eliza, of course." Both of his eyebrows raised as he looked at me over the top of his glasses. "I know, I know. She's gotten under my skin before."

Fio made a rude noise.

"Just bear with me a minute," I said, biting back a chuckle. "We know beyond a doubt she was partners with Donagan from our last case. And they were definitely more than just business partners."

"Absolutely."

"And we know that she's fabulous with disguises and dramatic skills enough to fool her own mother, let alone a couple of guards. She sure fooled all of us."

"I actually agree with you. We don't have proof, yet, but I think that's a reasonable assumption. And uh, Lane . . . Thanks for catching me in our meeting. I was about to erupt. I specifically told the warden to notify me of *any* visitors, but the guards were just looking for visitors who stood out. However, they don't need to carry that extra burden. At least, not today. Today is dark enough already," he said contemplatively, as he looked out the window at the city he loved.

The next morning dawned cold, but sunny. It was Thanksgiving. Despite the sadness of the day before, we had a houseful of guests coming and already the wonderful smells of herbs, onions, bread, and coffee were wafting up from downstairs. Above me, I heard Aunt Evelyn in her studio with soft music playing and an occasional footstep making the familiar sound of floorboards creaking.

I still had my head on my pillow and my fingers stroked the soft cotton of the warm sheets. The air was a little frosty, so I longed to stay in my cozy covers. The pillow next to me was plump and untouched. I wondered what it would be like waking next to Finn. Every day. I smiled to myself thinking of his dark eyes smiling back at me, how he'd look all rumpled in the morning, the hair on his muscled chest as I'd run my hands slowly down . . .

And with that thought I got out of bed—no use torturing myself. I wrapped my big, fluffy pink robe around me and found my slippers. I walked sleepily up the stairs to the studio and plopped down on a pile of tarps.

Aunt Evelyn was painting a colorful scene of skaters on a frozen pond in Central Park. She usually painted in the abstract, but occasionally she would do an artful landscape or picture like this. You could see the individual skaters, but they weren't crisp and clear-cut. Each one had a modular, modern shape and was slightly blurred with the wind running through them. They had coats and hats as colorful as a bowl of jelly beans. The brown trees and buildings surrounded the scene, keeping them safe. And there was a couple in the middle of the rink. Something sweet and longing about them. They were reaching out to each other, about to embrace, definitely happy, with a beseeching tilt to the woman's head.

Evelyn looked at me and smiled knowingly. "You miss him a lot, don't you?"

I let myself fall straight over into the pile of tarps and said pathetically, "Yeeeessss!"

She laughed. "Yes, and I always think that all that talk of *distance makes the heart grow fonder . . .*"

"Grrrrr," I interrupted.

"Yes," she chuckled. "I always think it is quite a crock of . . . Well. Enough said." She tilted her head and looked at me closely. "You've decided to go back to Michigan soon, haven't you?"

How does she do that? I had just made up my mind last night.

"Yes, I'm thinking next week sometime, so I can be back here at least a couple of weeks before Christmas."

"Well," she began, "I think I can arrange something for you and me to go out maybe Tuesday or Wednesday—"

"Well . . ." I tentatively interrupted.

"What, Lane?"

"Well . . . I've been giving it some thought." I got up and slowly walked over to the large, colorful canvas that hung on her wall behind her. It was an experiment she and I had done a while ago, painting to music. I am no painter, but the experiment was something I would never forget. The polonaise by Chopin moved me, moved my body and my hands and my fingers to paint along with the powerful music. I went up to my canvas and reached out my hand. With a delicate touch, I brushed my middle finger along a wide stroke of dark magenta, lightly feeling the texture of the paint and the canvas underneath.

I thought of Finn, touching his face, the lapels of his suit coat, the feel of my face pressed up against his strong chest, the sound of his heartbeat and the perfect fit of his embrace. That feeling that our bodies were made for each other. That he felt like home.

I thought of that time when we had been covered in debris from a bomb blast, and we had shared deeply about our past: of the death of my parents and about the painful betrayal of his brother, Sean. Not only had he betrayed Finn, but there was something else that we hadn't even talked about yet. It was obviously a painful secret, that would take time to carefully unfold. Sean had done something that had profoundly harmed Finn both physically and mentally. When Finn and I had that moment with each other, I had the feeling that if we could talk about and work out those things, that *one extremely difficult time*, then we could move on.

It felt the same now.

"Aunt Evelyn, I don't understand what happened at the Rochester house. But I feel like it's something I have to overcome. And it's something that I need to do on my own, or I'll never be able to move on."

She took a deep breath, not at all pleased that I had just suggested going alone.

"Please, Aunt Evelyn, I don't need a long time by myself. Maybe just a few days. But I feel very strongly that . . . that if I can figure this out and work it through, this one difficult time, that I might be able to move on. And after yesterday . . . Damn it, Aunt Evelyn! If there is any way that I can find clues about what's going on with Rex Ruby, I want to help. I know that there are more parts to the puzzle of my parents' death and what the hell is behind that silver gun and the gold pawn. And I need to figure it out."

Her eyes sparkled, her mouth set in a determined line. "Lane, if you feel strongly about it, I'll support what you want. And I'd much rather have you angry and spunky than downcast. But I think it would be unwise to have too much time there by yourself. Besides, we don't really know who was behind the death of your parents. That perpetrator could still be around."

I hadn't thought of that.

"But, I completely understand the need to tackle and overcome something on your own two feet. What would you think about going out this Tuesday or so and then I could come out a few days later, perhaps by the weekend?"

"I think that would be great. Oh, and I can also find out if Tucker will be around. He said that he goes to Detroit frequently and he would be around if I needed anything."

Aunt Evelyn didn't look exactly pleased about that.

As I headed down the familiar staircase to my room, I firmed up the notion of going on my own. It was just easier to do it by myself. I wouldn't have to keep explaining my feelings or find all of them looking at me, wondering if I was okay. Yes, I really wanted a few days to myself. As I stepped across the threshold into my blue and white room, a line from my Book came easing its way into my mind: *". . . you must not be surprised, nor must you doubt my friendship, if my door is often shut even to you. You must suffer me to go my own dark way."*

CHAPTER 20

"It is one thing to mortify curiosity, another to conquer it."

The festivities of Thanksgiving Day began bright and early with Valerie dropping by to help with preparations. She also brought the new magazine that had just come out this week: *Life*. I took it in my hands with great expectation. It was to be a photo journal of all of life's various activities *and* I was excited about the fact that some of the photojournalists and writers were women.

There were more and more of us women working in professional roles, but the career world was still a boys' club. Even with my job being a bit more than a secretary's, which seemed to be a profession tolerated by men, I had responsibilities that usually fell to men and believe me, it was a tough arena. I conducted interviews and wrote community relations articles, crafting words to my own views and opinions. And I had to fight for respect. Respect is always something you earn, but as a woman in a man's profession, I had to work three times harder than a man, with four times the excellence, to get the same degree of respect. At least with my role working so closely with the mayor, I was usually exempt from the degrading fanny pats that a lot of secretaries received when going around delivering coffee and lunches to a group of men at the table. I may have let it slip once or twice that I was good with a knife. Maybe. And I had a definite plan worked out if it did happen. I'd only had to use it once.

Life magazine had a unique cover of what looked like an industrial site, the light on the sides of the great factory making the massive structures imposing and strange. Inside were wonderful articles, but I also loved the advertisements. The *cars* coming out next year looked incredible. The '37 Plymouth looked fabulous, but the new Ford V8 was amazing. However, new cars were almost seven hundred dollars, a pretty heavy chunk of change on my salary, not that I really wanted a car in the city, I hadn't learned to drive yet. But they *did* look marvelous. Then there was an ad for Thanksgiving dinner, and to aid in the digestion, it recommended smoking Camel cigarettes. I only smoked once in a while. With my fall into icy waters when I was ten, sometimes my breathing wasn't up to par, so smoking wasn't my *thing*. Most people casually smoked but Aunt Evelyn, extremely outspoken on issues of smoking, never let *anyone* smoke inside. She made a fuss over the smoke harming the artwork we had in the house. So there would be no helpful smoking to aid our digestion tonight.

Another early arrival that morning was—I have to admit a most excellent strategy on my part—Morgan. I asked her to come and help this Thanksgiving Day, assuring her that we needed the help and as it was a day for friends and family, we wanted her to come. She still looked iffy, so I made it seem that it was a working arrangement, that we needed her help and would be paying someone else to come anyway, so why not her? *That* seemed to help her get over the hump of pride and awkwardness. She arrived on our doorstep clean and nice-smelling, with a pink blush to her face from what I presumed was rigorous scrubbing. I hid a smile that would have definitely offended, and thanked her for coming.

Valerie, Morgan, and I all jumped in chopping vegetables, peeling great mounds of potatoes, prepping the humongous turkey, cutting up fresh fruit for a salad, setting the table, washing the silver, dusting and cleaning, etc. It was a wonderful bustle of activity with a lot of laughter and after a couple of hours, I was happy to see the set of Morgan's shoulders relax.

Only one time had I seen her in action, with a few of her other urchins running around the city here and there. I could immediately see what pulled her back to the streets: She was their captain. She was one of the older ones and had probably taken quite a few under her wing. The streets were very dangerous. I had no doubt she tried with everything she had to keep her followers safe. With her hair tied back and a cap upon her head she'd looked just like a boy; a smart move on her part. She was a funny mix of tender youth and hardened maturity. When we rescued her, we thought she might be younger, but I think she was about sixteen or so.

As I looked over at Morgan wiping a small bit of soap off Valerie's nose, I glimpsed some happiness in her. Probably being part of a big family event, being useful, but also *not* being in charge. Just for the day. Every leader needed a break now and then.

Later on, everyone started showing up: Roxy and Roarke, the La Guardias, and a few surprise guests whom Aunt Evelyn had adopted for the day. There was a man named Albert and his wife, Elsa Einstein; Big Sam, whose wife and kids were visiting his mother-in-law; Nina Mittman, who was an artist and fellow women's rights advocate; and another man whom I recognized but couldn't figure out from where, Bob something or other. I missed his last name. Bob was the life of the party, making funny quips the entire time, with Big Sam's deep and booming laugh punctuating the time, making us all smile wider. Or was Bob's name Leslie? Bob Leslie? Something like that, but he seemed awfully familiar. I think I had heard his voice on the radio . . . Albert apparently never left home without his violin, which he affectionately named Lina. We got to hear all sorts of songs, but you could see by the rapturous look on his face that Mozart was his favorite.

At the dinner table, Mr. Kirkland said grace and we dug into the bountiful feast. Albert and Bob sat next to each other, neither of them knowing what to say to the other. They were complete opposites. Bob was a single man of about thirty, funny, and definitely a lady's man; Albert (whom Aunt Evelyn insisted on calling "Albie," which resulted in a confused look from the brilliant man) a scientist of sorts with a great white mustache and matching unkempt hair. Bob and Albie eyed each other dubiously from time to time and at last, after the wine took effect, started to talk and joke together. Big Sam and Nina enjoyed watching those two, a smile tugging at their lips.

My favorite part of the day was when I walked in on a group gathered in the kitchen, all talking earnestly: Bob, Albie, Roxy, Morgan,

Big Sam, and Aunt Evelyn. It was a ragtag group of assorted indi-
viduals and Aunt Evelyn had attracted them all and made them fast
friends. Completely typical. I loved it.

I joined Mr. Kirkland, Val, and Roarke in the parlor. Nina and
Elsa were having a quiet little chat in the corner. In all the bustle
of getting ready and Morgan coming over, I hadn't made it to the
Thanksgiving Day parade like I usually did. Roarke, who had covered the event, started to tell us of the annual mishaps that *always*
occurred, especially with the massive balloons that they started
to use about ten years ago. Rain, wind, lampposts . . . all wreaked
havoc on the balloons, but somehow made the celebration that
much more fun.

Everyone was already laughing with Roarke's account and I
caught up the discussion at, "And *then*, good ole Knickerbocker
started to look a little dodgy, his nose drooping lower and lower. I
nudged my photographer buddy next to me and he started taking
pictures. In a few minutes Knickerbocker had *completely* deflated,
the human anchors moving out of the way, letting the massive rubber man slowly fall down onto Broadway."

Valerie snorted as she laughed.

Roarke continued after addressing her snort with a grin, "And
the damn rubber or canvas, whatever it is, weighed so much without the helium to hold it aloft, the entire parade had to be stopped
so they could haul the carnage off to the side with the help of about
twenty extra men from the sidelines."

We all laughed, then talked and laughed some more late into
the night. Everyone went home and after a lot of convincing, I
coaxed Morgan into staying on our couch for the night. We had
a guest room, but somehow the couch made it seem like less of a
long-standing or permanent situation, which she was agreeable to
accepting. I noticed that she had continued her reading. She had
surprised us all with being able to read when we first met her; she
must have learned at a very early age with her parents. Most kids
on the street, whether homeless or just poor, were illiterate. Before
bed, I gave her the latest copies of the Tarzan series, *Tarzan's Quest,*
and a Kenneth Robeson *Doc Savage 27: Mystery Under the Sea.* Morgan's eyes grew large and glossy at the attractive, brand-new books.

By the look on her face, her first inclination was to not accept the gifts, but the temptation of the crisp books along with the enticing mysteries within rendered her incapacitated.

Morgan ended up staying that night and the next with us, but on early Saturday morning we arose to find her couch empty, her blankets folded neatly in a pile. It was to be expected, yet it was still a little sad for us.

Those first two days of the holiday weekend had been idyllic: full of friends and family, good music, laughter around our radio, rest, reading, and sumptuous food. Little did I know that those days would soon be distant memories, like the sunny, sweet calm before a potent and dark storm.

CHAPTER 21

". . . my blood was changed into
something exquisitely thin and icy."

Saturday night, Valerie and I went out dancing with Ralph and a crowd from work. Peter showed up with several of his police buddies including Scott from Central Park. I spotted him as he walked over with a big grin.

"Hey, Lane, how are you?"

"Great, Scott, good to see you."

"Gee, seems like a pretty dull night, huh?" I looked around the colorful, bustling, noisy crowd and then looked back at him with a cocked eyebrow.

He laughed, and then I got the picture.

"Oh, I get it," I said with a smirk. "You mean you're surprised that I'm not covered in dirt or tackling a guy who stole my purse? Well, buddy, the night is young!" After that we danced a few dances and had a couple of drinks with several of his friends and mine.

It was a fun night. Val had danced with Peter a couple of times, but there wasn't the same kind of spark that had been there before. I smiled to myself as I wondered if maybe that moment at Penn Station where the stranger with the dark blue eyes caught her in midair had a more intriguing effect on her after all.

Late in the evening, Valerie and I pulled over to the side, away from the dancers, to rest for a bit. We sipped our drinks, deciding to sidle over closer to the entrance of the club where fresh air poured in, dissipating the clouds of cigarette smoke. We watched the rollicking crowd for a few minutes in companionable silence.

I smiled at Val, about to suggest one last dance before we headed home. Suddenly, I wasn't smiling. Val's face blanched and I simultaneously felt the cold barrel of a gun poke into my back.

"Good evening, ladies. You need to come with us," said a slick, deep voice from behind me. A small but effective group of men surrounded us, all wearing black overcoats. The man behind me stood close enough that no one could see that I was being held at gunpoint.

"What do—" I started to say, but he cut me off, taking my arm and pushing me from behind with the gun. I'd been working with Mr. Kirkland on some self-defense moves, but it would have been stupid to try anything. We were in a packed club. If his gun went off, it would definitely hit someone, most likely me.

"Okay! Okay, here we go," I said calmly, trying to get him to relax and quit pushing.

They ushered us outside. We tried to make eye contact with anyone who might look at us, but they effectively blocked everyone with the precise movements of people who had clearly done this sort of thing before. Just outside, we walked down the sidewalk and then turned into a wide alley that opened into a deserted lot.

My skin prickled with the dangerous predicament I was in. Again. Things were getting desperate fast. If we didn't do something quick, we were dead meat. Val was just about to faint, her legs looking as wobbly as a newborn fawn's. I was getting angrier and more scared as each precious second ticked by. The men were getting rougher, pulling and pinching hard on my arm. They were cackling to themselves and making eyes at each other in a way that didn't bode well for us.

"What do you *want*?" I demanded.

The one holding me laughed menacingly as he said, "Well, Miss Sanders, our boss said to give you a message and then as long as we didn't kill you, we could have a little *fun* with you."

I felt the bile rising in my throat as his little speech made his buddies laugh along with him. My mind raced, thinking of ways to get out of this. Suddenly, up ahead in the alley where the bright lights of cars went back and forth, a large sedan pulled in and slowly rolled to a stop right before us, its hood glossy and sleek. The guys holding my arms came to a dead standstill and as my hopes started to rise, looking for salvation, the car doors opened and out stepped Donagan Connell and Eliza.

My hopes came plummeting down.

"Well, well, well . . . Little Lane," crooned Donagan, in a mocking voice.

All the men were ogling Eliza as she came around to the front of the car wearing an extremely tight-fitting black dress, a mink stole casually slung around her shoulders, her long red hair curling down her back, and the headlights shining through the skirt on her dress highlighting the silhouette of her legs.

"Hiya, fellas," she purred. They all seemed to know her *quite* well. Then she looked right at me. "Ahh . . . that's the look I was hoping to see," she said with a sneer.

I quickly straightened the shocked look on my face and I turned to take a quick look at Val. With Eliza in her sight, my sweet friend had abruptly turned from fearful to incensed. Her tight, petrified lips turned into a snarl and even Eliza found it rather disconcerting as she looked at Val and then took a subconscious step backward. Valerie was extremely loyal and she was probably thinking through the torture that Eliza put her through when she had Roarke and me kidnapped a few months back.

I'd known that Eliza had eluded capture when a body with red hair had been taken to the morgue in her place, and Fio and I knew deep down inside it had surely been she who had posed as Donagan's mother at Sing Sing. But seeing her right before my eyes was a shock to the senses. Now we were eyewitnesses to the fact that Eliza was absolutely alive and well. Quite rotten, but well, I supposed.

"What do you want, Donagan?" I asked, looking at every angle, every possibility, and all the guns in the hands surrounding us.

"It's simple, really. You have something of mine. And I want it back," he said, the artificial lighting of the headlights creating awful shadows on his already disturbing face. He had an overcoat slung about his shoulders like a cape, making his large body frame even more menacing. His scar that pulled his lip down and the thick makeup on his face combined to create the feel of a morbid masquerade.

"Yours. What could I possibly have of yours?" I asked, as I was starting to get an inkling as to what he could be talking about.

Something in my tone, probably the absolute loathing I felt, made his cool demeanor slip away. His eyes hardened and he shut his smirking mouth with a snap. In three quick strides, he came right up to me and pulled out his gun, leveling it at my chest.

"Holy—" I blurted out. Eliza was cackling with delight. My eyes shot to her and she suddenly mimicked an old lady walking, holding her back, with an invisible cane. She was such a prima donna.

"I knew it had been you," I murmured.

Donagan came a few more critical inches closer and growled, "Now, give it to me. I know you have it."

Right at that very crucial moment, three cars behind Donagan and at least a few behind me all came suddenly screeching and racing into the alley at the same time. The ruckus and the bright lights everywhere at once confused all of us and even Donagan pulled farther away from me. I slipped to the side, desperate to get that gunpoint off me. About ten guys in front and just as many behind leaped out of the cars, every single one of them bearing machine guns—all of them pointing directly at Donagan and Eliza.

I recognized a few of the guys and I bit back a hysterical laugh as it tried to bubble to the surface. The tall guy closest to Donagan, and clearly the one in charge, barked out orders. "Put your gun down, Connell. And if I were you, I'd tell the rest of your crew to get down on the ground. Now."

Donagan took in a big breath, let it out, and nodded his head. His men, who were greatly outnumbered and outgunned, fell straight to the ground. Donagan remained standing, the muscles in his face twitching with hatred. Eliza slunk backward and awkwardly halffell, half-leaned up against their car.

The guy in charge then turned his attention to Valerie and me and I heard a gasp escape Val's lips. "Ladies, you better come with us. The car right behind you," he directed, as he came behind Val and helped usher us over to the door.

"Okay," I said very shakily.

We were marched quickly back to the sedan. The door opened and we jumped inside.

"Well, girls. Seems like you got yourselves in another bit of trouble," said a gravelly voice across from us in the car.

"Oh, my God," whispered Val.

My heart tried hard to start beating again. "I . . . I . . . You have impeccable timing, Mr. Venetti."

CHAPTER 22

"My head goes round."

We returned to the club and Mr. Louie Venetti, notorious gangster, let us out of the car about half a block away. As we walked toward the club, our knees a little wobbly, the adrenaline began wearing off. Our friends were outside looking around, presumably for us. Peter was in the front of the crowd, his brown hair and black hat a head above all the rest. A look of relief spread across his face as he spotted Val. I knew his detective instincts would know that we had been in trouble. Besides, he was holding our coats: a sure sign that we had left in something of a hurry.

"You girls all right?" he asked seriously, but quietly, trying to be discreet. We nodded and he added another question. "Do I even want to know where you've been?"

"Probably not," I replied as I shrugged into my coat.

"Oh boy."

The rest of our group came up to us and we made up a story to keep them out of the rather terrifying loop. Scott, the policeman who always got to see me at my best, was grinning widely, not buying it at all.

Peter took us to my place and we all circled around our safe and cozy kitchen table with Evelyn and Kirkland. We explained the full story about what happened with Donagan and our most unlikely rescuer. They were all shocked into a most uncustomary silence. Val and I looked at each other uneasily and I took refuge behind my great mug of hot tea, taking a long swig.

"W-well . . ." stammered Aunt Evelyn. "What did Uncle Louie say exactly?"

I shook my head, still bewildered. "Not much. He asked if we were all right. We said 'yes' and thanked him. A lot." Val nodded vigorously, but was still very silent. "And then he asked us what Donagan wanted. I told him he said that we had something that was his . . . and I told him I didn't know what that meant."

"Did Donagan believe you?" asked a dubious Peter.

"I'm not sure. There wasn't time to find out. It has to be the silver gun, right? Eliza lost the gun over the bridge, and she and Donagan were a team. Maybe he knew of the second one and is making a guess that I have it . . . But why does he think it belongs to him? Ever since he appeared a few months ago, it seems he might have had ties to Rex's network. Do we have any hard evidence that he was part of the Red Scroll when Rex Ruby was around?" I asked the group.

No one knew.

Aunt Evelyn surmised, "Well, it could be the gold pawn, too. It was on Rex when your father and Kirkland killed him. Maybe it means something." I nodded. That was definitely possible.

"And!" I declared loudly, making heads turn. "I recognized two of the guys with Venetti. They were the two who chased Roarke and me in Central Park. I asked Venetti about it. He wouldn't answer my question about the meeting with Marty and why he'd wanted to assure Marty that the bank business was okay. But he confirmed that his goons were not interested in us. Supposedly, they had been following Marty, but then they spotted Roarke and me. When we took off running, they decided to pursue." I rolled my eyes, nerves making me joke, "I think Roarke and I just have that effect on people." They laughed, albeit uneasily.

I shot a look at Val, wondering if she was going to speak up about the tall gangster who looked to be Venetti's right-hand man, the one who ushered us to the car, a hand on the small of Val's back. He also happened to have dark blue eyes. I wondered if he was the man who caught her at Penn Station as she tripped and was about to fall. She just sat there looking innocent. *Hmm.*

After a long and drawn-out pause, Mr. Kirkland clasped his hands and put them on the table as if he had come to a decision and was about to make a declaration. With a stony face and a resolute sigh, he said, "Lane, this encounter has made one thing absolutely clear. You need to get to Michigan. *Tomorrow*."

I pondered over these events as my train click-clacked over the States once again. It was a whirlwind getting ready to leave on such short notice. Mr. Kirkland and Aunt Evelyn had been going over some plans for the Michigan trip anyway and with this new-found interest of Donagan's, we felt an increasing pressure to figure out what my parents had been involved in and what the meaning was behind the gold pawn. *Why was the date they were killed marked on that bridge?* Also, it seemed I was a target once again, so it would be much safer for me to be in Michigan. Even if Donagan got wind of it, I could be there for a few days before he would find out. We devised a plan where no one else but those of us at the table that night (of course informing Fio as well) knew the timing and my destination. I would call in sick Monday and Tuesday, and by leaving right away on Sunday, I would have an excellent head start.

Mr. Kirkland and Aunt Evelyn were still willing to have me go alone the first few days, but they would be there no later than the weekend.

The funny thing was that I felt more at ease than I suspected I would. With the high drama of the night before, I had a tangible problem and a concrete foe to work against. It was far less disorienting than my invisible enemy of my odd reaction to the Rochester house the first time. I felt a confidence of surer footing than the last time. And despite it all, I wanted to go back. I truly wanted to see some of those places that were vivid and real in my dreams and memories. Maybe I would find solace in seeing and touching the favorite things of my parents.

The only part that gave me pause was thinking of Finn. I sent him a telegram to tell him of my plans, but you can only get so much across in a telegram. It felt so inadequate. And there was something strangely wrong about going without him. But I felt like my hand had been forced. I would just have to make the best of it.

I took out my beautiful and eerie Book, caressed the leather cover with its golden scrolls, and opened it to the page where I left off.

CHAPTER 23

Finn had been shaken when he ran into Gwen. Especially outside his grandmother's nursing home. He had asked his grandma about it, but she was evasive, saying that Gwen had come to visit several times over the years.

He wasn't prepared to run into his younger brother, Sean, Gwen's husband. It had been nine years since he'd seen him last. Sean had masterfully manipulated their parents for years, Finn only realizing the evil intent and cruel twisting of the truth after it was too late. Sean had successfully turned everyone in his life against him. Right when he needed them most.

Everyone, that is, except Grandma Vivian. He hadn't realized that she had been a constant ally his whole life. Even his own parents had been duped by Sean, and they had cut Finn out of their will and out of their lives.

Finn had scrimped and saved his entire life, not being one to purchase little and inconsequential trinkets, so being cut off financially from his parents wasn't that heavy of a financial burden. He had always lived independently anyway. It was the intent behind it that had stung. Eventually, when Grandma Viv was no longer able to take care of herself in her own home, Finn had her moved to the Belmont Nursing Home. She seemed happy. He had tried to convince her to come to America to be closer to him, but she wanted to stay in her home country.

They had spent a lot of time together during his weeks on

assignment in London. He had told her almost instantly about Lane. She took one good look at him when he came to visit the first time and said, "By golly, Finn, you're in love!" He had turned bright red convincing her of that truth more than any words could have done. She asked question after question about Lane, about the last couple of months, their limited time together and, most of all, about Lane herself. What she was like, what she looked like, what kind of job she had, what she loved to do, etc. . . . It had surprised him how he knew all the answers. She had insisted that he must bring Lane to visit her within the next year. He promised he would.

After leaving the warm and cozy side of his grandmother, he found himself walking toward a darker end of town. Tonight, the fog stayed away, but now that it was the end of November, the winter chill started to make a more stalwart and frequent appearance. His breath huffed in the cold darkness as he turned the corner, going down closer to the Thames.

He squinted in the night and ah . . . there it was. The little hole-in-the-wall pub that was downstairs from the apartment he secured for Miles. He had met him two times since their first meeting and Miles began to look more and more like a human being. He was cleaner and smelled better, that was for sure, although it would have proven difficult to be grimier than at that first meeting. Finn had been stunned that underneath all that dirt had been pink skin and black hair only graying at the temples, despite Miles's many years. His darting eyes hadn't changed, but the intelligence that had been covered over by years of terrible anxiety, paranoia, and purposelessness started to make its brave way to the foreground.

Finn was anxious to get to this next meeting; he had received Lane's telegram about her findings at the bridge. He had no idea what the pawns meant, but he was certain that the date on the seventh one, being the date of her parents' deaths, was not a particularly good sign. Something happened that day that involved the mark of the scroll—the scarlet scroll on the silver gun and that same scroll on the bridge. He was getting the feeling that this was much bigger than any of them had suspected. Well, at least bigger than *he* had suspected. Fiorello, not to mention FDR, must have had their suspicions. They had sent him on this errand after all.

He pushed open the thick brown wooden door that had probably stood there for over a century. Inside, the pub was warm and the amber light flickered from the fireplace casting homey shadows on the masculine occupants. The familiar smell of beer spilled on wood flooring made him think of the hundreds of times he spent with mates in just such a pub. It was a pleasing little tavern and he spotted Miles sitting in an inconspicuous corner. Finn had picked this out-of-the-way place himself and he told only one person about it besides Miles.

Finn crunched over scattered hay and peanut shells to the stool awaiting him at the small table. He greeted Miles and they chatted awhile as they ordered their pints and a couple of pasties.

"Miles," Finn began as they got down to business, "I heard from my contact in New York. We found a scroll on the railing of a bridge in Central Park that was an exact replica of that red scroll on the gun I told you about."

"Sounds just like something Rex would do, yeah," rasped Miles as he brought the frothy pint to his lips for a long draught.

"After they took a closer look, they realized that the railing was made up of figures that looked just like pawns. Pawns from a chess game."

Finn saw recognition in Miles, that he knew what those pawns meant, but he only replied, "Go on. Did they find anything else?"

Finn nodded. "Well, first, when Rex was killed, they found two gold pawns on him that are identical in shape to those on the bridge. On that railing, there were ten larger pawns in the middle of the bridge. After close inspection, seven of them had an X marked near the bottom, on the side of the pawn. Three were blank. Lastly, on that seventh one that had the X, there was a 1-22-23 marked on the back."

"Sounds like a date," remarked Miles, with his quickly returning cleverness.

"Mm hm," agreed Finn. "My contact's parents were killed on that date."

Miles's head moved back in surprise. "Really," he said with his brow furrowed. "Are there any more links with this contact of yours?"

"More than I like to admit and growing every day," said Finn with grave apprehension.

"Is it possible that those parents were part of this?" asked Miles, thinking hard, but enjoying his pasty. Then something obviously dawned on him and he put his pasty down and placed both hands on the table. "Hold on a minute," he said quietly, but sharply, which made Finn dart his eyes to Miles's face with an intense stare. "Those parents. You don't mean Matthew and Charlotte Lorian, do you?"

"Well, wait, do you mean Matthew and Charlotte Sanders?" he asked, confused. How many Matthews and Charlottes could there be?

"Yeah, yeah. But their real name is Lorian. You know their child?" Miles asked.

"Yes," said Finn. "She's the contact. Their real name was Lorian?"

Miles shook his head in concern and said, "I knew that they died, but I had heard it was an accident. Knowing them, I always did have a doubt that it was truly accidental. The Lorians became very well-known in the underground crime networks. So, later on they decided to change their name. Yeah, yeah. Let me think about this, let me think about this . . ." He tapped his finger on his chin, then took a deep draught of his pint.

Finn took another drink, trying to be patient, wishing for something stronger.

Miles went on as he reflected on the problem. "Okay, yeah. So, I knew Matthew and Charlotte, they were part of our team. There is no way that they were with Rex. No way. So it has to mean something else. I have a thought. Let me do some checking around and we'll talk more." Finn nodded, thinking through the elusive bits and clues.

Miles took a bite of the piping hot pasty that was placed before him, ruminating on the case. He wiped his mouth with a napkin then continued. "But I do know about those pawns. Not many do,

THE GOLD PAWN   131

I can tell ya that. But what I know is, they were Rex's calling card. Whenever he made a hit, he would leave a small gold pawn on the body. It was perfectly fitting for him, too, yeah. He used everyone. Everyone was a pawn to him." Miles munched on his dinner thoughtfully, still carefully thinking and considering.

"Anything else to add?" Finn asked. He noticed Miles's original Cockney got more and more pronounced as he thought deeply about all of this.

"Well . . . those pawns. See, they were his calling card, yeah. But they were more than that. Rex always had one in his hands. At all times. Rolling it around, passing it between his fingers, tossing it about when he was thinking. And after people realized it was his death card, it was a threat, too. He knew that. He liked having it in his hands to play with, just like he toyed with people.

"I only laid eyes on Rex once. I had been sent out on surveillance, hoping I could get a chance to see his face. He was at a restaurant, meeting with one other man. I can still see that cold face of his, rolling that pawn around and around in his fingertips and on the table, the light from the restaurant glinting off the pawn and his ruby ring. Once in a while, he'd catch that the poor sod in front of him was almost hypnotized by that damn pawn and he'd grin from ear to ear, teasing and testing. Like a cobra teasing a mouse. Sure as hell scared the living daylights out of *me*, and he wasn't even talkin' to me."

Finn took it all in, more pieces clicking into place. He asked, "So do you know much about Rex's son?"

"Well, not much. He wasn't a big player. In fact, rumor had it that Rex was highly disappointed in him. Didn't have that same drive that Rex had. Rex ended up seeing the writing on the wall and handpicked a young apprentice of sorts. Figured his son would never cut it, so he wanted someone else to invest in. After a while, the son just disappeared and I think he died along the way somewhere. But his son had a kid, or a few or something. I'll check on that, too. I had heard at one point that even though Rex had given up on his son, he had been thrilled with the prospect of grandkids. I have no idea if amends were made with that son or not."

"Okay, you check on those things, Miles. Same time, same place Friday?" asked Finn as he shrugged into his coat.

"Sounds good, mate. And, uh . . . thanks."

Finn caught Miles's deep eyes piercing his own, the light from the candle glinting off them, and knew that the *thanks* meant a lot more than just the pint and the pasty.

CHAPTER 24

"Certain agents I found to have the power to shake and pluck back that fleshly vestment, even as a wind might toss the curtains . . ."

The train pulled into Detroit right on time. I got a cab from Michigan Central Station to the Statler, then dropped my bags at the hotel and decided to do a little Christmas shopping. I left a quick message for Tucker at the front desk in case he was in town. I walked along bustling Jefferson and Woodward and went into Kern's. I bought beautiful silver-plated compacts for Valerie and Evelyn. Valerie's had several delicately carved violets on the top. Evelyn's had lovely lilies of the valley sprinkled over a dark blue cover. I of course hit the Sanders soda shop and splurged on a hot fudge crème puff. Vanilla ice cream was tucked inside a large profiterole, laden with the famous and ridiculously delicious hot fudge.

I also stopped and inquired about taking a train out to Rochester instead of asking Tabitha to retrieve me. Later, as I walked back to the hotel, I stopped at the front desk and there was a message waiting for me from Tucker. He was in town and was delighted that I contacted him. He said that he would be having dinner at an Italian place near the hotel and that if I was available, to just meet him there at eight. Sounded great. I went up to my room and rested for an hour, easing my sore feet.

The phone jangled obnoxiously, startling me out of a deep slumber, my heart racing. Sure, I had asked for the wake-up call, but I still luxuriated in a daydream of chucking the offending piece of equipment out the window. I took a quick shower, reapplied my makeup, and swept my hair to the back of my neck. The restaurant wasn't as chic as Carl's, but I wanted to wear something that was dressy enough to go dancing. I put on a favorite black dress that I spiffed up with sparkling jewelry. And of course, my red high heels that matched my little hat with sparkling jet beads on the netting.

I had done all my ablutions in record time and it was only seven thirty. I decided to go to the restaurant a little early and get a drink at the bar while I waited for Tucker. The restaurant was only a couple of doors down from the hotel, so I walked. It was chilly and I was glad to have my black and red wrap around my shoulders.

As I sipped my sidecar, I enjoyed the atmosphere. It was very different from my favorite place back in Little Italy, Copioli's. Here there were high ceilings that were softened just a bit with fabric draped in great sweeps and large potted plants stood in the corners. The walls were a natural stone color that gave the place a European feel. A few jazzy Christmas songs played lightly from a phonograph.

I caught a glimpse of Tucker at the other end of the restaurant in a meeting with three other men. The candlelight and chandeliers shone off his strawberry blond hair. He looked handsome in his black suit and black tie. He was deeply intent on his discussion. Just then, as he put out his cigarette and was about to take something from his inner jacket pocket, he looked up abruptly like he had felt my gaze. I smiled at him and his face faltered with surprise. He took his hand out of his pocket with a quick pull and I saw a flash of red as he patted the red pocket kerchief in his jacket. He nodded and smiled in my direction, telling me with his eyes that he'd be over in a minute.

There had been something familiar about that look on his face when he caught me looking at him. What was it? I had seen it before . . .

I took another sip of my drink and turned back to the bar so that he didn't feel rushed. The sidecar cocktail, very popular right now, was made with brandy, Cointreau, and lemon. Cocktails were all the rage. I usually preferred wine, I guess with Aunt Evelyn's European influence that came naturally. But in New York? It was all about cocktails, cocktail parties, and more cocktails. Burke's cocktail guide had just come out and I bought myself a copy so I could look through the massive selection. But I was still a little nervous about drinking absinthe too regularly. It wasn't outlawed anymore and they said that the psychotic effects of it were fabricated and greatly exaggerated; it was just another spirit. But still . . . that green fairy business.

I looked at the bar with its Christmas decorations and little fairy lights woven in and out of the glossy bottles of liquors and spirits. It was a pleasing sight and eased a smile to my lips. But then my mind went to the train ride tomorrow and the house. My feelings were riding on a swing, greatly lilting from side to side. One moment I was feeling confident and even happy, sitting here, enjoying the aromas of the meals being cooked, the chatter of the crowd, the warm taste of the brandy . . . Then the thought of that train ride. A prickle of fear ran up my spine, an unexpected shadow of apprehension that quickened my pulse.

What would I find in Rochester? I was plagued with a daunting list of questions. Where did the power of the silver gun come from? What was the meaning behind the gold pawn that twisted and twirled through my dreams? Rex Ruby was integrally involved; I needed to find out more. And what about Uncle Louie? He kept making an appearance. It didn't really make sense, but he was involved somehow. He wasn't involved with Donagan, they seemed more like enemies. So what was he doing? Again, he was helping me, hell, even saved my life. Twice now. But he was not a nice guy, to put it mildly.

I set my glass down with a firm clink.

"That sounds like you've come to a decision, Lane," said Tucker, suddenly at my side.

I laughed. "I didn't see you come up. I hope I didn't make you rush your meeting. I just finished getting ready quicker than expected and thought I'd come early for a cocktail."

He smilingly searched my face. Coming to his own decision about something, he replied, "Oh no, not at all. I was surprised to see you across the room, but quite glad to see your familiar and quite lovely face." I felt a blush creep up my cheeks as he quickly continued, "Come on, our table is ready."

He took my hand and led me to where he'd been sitting; now a small table for two was set with crisp napkins and bright silverware. We ordered chicken parmigiana and penne with vegetables and garlic with great, creamy lumps of mozzarella cheese.

We had a nice evening, but we were both somewhat distracted, our minds elsewhere. However, once again, it was good to have an evening with a friend before I opened doors that could be hard to close. It was a pleasant change being in a different city, with new and exciting things to discover, but I felt like a tourist. New York had become a large friend. Even though it was always changing and moving in a rhythm all its own, it was a rhythm I knew and understood. So it was a special feeling to have the comfort of a New York friend here in Detroit. Someone who spoke my language.

I told Tucker about my plan to take the train tomorrow to Rochester. Unexpectedly, he chimed in, "Well, Lane, if you'd like a little company, I have a couple of days to myself. A meeting got moved to next week. I used to do business with some people who live out in Rochester now, they bought up the woolen mill there. I could ride out with you and then meet up with my friends, leaving you to your exploration."

I wasn't sure how I felt about that. I was already feeling awkward about being there without Finn, yet I also felt exposed and vulnerable, like I was going in without backup or something. It would be nice to have a friend along. But Tucker?

"Lane, I don't have to come, I can go on my own another time if it makes you feel uncomfortable," said Tucker with an earnest crinkle to his eyebrows. I didn't want my adolescent fears to get the best of me. It already felt like something outside of me was taking advantage and it made me feel hapless. I detested that feeling. It even *sounded* stupid. Hapless.

"Well, you know? I think it would be good to have you along, if you don't mind. I need some time on my own, but I would love the company on the train ride. I don't know how long I'll be in town, and I have to admit I don't really know anyone there."

"Great!" he said. "It's settled then."

The next day, we got to the train station and had an enjoyable ride out through the countryside. The large mansions of Grosse

Pointe, home of Detroit's wealthy socialites, were left behind along with the many closely situated smaller homes that made up the outskirts of the sprawling city. Clean white wooden siding mixed with red bricks and picket fences dotted the landscape here and there.

I spent most of the time holding my Book in my hands, looking out the window. Waiting. Tucker had tried to start up a conversation a few times, but I wasn't cooperating. I was in a quiet mood. As the train chugged over the sure and solid tracks, it was taking me closer and closer to my fate. I was a willing passenger, but it was a somber journey. I knew there would be familiar and loving things to be found. But there was also that image of the diving board front and center in my mind—that courage needed to climb up, the decision to walk to the end, the profound finality of jumping.

We pulled into Rochester and got off the train. Tucker put his arm around my shoulders as he asked, "Are you ready, Lane? You were awfully quiet. Are you all right?"

"Yes, thanks, Tucker. Sorry I wasn't the greatest conversationalist. I have a lot on my mind," I said with a self-conscious smile. "Oh look! There's Tabitha. I phoned her to ask if she could pick up both of us."

She had met us with the car at the train station. I waved to her and she had an odd, disgruntled look on her face. Maybe my arrival had been poor timing for her.

As we made our way over to her I said, "Hi, Tabitha, I hope we aren't coming at a bad time for you. This is Tucker Henslowe. Tucker, this is Tabitha Baxter, our next-door neighbor."

They shook hands and Tabitha made noises that said she wasn't at all inconvenienced, but her surly teenage face said otherwise. Tucker removed his arm from my shoulders and took our bags to put them in the trunk.

We pulled into downtown Rochester, onto Main Street. I spotted the opera house up ahead, the barber shop, the trees lining the streets. I thanked Tucker for coming with me and we made plans for dinner about six o'clock before we dropped him off at the mill for his meeting.

Tabitha didn't spare him a glance. We turned left onto a side street off Main and approached the house from the other side this time. We pulled into the back of the house, where the garage was located and the side door, instead of the front of the house. It instantly felt natural, like the front door entrance was for guests. I must have come in and out this side entrance thousands of times.

We got out and Tabitha told me that her mom had made up the beds in my parents' room and my old room in case I wanted to sleep in either one. She had also dusted and vacuumed and left some food in the refrigerator. There was a chicken and rice dish in the oven that could be heated up anytime I was ready.

Tabitha gave all these directions without once looking me in the eyes. I was doing that bobbing and weaving again to try to meet her gaze. I couldn't tell if this was a bad habit or if she was *trying* not to look at me.

At last she said she was going to leave but then remembered something. "Oh and this came for you today." She handed me a yellow telegram and turned around and left.

I wanted to open that telegram, but I also wanted to savor it. It had to be from Finn, and I'd only had one other telegram from him so far. I pocketed it for later.

I turned and took a good look at the house. My house. I inhaled a large, bracing breath and walked to the side door. Oddly enough, I had had a dream a few months ago where I had come in this door. It was strangely sweet and comforting to remember that dream, like when a normally aloof cat makes the affectionate overture of curling his head into your hand. A good omen.

I took out the keys. Mr. Kirkland had given them to me, the ones he used every time he came. There was a key to the side door, the front door, and several other keys of unknown use. They used to be my father's. I liked that. I felt the weight of them in my hand, I touched the silver *M* that was on the key ring. It was slick with use and cold to my fingertips. I felt along the lines of the molded *M* and thought about my father's hands doing the same thing, once upon a time.

I inserted the key, turned the oiled lock, and walked in.

CHAPTER 25

"I thus drew steadily nearer to that truth . . .
that man is not truly one, but truly two."

It was wonderfully, exactly, like my dream. I was greeted by the familiar ticking of the kitchen clock. I drank in the soft yellow walls, the table, the brass knobs on the doors. In the silence, I breathed. It was like I had stepped back in time and was ten years old again. It was a perfect, stolen moment. One of those unusual times where you're suddenly very alone in what is typically a busy house, a busy life. Where it feels like time has decided to stand still, allowing for a precious moment of deep awareness. Where you are intensely perceptive of every soft noise, the scent, the essence of the room, but more so . . . of life itself. I whispered, "Thanks."

I listened some more. I smelled wood polish and the scent of recent vacuuming. Mr. Kirkland, with his love of gadgetry, must have bought a vacuum for here. He loved our Kenmore back in New York. Just for the fun of it, he took that thing apart and put it back together again more than he vacuumed with it. I soaked everything in; remembering, wooing the memories and feelings of so long ago to come back to me.

I had often dreamed of getting a wish from a magic genie. That with my adult mind, I could travel back in time to this place for just one day. To enjoy and drink in the essence of what it was like to be here with my parents, with the things that seemed huge back then but were small now. To hear the sounds of my school, my friends, my teachers. To enjoy with the clarity and appreciation of an adult, the mundane and ever-so-sweet, poignant bits and pieces of childhood.

This wasn't quite it, but it came very close. My house had stood still in time, even though everything else around it had continued on.

I walked through the kitchen to the bottom of the stairs. I put my left hand on the banister and as I ascended the stairs, I closed my eyes, trailing my hand along the banister just like I did in my favorite dream. Knowing every single nick, every curve before I felt it. I listened to the creak of the stairs, knowing exactly which ones would click and which ones would creak. It was intensely quiet. This time I went to all the bedrooms and saw firsthand my parents' room, the old bathroom with the blue tile, my room with the interlaced circles chiseled into the white pine headboard, and lastly my father's study.

Renewed energy and elation that I was handling this all right coursed through me. Whether it was because I was more prepared this time or because I had a purpose in being here to help my friends and family in New York, I didn't know. But I knew I needed to figure out the mystery of my parents' past and to search for clues that might illuminate who was behind the uprising of the Red Scroll Network. This mission filled me with great enthusiasm. I looked at my dad's study with loving eyes, but also with the hungry eyes of a detective intent on figuring out a particularly tricky mystery.

I took the key from my pocket that my parents had left me along with the key to the safe deposit box. This key was to my father's safe. I figured I'd start searching in his study first, but there was no safe out in the open, of course. His desk was the focal point, perhaps just as he had left it. This room was very different from the soft elegance and light colors of Mr. Hambro's study way back in New York. My dad's study was more typically masculine. Deep evergreen walls, dark walnut moldings, a petite fireplace, and the Victrola! I remembered its glossy sides, and the decorated brass edges and woodwork. I went over to it and happily saw that there was a thick, vinyl record in place.

I turned it on and set the needle. And with that small gesture, the house came alive with music like it was eating it up, happy once

again to have life here. "Für Elise" played, making me remember
the hours and hours that I toiled away learning that on the piano. To
this day, it's still the only piece I was ever able to play fully, probably like thousands of other childhood piano players. It was surprising that my dad could even handle listening to it, I had played
it so frequently. But he never tired of hearing it. Anytime we had
visitors, he'd proudly ask me to play it for them. I knew it so well,
I could play with a lot of emotion. It made it seem like I was quite
an accomplished pianist, despite it being the *only* thing I could play.

The piano. I suddenly remembered a game my dad and I used
to play. While I was toiling away at my songs, he'd sneak up on me,
suddenly appearing out of nowhere. It used to irk me that I could
never figure out how he did it. The memory was pressing on my
mind, insistent as a nagging child. I finished with a cursory search
of his study. He was crafty enough that I was gaining the convic-
tion that he would hide his safe *quite* well, so I figured I'd do a more
comprehensive search later. For now, I decided to go down to the
front room to the piano.

Mrs. Baxter must have dusted this room well because the scent
of wood polish was even stronger here. I loved that scent. I put
up the keyboard cover with a familiar thump. My right hand went
automatically to the correct place and I started to play "Für Elise."

I got to the passionate, driving part that I used to love to play
in my robust style and I suddenly stopped. I looked slowly up and
then turned around to my left, to the paneled wall behind me. That
had to be it. I smiled and walked over, listening to the soft sounds
of Beethoven still floating down the stairs from the Victrola. Golden
paneling lined the walls throughout the front room, matching the
wonderful beams along the ceiling. The idea of a secret passage
hidden behind there was enticing and just plain fun.

My dad always appeared to my left and from behind, so it just
had to be there. I ran my hands all along the woodwork, pushing,
prodding, sliding, but I didn't feel anything like a release. Hmm . . .
I stood rooted to the spot, puzzling and forcing my mind to search
through memories. I remembered him saying something whenever
I tried to get him to tell me about how he magically appeared out of
nowhere. He used to say, "Oh Lane, just enjoy the magic, it comes

from above!" I knew he meant God, he always used to talk about God in creative and magical terms. But he used the word *above*. My fingers thrummed the top of the piano as I looked around. *Thrump, thrump, thrump.*

I took a step back and looked at the wall again. The warm, golden brown paneling went along about six feet off the ground; above it was painted a soft cream color. I ran my fingertips along that top molding. The dust was pretty thick along that ledge. Understandably so, *I'd* certainly never think to dust along there. And there it was, I felt a very slight indentation and I pushed it. It made a soft click and I pushed against the paneling. It opened.

The cracks of the door were cleverly hidden in the woodwork, so unless you knew it was there, you'd never find it. I walked in and a circular stone staircase wound downward.

As I reached the bottom, it felt much cooler than the floors above. I pushed on the door and it opened inward to a very dark room. I wished I had brought my flashlight. I felt along the wall beside me, apprehensive about inadvertently feeling the skitter of spiders, and felt the thick buttons of the light switches. With a loud click an overhead light went on.

And here was the man's castle. It was a game room mixed with some homey, masculine touches. I didn't even remember we had a basement let alone a place that was clearly designed for my dad and his friends. I grinned looking at a pool table, a dartboard, and two big comfy couches facing each other in front of a fireplace.

I plopped down on one of the extremely comfortable couches, putting my legs up. The room needed a good dusting, but Mr. Kirkland must have known about its existence because there was not an accumulation of thirteen years of dust, that was for sure. I brought a pillow into my arms for warmth and I took a good look around. I thought about my dad down here enjoying man-time, probably with Mr. Kirkland. The dartboard looked like it had seen a lot of use and a fleeting memory came back about hours and hours of playing darts with my father. But it wasn't down here, it had been in the garage.

I scanned the room again, knowing there was more to find. I just knew it. I suddenly had an idea. In the far corner, I spotted a painted portrait . . . of me. It had the wispy strokes of an impressionist and it was given an old-fashioned, Victorian flair. I was only about three years old, and I had on a white, long dress. I was playing in tall green grass, the suggestion of a small house in the background and flowers in the front. All around the edges of the portrait was a white vine that brought in more of the floral theme. There was no frame, just the beautifully stretched canvas, allowing the vine to delicately encase the piece.

For some reason, I knew my dad had known that I'd be hunting around here one day. And he left me a clue that pretty much said, "Lane! Over here!"

I stood up and walked toward the portrait, smiling back at the child that was supposed to be me, but felt like someone else. I felt along the paneling above and below the portrait and this time it took a few minutes to find it. But I did. I felt a very small button that was flush with the molding way up high. I pushed it and had to step back as the entire rectangle of molding, with the portrait, slowly opened outward—it was actually a door.

Inside was a large steel vault.

I looked at the other keys on my dad's key ring and took the largest, sturdiest-looking one and sure enough it slipped right in. I turned it and with a mighty heave, I opened the door. It was heavy, but opened smoothly.

Inside were rows and rows of . . . booze. That devil! When my parents were here in Rochester, it was in the middle of Prohibition. I carefully looked at the door of the vault and there was a handle on the inside, but I wasn't taking any chances getting locked in there by myself. I pulled over a large ottoman to prop open the door. Inside, a bare light bulb with a string hanging down seemed to be the only lighting. I pulled on the string, but it was burned out. So after some digging around the newly discovered basement I found a light bulb stash and replaced it.

Inside the vault, the walls were covered with shelves of alcohol. Including wine. I took a good look at those and recognized some interesting dates. I pulled out one and set it aside for later. But there was no safe to be seen.

I must have studied that place for an hour. Maybe more. But I was determined to find that safe and I just knew it was in here. There were a couple of obvious places that I tried first, places where there weren't shelves. But nothing. I felt along all sorts of dark nooks, fighting a battle of squeamishness. I sat down on the floor with my arms crossed, thinking hard, my mouth set in a resolute line.

There was one wall that I had examined, but it seemed like it would be too difficult for a safe to be hidden there. It was by an electrical box on the wall. I went over to it and scrutinized every inch of the box, the cords and tubes going in and out of it, up and down the wall. Ever since an old neighbor of ours had unplugged a vacuum cleaner and was jolted with an enormous shock that badly burned her hand from faulty wiring (that was a pretty common thing), I was very uneasy around electrical things. I brought a stepstool over so I could see above the box better. I wasn't keen on running my hand around in there.

But along the top was an indent similar to what I had felt along the previous moldings. I drummed up my courage and pressed the tiny indentation.

The entire box and wires around it came cleanly away from the wall. It was a fake electrical box. The opening was about two feet square and behind it was the door of a safe. This was it. Out of my other pocket, I pulled my key. I slipped it in, turned it, rotated the circular safe handle, and with a *clunk*, the safe opened.

Inside lying flat was a single ivory envelope. And right on top of that envelope stood a shiny golden pawn.

Chapter 26

"My devil had been long caged, he came roaring out."

I slipped the pawn and the envelope into my pocket with the telegram, grabbed a couple bottles of wine, and went upstairs. Just like the telegram, there was something that made me want to have a proper moment to think about what I would discover written on that paper. It was such a satisfying day of discovery; I wanted to make that moment as perfect as possible.

For lunch, I heated up the chicken and rice dish in the oven. With the music from upstairs and the good smells wafting from the kitchen, the house was feeling alive again, like a home. Louis Armstrong's jazzy smooth trumpet floated throughout the place.

I spent the rest of the afternoon poking around and just looking at everything, retrieving lost memories. From another story, another past. I remembered making cookies with my mother, in fact I'd found her recipe box. I quickly looked up my favorite recipe of hers that I hadn't had in ages: her peanut butter pocket cookies. I could hardly wait to try to make them for Valerie.

I also found a few of my mom's little bits and pieces: petite needlepoint and beaded purses, and some jewelry that I didn't remember but looked unique and delicious to wear. I also found a few of her dresses and discovered to my delight that we wore the same size. I even put on one of her gowns, a gorgeous slinky satin in a deep rose color. It was like it had been made for me. I also found a small bottle of Chanel No. 5 on her dresser atop a doily with a beautiful silver brush and mirror set.

I wanted to while away days and days in just their room alone, but I knew I needed to look around everywhere. Hours later, back in the cozy living room, I set a fire and opened the bottle of wine. I fingered the pawn, feeling its pleasing weight and smooth sides. The *RR* at the bottom was deeply etched as my fingertips crossed over the letters. It was identical to the one Mr. Kirkland had in his rucksack.

Rex Ruby's pawn, huh? His hands had held this. My dad's hands had held this. And now I was holding it. It felt like time was suddenly rushing toward me. The events of the past barreling down on me like a freight train while the future direction would all depend on the impact of the past meeting the present.

All day, I had purposely waited and now I finally placed two things before me on the coffee table: the yellow telegram and the folded letter from the safe. Which tasty tidbit to open first? I took a sip of the deep red cabernet. It was a full-bodied wine that tasted like Paris. I took the telegram into my hands, feeling the delicate paper, and carefully opened it.

HI LOVE STOP PAWN WAS LEFT WITH REX
HITS STOP SCARE TACTIC STOP RR HAD SON
STOP BE CAREFUL STOP SAW GWEN NOT
SEAN STOP WRITE SOON STOP
FINN

Saw Gwen. *Well, how nice.* That wasn't what I'd hoped to hear. *I wonder how he ran into her?* And I wondered darkly about his brother, Sean. He was the kind of man that didn't just go away. Finn would have to deal with him sooner or later.

So, Rex Ruby left the pawns with the people he killed. And Rex had a son, huh? Who was that? Could there be a connection with the silver gun, the gold pawn, and a possible heir? Maybe a legacy had been handed down . . . Perhaps that new *über* gangster in town? Maybe those pieces, the gun or the pawn, were a kind of proof-of-ownership of Rex's legacy.

I was suddenly very, very tired. Gwen, Sean, Rex, Rex's son, Uncle Louie, Mr. Hambro . . . Gwen.

I was weary of trying to figure out who the real enemies were. And why they were often coming after me, all because of things I couldn't control such as the choices my parents made decades ago. Trusting, not trusting. Even with my love of the hunt and figuring out the mystery, there were times I wanted to throw off the clinging heavy cloak of intrigue and run away. Abandon the complicated, cloying feelings. Be free. *Escape.*

Of course I'll be careful, I thought irritably. *Where is he? What is he involved in?* We'd only been dating a little while, but I could always count on Finn to be there when I needed him most, watching out. But now he was across an ocean. It felt wrong. *I* felt wrong and fragmented. Fractured somehow. What if . . . What if I'd read him wrong?

Heat started to climb up my face. I took another drink. I'd been wrong about my parents, about what I'd thought had been a simple life. Everything that I knew about them had been a lie.

I'd always prided myself on seeing the truth in people and yet I'd been wrong about my own mother and father. What if Finn wasn't who I thought he was either? I was so in love with him, it hurt. What if it wasn't real?

Saw Gwen. My thoughts went bitterly back to that damn telegram and those two words. Was there anything written there between the lines? *Did seeing her again after all these years bring back those feelings he had for her? Did he long for a shared past that she could understand—that I could never be a part of?* I took another long drink of wine, poured another glass, and grasped the envelope from the safe.

I quickly ripped it open and in my haste, I slashed a deep paper cut into my finger.

"Damn it!" I yelled, a few tiny droplets of blood splashed onto the crisp paper. I sucked on my finger and grabbed a napkin, holding it to the cut. That tiny slice hurt like hell, making me utter a few choice words.

I took a good look at the note from the safe, taking a moment before I unfolded it. It was a letter from the past, written to me. My name had been written on the envelope in a masculine hand, with sharp upstrokes in the cursive penmanship. It was my dad's writing.

I felt that imaginary train of time rushing up, the wind hitting me hard, the horn blast loud and cautionary.

I opened the letter.

> *Dearest Lane,*
> *We knew you would find your way here. You're*
> *probably about twenty-five. Even at your young*
> *age, as I write this, I can see that you will be quite*
> *an amazing woman full of imagination, life, and*
> *intelligence. This letter will be frustrating to you, Lane.*
> *I know you and you will be angry. I can just see your*
> *scrunched nose and furrowed brow.*

I fought off the urge to look around as if the writer of the letter might possibly be watching me. I straightened my scrunched nose and scowling face and kept reading.

> *This letter can't come close to telling you all that I wish*
> *to tell you. It's not enough. I know that, and I hope I'll*
> *be able to tell you more later. Our business requires us*
> *to be extremely careful. For now, my sweet girl, this is*
> *all I can say: Follow what we <u>pointed</u> out to you. Do*
> *you remember those lessons? Keep looking up, <u>have</u>*
> *<u>faith</u>. It will all work out. We love you.*
> *—Mom and Dad*

Follow what we pointed out to you? And why was the word *pointed* underlined with a dark black line? Sure, I remembered a lot of lessons they taught me. Survival skills, archery, the many puzzles we pored over . . . And they were always taking advantage of those parental teaching moments. As a kid, I rolled my eyes when they made a point of a lesson. Now I was wishing I'd kept a log of each of those lectures. *Keep looking up.*

I understood why they couldn't be straightforward. Their work, their business, as he said, required hidden meanings and mystery. But he was right: I was so frustrated. *Damn damn damn.* That heavy cloak was getting claustrophobic. The heat from the fireplace was stifling. I longed to fling off that cloak in rebellion. I was so angry, and so stuck. I didn't know which way to turn. I swiped at a small tear that pricked at my eyes. He was right. It wasn't enough.

I looked around. The music had ceased playing. The silence was heavy and hung about my shoulders, weighing me down. I was very, very alone.

Behind the letter was a second piece of paper. I slipped it out. It was my birth certificate. I saw my birthdate, birth city, birth parents. Then I gasped and almost dropped the papers. It didn't say Sanders. It said *Lane Lorian*. Parents: Matthew and Charlotte Lorian.

Nothing, not one single thing that I had counted on in my life, was as it seemed. Not one thing. *Not even my name.* I put my hand to my heart, as if making sure I was still who I thought I was. That I was still here, still substantial. My head was pounding, heart aching, and it felt like a tormenting shadow had crept into the room with me.

The doorbell rang, a clanging dissonance that made me jump. It must be six already. I stood up, slightly tipsy from the wine. I took a deep breath to try to clear my head and made a firm decision. I straightened my sweater, patted my hair, and swept my hands down my slacks, making them crisp and orderly. I nodded smartly.

I took the telegram, my dad's letter, and my birth certificate and put it all under a heavy, brightly polished lapis lazuli stone upon the mantel. I let the stone clunk down upon those goddamn papers.

Then I went to the front door and let Tucker in.

"Just a second! Let me get my coat and we can go," I said as he stepped into the foyer.

"Great! Did you have a good day?"

"Yeah. I guess. I did, overall. It was nice being here." I shook my head again, clearing my mind. I was in a bad mood, surly and irritated. My finger throbbed. I struggled to make sense of things.

I slipped on my coat and buttoned it up. I guess Sanders was a good, blending-in kind of name, just shy of Smith. My parents had come here to get away from danger, after all. It would make sense that they'd use a different name. *Right?*

I clenched my jaw. *No. Not all right.*

"Good. I'm glad," said Tucker. "Hey, there's a little mom 'n' pop restaurant downtown, want to give it a try?" asked Tucker.

"Sure. Sounds great." I didn't really care where we ate. I put the screens in front of the fireplace as low, red-hot embers were still burning. I grabbed my keys and purse and headed out.

"Okay, Tucker, let's—" As I closed the front door behind me, the words died on my lips. I dropped my purse and fought the feeling that my knees might buckle.

"Lane, are you all right?" asked Tucker.

I slowly walked over to my precious purple maple tree. The place I played a thousand times as a little girl. The place where I could climb, be alone, look out over my house, my home. The defining place of my childhood. The leaves were completely off the branches now, but that wasn't what I was looking at. We'd driven up to the back of the house this time and entered in the side door, so I hadn't seen my tree yet.

The large branch that I climbed up on, the branch that was like a friend, the arm of a friendly giant beckoning to me to come and play . . . had been completely chopped off, leaving an enormous, shockingly white, new, smooth scar upon the dark trunk of the tree, about four feet from top to bottom.

It was like I had been sucker punched in the gut. The air came right out of me, leaving me unable to breathe, a racking pain in my chest. I walked numbly over to the tree, stumbling once over a root in the ground. I wanted to shout and cry and hit something. But I couldn't do anything. I was cold. I slowly, numbly lifted a hand trying to touch the scar. I couldn't bring myself to do it. It was like the tree's very heart had been amputated. One solitary tear slipped down my cheek. Just one.

I looked down at the ground and as I breathed in and out, in and out, I slowly, one at a time, clenched my fists. I set my jaw and lowered my eyes. And I built up that goddamn thick, solid, impenetrable wall again. One heavy, vile stone at a time. This time it wasn't just a wall—it was a fortress. And I dared anyone to come and get me.

CHAPTER 27

*"I was conscious of a heady recklessness, a current of
disordered sensual images running like a millrace in
my fancy, a solution of the bonds of obligation, an
unknown but not an innocent freedom of the soul."*

On the way to the restaurant I saw that the apothecary was still open and with a determined step I decided to send out a spicy little telegram of my own. *Gwen. Bah.* It wasn't too late to send it despite the late hour; they were just happy for the business of an expensive telegram. I sent it off, banged out the door into the cold fresh air, and looked forward to my evening with Tucker.

The restaurant was a nice little place, Merchant's Restaurant. They served alcohol. Perfect. I ordered a steak and suddenly missed Roarke a lot. I thought about that time we ate at the little French bistro after the Randall's Island incident. I wondered what he was up to. I ordered some cocktail or other that looked good and potent. Tucker smiled, ordering one for himself, but he also looked . . . wary. An odd look for him. *Huh, maybe he had a hard day with his business deals.*

We both ate our dinners with relish and ordered a bottle of wine with it. I started to laugh a lot. I didn't realize Tucker was so funny. It reminded me of that day in the rowboats at Central Park.

"You know, Roarke . . ."

"Tucker," he reminded me, which I thought even funnier.

"Yes, of course, Tucker. You know, Tucker, that day with the rowboats was really fun. I was thinking that that's just like shledding. I mean, sledding."

"Sledding?" he asked with a chuckle. He was almost giggling. *Honestly, some people just can't handle their liquor.*

"Exactly, except for the part with the oars and the water," I said matter-of-factly.

"Naturally."

"What I mean is, I love sledding, except for those horrible sleds with the big iron runners on the bottom. What exactly are they supposed to go over? They just sink right into the snow. It would be faster to ride down on your bum versus a slow metal runner digging into the snow. I don't get it."

"Well, from the looks outside, we may get that chance tomorrow," he said, nodding to the large front window.

We were just finishing up our meal, and as I looked out, I glimpsed big, chunky flakes of snow coming down. It was beautiful. The anger and steam inside of me had been waning just a bit. But there was a part of me that liked it, I liked that bastion that wouldn't let anyone or anything in. They could all go to hell. I didn't need anyone and I would figure out this shitty mystery all on my own. And maybe I'd have some fun doing it, too.

I looked at Tucker in the flickering candlelight. He was about to say something, but then he stopped and looked at me. Really looked at me, and his eyes grew dark.

"Come on, let's go take a walk in the snow," he said, helping me up and putting my coat around my shoulders as I shrugged into it. Now I was more than slightly tipsy and Tucker kept his arm around me.

It was pitch-black outside as the days had grown short. The snow was falling with the muffled, soft sound that is unique to snow. The little downtown was already blanketed in a covering of white; the cottony flakes coming down in a heavy, steady pace. I was cold; I hadn't put my boots on. But the snow wasn't deep yet, so I managed all right. I slipped a few times, but Tucker kept me upright. The cold air cleared my head a little. I couldn't decide if I liked that or not.

We slowly made our way to my house past dark, spindly trees outlined in white, and bright spots of gold shone out from the porchlights of the houses we passed. We came up to the doorstep of my little Tudor-style house. Tucker took me by the shoulders and looked down into my eyes.

"Lane, I . . ." He paused and the sense of wanting to surrender was powerful. I wanted to do something reckless and defiant. "I want to come in," he said.

"I . . ." Tucker started to lean into me. I looked at his lips, wondering if they'd feel warm or cold from the night air. That's when I heard it. "Where's that coming from?" I asked, turning in the direction of the beautiful sound.

Echoing eerily in the blue night, bagpipes played their steadfast, noble tune across the snowy fields, past the glowing street lamps, and throughout our sleepy neighborhood. And what the cold air couldn't do, that sound did. I didn't know what I wanted, I didn't know what I was searching for. I just wanted so badly to run away. The bagpipes were in the distance, but not too far away. It was the Christmas carol, "The First Noël."

I felt Tucker's eyes on me, his face altering a bit in the night, the mood having changed. "Good night, Lane," said Tucker. "Thank you for a . . . good evening."

I nodded. "Good night, Tucker."

"Maybe sledding tomorrow?" he asked.

"Yeah, maybe. Good night." I closed the door and turned toward the dying embers in the fireplace.

CHAPTER 28

*"I sat on a bench; the animal within me licking the chops
of memory; the spiritual side a little drowsed, promising
subsequent penitence, but not yet moved to begin . . ."*

I woke up freezing cold the next morning with a pounding headache. Not surprising on both counts: I had slept on the couch—which my dad called a davenport—in the living room but the fire had died midway through the night, and well, the headache just made sense. I stacked the large fireplace with fresh wood, nice and dry and ready to burn. It came up to an orange, crackling fire quite quickly. After I warmed myself sufficiently, I went to the kitchen to put the kettle on. As my tea brewed, I grabbed a couple of slices of nut bread that Tabitha's mom left for me and the whole kettle and my cup. I raced back for milk and sugar, ran to the couch, and quickly wrapped up in a thick blanket.

Later, I managed the courage to run to the frigid upstairs bathroom and got a hot shower going. After I dressed and had another cup of tea, the doorbell rang. I went to the door and there stood Tucker with two sleds in tow.

"Come on!" he yelled, and turned around and started walking off.

"Okay! Wait a minute!" I yelled, and quickly put on my boots, coat, mittens, and hat. I got outside and he looked at me with a funny expression on his face.

"What?" I asked.

"Your hat."

"What about it?"

"It's . . . very pink and . . . very long."

"Yes, it is." I smiled impishly waiting to see if he would out-wardly make fun of my goofy hat or just keep it inside.

Kept it inside, much to my amusement. "All right then! Let's go!" he declared.

He seemed to know where he was going and off to the right of our house we tromped through the white snow. It had left a thick blanket of at least eight inches or so through the night. Just past the old cemetery, we eventually came to a big hill that already car-ried several laughing, rollicking children racing down with gleeful shouts. We slowly climbed the big hill with minimal grousing on my part, puffing and out of breath once we reached the top.

He handed me the dismal sled with the heavy iron runners.

"You've got to be kidding."

"Nope! Just like the rowboat, you've got to give it a try."

"Hmph." In my head, I was whining that he got to use the tobog-gan with the slick underside that was sure to go skimming effort-lessly over the surface of the fluffy snow.

One of the helpful boys at the top of the hill turned to me and said, "Don't you like your sled?"

"Not really, I can never make the ones like this with the runners go fast," I answered.

"Aw, it's easy, lady! Here, see how I do it. And great hat, by the way."

"Thanks." I grinned smugly at Tucker.

The boy took his sled by the wooden body and went running to where the hill dipped, slammed the sled down, and did a graceful belly flop right onto the top of his sled, which had runners identical to mine. He shot down the hill at full speed, whooping and yelling as he passed several kids on slower sleds. My spirits lifted and I thought that maybe I could do it.

First, Tucker went down the hill on his toboggan just as quickly as the other kids. He reached the bottom and waved enthusiasti-cally at me, excited for me to give my sled a try.

I backed up a few feet just like the boy did, trying to take the ex-act steps he took, and adjusted my angle a little. *Okay, I can do this!*

Stupid sled.

I ran, bending my knees, getting ready to do a graceful belly swoosh onto my sleek sled. I did everything perfectly: The sled hit the ground smoothly, I angled myself down and *POOF*! My belly sure did hit the sled perfectly and at top speed—but also with maximum momentum. I crushed the sled into the snow, digging the damn runners deeply in. It caught fast. But I didn't.

After smacking the top of the sled with all my might, my body rebounded up and over the sled, into the snow. But now I was on the slick, packed-down part of the hill from the sledders before me. I continued to roll and *poof* my way down the long, long hill. A litany of profanity rang through the air, sprinkled with general shouting. I finally landed at the bottom with an even bigger puff of snow, completely covered in the cold, glittering frosting.

No one spoke a word.

Then the boy who showed me so expertly how to sled said, "Uh, you lost your hat."

I said with a mighty laugh, "Ha! You're all dead!" I got great loads of snow into my hands and, being an expert snowball thrower, started to slaughter them. They cheered and yelled happily as I ran around plastering them all, including Tucker, with snowballs. I may not sled with grace, but I can throw a good snowball. Tucker was laughing harder than I'd ever seen him laugh.

"All right," I declared after we had all fallen down exhausted in the snow. "Now hand over the toboggan and no one gets hurt."

"Yes, ma'am," said Tucker with a chuckle.

Then we all happily sledded, not one of them continuing to try to convince me of the merits of the runner sled. After all our feet were cold and our chests were heaving with the exertion of sledding and climbing the hill over and over again, we said we'd see them tomorrow and departed. On the way back to my house, Tucker and I talked about the sledding and he no longer made fun of my hat. He had far more significant material with which to jest.

He and I said good-bye, making plans for more sledding the next day. That afternoon I wanted to be by myself again. I had some reading to do.

The fresh air and sledding had been a release. It was fun and it wasn't wrapped in mystery and intrigue. But the isolation and anger from the night before was still coursing through my system. The thought of my tree being forever altered, never being quite the same, had been the last straw. I swallowed a lump in my throat. I hated the thought that maybe I had a false sense of security with Finn. I'd been duped by my parents; who's to say that Finn hadn't duped me, too? It stung my ego, that I could be played. Other than the two scanty telegrams, I hadn't heard from Finn in weeks.

Well? The quicker I figured out the ties my parents had with the Red Scroll Network and any clues about the gold pawn and their ultimate plans, the quicker I could get back to my job and to New York.

I had brought my journal from my parents with me from New York. It was now dawning on me that my parents put that album together to keep their memories, but it was also *for me*. They meant it for my eyes; they'd taken me through that album countless times when I was a kid, pointing out significant places and moments. It made me wonder what else they had taken me through countless times. Is that why I had memories of the silver gun and the gold pawn? Had they worked to make sure that I would recall certain crucial clues? Was that what my dad meant when he wrote *Follow what we pointed out to you*, then asked if I remembered those lessons?

In front of the fireplace once again, I ate more of the rice and chicken for an early dinner. Tabitha's mom had also brought over some fresh salad ingredients, bread, and oatmeal cookies. But with raisins. I had to pick out all the raisins. I still found it a worthwhile endeavor, though; I hated to waste a good cookie.

I flipped through the journal, looking at the photographs from my parents' life before I came along, trying to find patterns, anything that might point me in the right direction or rekindle memories of those lessons they taught. But nothing. I finally dozed off, snuggled up in my blanket. The davenport was sublimely comfortable and for some reason I felt the safest and the happiest there instead of in one of the bedrooms. That night I dreamed again of the twirling pawn, the silver gun, and the ghostly white hand that was pointing to something.

I awoke in the early morning with a feeling of the right timing, that things were coming together somehow. And, for some reason, I was certain that I would discover the meaning of that mysterious hand *today*.

CHAPTER 29

*". . . I chose the better part and was found
wanting in the strength to keep to it."*

I was just about ready for more sledding. I had a cup of coffee, I
put on an extra pair of socks, ate a Skippy peanut butter sandwich,
and was ready to go. I was rinsing out my cup at the sink, looking
out to the front yard, but over to the right, avoiding my tree. I could
hardly bear to think about it. With determined and calculated anger, I tamped it all down, using it to fuel my need for vengeance. I
reveled in that solitary feeling. I didn't need anyone. I could figure
it out on my own.

As I pondered all this, I went to the laundry room in the back and
looked out the small window toward the rear of the Baxters' house and
saw Tucker talking to Tabitha. He had his sled in his hands,
about to come over and pick me up. His back was to me and he
raised his right hand to sweep a lock of her shiny black hair off her
face in a very *friendly* gesture.

After a bit, he came over to my door and I was all set, ready to go.

I opened the door and he greeted me, "Morning, Lane!" His
gaze instantly went up over my eyes.

"Morning, Tucker," I said, smiling.

"Ah. You have a new hat."

"Yes, I do."

"All right then, let's go!"

We walked to the right again. I was surprised to feel that my legs
and back were not tired or stiff. I had been wondering if all that

climbing yesterday, not to mention my graceful tumble down the hill, would leave some uncomfortable reminders.

"Hey, what's in the bag, Lane?"

"Oh, a little something I cooked up for our friends," I said, a wicked smile creeping over my face.

He laughed, "I can only imagine."

After a little while of enjoying the bright day, our boots making great clomping noises as we proceeded down the sidewalk and the sun sending rainbow-colored glitter all over the white snow, I nonchalantly said, "So Tucker, did you know Tabitha before this visit?"

"No, why do you ask?" he responded quickly, casually.

"Oh, no reason," I lied. "I knew you said you'd been to Rochester on several occasions, the town is so small, you know . . ."

"Nope, she seems like a nice girl," he said in a friendly manner. So. We were both lying. But why?

We came up to our hill and our little friends were ready and waiting for us. I waved a hearty hello and greeted them all by name.

They were waving merrily until they saw my hat. They put their hands down at their sides and gazed in wonder at my head. They all murmured several things like, "Wow, that's the biggest puff ball I've ever seen . . . Nice, very blue hat." More or less . . .

I ran up the hill as fast as I could to beat the boys to the top. I took the toboggan out of Tucker's hands and he jumped on behind me. With our combined weight, we raced down the hill at breakneck speed to the cheers of all the boys. I wondered why there weren't any other adults out. Finn would be here with me.

My heart felt a swift pang of emptiness. I shook my head, shuffling off that emotion. I made my way back up the hill.

After we all went down the hill a dozen times, I declared a little breathlessly, "Okay, guys, I have something for us to play with."

They were delighted, but a little dubious. I went to my bag that I brought and unzipped it. With a great flourish, I pulled out a leggy bunch of thin, rubbery tubes with a connected square of canvas.

"What the—" said the biggest boy, Jack.

"Trust me, gentlemen," I purred.

I took Jack and gave him the makeshift handle on one end of the tubing. I took the next biggest kid, LJ, walked him over about five feet away, and gave him the other handle. Now the tubing wasn't so coiled and knotted; it was making one long, stretched-out loop with a kid at each end. In the middle was the canvas square that made a sort of pouch.

"Aha!" said Tucker.

"Yep," I said with relish. "It's a giant slingshot."

All the boys' eyes opened wide with anticipation and they practically drooled, instantly dreaming of blasting enemies and friends alike with all sorts of things like snow, rotten apples, mud . . . The possibilities were endless.

I loaded up the center with a giant snowball, telling the two end boys to hold steady and strong. Then I took the handle that I had sewn to the back of the canvas pouch, pulled it back, and yelled, "Ready! Set! Go!" To many *oohs* and *ahs*, the snowball arced high in the sky and landed with a momentous *poof* a couple hundred feet away. All of us cheered. I figured I might have some explaining to do with the parents in the neighborhood, but what the heck. If they wanted in on the fun, they could play, too.

We launched about twenty huge snowballs, seeing how far we could get them. Then one of the kids thought we should have target practice with some of us out in the field. The snowballs weren't icy, so it was all right with me. I got pelted a few times as well as Tucker. I think they were aiming for my hat.

I had also thrown some of Mrs. Baxter's cookies into my bag of tricks. After we all dined on those, we decided we were cold enough and everyone headed for home. Tucker and I were starving, so we went to Knapp's opting to just lug the toboggan with us instead of backtracking.

We didn't talk much, just about the sledding, the boys . . . and we ate our extra-wide, thin hamburgers and fries. I was in a thoughtful mood, putting together and taking apart several things that I'd come across lately; several hunches, thoughts, ideas. None of it made sense yet, but I knew that some of them would turn out to be valuable clues. So as I sipped my chocolate malt, I kept sliding them together, putting them in a different order, testing them out this way and that.

Tucker didn't seem to mind; he seemed to be deep in thought, too. On the walk back to the house, we decided to go a different route so I could see the Chapman House. It was a lovely home just a couple of streets away from mine. It was the biggest and grandest house in town with beautiful creamy gray stone walls, large curved windows, and columns in the front. Very pleasing to the eye. I wondered what it looked like inside. It used to have a small pool in the back, a neat little thing. But I heard that one of the children of the house had tragically drowned in it, so the family had it filled in with cement. Such a lovely home, but such sadness.

The house had the look of being closed up for the winter. They were probably somewhere south. But out of the corner of my eye, I saw the branches of a fir tree rustle. I thought it could have been a squirrel, but Tucker tensed. My eyes darted to him and then back toward the tree by the corner of the house.

Three large men came around the corner with menacing grins on their faces—two of them were the same guys from Carl's Chop House who had chased us off the dance floor. The block was eerily quiet like everyone was indoors taking a winter's nap. The men had beefy arms accentuated by their thick wool coats, which reminded me of the thugs that Roarke and I ran into in Central Park. All eyes were on us and they were not friendly.

"You there, with the weird hat!" said the leader, pointing at me.

"Hey! Whattaya mean weird hat?" I said indignantly.

I could feel Tucker tense even more, taking in the situation.

The big guy growled a laugh. "You sound tough, but are you really? Let's just see about that. You've got something we want and when we want something, we get it," he said, starting to come closer. In this heavy snow, running was going to be slow going. I wasn't sure we could make a break for it. I might usually be able to outrun them, but my legs were a bit rubbery after the long hours of sledding, and I had on heavy snow boots.

I was wondering if Tucker was ever going to do *anything* when he finally said, "All right, guys, we don't want any trouble." Not the wittiest remark.

As the men kept advancing, we took tentative steps backward. The biggest guy stepped onto a patch of ice and slipped a little. Tucker murmured confidently, "I got it, Lane, don't worry." He took the toboggan and swung it sideways, walloping the big guy. The man put up his arms to block the blow, and as the toboggan made contact, the momentum mixed with the ice made his feet go right out from under him. He came down hard, all three hundred pounds of him. It stunned them all and I yelled, "Run!"

We ran down the sidewalk. The big guy was still prone on the ice—his hulking form obviously difficult to pick up. One of the smaller guys made a leap and grabbed me from behind, giving me a breath-whooshing bear hug. The third one grappled with Tucker.

My arms were pinned, crossed in front of my chest. I took a big breath and with a mighty thrust, I pushed my arms down—palms to the ground—and bent over as hard as I could at the same time. Kirkland's self-defense maneuver broke the guy's grip and the way I bent over so suddenly, my rear end gave him quite a big punch to the gut. *Actually, it was probably a bit lower than his gut,* I thought happily to myself.

I could see that the guy Tucker was grappling with was the meanest and the cleverest and he was not going down easily. I watched as Tucker punched him with a mighty blow to his jaw, allowing him to break away from him and we ran like gangbusters. I wanted to shout for help, but my lungs just couldn't do it.

We ran around the side of a large, white building that looked like a rambling house with black shutters. Then I saw the sign; it was a funeral home. As far as omens go, it didn't seem like things were boding well for us. We found a small shed that was attached to the side of the building and we stepped inside. We had been on a cleared part of the sidewalk for a while, so we didn't leave any telltale footprints behind.

We got in, both of us panting, trying to do so as quietly as possible. Tucker turned to me, his eyes dark and inviting. He walked me backward until my back came up against the wall. Taking my hat off and placing his warms hands on either side of my head, he whispered intensely, "Are you okay, Lane?"

I liked this danger, even though I knew I shouldn't. It was simple. It made me despise the complex and heavy cloak of mystery and obligation even more.

Everything was so confusing. *Damn*, I missed Finn, and I hated myself for it. I looked at Tucker, his pleasing face. I wanted to surrender, to feel something that wasn't complicated.

His right hand slowly came down the side of my face and his thumb traced my lips, lingering on my lower lip as he bent slowly closer.

A harsh voice came from outside, not too far away, freezing Tucker about two inches away from my lips. "Guys! I lost 'em! You see 'em?" We heard two others cuss in frustration. Then the same harsh voice: "Come on! We better get movin', we're gonna have some company soon."

Tucker never stopped looking at my eyes. "Tucker," I whispered. "We have to go."

I looked at his lips. He took a ragged breath in. Just then, the door to our shed opened abruptly. In the bright light, I could just see a man's shape. Tucker stepped in front me with his arm out.

"You kids okay? I saw those guys coming after you—called the cops." It was a middle-aged man with wispy strands of hair covering his balding head.

"Yeah, we're okay. Thanks," I said as I walked around Tucker and out of the shed into the white sunshine.

The man was the manager of the funeral home. We told him what happened. As we walked along the side of the building, I heard the swish of footsteps and turned back. The biggest guy that Tucker had clobbered came stealthily around the corner. He had a gun in his hand and it was pointed right at us. Tucker turned his head back at the same moment and dove to his left, directly at me.

"Lane, get down!" The gun went off, the bullet zipping over our heads.

Tucker landed right on top of me. He looked down at me, my face just inches from his own, and it might have been a dramatic and romantic moment—but he had knocked the wind right out of me. I struggled not to panic. It was awful. It felt like I was going to die and I was absolutely willing my lungs to kick in and start working again.

"Oh, my God!" yelled Tucker. "Are you hit? Are you hit, Lane?" He started pawing at me, looking for a bullet wound.

I croaked, "Stop it."

"Oh God, oh God, you're okay?"

I nodded and croaked again, "Get. Off me."

He did and I saw that the gunman had departed and *at last* more people started coming out to see what the fracas was all about. My body was in the euphoria of being able to breathe freely once again. I didn't much care what else happened; I was just so happy to breathe in great gasps of air.

All three of the attackers disappeared, slipping away unseen by anyone. We gave a report to the sheriff who showed up, the events sounding ludicrous even to me. The look on his face spoke volumes about what he *really* thought: We clearly had been drinking too much. After everything, which took much, much longer than I thought necessary, we at last wearily headed home after we retrieved our toboggan and my bag of tricks, dropped during the pursuit.

The darkness of night was beginning to close in on us even though it was only about four thirty. That whole afternoon, I had a feeling like I was just missing something. Like knowing a face in the crowd, but you just can't remember where you'd seen them before. As we walked, I kept turning over those little pieces to the puzzle, trying to find the right places, the right angle where everything would fit perfectly. I was close.

We arrived at my door and I thanked Tucker for the robust day. He chuckled.

"Lane, maybe I should come in. Do you want me to make sure the house is locked up?"

"No, no, I'm sure the house is fine. I checked all the locks this morning. Besides, I'm exhausted and I really want a nap." He didn't look at all like that was okay with him. But I desperately needed some time alone to sort out my thoughts.

"*Really*, Tucker, I'm fine and I want to be alone," I said.

"Okay, Lane, I give up. Get some rest and I'll . . . see you tomorrow. You sure you're all right?"

"Grrrr . . ."

He put his hands up in a posture of defense. "Okay! Okay! I get it," he chuckled.

"Good night, Tucker." I closed the door softly. And locked it.

CHAPTER 30

"And now," said he, "to settle what remains.
Will you be wise? Will you be guided?"

I double-checked all the locks and windows in the house, as well as the closets, so I could be at peace, wishing the entire time that Ripley was with me. I stoked up the fire and was all at once so weary, I lay down on the couch and fell directly to sleep.

I awoke a few hours later with that odd sensation from sleeping deeply during the day, where you can't figure out what time it is, where you are exactly, and if you slept through several days. I felt the soft, cream-colored blanket between my fingertips, nuzzled into the chocolate brown velvet pillow and gazed into the fire. I sleepily looked at the clock on the wall and saw that it was about eight o'clock. I felt quite refreshed and I decided to take a hot shower. I washed and dried my hair and put on a sumptuously soft taupe sweater with a very wide neck. It felt lush and comfortable and pretty.

Mrs. Baxter had brought over some more food. I made a plate with stuffed cabbage rolls and some freshly baked bread, then took it to my fire. I ate with the soft strands of Cole Porter floating down the stairs, enjoying the good food as I thought through the remarkable events of the day. Things were not making sense and it was pressing on my mind.

As I ruminated on it all, I drew out my journal from my parents, slowly turning the pages, taking a close look at each photograph by itself, then in comparison to the ones around it. Looking for . . .

something. Patterns, things that stuck out, anything that drew my attention in a unique way. I finally got to the page that had first started my mind churning about my parents' past: the photo of my chic mother, in front of Jimmy Walker's casino in New York City. With the notorious mobster Louie Venetti directly behind her.

Her hand. Her hand was flung out to her side in a rather glamorous pose. I made a small square with my fingers and placed it onto the photograph, framing her hand. When I looked at the hand alone in the black-and-white picture, it was the ghostly color of white and gray. Her index finger was pointing off to her side, to the right. *That* was the hand in my dreams. Maybe it was what my father meant in his note, about what they had pointed out to me . . . Her hand was *pointing to something.*

I looked very closely at the right side of the photograph, and lo and behold, that picture had been perfectly folded. It looked like it was a full-sized square photograph with the corners pinned back with black corner tabs, but in fact the photograph had been bent.

I carefully took the photograph out of the corner holds and pulled it out. I unbent the photograph back into its original rectangular form. There was a man standing there, someone I had never seen before. I knew exactly where to start looking for someone who *had.* It was too late tonight to check it out, but it would be first on my list for tomorrow.

Later on that night, after I combed through the rest of the album, not finding anything else of interest, I went to the piano. The snow was starting to fall again. The house was silent and I craved some music. Some life.

I thought about the years here in this house. What my life looked like back then. What it looked like now. What it would have been if my parents hadn't been killed. I loved my life, but I wondered what I'd missed out on. I ached for the things that would never be, the questions that would never be answered. And who. Who was responsible for bringing this upon all of us, upon me?

My thoughts drifted to my friends back home. My real home. And I discovered my fingers hunting and feeling out notes to a song I had heard only once. A song Finn and I had danced to in the foyer of our townhouse in New York. An achingly sweet dance. I couldn't quite figure out that song, so I played a different tune, and sang a few soft words, trying to convince myself that I didn't miss him.

I had opened a bottle of wine, pouring a single glass this time, and I sipped a little. I had been arduously avoiding thinking of Finn the past twenty-four hours. That anger that had boiled up and over when I'd discovered my tree was still walking with me, a constant companion, yet something I feared at the same time. But truthfully, I longed for Finn. His friendship, his embrace, and his laugh, which had become so much easier than when we'd first met and he'd been so serious. I wanted the simplicity and sweetness of our friendship. But the anger was powerful, hot, and seductive.

And Finn was not here. He had chosen not to communicate hardly at all. And he *did* communicate that he'd been with Gwen. It had been a couple of days since I'd sent that telegram to him. I wondered if and when he'd get it.

A memory fluttered into my mind of that summer night that I had been sitting on the loveseat during a thunder storm, listening, absorbing the rumbles and the electric, velvety atmosphere. Enjoying the sounds, but feeling endlessly lonely. And Finn came to me. Once again, I was very alone . . . and lonely.

There was a knock at the door.

I walked cautiously over to the front door and peered out the small side window. It was Tucker.

I opened the door and looked at his nice face. The snow was blowing about in gentle gusts, the white making that special bluish glow in the moonlight with countless tiny white crystals reflecting off the smooth surface. Behind him, to the left, my eyes were drawn to my scarred tree. The resentment and bitterness started to painfully rise in my chest; becoming sturdier, more substantial. That tree had been my *friend*. In a childhood where I had spent so much time alone, it was a constant partner. I felt at home there. Safe. Even in the emptiness that the loss of my parents created, it was one monument that had remained the same. Until now.

And here was this tantalizing new emotion. This anger. This red-hot, seething, pulling, effortless delight. I hated it and I loved it. I craved it. There was a kind of drunken strength that came from it and a tempting wickedness that swirled within. A throbbing desire to give in, to let it seduce me, let it consume me.

I raised my eyes, slowly, with great care. To Tucker. He'd been watching me intently, silently, not moving a muscle. I wondered if he was reading my inner turmoil, not budging, trying not to break the spell. His eyes were dark with desire. Neither of us said a word.

He leaned in and kissed my neck right below my ear and I trembled with the softness and the heady desire. He pulled his head back and looked into my eyes. He gingerly put out his hand and tenderly brushed a lock of hair from my face. *I'd seen him do that before.* A crack of reality shone a tiny shaft of light into the darkness, and the temptation ebbed the slightest bit. Then, thin tendrils of music once again wafted through the frosty open air. The bagpipes. Like an ethereal, mystical messenger sent specifically to speak to me. To remind me. To wake me.

Tucker said with a husky voice, "Lane, I want to come in."

"I know," I said softly, and paused.

"Lane, it's not safe for you to be alone. We didn't catch those men who attacked us today, I really think I should come in."

Another idea took shape in my mind of those men who were chasing us. Something was up with them; I thought I had seen them before. It was a rather frightening thought, which brought even more clarity to me. Like cold water splashed on a hot face.

I had made up my mind.

"No, Tucker. But thanks for coming over to check on me. See you tomorrow . . . For one more day of sledding?"

He took a deep breath. Then he exhaled a soft sigh. "All right, Lane. See you tomorrow."

CHAPTER 31

They met in the same pub. This time snow was falling, making the streets just as dank and chilly as the rain, but with a softening beauty. On the walk over, Finn wondered what Lane was doing, wishing they could share a walk through the snow together. His mind shifted to that summer night he had walked over to her house, incapable of staying away one moment longer. It would have been safer for her if he'd stayed away. He'd tried, but he just couldn't. He had gone with not a little trepidation to her townhouse. He could hear the low rumble of distant thunder, sending static chills down his spine. There was nothing sweeter than a summer thunderstorm. Until he got to share it with Lane. He marveled at how hard it was being apart from her. He'd never felt that kind of connection or devotion to anyone.

Finn was hoping to finish up his work in London soon and head home to New York. Miles was making headway on some of the questions they had about the Red Scroll Network. He was almost at the end of his mission.

The snowy white flakes frosted the top of his black hat and shoulders and he hunkered down deeper into the collar of his long wool coat. He pushed open the door to the pub and saw Miles in the same corner, the same table. They greeted each other, ordered some Guinness and fish and chips.

The place was no gourmet restaurant, but had decent, earthy food. He was starving. And he was anxious to hear what Miles had discovered. He hoped that it would be enough to wrap it all up. Maybe he'd fly out to Michigan directly from New York to meet Lane there.

"I found out quite a bit, Finn," said Miles in his raspy voice. His hands and face were much cleaner now, as well as his clothes. But it was also something within that had changed, as if the soap had washed his exterior and some kind of cleansing agent worked away the paranoia and the anxiety on the inside.

Finn nodded, encouraging him to continue. "Yeah, my contact gave me more than I expected. Okay, this is the deal, Rex definitely had that one son. I knew I could find out his name, but it took some real digging, yeah. But I found it. It was Rutherford."

That name rang a bell with Finn, but he couldn't remember where he'd heard it, it was on the tip of his tongue. They kept eating their fish and chips, both enjoying the crispy crust on the tender cod and large chips that Finn had come to call fries. They both shook malt vinegar over the fish. Finn licked the salt from his lips.

"Oh, and I found out that, for sure, Rex had two grandchildren from Rutherford. One boy, one girl."

"Great, that will help. The more details the better in figuring out this tangled mess," said Finn. Miles gave his craggy smile, clearly gratified to hear the praise.

They slowly finished their simple dinner, the flames from the fireplace creating flickering shadows on the walls, the wood floor crunching as people walked back and forth over the peanut shells and hay. It was pleasant, but there was something nagging insistently at Finn's mind, leaving a mark of uncertainty over their companionable time.

Just then the barkeep, who was also the landlord of the building, came over to Finn. "Mr. Brodie, this came for you today." He set down a telegram. Finn looked at it with great expectation as he hoped it would be from Lane. He had given her the address of this out-of-the-way place so he could be as sure as possible no one would intercept any messages.

But before he could read it Miles said, "Oh, I almost forgot. It was by great luck that I actually got a photograph of Rex's grandkids! My contact used to be friends with the family and he was an amateur photographer, so he was always taking photos, practicing, you know. Here ya go."

He handed Finn the photograph, grinning in satisfaction at the look of astonishment on Finn's face. There were two children playing outside, possibly in Central Park, the son quite a few years older than the girl. He focused first on the girl in the rather fuzzy, old photograph.

Finn's stomach dropped and all at once he remembered where he had heard the name Rutherford. Rutherford *Franco*.

"Wait," said Finn. "So you're telling me Rutherford Franco was Rex Ruby's son?"

"Yes. Exactly," said Miles, a bit mystified at Finn's strong reaction.

"Well, this is the thing, Miles. We had a whole different case a few months ago, and Eliza, Rutherford's daughter, was up to her eyeballs in it. So that means Eliza is Rex's granddaughter, right?"

"Yes."

Finn thoughtfully pulled his hand through his hair and murmured, "I guess that solves how Eliza got her hands on the silver gun. . . ."

Miles piped in, "And Rutherford had a son, too, don't forget."

Finn turned his focus to the young teenage boy in the photograph.

In that picture was, beyond all doubt, a young Eliza and . . . Tucker.

"Oh, my God," he said in a horrified, hushed voice. Miles's eyes looked up from his pint with urgency, very aware that their conversation just turned grave and of paramount importance.

Finn grabbed the telegram and opened it with a violent slash. Inside it read:

IN MI STOP FINDING CLUES STOP ITS HARD
STOP SAY HI TO GWEN STOP TUCKER HERE
WITH ME STOP
LANE

It didn't seem possible, but his stomach plummeted even further. His heart almost broke at the despairing sound of those two words from Lane, *It's hard*. And Gwen, why the hell had he mentioned her in a telegram, without context or grace? *Tucker here with me*. My God.

"Holy shit," he muttered in mounting fear and agitation as he fingered the photograph of this cunning enemy that now had a name and a face. And he was within reach of the woman he loved more than he thought possible. His voice turned almost savage. "Miles, I need to get to the States. I have to get to Michigan. Now."

CHAPTER 32

*"I loaded an old revolver, that I might
be found in some posture of self-defense."*

I awoke the next morning still on my davenport, contemplating, calculating, pondering. It was like my mind had never stopped working even while I slept. I closed my eyes last night thinking through everything and woke up without missing a beat. I was refreshed. I was ready.

After a hot shower and putting on my favorite black skirt, dark red blouse, and tall black boots, I felt like my New York self again. I brushed my hair, letting it cascade over my shoulders. I put on some eyeliner and mascara, and finally my red lipstick. I was ready for the battle that I knew would come today.

Lastly, I took my father's dagger that Mr. Kirkland had given me. I held the small knife in my hand, feeling its pleasing weight, appreciating the bright, razor-sharp silver blade, and the exceptional handle. It had a pearl inlay of swirls and fleur-de-lis with a black background of ebony. A thing of dangerous beauty. My skirt had a wide belt around the waist and I slipped the dagger with its thin scabbard in on my right side so I could quickly grab it with my right hand.

I had practiced that maneuver over and over again with Mr. Kirkland. Most people thought you fought with a knife by holding it point-side up in your fist. But that was for amateurs. The best way to wield a knife in a fight was blade-side down. My deep red sweater overcoat with a matching fur collar could give me issues if I need to get to my knife quickly, but I'd just have to figure that out on the fly. If all went well, I wouldn't have to.

All right, I was ready. I had some sleuthing to do, but this time I was on my own. I hoped I was early enough to miss Tucker's sledding visit; I needed to ask my probing questions without an audience. I took my capacious purse, heavy with the *present* I had placed carefully within along with the photograph of the mystery man from my mother's picture.

Time was running out yet again. It was still another day or so before Aunt Evelyn and Mr. Kirkland would arrive. The pieces to this particular puzzle were falling into place, but there were a couple of gaping holes I intended to fill in today. I could feel the fog around me forming shapes that were starting to come together into disturbing images. I needed to send two more telegrams. That would be my first errand of the day.

I opened the door and walked out into the crisp, refreshing air. There were a few people around shoveling snow or getting into their cold cars, but it felt so empty. I was used to the energy of the hustle and bustle of the purposeful New York mornings. I missed it. It was lovely here, but drowsy.

I walked over to the apothecary and sent my two telegrams. I was giving them quite a good business my few days here and they seemed to like that a lot. I received nice big smiles in return. But then again, everyone had heard about the ruckus and the odd story yesterday with the two crazy New Yorkers who were visiting. Word spreads quickly in a small town, and I noticed a little hesitation to be *too* friendly with me.

I headed to my next meeting a couple of blocks farther down Main Street. Just as I was crossing the street, I saw a familiar form and I ducked alongside the building. Tucker was coming out of the diner. I peeked around the corner and there were two men about to enter for a late breakfast. As Tucker passed them, he nodded his head in a *good morning* gesture. The tallest man nodded back, clearly knowing Tucker, and said something to him that I couldn't hear. As he turned into the diner door, I saw his profile. *Wait, was that one of the guys who attacked us by the funeral home? No, it couldn't be.*

When the coast was clear, I walked the two doors down to my destination, my mind reeling from what I thought I just saw. There were a few men inside the shop, the snow collecting charmingly in the corners of the windows. The blue, red, and white stripes spun around and around on the pole next to the sign. I opened the door with loudly clanging bells that announced a visitor; which was funny to me because everyone who worked at this place of business was just a few feet away and in full view of the door. It was Baldy Benson's Barber Shop.

There was one man reclining in the chair, getting a close shave. There was another barber sweeping up the hair from an early morning clip. Even though none of them looked up, they must have sensed the out-of-place feminine presence. They all stopped and slowly turned questioning faces to me.

"Hello, gentlemen."

"Uh, hello," said the man sweeping up. The two barbers looked like they were in their eighties, but very spritely. They were instantly suspicious of me. So, I reached into my bag, taking the advice that Roarke had given me from his last visit with these gentlemen, and I pulled out a bottle of forty-year-old scotch from my father's vault.

I suddenly had three very good friends.

It wasn't quite afternoon, but hey, you don't pass up scotch like *that*. I poured generous helpings for the three of them. They just happened to have some glasses available. I abstained. Fire didn't sound appetizing at the moment.

After they fully appreciated the amber nectar, we got down to business. Benson, who was indeed bald, Fred, and Jasper gave me their full attention, all three sets of eyes twinkling with this newfound and bountiful friendship.

"What's your name, dollface?" asked Jasper, the man who had been getting a shave. He looked younger than the barbers. A boyish seventy. I smiled at the "dollface," remembering my dad calling me that once in a while.

"Well, that's what I'm here to discuss. I believe you met a friend of mine a while back, Roarke—" But before I could even say his last name they cut me off.

"Sure! We remember Roarke! Nice guy, had a lot of laughs with him." I bet they did.

"Well, I know he asked about a cousin of his. Lane Sanders?" I said.

Their faces turned slightly downcast, wary. "Oh yes, we remember," said Fred.

"Well, I'm Lane. Lane Sanders." They all looked at me closely, like they were looking for someone deep down, to see if I was who I said I was. I smiled as recognition hit the sweeper first.

"My God, Charlotte's smile," said Benson.

"Damn," said Fred appreciably.

I laughed, making them smile broadly. I told them briefly about getting things in order here now that I lived in New York. They nodded as they listened closely. I was attempting to sound light and airy, but these men were smart. Like Roarke said, they knew that there were fishy things that happened back then and that the mystery of my parents' death had never come to a satisfactory conclusion.

"Could you take a look at this?" I asked as I pulled out the photograph of my mother, pointing to the previously hidden man next to her under the fold. He looked young like my parents and handsome with a large, hawk-like nose, but his angular face could handle it. It made him look distinguished.

"Wow! Charlotte was quite a looker!" Benson blurted out. "Oh, sorry, Lane," he said sheepishly. I just laughed. She *was* a looker.

"Actually, do you know who this man is next to her?"

Both barbers took off one set of glasses and put on another, presumably stronger, set of spectacles and peered closely. They both looked at each other with dubious glances and Benson spoke for them all. "Why, that's Rutherford. Rutherford Franco."

I'm not sure what I was expecting. I had a vague notion that these all-knowing barbers might be able to shed light on this man, but *Eliza's father*? The man who had perished on the lake with my parents? What were they doing in a photograph with him? My parents had been killed outright, it was no accident. There had been a small explosion that went off as my parents and I skated close to the outskirts of the rink, out toward the middle of the lake. We all fell into the icy waters as well as another man, Rutherford Franco. But whether it was intended to kill or just be a distraction, a bullet is what killed my mother and father. I was the only one rescued. Was Rutherford's death intentional as well? I'm really not a believer in coincidences, but why this small-town man? And why was he in a photograph in New York with my parents? And most intriguingly, why was it imperative for my father to point this out to me and in such a clandestine way?

"How long had the Francos lived here?" I asked.

Benson, the obvious spokesman of the group, replied, "Well, let's see, a few years. In fact, maybe just a little after your folks moved in. Their daughter Louise was just a bitty thing when they moved in. And lemme think, their son was much older than the little girl, and he was about . . . Oh, I'd guess about ten years older." Louise had been Eliza's original name. The first of many.

"They had a son? What was his name?"

"I think it was Tom. That sound right, boys? Tommy?" he asked his cronies. They replied that yup, sounded right, but more than anything they started eyeing the delicious scotch again.

I murmured, "Tom, huh . . ." while I poured another glass all around. This time I poured myself a small, restorative swig.

"Anything else you can tell me about the Francos?" I asked.

"Well . . ." The other barber, Fred, spoke up in an intense and thoughtful voice. "You know, I don't mean to be disrespectful, but that wife of Rutherford's, Daphne, she was a bit of a twit."

"Hah!" barked out the seventy-year-old Jasper. "Scary twit! Something not quite right about her. Always used to feel sorry for those kids. Course that son, Tom, went away and really it was the little girl that was around most of the time. That Thomas, boy oh boy, he could charm the skin off a snake. But there were times, though, there was somethin' deep down in him that was off . . . kind of scary, like his mother."

I took all this in and then asked the most important question I had now that they were warmed up, hoping that the question wouldn't scare them off. "When the ice skating, uh, *accident* happened . . . was there anything or anyone out of the ordinary around town? Or just anything at all that comes to mind that was out of place?"

"Well, there was this friend of your folks; real tall guy, bright blue eyes, gray hair even though he didn't look that old. Looked like he could have been a sailor or somethin' . . ." Mr. Kirkland. For sure.

"Anyone or anything else?"

"Well . . ." said Benson hesitatingly, as if he wasn't sure he should say something.

"Spit it out, Benson," I said with a smile.

"Oh, ah. Well, this happened a long time ago, but it might mean something. I remember going out to eat one night. Me and the missus, took her out to a fancy night on the town down in Detroit. And across the room, I saw that young Tom Franco—had to be about eighteen then. He was with an old man, looked like his grandfather or something. But Jesus, that man had an *evil* look about him. And Tom, he was eager; eyes wide like he'd do anything at all to please the guy. The only reason I remember that meeting, was that I had thought to myself that the old man was trouble. Bad things would happen around him.

"I only saw Tom one time after that, much later. In fact, come to think of it, it was just a day or two before your parents' accident. In Detroit again, saw him across the train station. I made a run down there to pick up some sick relative or other who wanted to come out to the country to visit. After the accident, I felt awful for Tom. Hard for a boy to lose his father. But I never saw the boy again. He never even went to the funeral."

"Hard to imagine . . ." I whispered, thinking hard. "Anything about that old man that stood out to you? What did he look like? Besides bad."

"Well, he was sitting down, so I don't know how tall he was. Looked average to me other than the criminal feel . . . But I know! He wore a lot of jewelry."

"What kind of jewelry?"

"I don't know."

"Necklaces? Rings? Bracelets?"

"I don't know. Just jewelry." Such a guy. "Wait a minute, lemme see that picture of Rutherford again." I handed it to him and he looked up at me after looking closely at it. "You know, I think it really was Tom's grandfather. He had that same big nose as Rutherford. Didn't remember it until I saw that picture just now of Rutherford up close."

"Well, thanks, gentlemen. I've really enjoyed meeting you," I said getting up, feeling that I had gotten all the information I could. "And keep the bottle," I said, laying a hand on the beautiful amber glass. "I don't have many friends here yet, and it meant a lot to talk with you."

"Mighty nice of you, Lane, thanks!"

I smiled as I walked out the door, hearing the clanging bells clunk against the glass door, making an audible bookend to my time with new friends in this familiar, yet strange town.

I needed to think. I took a winding walk away from Main Street, in the opposite direction of my home. I meandered along the quaint streets as I continued to slide the intriguing pieces of my puzzle around, trying to find a shape that would make sense.

As I walked down the sidewalk, a cardinal pattered down a branch with his showy bright red feathers, brilliant against the snow. In a fenced-in yard, a couple of joyous black dogs romped around in the snow together, with huge mounds of snow piled up on their noses from shoving their snouts into the cold, delightful white stuff.

Past the house with the black dogs, a lovely little church came into view with what looked like the winding branches of wisteria trees by the entrance—a beautiful sight, I was certain, come spring. I was admiring the charming little building made out of brownstone with a large, curving stained glass window, when the door opened and a very large man who must have been the rector came stomping out into the frozen air. He was carrying bagpipes.

"You!" I said loudly, making him jump as his back had been turned to me to close the door behind him.

He whipped around. "Oh . . . pardon?" he asked.

"Sorry about scaring you. I've heard your bagpipes a couple of times the last few days I've been here. They're *wonderful*," I said earnestly. Those hauntingly beautiful sounds, slipping their way through the winter night like cool silken ribbons, right to me.

He was a balding man, probably in his forties. A large, burly guy with a very friendly, open, and capable face. His warm brown eyes looked like they laughed a lot. He had a lively Scottish brogue, which made sense with the bagpipes and all.

"Hi, I'm Lane Sanders," I said, holding out my hand.

"Father Alan MacQueen. Nice to meet you, Lane." We shook hands slightly awkwardly as he held the leggy instrument that looked like it was trying to make a run for it; his hands were enormous and warm.

He took a good look at me and his searching gaze made me wonder what he saw. Kindness shone out of his eyes, just like the sun was shining down, warming our heads. I liked him. I was reminded of Little John in *Robin Hood*; he felt safe and perfectly capable of handling any evil sent his way. Still smiling, he cocked his head in an earnest way and said, "Is there something troubling you, lass?"

I was shocked at his forthcoming question, but found myself blurting out, "Yes!"

He grinned even wider at my exclamation and said, "Come! Let's sit for a moment. It's chilly out, but such a glorious day, I hate to be inside." He ushered me over to a little bench that had been brushed off along with the front walk to the church, and we sat down.

"So, you heard me playing my pipes, eh?"

"Yes, in the moonlight. They were glorious."

"Thank you."

He waited for me to say what was on my mind, unafraid of pauses. "You know," I ventured. "Your bagpipes helped . . . stop me from making a big mistake. It's hard to say what I was wrestling with, but it was powerful. And a large part of me wanted it. I don't really understand, but I was considering . . . I'm not sure how to put it . . ."

"Darkness," he supplied.

"Exactly."

"I can understand that," he said simply.

"Really?"

"Of course, Lane." His Scottish brogue was thick and pleasant. His muscular frame and broad arms and long legs made me think of Highland games and how he looked like he could easily toss around a caber.

We sat in comfortable silence a few seconds longer, his gentle presence inspiring patience and stillness. Then he said, "You know, Lane. It occurs to me to tell you about a sermon I was just preparing inside before you came. You see, there are things in life that we have to fight and conquer on our own. And then there are times when we need other people."

I nodded. He sounded like Morgan.

"I was studying the account of the fall of Adam and Eve in the ancient Jewish scriptures. And it's always made me angry that people, men mostly, I hate to admit, have made Eve to be the villain."

I was surprised to hear that, because even though I could completely understand the plight of Adam and Eve and certainly had my own moments of specifically choosing things that I knew were wrong . . . the story agitated me.

"You see, when Eve was being tempted . . . and she took a bite of the apple as she was being seduced and deceived by the enemy . . . where was Adam?"

"I have no idea," I said.

He smirked. "He was *right there*. Eve should never have listened to lies, listened to tempting evil that she certainly knew was wrong and corrupt. But Adam should have picked up his bride and whisked her away from the enemy. He should have helped her see evil for what it was, to save her. She couldn't fight that battle on her own. *And neither could he.* She should have protected him, too. That was the point of God creating them for each other."

Before I could chew on that, he abruptly declared, "Well, Lane? I must be off. Come again, I would love to chat some more. But if I am to get in some practice, I had better be going."

"Don't you practice in the evenings?"

"Sometimes. The last few days I wanted to get in a little extra practice for the Christmas service. Most often I practice in the morning or afternoon. But I'm sure you noticed, music in the dark is magical. Right, Lane?"

"Yes, it really is. I have to get going as well. I have a couple of appointments in town. I need to find some answers to a perplexing problem."

He briskly replied, "And you can count on my prayers for you. See you soon, Lane."

I shook his hand warmly and walked toward Main Street. I wondered about getting lunch before heading back home. The heels of my black boots *click-clacked* along the shoveled sidewalks. The town looked empty; most people were inside on this frosty day. I pondered the things my new barber shop buddies had told me about that Tom Franco, the meeting with Father MacQueen, needing people, certain battles that you just can't win alone . . . I watched my feet walk in their rhythmic pattern, deep in thought, my hands stuffed into my pockets as I hunkered down into my fluffy red fur collar. A movement caught my eye up ahead and I looked up.

Tucker.

CHAPTER 33

"Between these two, I now felt I had to choose."

Tucker's intense eyes pierced into mine as he nodded a greeting, motioning for me to come over. I walked toward him with a little wave.

"What have you been up to, Lane? I thought we were going sledding again," he said with a low voice. He wasn't his usual, charming self. But there was something familiar about the way he was acting, albeit *off.*

"Well, I went for a walk and then I ran into the rector up the street. *He's* been the one playing the bagpipes the last couple of nights. We chatted for a while and now I'm just making my way back," I said, consciously making a cheerful effort to soothe his obviously agitated stance. *What's wrong with him today?*

"Are you okay, Tucker?" I asked.

He took me by the shoulders and looked at me intently. "Lane . . . I just . . . I'm just worried about you. I was worried that something might have happened last night."

"Oh no, I'm fine, Tucker. Really," I said, watching his charm slowly return. Back in place. An ability that reminded me of the effortless sleight of hand of a magician. His affable countenance nicely tucked back into place.

And then it hit me all of a sudden, like an avalanche. Thoughts started to flood through my mind, all the things I had seen in bits and pieces coming together into one fluid line, one terrifying whole. Tucker's friendly nod to the man today outside the diner; the man I thought I recognized as one of the attackers the other day. Tucker's familiarity with Tabitha while brushing the lock of her hair off her face; he'd met her before. The *RR* on the pawn being Rex Ruby. The fact that Eliza had a big brother, Tom; Tom meeting with his evil-looking grandfather who wore jewelry, perhaps a *ruby ring*. That familiar *something* about Tucker's face in the bar when he saw me unexpectedly and today when his charm had not been securely in place. The fact that someone powerful—an *über* gangster—must have been in play to extricate Eliza when she was shot, someone Uncle Louie knew to have been around and yet invisible. The flash of red on Tucker's finger at the restaurant . . .

My eyes locked onto his; his smile faltering as he saw what was behind my gaze. I said quietly, "Tom?" His eyes dilated and he sucked in a breath. I whispered slowly, determinedly, "You're. The new. Rex Ruby."

In an instant, that familiar thing about Tucker's face fell. Just like *hers*. His veneer of charm and control came crashing down. That was *his* mother, Daphne, I had met in the insane asylum. My God, Eliza and Tucker were brother and sister. The grandchildren of Rex Ruby.

His fingers tightened painfully on my arms.

"Lane," he growled with primal urgency. "Don't do this. We're made for each other. I saw the anger in you. I hated it and I loved it. It's what you want, you *know* it. You want *me*," he said raggedly.

It was true. I loved that anger. I had wanted to dive into it. I wanted it to consume me. It was so tempting. Tucker was tempting. I could definitely choose anger—I was capable of it. But there was a choice to be made. One thing or the other. Their natures so completely at odds they could not coexist. Anger was a solitary thing, pushing, clawing, ripping at everything else. The other . . . well. The other.

I made my choice.

I took a powerful inhale of crisp air, refreshing and bracing my heart and my mind. What these past days of searching and fighting had painfully but perfectly shown me, culminating into one powerful idea, was simply this: *I loved the man more than my anger.*

"No, Tucker."

He was livid; his loathing and his rage pumping through his body in an almost palpable throb. He took a hand away from my shoulder and brought it back. I saw hatred and confusion in his eyes. I saw a lot in his eyes.

In his anger, his draw back was slow like he was enjoying the thought of striking me. All my defense practice with Mr. Kirkland just left me like a lifeless leaf tossed away in the wind, but I was enraged that Tucker was going to try to strike me. With a savage shove to his chest and an unladylike growl—"Unh!"—I shoved with all my might, totally indignant, completely changed. I saw my choice clearly for the first time.

"Lane!" I heard a shout from behind me and I knew that voice, like a voice from inside my soul, and I thought my heart would leap right out of my chest.

I whipped around. "Finn!"

I took a step toward him and he started running toward me. He yelled desperately, "No!"

There was the click of a gun being cocked behind me, and then a hard arm wrapped around my shoulders and pulled me against him. I felt the cold barrel of the gun just beneath my ear.

"Tucker!" I said, with a pained voice that begged, *How could you?*

"Lane, I'm sorry. This wasn't my plan. It's not . . . *what I wanted*," he said in a choked voice.

In a flash, Finn pulled his gun and was pointing it at Tucker.

"Put it down, Brodie!"

"Tucker . . . Okay! Okay! It's going down," said Finn, not taking his eyes off Tucker's gun, his voice trying to soothe the savage beast.

"Throw it on the ground!" Finn did.

Just then, the three attackers from yesterday came around the corner from across the street, guns drawn, backing up Tucker. And that hunch was confirmed: Tucker had been working *with* them, engineering those scenes of danger and pursuit . . . *Why?*

"Yo, boss, you okay?" they asked Tucker as they took up their position behind us. Goddamn it.

Finn's eyes were darting back and forth between Tucker and his henchmen, summing up the pitiful situation, his posture tense and defensive, ready to react to anything.

Things were already out of control, but then a new element added another degree to the chaos. My three barbershop friends came out of their shop directly behind Finn—each of their elderly hands holding guns. Two shotguns and one rifle, to be precise, pointing them directly at the large men behind me, the rifle on Tucker.

"Holy shit," said the big guy who had taken a shot at Tucker and me yesterday. Summed up the situation quite well.

Tucker, who was no dummy, could tell things were deteriorating rapidly and said, "All right, nobody panic. I *won't* hurt Lane."

"Prove it!" demanded Benson. For rather shaky octogenarians, their capable hands didn't waver the slightest. They meant business. Sirens sounded in the distance.

"All right, all right," said Tucker releasing my shoulders but keeping the gun on me.

One final crazy element happened that set everything into motion, like the tip of the first domino that begins the falling of a thousand pieces. One more player. One more distraction. Finn's mouth quirked slightly on one side and he looked at me, his glittering eyes telling me *get ready*.

An incredibly loud *BOOM* sounded from behind me. I felt a great shove from behind and simultaneously heard several guns going off, a lot of grappling and running feet. I had been painfully shoved, and was launched forward practically into the air. Finn caught me up in his arms before we both landed hard on the ground. He put a hand over my head, crushing me to his chest, sheltering me from the ruckus and the bullets that were flying. I held on as tight as I could. Despite the fear and the pulsing adrenaline and desperation, I was never so happy in my life.

The noise died down, I felt Finn relax his muscles slightly, and we both started to sit up. He pulled me to my feet, both of us looking around to find out what had happened.

Father MacQueen. *He* had been the rather large domino that started the pieces falling, the cornerstone that threw everything to our favor. He had an enormous shotgun in one arm, one of the attackers in an effortless headlock with the other arm, and an ear-to-ear grin plastered to his pleased face. My elderly friends had come to form ranks around me and Finn. Tucker and the other guy were gone.

Everyone looked at everyone else.

Benson said loudly, "Everyone all right?"

We all looked down at ourselves. Father MacQueen grinned even more, like he hadn't had this much fun in years. Benson, Fred, and Jasper all nodded, and Finn turned to me.

"Lane," he said in his deep whisper, looking deep into my eyes. "Are you all right?"

I nodded, smiling, tears slipping down my cheeks. "Yes. I'm very, very good."

"Oh God, Lane," said Finn with a loving look. He stepped forward and with his right hand behind my head, he pulled me toward him. My arms went around him, his arms fully embracing me and we kissed, moving into each other, finally together, at last. All those confusing feelings of wondering if I'd been misled or duped by Finn slipped away as I realized them for the lies they were. The loneliness and anger had deceived me, not Finn. And once I realized what was going on, what the choice truly was, I knew I loved him and that he loved me.

I never wanted to stop kissing him. That is, until I heard Father MacQueen start to whoop and holler in great appreciation. Benson, Fred, and Jasper all joined in the cheering.

I looked up at Finn's almost bearded face; his dark jawline, his gray green eyes, and those crinkles in the corners that I loved so much. I stroked his jaw.

"I missed you, Finn. So much."

Then I heard the sirens come closer with loud horns honking. Several cars and police cars came barreling down Main Street, coming to a screeching halt beside us. I half-expected Fiorello to jump out, but instead my eyes blinked hard trying to decide if what I was seeing was possible. The lead sedan had Mr. Kirkland in the passenger seat and *driving* the car was a disheveled, crazed lady. She jumped out of the car and ran toward us.

"Aunt Evelyn?" I shouted, barely recognizing her in her manic state. She rammed right into me, whooshing the air out of me as she embraced me with all her considerable might. Then she started to ruthlessly pat me down, presumably looking for bullet holes.

"Cut it out!" I yelled with a smile. "We're okay. Really, Aunt Evelyn. Stop," I said, using *my* soothing tones to calm *this* savage beast. I put my hands on either side of her shoulders, making her pause, and looked into her fierce, flinty eyes and smiled. "Really," I whispered earnestly.

"Really?" she squeaked. "My God, I've never been so worried in my life!"

By then Mr. Kirkland had made a wobbly journey over to us. He was muttering to no one in particular, "She wouldn't let me drive, grabbed the wheel and took off . . . had to jump in . . . she . . . she . . . went through about fifty lights . . . almost took out an old lady . . . more scared than when I was in the war . . ."

Benson, taking in the situation with perfect acumen, ran into his shop and came out with a couple of glasses and the bottle of scotch I had brought him. Finn chuckled as Mr. Kirkland skipped the whole glass idea, blindly grasping the bottle, and took a great gulp of the fiery liquid. Benson laughed, but Fred wasn't pleased.

I winked at Fred and mouthed the words *I'll get you another one.*

CHAPTER 34

Well, everything was such a mess, we decided to get everyone back to my house to get organized. Finn and I were never apart. He always had his arm around me, we were holding hands, or just pressed up against each other.

I quickly talked with Father MacQueen and between the two of us we made a plan to get the grocery store to deliver a bunch of food and drinks to the house, then the local butcher was to bring over a large selection of deli meats and cheeses. We had a lot of explaining to do, so we also invited the confused sheriff and his crew that had arrived directly after Evelyn and Kirkland.

We held a debriefing that didn't include *all* the juicy details, but the ones that the police were most interested in. I think the sheriff knew there was more to the story, but being a man of simplicity, he was just fine with knowing a vague outline. What mattered to him was the bad guys who got away. He put out an APB on them for disturbing the peace, attempted kidnapping, and several other grievances he thought up.

After a lot of eating, pats on the backs, and some general partying, our new friends took their leave. I promised to come around to the barber shop and the church the next day. And I did remember to give Fred, Benson, and Jasper *each* a special bottle of scotch from my father's lavish collection. I brought one up for Mr. Kirkland and Father MacQueen, too.

Later that evening, Aunt Evelyn, Mr. Kirkland, and Finn and I sat around the fire, enjoying the warm ambiance and being together once again. I was sitting close to Finn on the couch, his arm around my shoulders and my hand on that side in his, my head resting on his shoulder. I hadn't known this sort of peace in quite a while. It felt so good. I was finally *home*. I kept taking deep breaths, taking it all in. Relishing it, loving every sensation of warmth, completion, and happiness. Loving my family around me.

Mr. Kirkland leaned over, resting his elbows on his knees. "Now that we're alone, I think we have a lot to discuss," he said in his gravelly voice.

"*How* did you get here so fast?" I exclaimed, still in disbelief and still very much amused at the crazy lady: my aunt Evelyn.

That crazy lady said, "Hah! *That's* what you want to discuss? With all this insanity, *that's* what comes to your mind first?" She guffawed and slapped Mr. Kirkland's knee. I didn't think it was *that* funny.

Mr. Kirkland took the reins. "Well, Lane, the day before yesterday we received a disturbing telegram from Finn that he was on his way back as quickly as possible, and that we needed to get to Michigan as soon as we could." He raised his eyebrows at Finn, acknowledging him. "We raced here and got to Detroit just this morning. We decided to go to our hotel front desk, even though we hadn't checked in yet, just to see if there were any messages—"

"And you got *my* telegram from this morning, saying that I was concerned and to come here immediately," I cut in.

"Exactly." Then Mr. Kirkland gave Evelyn a rather shifty glance, obviously remembering their outrageous and scary-as-hell ride from Detroit to Rochester. I daresay he figured it took a few years off his life.

I could feel Finn's silent chuckle as he'd been reading Mr. Kirkland's face, too. Mr. Kirkland asked Finn, "Say, Finn. How did you get here from Europe so fast? The *Queen Mary* takes five days to New York."

Finn's eyes sparked with mischief and he grinned when he said, "Oh, my military buddies helped me out."

I'd have to ask him more about that later, but for now, I decided to go get a bottle of white wine and some glasses. I also grabbed a little box of chocolates from Sanders. Wine and chocolate. Just seemed right. The firelight made the light yellow-green wine gleam and shine. We all clinked glasses, and then between Finn and me, we explained what had been going on. Well, most of it.

"Well," I continued, "I knew things were coming to a head. I had no idea what was going on, but just in case you arrived early, or if something happened . . . I wanted you to know that things were looking dicey. So, I sent two telegrams to you, one to you in New York and one to your hotel just in case."

Finn told us about his new contact and obvious friend, Miles. That he had been the one to shine light on Rex's fondness for architecture and self-aggrandizing embellishments on public property. And of course, what the gold pawns meant when Rex would use them. Lastly, he told us about the photograph of Rex's grandchildren. That's when it all clicked for Finn, that Rutherford was Rex's son, which meant Eliza was his grandchild. And in the photograph, right next to Eliza had been her brother. Tucker.

"But I didn't know that you even knew what Tucker looked like," I said, perplexed.

Finn grinned mischievously. "Roarke and I had a funny . . . *feeling* about him. We staked him out right before I left for Europe."

I smacked him on the chest. "You did not!" I said with a smirk.

"Oh, you better believe I did."

"I like it," I said approvingly.

Finn went on to say that at that very moment, he received my telegram that things were difficult in Michigan and that Tucker was with me. He left immediately and raced to Rochester, having sent a telegram to Evelyn and Kirkland as well.

I then filled in everyone on my findings here. "You know, Mr. Kirkland, I found my dad's *game room.*"

"Hah!" He turned abruptly to Evelyn and said, "You owe me five bucks!" She just rolled her eyes. "She didn't believe me when I said you would find the room. I knew you would."

I laughed and then added slyly, "But did you think I would find his *second* secret room?"

"Secret . . . what?" he asked with disbelief. So satisfying.

"Uh huh. His booze room. *And* his safe."

"Holy—"

"We'll go exploring later. But this is the deal: Dad left me a letter, my birth certificate, and this." I held out the gold pawn piece in my palm, the light from the fire giving it a glowing life all its own. I handed it to Finn to scrutinize, mesmerized by his fingers gently touching the gold piece and stroking it.

I went on, "The letter said a few cryptic things, I'll give it to you to read yourselves. But the gist is that it led me to look at that photograph of my mother in my journal, the one in front of the Central Park casino in New York. The note had said to remember what they'd *pointed out to me*. When I took a closer look, her hand was pointing to the right and, sure enough, that picture had been folded. I took it out of the corner tabs, opened it up, and next to her was a picture of a man I had never seen before. I took it to my barbershop friends and they recognized him: Rutherford Franco. Father of Eliza and Tucker. Of course, at that moment I hadn't realized Tucker was actually his son, Tom, yet. It was right on Main Street today that everything slipped into place. There had been something familiar about a few of Tucker's gestures the past couple of days." I went on and explained everything that happened, including the attacks from Tucker's cohorts. Everything had been so confusing until put together the right way. "Suddenly, everything came together."

"Wait a minute, you were attacked by gunmen yesterday, *too?*" blurted out Finn.

Mr. Kirkland murmured something indescribable.

I replied, "Tucker must have set it up. They didn't hurt us, just put us into a sticky situation. They were the same guys who were *with* him today." I didn't bother to mention they were also the same guys from the restaurant earlier in the week. "I don't get it. He set it all up . . . but *why?* If he wanted the gun or the pawns, if he thought I had them, why not just barge in here and try to steal them?"

Finn murmured, "I know why . . ."

Aunt Evelyn's eyebrow cocked cynically, "Mm hmm . . . First of all, he probably knew they'd be hidden in a place only you could locate. Secondly, Lane, he's been targeting you all along. A while ago, you went on a couple of dates with him, right?"

"Yes, before Finn and I were together. But it was never anything serious."

Finn and Mr. Kirkland shared an all-knowing expression, evoking in me the desire to kick them in the shins.

"What?" I asked accusingly.

Aunt Evelyn continued, "Lane, dear, you obviously hold the key to something that he wants or needs, and it's probably the gold pawn. They must know that your father killed Rex and he always had one on his person, so it's likely they took it. But there's something else there, too. From what I gathered when I met him, I think you're . . . *important* to him, Lane."

"*What?*" I choked out. "You *met* him?" Finn and Mr. Kirkland looked at her in astonishment.

"I caught him on his lunch hour one day, had to see him for myself. Let's just say *I* had a funny feeling about him too," she said provocatively.

"Pour me another glass of wine, Lane," Mr. Kirkland directed. I did and I handed him two chocolates.

"And getting back to Rutherford . . ." said Finn, deciding we'd taken this part of the conversation far enough. "Okay. Let me summarize this mess. The original Rex Ruby started the Red Scroll Network to pillage artwork and national treasures through war-torn Europe during the war. He had a son, Rutherford Franco. Miles says that Rex was never inclined to appreciate his son. I believe that Rutherford didn't share his violent nature as much as Rex desired. Rutherford had two children with Daphne: Eliza and Tucker.

"Somewhere along the line, Rex starts to induct his grandson, Tucker, into the family business, probably seeing his proclivity for charm and deception. But even before then, Miles told me that there were rumors of Rex finding an apprentice of sorts, after the great disappointment of his son. We'll talk about that in a minute. We know that Lane's father and Mr. Kirkland killed Rex Ruby, beyond a doubt. When was that, Mr. Kirkland?"

"About two months before Matthew and Charlotte were killed. We got word that Rex was hunting us down. An informant of Matthew's revealed to us Rex's general whereabouts and since taking him out had always been part of our mission, and now with the added incentive that the family was in danger . . . Matthew and I went to Ireland, located him, and finished it. He had two gold pawns in his hand when we killed him. At the time, we didn't know what they represented so we each took one." Our eyes were glued to him, he looked impassive and his eyes held a red and determined fire. Finn filled us in on what Miles had explained to him about those pawns being Rex's calling card.

"All right," continued Finn. "So now Rex is out of the picture. But we are left with many unanswered questions. If Rex did select an apprentice, in addition to Eliza and Tucker, who then? If Rex was taken out, then who is responsible for Matthew's and Charlotte's deaths, not to mention Rutherford's? And how did Rutherford end up in the same exact town as Matthew and Charlotte and what was their relationship?"

"Hey!" I exclaimed, with sudden inspiration. "I've got it. There are three of those larger pawns on the center railing of the bridge in Central Park that don't have the *X* on them, right? Ten altogether, seven with an *X*, and that seventh one is marked with the date of my parents' deaths."

"Yes . . ." they all murmured, tracking with me.

"Those pawns must represent the Red Scroll Network members, at least the leaders. You said that you took out six members, Mr. Kirkland. That seventh one must have represented Rutherford—he died the same day as my parents. He was special because he was Rex's son, thus earning the date marked on it. The three remaining ones have to represent Eliza, Tucker, and perhaps that rumored apprentice."

"Oh no," said Aunt Evelyn, with a look of incredulity.

"What?" I said.

"That apprentice. Who is the only other key player who keeps popping up, who has been working against us *and* working with Eliza . . ." she prodded.

Finn finished the thought. "Donagan Connell."

CHAPTER 35

After going over everything, we all decided to take a break and Evelyn and Mr. Kirkland informed us they were going to go to dinner that night with Evelyn's close friend. I had a notion that they wanted to give Finn and me some time alone. They quickly changed and began to head out for the evening.

Right before they left, I pulled Aunt Evelyn aside. I took her by the shoulders and looked right into her eyes. "Aunt Evelyn, thank you for coming to rescue me." Her hand came up and clasped my hand on her shoulder. I continued, smiling, "I recently learned from a friend, that there are just some battles we were not meant to fight alone. You have always been there for me. I want you to know, you have been the best mom I could have ever asked for."

Her eyes brimmed with tears as she smiled. "Oh, Lane . . ." was all she could manage.

I hugged her tightly. "But next time . . . let Mr. Kirkland drive."

"Bah!" she laughed in her funny way. "Hold on. Next time?"

For a long while, Finn and I sat on the couch near the fireplace in silence and peace, sipping wine. His long, strong legs stretched out, I fit perfectly next to him, my head up against his chest, my hand on his thigh. The snow was falling softly outside in large chunky flakes against the dark nighttime sky. I had an idea from a memory that came flooding back to me from when I must have been six or seven.

I turned to Finn and said, "Come on, let's go outside."

He looked out the window a little dubiously, but then turned his eyes to mine and smiled. "Okay. Let's go."

We bundled up and went to the door. We stepped out the side door onto the porch and I took a gulp of the crystal-clear air, feeling the large flakes alight on my face, my eyelashes, my lips. "Come on, I have to do something," I declared to Finn, taking his gloved hand in mine.

I walked over to the side of our house where the drifts were especially deep. I still had on my knee-high New York boots, not quite snow-worthy, but we wouldn't be long.

"I remember doing this *right here* when I was a little girl. It was a night exactly like this one," I said, hunting for the precise place.

I took us over to where the canopy of the trees opened up and we could see the sky, feeling the full force of the gently falling snow. I stood up tall, made sure nothing was behind me, and fell straight back, landing smack in the middle of a deep drift of snow. I wiggled and shifted around making a trench in the thick snow, my face eventually even with the top layer. Then I turned my eyes over to Finn. "What are you waiting for?"

He laughed and even at the odd angle from within my trench, I could see the crinkles at the sides of his eyes as he smiled and it flooded me with a thrill of warmth. He clomped over in his big boots, putting his feet right next to where my boots were. "Like this?" he asked with his arms out just a bit.

"Yeah! Great. Now fall backward."

"Hmm . . ." he murmured uncertainly. He fell with a poof.

"Now . . . listen," I whispered.

In the heavy, thick silence the snow softly fell to the ground with a muffling, otherworldly sound. It was a powerful and sweet sensation to know I had done this, at this exact spot, a long, long time ago.

We stayed that way for quite a while. Then I rolled over and propped myself up on my elbow and looked down at him.

"What do you think?" I asked softly.

He smiled with deep thoughtfulness in his eyes and leaned up on his elbow so that we were face-to-face. "It's wonderful." I smiled at him.

"Lane, I . . . I thought I might have lost you."

"My telegram?" I asked.

He nodded with his brow furrowing. "I could tell your heart had been broken somehow. I knew something was very wrong. And I had just learned the truth about Tucker, just a moment before I read your telegram. I thought I might have a heart attack right then and there."

"Finn, I'm sorry. And I'm sorry I mentioned . . ."

"Gwen?"

"Yeeeessssss, Gwen," I softly whined, which momentarily eased away the creases in his worried brow as he chuckled.

"Were you jealous, Lane?" he asked, with a slightly pleased edge to his voice.

I put my face in my gloves and said a muffled, "Yes."

He pulled my hands away from my face, smiling, and said, "I've known for a long time that there never really was anything between Gwen and me. I'm sorry. I never should have mentioned her in a telegram, it was thoughtless. Especially with everything you were going through back here." In the moonlit glow of the night, his eyes looked intense and kind. He leaned over and slowly, softly kissed my lips. He pulled away and opened his eyes.

I looked up at the sky for a moment, collecting my thoughts. "Remember when I wrote to you about that first visit here? And how I had that strong reaction? It felt like it was a powerful force outside myself that made me want to put up a kind of *wall*, something to keep everyone out and my emotions at bay. When I came back this time, it was different. I felt good and I thought I had gotten over that wall, or whatever it was. But then . . . later, I had found that letter from my father. And my birth certificate."

I breathed out, resolutely. "Nothing was as it seemed. It felt like everything had shifted and I couldn't count on anything. Or anyone. And that was when I read your telegram."

"Oh, bloody hell."

I rolled my eyes. "I know. Perfect timing," I replied. "But that was just the setup. See, I hadn't been out the front door yet. We arrived at the side door and I had spent the day inside searching around. But then, I stepped out the front and I saw *my tree*.

"Here, I'll show you," I said with resignation, getting up and brushing some of the snow off my coat. He had been quiet, listening carefully. He put his arm around my shoulders as we walked around the house and over to my tree. He knew all about how I grew up climbing that tree, knowing every branch, every foothold, loving it like a friend.

I heard him take a quick breath of surprise when we got close enough to see the cut limb. The scar was massive and bright against the deep, dark bark. I was finally able to walk over to it. And this time, I put my hand right on the place where the limb had been. And I patted the large scar, just like I would have patted Ripley's head.

"I'm sure the Baxters were just maintaining the landscaping like Kirkland hired them to do, *but damn it's hard.* I know it's just a tree . . ." I said, with a self-deprecating smile.

"Oh, Lane, it's more than just a tree," he said as he came over and wrapped his arms around me, hugging me and making the red fur of my collar tickle my face.

We stood there for a few moments and then I walked a couple of steps back, and I sat on a large rock, leaning my elbows on my knees. "When I came to Michigan the first time, I climbed right up the tree and it felt just like it used to. My hands were bigger, but the branch, the trunk, the footholds . . . it was like I could have climbed it blindfolded. It was so sweet that something tangible, real, and alive hadn't changed." I smiled at that first memory, remembering the sweetness of it.

"I sat up there," I said, pointing about halfway up the tree. "I looked all around. The flower planters were there, the big pine, the funny little black fountain. But then it hit me. There was no mother looking out the window. There was no father standing at the bottom of the tree smiling up at me telling me to be careful. And it wasn't right," I whispered.

I doggedly pressed on. "And then this time, when I came out and saw what had been done to my tree . . . It was one more loss. The thing that symbolized my childhood had been cut off. And I was *so angry.* And my damn birth certificate! I'm not even Lane Sanders. My real name is Lane Lorian. This time I put up the wall stronger, harder. Every single goddamn stone, I put there because I wanted it. I wanted the anger. I wanted the darkness."

He let that sink in and walked a couple steps closer, sinking down to my eye level on his haunches. He asked in a low voice, "Is that where Tucker comes in?"

I sighed and looked him full in the face. I had to be honest with him, I needed to have him see me as I was, faults and all. "The anger was overwhelming and dark. I wanted to dive into it and run away from everything. And I knew I was capable of it. But I . . . hesitated. And then there was music," I said, with a little mischief in my voice.

He tilted his head. "What do you mean?"

"It was kind of magical. There were two times that I was faced with turning to darkness, or not. And right there late into the evening, someone far away started to play the bagpipes. Turns out it was Father MacQueen."

"Of course it was," he said as he shook his head with a smile.

"He played 'The First Noël.' This is the thing, it helped me see what my choice *really* was."

"What was it?" he asked.

"The choice was never Tucker or you, Finn. The choice was *anger*, or you. That real choice came to me in bits, and then in full today, right on Main Street: I love you more than I love my anger, and the unfairness of all this. And I couldn't hold on to both. I had to let go of something . . . and there's *no way* I could let go of you. I wouldn't." His face slowly cleared. He gradually smiled, starting in his eyes and going all through him. It was contagious. Our eyes locked, sharing our delicious secret.

He suddenly dove at me, grabbed me around the hips and hoisted me into the air, "My God, I love you, Lane!" We were both laughing as he set me down, then he put his hands on either side of my face. "And you will always be Lane Sanders. It doesn't matter what a piece of paper says." I smiled up at him. He was right. "Actually, that gives me an idea," he said, with a sudden stroke of inspiration. He walked around the tree, stroking his chin and thinking, muttering things like *mm hm, uh huh, let's see* . . .

I cocked my eyebrow at him and said, "What are you doing?"

"All right, this is it, come here."

I walked over and looked up at the branches that he was staring at, my eyebrow still skeptical.

"Ready?"

I replied slowly, "Sssssssure."

He held out his clasped hands in the universal *hoist up* pose. "You, love, need a new way to climb up. This is it."

A new way.

I put my hands on his shoulders, my foot into his hands, and he lifted me up so that I could easily grasp the two branches he'd been looking at. My foot found a natural hold and I was there, in my tree once again. I still had my skirt suit on, making me wish I'd changed into trousers. I hiked the skirt up a little and grinned at Finn watching me from below as I was certain my garters were showing, then climbed up higher. As I looked around, the view was indeed different. The house was the same, all the things I loved about it still remained. But now, inside, I saw the wine bottle and glasses from when Finn, Evelyn, Kirkland, and I all shared our stories. I saw the fireplace warm and inviting, glittering off the glasses. I looked down and there was Finn, smiling up at me.

"Is it good?" he asked.

I smiled and nodded.

"Any sightings of your wall, love?"

"No. No walls."

I stayed up there for a few more moments. Having taken off my gloves, I touched the cold, familiar bark of the trunk of the tree. I said very softly, low enough for Finn not to hear, "Hey, buddy, I'm back. Thanks for waiting for me."

I enjoyed the moment and eventually climbed downward to the lowest branch and sat on it, dangling my legs, holding another branch with my right hand to keep my balance. I looked at Finn, with his hands on his hips, looking back at me with a smile on his face. Our eyes locked and my heart gave a thud. "Help me down?" I whispered.

He walked over, keeping his eyes on mine. I reached down to him, he reached up and I slipped off the branch into his arms. He slowly, slowly lowered me down. My lips brushed his forehead, his eyelids. And finally, his lips.

I kissed his lips with a hunger, a heat that was overwhelming. Somehow my feet reached the ground. He opened the top of my coat and his mouth went to that incredible spot where your neck meets your shoulder and slowly kissed his way up to my lips, making my knees buckle. He brought his arm around my lower back. I slightly pulled away, panting just a bit. I took his hand and whispered, "Come here."

He slowly walked me backward toward the door. I managed to open it, grasping the handle behind me as he swept in for another long, deep kiss. Inside, he didn't stop kissing me, he brushed the hat from his head and ditched his boots like magic. My hat had already come off outside somewhere and I shrugged off my coat as he started to unbutton my deep red blouse.

As his kisses grew hotter and deeper, my hands easily undid his buttons *one, two, three* . . . I unbuttoned his pants and opened them as he nibbled on my ear. He quickly took off his shirt as I slunk out of my blouse. I *really* liked his muscled chest and arms, with his dark chest hair nicely accenting those muscles and his enticing flat stomach. I still had my pearl dagger in the waist of my skirt. As I took it out of my belt I heard his deep chuckle. "Honest to God, Lane . . ."

"Luck favors the prepared, Finn."

I unzipped my skirt and slipped it off to the ground. He groaned as he looked appreciatively at my black lingerie and garters holding up my nude stockings. Finn was instantly up against me, the feel of his hot chest making me gasp. As we kissed, he gently walked me back to the chaise longue. He went to the foot of the chaise and slowly took one booted leg into his hands. He slowly, slowly unzipped the boot and pulled it off.

He knelt and started with the second boot, this time bringing his lips to my thigh and slowly kissing his way down as he unzipped the boot, then carefully brought it up over my heel and off my foot. He stood for a moment, looking at me. The warm light of the fire glimmered off his chest and arms.

"Come here," he whispered as he pulled me up to standing. Both of his arms enveloped me, coming completely around me and we melted into each other. He lifted me off my feet and carried me to the couch.

After lying in each other's arms by the firelight, and a second round of enjoying each other at a slower, lingering pace, we fell asleep peaceful, content and happy.

I awoke to the harsh sound of the phone ringing. We both jolted upright. I quickly made my way to the phone. After I hung up, I said, "Well, that's helpful."

"Who was it?"

"Evelyn. The snow is keeping them at their friend's overnight."

"Oh, thank God," said Finn in a rush.

I casually leaned my shoulder up against the bookcase, my heels crossed, completely naked except for a small blanket barely covering me. "Why? What's the problem?" I smirked.

Finn laughed. "Well, I'd like to keep Evelyn and Kirkland liking me and he *does* carry a gun, so . . ."

"Very true," I laughed.

"You're so beautiful, Lane."

I smiled in appreciation. "And hungry."

CHAPTER 36

After they had a snack and Finn stoked up the fire to carry them through the night, Lane had fallen asleep quickly, utterly exhausted and spent. *And not just from their rollicking good time*, he thought as he smiled happily to himself. They lay entwined together on the couch, Lane preferring this room to any other. He let her fall asleep, then moved to the floor where he'd set up a padding of blankets and pillows.

He lay on his back with his arms behind his head, watching the flames sway against the creamy ceiling with its warm, deep golden brown beams. He thought through all that transpired that day: of his great fear of a loss more substantial and crippling than he could conceive . . . Of his fierce rage in seeing Tucker put his hands on Lane, and his equally fierce joy at their escape . . . Of their reunion and satisfying sense of completion. Their funny, new-found friends. Especially that Father MacQueen; he was a special character indeed. And finally, of being together with Lane. Finn smiled in the semidarkness. His eyes grew heavy and he soon fell asleep.

Later, in the middle of the night Lane didn't make a sound, but suddenly, she sat bolt upright, looking wildly around her. He awakened immediately, touching her arm, saying softly, "It's okay. Are you all right, Lane?"

Her eyes focused on him in the dim firelight. She sighed deeply and whispered, "Yeah. I'm all right."

"Come here," he whispered.

She came down off the couch and lay down facing him, her head just below his chin, her hand on his chest, his arms around her. Her fingers softly stroked his chest.

He looked down at her, appreciating her dark hair falling back from her face, the curve of her brow and her long eyelashes, the way the firelight made her glow with warm colors. His desire for her was great, and she murmured, "Finn." He knew her desire was just as great, but the poor thing could hardly keep her eyes open. The things she had been through these past weeks . . . and yet she seemed whole again. There wasn't a strain showing through her beautiful eyes like he had expected. She had dark smudges of fatigue under her eyes, but her spirit was untouched and luminous. He couldn't fathom all the thoughts, struggles, and demons she had faced.

Now there was a calm stillness in her. She had made peace with her past, accepting the imperfections, finding the strength within to see the real question before her: to accept the past and move on—or not to.

She said softly, "I want you."

"I know. I want you, too," he whispered.

He gently kissed her forehead, her cheek, her chin; his hand coming up along her waist, slowly caressing her soft breast, up her throat, cupping her face.

She sighed and made a small, contented sound.

"It's all right, close your eyes," he whispered.

"I don't want to close my eyes," she said with the ghost of a smile, as she slowly closed her eyes.

"We're together, you're safe, I'm here." He slowly stroked her hair and let his quiet, steady whisper lull her to sleep. "Just rest. Fall asleep. I love you. I'll be here."

"I love you," she whispered as she fell asleep with a smile that lingered on her lips and a soft sigh as her body relaxed fully, snug against him.

CHAPTER 37

The next day, Mr. Kirkland and Aunt Evelyn made their way home just before lunchtime. We ate sandwiches from the day before, then I took them all on an adventure around the house. I told them about my childhood game with my dad appearing out of nowhere when I played the piano (much to my horror, they wanted me to play "Für Elise"—I said no). I spied the box of chocolates that I had placed on top of the piano that morning. And it hit me.

"You have got to be kidding," I said, my hands on my hips.

"What, Lane?" asked Aunt Evelyn.

"So my parents' names and my birth name was Lorian, right? And then they changed it to blend in and become more anonymous," I said.

They all nodded. "They picked the name Sanders because of the chocolate, didn't they?" I stated, knowing it was true without even asking.

Mr. Kirkland started to truly guffaw, his arms wrapped around his stomach. "Hah! Hah! Hah! Matthew never told me, but you *have* to be right. It never dawned on me!"

Aunt Evelyn thought it was funny, but Mr. Kirkland's amusement knew no bounds. She looked at him with a grin and a little consternation. Finn just shook his head, silently laughing.

Wiping a tear, Mr. Kirkland said rather breathlessly, "Those two. They always had a box of chocolates lying around and at least three, *three, I tell ya*, bottles of hot fudge in the pantry. You should have seen Charlotte's panicked eyes whenever they opened the last bottle. They'd run down to Detroit to the Sanders Soda Shoppe the very next day! Hah! I have no idea why I never put two and two together about their name. Oh, Lane. They were just as incorrigible as you."

I was laughing, perhaps more at Mr. Kirkland's reaction than anything. But inside, a satisfied feeling warmed my spirit. It was moments like this, these rare and sweet times, where I felt a powerful bond with my parents. That our stories were definitely entwined in a way that death couldn't separate. Even the fake name, which Evelyn informed me was a fully legal name change so I was still indeed Lane Sanders, had a link to something I loved dearly. My Sanders hot fudge. And that made everything all right.

I smiled and sighed happily. Finn looked at me and shared a knowing smile. "You would have picked that name, too." he said.

"*Pfft.* No question."

"Of course you would," he snickered.

With a flourish, I showed them the hidden door that led to my dad's special room. Mr. Kirkland had of course been down there, but Finn and Evelyn loved the secret passage with stone spiral steps leading down to the game room. The game room took on a whole new life as Mr. Kirkland regaled us with stories of the many, many hours that he and my father spent down there.

I challenged Mr. Kirkland to find the secret room with the safe, but he declined, having thoroughly looked for it himself many times.

"Here's the door and the button is up here," I said, showing him the button I found above the portrait of me as a little girl.

"That rascal," he exclaimed. Turns out, my dad made the button so small a man would have to use his pinky to depress it. A larger finger wouldn't do the trick; it would float right over the minuscule depression. A woman would have naturally found it easier, and a man would be given fits trying to find it. Like it clearly had given Mr. Kirkland.

I opened the door with a big grin. They all stepped in and regarded the copious amounts of alcohol my father had stored up. All their eyes grew large with surprise.

Finn eloquently said, "Whoa."

They got distracted looking at all the booze and wine, obviously amused at my dad's almost greedy collection. I went over to the safe behind the false electrical box and showed them that as well, although it was now empty. He had been surprised up to this point, but now Mr. Kirkland looked infinitely self-satisfied and I wondered what he had up his sleeve.

"Okay, Lane, you discovered far more than I ever did. But did you know about *this?* Matthew and I always used this trick." He looked closely at all the walls of the inside of the safe, took out a playing card he had in his pocket, and slipped it in the back right groove in the corner.

"Okay, you got me," I declared.

He carefully pulled at the card, and sure enough, there was a false side in the safe. But then, as he revealed what was behind it, even he was surprised. We crowded around him. In his large capable hands, he held a small photograph with three men sitting casually on a park bench overlooking the Brooklyn Bridge: my father, Louie Venetti, and . . . Mr. Hambro.

"Oh my," said Aunt Evelyn.

CHAPTER 38

With the photograph of my father, Venetti, and most shockingly, Mr. Hambro, the pressing issues back in New York City were most definitely linked to Rochester. Ever since Hambro received a red envelope, we'd known he'd been involved in the Red Scroll business. *Of course.* But it had never occurred to me that my father and mother might have known him and worked with him. It had always seemed like they were in a different world than me. But really, we were all connected. And so was this whole Red Scroll business.

We only had a couple of days left, so I decided to visit my new friends and took a walk to both the barbershop and Father Mac-Queen's church. Benson, Fred, and Jasper and I had a great laugh and promises were made to keep in touch. I walked over to the quaint little Episcopal parish and sat on the bench that Father MacQueen and I sat on just the day before, but already felt like weeks ago.

I enjoyed the sunlight warming my face while I took a moment to reflect. It was cold out, but the sun made everything cheery. Father MacQueen opened the door and peeked around the corner.

"Lane! Good to see you!"

I smiled up at his hulking frame, his open and honest face. His eyes were a melting, chocolate brown and utterly friendly. Little John in the flesh.

"Have a seat," I said as I patted the bench next to me. "Pretty exciting day yesterday, huh?"

"Oh yeah. You could say that again, little lady." He chuckled a silent laugh.

"So . . . how . . . How did you know that there was trouble brewing, that you should just take a little stroll with your loaded shotgun?" I asked incredulously. He had been the key to our victory yesterday, swinging the advantage to our side by his imposing presence and enormous shotgun.

"Well, Lane, after we talked I was planning on practicing as I told you. But I got to thinking about you, and being one of the town's reverends I know a lot of what is going on. I had heard about the scuffle by the funeral home and knew that there were some folks about the place that were up to no good. And I do know about your past, lass, and your parents. I'm so sorry that you had to deal with that tremendous loss. It is a hard, hard road." I appreciated his honesty instead of beating around the bush. He continued on, "And after we got to talking about darkness and the feelings you were having, I got to worrying about you. It seemed like something was brewing, so I headed down to talk with the barbershop lads. I figured taking a little ammunition couldn't hurt either. Just in case." He gave me a sidelong glance and grin that reminded me again that he had a very good time yesterday. I smirked back at him and he landed one more statement. "And, Lane, lastly . . . I get the feeling that trouble follows you around a bit."

"Hey!" I exclaimed indignantly, laughing. But what could I say? He was right.

"Anyway, it was good to meet Finn. I like him. Did he help you figure out some of that darkness you were struggling with?"

"Yes," I said as I smiled thoughtfully. "He did."

"Good. Very good."

After more promises of keeping in touch and one enormous rib-cracking hug, I walked back to the house. I strolled, taking my time, thinking about my new friends, the whereabouts of Tucker, the alarming photograph of my father, Louie Venetti, and Mr. Hambro . . . And then a thought occurred to me, that with all the ruckus of the past couple days, I hadn't finished looking around my father's study. And knowing my parents, as I was beginning to form a better picture of them as the adults that they were versus merely the memories of my ten-year-old mind, I knew I needed to leave no stone unturned.

When I got back, the house was empty and silent. I called around with no reply, then saw a note on the kitchen table. Evelyn and Kirkland were out to lunch, Finn went for a walk down by the sledding hill and said to join him if I got back soon. I figured I could put aside the search for a little while. Some lighthearted fun sounded wonderful.

I put on my snow boots and gear and walked down the street toward the big hill. Even from a couple of blocks away, I could hear the din of laughter and yells and whoops from little kids enjoying themselves. As I got to the hill, Finn was, of course, in the middle of the throng of excited boys. They had been working with my sling shot and added to the mix a couple of pumpkins that had been left over from the fall harvest. They made a wonderfully messy explosion. The boys were almost to the top of the hill, about to come down when they saw me.

They yelled and waved and cheered me up the hill to join them.

"Hey, love, glad you made it!" said Finn, with a kiss to my cheek. One of the little boys made a *that's so disgusting* face. I saw a toboggan and asked if I could use it. I turned around in time to see Finn as he picked up the damn runner sled, ran to the hill, dove, and landed on it smoothly, racing down the hill like a professional luger.

"Show off," I said. The boys were all sniggering but when I turned abruptly to them, they pretended to be suddenly consumed with getting their sleds prepped.

We had a great time going up and down the hill, then Finn and I said good-bye and headed back to the house feeling reenergized and fatigued at the same time. As we neared the house we ran into Mr. Kirkland and Aunt Evelyn coming back from their errands.

Evelyn said, "We made plans to take the train back day after tomorrow. But in the meantime, I have a friend I want you to meet. I phoned her and she invited us over for dinner tonight. How does that sound?"

Finn nodded and I said, "That sounds wonderful. Which friend?"

"My friend Mattie. We go way back. And I really want you to see her house, you're just going to love it. They're a little formal, so wear something nice."

A couple of hours later, after we had time to rest and then change into our dinner attire, we were on our way to Mattie's house. It wasn't very far, still right in the Rochester area, but out of town. We took Evelyn and Kirkland's car. Mr. Kirkland had taken the keys into his possession and I don't think he ever let them out of his sight. As far as he was concerned, Evelyn would never drive again. At least, not with him as a passenger.

Finn and I sat in the back. I enjoyed the soft feel of my dark blue dress against my legs and the silky feel of my stockings. I crossed my legs and sat closely to Finn, intertwining my fingers with his. He looked smashing with his black suit, bright white dress shirt, black tie with a small indigo stripe, and matching pocket handkerchief. With his fedora, of course.

Our car went up and down gently sloping hills and then turned onto what looked like a private road. We had to check in at a gate with a guard who asked our names and then allowed us entrance. I turned a quizzical look to Finn and he shrugged his shoulders. I caught Mr. Kirkland's impish eyes in the rearview mirror. He winked at me.

We rolled down a long drive, through the snow and wintry trees devoid of their leaves. I caught glimpses of golden lights, flickering in and out of the tree space. Our car turned to the right and then circled around to the left. In front of us was an enormous manor. Almost castle-like. There were turrets and a large stained glass window, about fifty chimneys poking out of the top of the long house, and I suddenly had the feeling we had been transported to Europe.

"What the— Where *are* we Aunt Evelyn?"

"I told you, Mattie's house," she said in a *don't be ridiculous* tone of voice.

I could feel Finn's chuckle beside me. I should be used to Aunt Evelyn's friends-in-all-places by this point.

Mr. Kirkland said, "Welcome to Meadow Brook Hall."

CHAPTER 39

Two men came out to open our doors for us. Mr. Kirkland handed one of them the keys. I looked way up to the top of the English manor house and then off to the left where another long, low building stood where the carriages, cars, and horses were kept. We went up to the front door, which another servant opened. She took our coats and hats and then we walked in.

We came into a foyer of magnificent proportions, with dark woodwork on every wall and an intricately cut ceiling, rich floors with oriental carpets placed about, and glistening windows looking out at snow-covered fields glowing white in the moonlight. My eyes couldn't take it all in; I'd already noticed a Rembrandt in the corner and several striking bronze sculptures. I had to fight the urge to start running over to everything at once to touch the fabrics, to let my fingers absorb this moment rich in sensory overload.

A very tall man and a very petite woman both probably in their fifties walked over toward us. The man had a friendly, open smile and the woman looked nice, but definitely more formal, more guarded. In a motion that seemed rehearsed, yet with a genuine smile, she held out her hands to her obviously dear friend, Aunt Evelyn.

"Mattie my dear! So good to see you," exclaimed Aunt Evelyn as she took her hands and then embraced the woman who came up to Evelyn's shoulder in height. I had to put a hand up to my mouth to hide my smile as I saw a fleeting look of long-suffering flash across

Mattie's face. Aunt Evelyn had pet names for all her friends, and I always wondered if they were on board with those names. In this particular case, I knew Mattie was not thrilled. But of course, love for Aunt Evelyn won out.

"Lane Sanders and Finn Brodie . . . please meet my dear friend Mrs. Matilda Wilson and her husband, Mr. Alfred Wilson." We shook hands. They were already familiar with Mr. Kirkland and shook his hand in a warm welcome. I was racking my brain to figure out who Mrs. Wilson was, who they were in society, because clearly, they were of importance.

They ushered us in, passing by a ten-foot-wide fireplace toward the expansive parlor with another vast fireplace at the end. Windows lined the beautiful walls of English oak with a mahogany Steinway underneath. They had been preparing for Christmas as holiday decorations were placed about with precision. Finn said in a low voice that he could fit about four of his apartments in the parlor.

Mrs. Wilson obviously ran a tight ship, yet it was a colorful one in which each piece of furniture and decoration had been selected with an exquisite taste for history, design, but also sentiment. Each piece was meaningful and she told us a little about a few select items. We all chatted and a drink cart was wheeled in by a servant to offer some refreshments. I could scarcely speak for looking around and enjoying the gorgeous atmosphere.

Finally, Mrs. Wilson had mercy on me and asked, "Lane dear, would you like a tour?" Her eyes were serious, but a ghost of a smile pulled at her mouth, clearly gratified that I was enjoying and appreciating their home. Mr. Wilson offered to stay with Evelyn and Kirkland as they were already very familiar with their grand house, but Finn and I followed Mrs. Wilson.

Her small frame took on the capable stance of a skilled tour guide. She had clearly done this hundreds of times.

"Finn and Lane, I would normally have more to show you, but officially we have not opened the house since we closed it up in 1931 to save on oil. But for the holidays, I open up most of this main floor for special guests. I hope to open the whole house for good next year some time. As there are about a hundred rooms, it's no small task. Here is one of my favorite rooms, the Sun Porch."

The porch was just off the parlor and I craved with all my heart to read in there for hours on end with the sun pouring in the curving windows, reclining on a chaise longue. Mrs. Wilson rattled off various things about the pieces in the room that were from Jerusalem, Spain, and Italy. Then we went back through the parlor to the library. It was there in the incredible woodwork, crafted to look like folds of linen, where a dignified portrait of a man was put in a place of prominence, that I figured out who Mrs. Wilson was. The portrait was of John F. Dodge. Matilda was one of the Dodge heirs.

I quickly pulled the incredible story back to mind. She and her sister had married the Dodge Brothers, John and Horace Dodge. But then at the 1920 New York Auto Show, Horace contracted pneumonia. John rushed to his side and then he, too, contracted pneumonia almost immediately. He died just ten days later. Horace lingered for a few months more and then he died as well. The two wives inherited the entire fortune, estimated to be worth something like sixty million at their deaths. But they didn't sell right away. Five years later, they finally sold the Dodge Company—for just under one hundred and fifty million, the largest transaction in history. I remembered reading an article about that sale. Mrs. Matilda Dodge—now Wilson—had quite an indomitable spirit.

We then walked back through the hall where we had entered and my breath whooshed out of me as I saw the staircase of the Great Hall in its full grandeur. Wide and in two flights, it worked its way up to the second floor, with an enormous stained glass window on the landing. The railings were of intricately cut cherry and the tapestries looked like they would have been right at home in a sixteenth-century castle. It was beautiful. The bedrooms were closed upstairs, the entire family having moved to the farmhouse on the property. The two Dodge children, Frances and Daniel, who were now twenty-two and nineteen years old, had their suites off to one side upstairs, guest rooms in the middle, then down a long hallway Mr. and Mrs. Wilson's bedrooms (the wealthy often had separate bedrooms), and the rooms of their two adopted children, Richard and Barbara, who were five and six years old.

We walked down a long hallway called the Gallery and saw Mrs. Wilson's study, called the Morning Room, feminine and efficient in the extreme. She ran a bank, several political organizations, and her farm and household with about twenty in-house staff.

Then we walked down toward Mr. Wilson's study. Finn was stunned into silence and I grinned at his awestruck countenance as we passed masterpieces by van Dyck, Rosa Bonheur, van Marcke, and C. E. Jacque. Finn was a lover of woodwork, so his eyes were drawn to the wood-paneled walls and interlaced wood-ribbed ceiling. Along the way, on our left, was a banister overlooking something. I walked over, and one story down was a full-fledged ballroom. I could easily imagine dances and soirees, loud music, chattering, and merrymaking long into the night.

We got to Mr. Wilson's study and walked into a masculine room of English burled oak that reminded me of Mr. Hambro's. All along the walls just above eye level ran a ten-inch-tall molding. The carvings in the frieze depicted incidents in the life of Mr. Wilson. I looked closer and there were humorous carvings from childhood into college days and his career in the lumber business. And right in the middle at the back of the office by his desk was a darling carving of a tall man wearing a top hat, bending down to a diminutive woman half his size, kissing her hand. Their wedding. I looked over to Mrs. Wilson as I had been admiring it, and was pleased to see a smile and a small blush creep into her pale and sophisticated face. She was a distant sort of woman, but she loved her husband.

"Oh, and you must see this, Lane. I think you'll find it . . . *interesting*," she said with a cryptic smile and keen glint in her eye. She had been using a well-versed tour guide tone up until this moment. Now she trained her penetrating gaze right at me. I looked over to Finn and received an eyebrow lift of support.

Mrs. Wilson was standing by the back wall opposite the desk and without looking, she reached her hand back and pushed in the molding. A secret door opened and revealed a hidden spiral staircase.

"Oh, my God."

She nodded, not taking her eyes off mine. "Familiar?"

"My dad's . . ."

"Yes."

The stairs went up and down. The upper stairway led to Alfred's bedroom. She led us downstairs. We got to the bottom level and walked into a masculine game room.

"You've *got* to be kidding me!" I exclaimed with all pretenses of formal behavior out the window.

She laughed a tight, contained laugh. She finally divulged everything, "Oh Lane, Alfred and your father had been friends for years. I never met your parents—Alfred and I married in twenty-five. We came to know your aunt Evelyn . . . Goodness, how did I come to make her acquaintance? For the life of me I can't remember; it feels like I've known her forever."

"She has that effect on people," I said with a knowing look.

"Anyway, we didn't really plan this house thoroughly until our honeymoon as we traveled across Europe. But early on, apparently, Alfred talked about certain aspects of a future home with Matthew, *certain aspects* that Matthew had already incorporated and Alfred admired."

I supplied with a smile, "The secret staircase, the game room. . . ."

"Mmm," she replied in the affirmative with raised eyebrows.

Alfred's manly room was much larger, but pretty much identical to my father's.

Matilda led us out the door, and we were on level with the two-story ballroom. We walked across the hall to it and our eyes were drawn directly to another huge fireplace with crossed spears above, a mammoth tapestry and . . . and . . . There were just too many wonders to describe. I went right to the middle of the room and looked up at the ceiling far above us, and the cut-out openings that were like windows in the hallway of the main floor. I enjoyed a moment of conjuring ghosts of past parties here, with big bands playing and couples dancing the night away.

We walked out of the ballroom to a hall that held the bathrooms and a fountain. She pulled open a small door and showed us a movie projector. "We have films brought in. For us, but the children specifically."

I remembered reading that many wealthy families would bring in entertainment rather than take their children out ever since the kidnapping of the Lindbergh baby. I thought of Frances, Daniel, Richard, and Barbara running around these fantastic grounds, always in the company—at all times—of a governess or guard. A life of incredible opportunity, but also a kind of imprisonment from the lack of anonymity.

On our way back to the stairs I glanced at an enormous vault— worthy of a bank. Mrs. Wilson saw my head turn, obviously gawking.

In response, she said, "Oh, we keep our guests' valuables in there, our silver, and during Prohibition, well . . ." I was amused as her stoic face gave a shrug of her eyebrows with a slight eye roll. For her, it was quite an ostentatious display of emotion. I rolled my own eyes as it came to mind that the vault was probably another design element to which my father contributed.

We joined the others back upstairs and had a wonderful time talking about the latest news from New York and the upcoming holidays; Mrs. Wilson would be going to New York soon to do her Christmas shopping. A servant came in to announce that dinner was served. We all started to walk down the long hallway. Finn and I were last in line, taking a small moment to look at each other in greeting. With no one looking, I put my arms around his waist for a quick embrace, enjoying the liberty of familiarity with him. We walked down the hall with his arm across my shoulders. We walked past Mr. Wilson's study and I stole one more glance.

I said quietly to Finn, "You know . . . have you taken a good look around my father's study?"

"No, I haven't," he said.

"There is a lot of molding. That carved frieze in Mr. Wilson's study makes me think we need to take a closer look at things."

"With the picture I'm gathering of your parents . . . Yes, we should most definitely take a closer look at that. At *everything*," he said with an incredulous look.

After dinner, we retired back to the parlor and Mr. Wilson surprised us by playing the organ—yes, they had an actual organ—that was at the back of the long living room. The hundreds of pipes were located directly underneath the organ, in the basement. The sound resonated through the room, our feet vibrating from the rumbling low notes. We sang Christmas carols and I enjoyed watching Mr. and Mrs. Wilson singing next to each other, her head barely coming near to his chest in height. After a long round of songs, a servant came in with a telegram on a silver salver. He brought it not to Mr. Wilson, but to Mr. Kirkland.

My eyes flashed to Finn. He returned my apprehensive glance with a furrowed brow.

I said quietly, "That seems rather ominous. . . ."

Mr. Kirkland opened it and Mr. Wilson inquired, "Everything all right?"

Mr. Kirkland handed it to Evelyn and said, "Well, it could be better, but nothing too dramatic. I do believe we should say our farewells, though."

We made a relatively quick departure, thanking our hosts for a delightful evening. Aunt Evelyn was able to smooth out our hasty good-byes with her consummate grace.

I had forgotten my purse, and as I went quickly back to the parlor to retrieve it, I ran into Mr. Wilson. "I'm glad you came for dinner tonight, Lane." He blinked, like he was trying to think of something. "You, ah, you look a lot like them, you know. Your parents."

"Thank you. I like hearing that," I said.

His earnest face blinked hard and a small smile crept out. "You're welcome, Lane. Please. Come and visit us again."

I turned to leave, but then he said, "Ah, Lane. It occurs to me to tell you something."

I looked up at him. "Of course. What?"

"Well, Lane. The year or so before your parents died, your father was having a very trying time with his uncle. He was a dangerous man and your mother wanted to trust him, but your father thought it would not be wise. He always had to talk in vague terms with me, but I suppose I was a good person to toss around ideas with. I have to say, being in lumber never looked simpler than when I talked with your father . . ."

"I bet," I said. "Well, I never knew much about my extended family other than Aunt Evelyn. I never heard of this uncle." And then it hit me. "Oh dear. Do you mean Uncle Louie?"

"That's it! That's his name. Uncle Louie. I don't know what they were involved in with him, but I would definitely say that your father thought he was a very dangerous man."

"Oh, he most definitely is that," I said. "I wonder why my mom felt that he was trustworthy?"

"I really don't know."

We walked back to the entrance and then hurried out the door into the cold air, huffing and blowing. Back in Mr. Kirkland's car, we were able to speak more freely. So I did. "What was *that* all about?"

Mr. Kirkland said, "The telegram was from Fiorello."

Finn and I said a collective "Uh-oh."

"He received a red envelope."

CHAPTER 40

Fio hadn't said what the red envelope contained, but he asked us to return to New York as soon as possible.

Back at the house, I decided I needed to perform a quick but thorough search to find anything that might help us. While Mr. Kirkland and Aunt Evelyn went out to check on returning to New York, despite the late hour, Finn and I split up. I knew where I was headed: right to my father's study. I brought in a tall stepladder and looked at the top molding along the ceiling. It was oak, therefore the wood had a lot of grain versus a clearer wood like maple or pine, so any carvings wouldn't be quite as obvious as it was at Meadow Brook Hall. But it was indeed carved just as Mr. Wilson's office had been.

As I studied the perimeter of the room, I saw that the curving floral vine carved into the molding was the same as the one that framed the portrait of me by the door to my father's safe. Over and over, I climbed up the stepladder, studied the molding, got down, moved my ladder over, climbed up again, and made my way around the entire room. Within the vine work, sprinkled about the molding here and there was a lovely sword delicately intertwined with flowers and something else I needed Finn's help with.

I ran downstairs to find him. "Hey, Finn! Come up when you get a chance!"

He came into the office right on my heels and said, "What is it? Did you find something?"

I pointed out the floral vine that was the same as on my portrait. "And here is a sword scattered about. It's the same sword around the room. But take a look at this."

"Is that a saying up there? I can barely make it out from here," he said.

"Yeah, it's Latin. It says *'pulchritudo ex cinere,'*" I read. I wasn't exactly sure of the pronunciation but I think I got it close.

"Well, I think *pulchritudo* means beauty. But I'm not sure of the rest," he said.

"I'll look it up when we get home. And you know? Before we leave, I want to do one more thing. Will you help?"

"Okay. Let's go," he said, ever ready for an adventure.

We went downstairs and got on our coats and boots and I led him outside to my tree.

"Can I get a boost?"

After a lot of work, I got up into my perfect spot. It was pretty difficult with my bulky snow boots, much easier in sneakers in the summertime. I leaned back and thought a bit.

"Needed one more time, huh?" Finn asked as he backed up and sat on a rock, leaning his elbows on his knees as he looked up at me.

"Yes!" I said, happily looking around. I got to thinking about our evening and the past few days, about my eccentric parents . . . So with me in my tree, and Finn sitting below, we took a good bit of time and discussed it all.

"Well, love, at least we know where you got your imagination from," he teased, his accent delicious.

After a while of feeling like I was able to put a kind of bookend on my time here, I looked down. I tried to figure out how exactly I was going to get down from there. Finn saw me searching and came over to the tree, still smiling. "Here, love, I'll give you a hand down."

But I was still quite a ways up. It wasn't as easy as just getting a hold of his hand and jumping down. In my heavy snow boots, I couldn't step around to that lower branch that I had sat upon the night before.

"Uhhh . . ." I said, not too sure about that.

"Here," he said as he came under me and held up his arms.

"Are you sure?" I asked, dubious.

"Positive. Just hop down and I'll catch you."

"Okay . . ." I shuffled to the edge. I didn't think it looked as easy as he was making it out to be, but I figured that at least we had puffy jackets on to break our fall.

And fall we did.

I jumped. He caught me. But he completely underestimated the vigor with which I would jump; I really didn't do anything by halves. His strong arms wrapped around me, but my momentum was considerable and I knocked him right over, falling on top of him. I was laughing but then I saw his face.

"Get. Off me," he gasped.

"Oh shoot." I had knocked the wind right out of him. I was half in horror, knowing *exactly* how that felt . . . and half wanting to laugh uncontrollably. My face was a contorted mask, being torn by two completely different emotions. I started to shake with trying not to laugh.

He got his breath back. "Are you . . . *laughing?*"

When we got back inside, we were covered head to toe in snow. A lively little snowball fight had taken place. Mr. Kirkland, just coming inside himself, watched us shaking snow all over the place as we took off our coats.

"Jeez, you two are as bad as Ripley," he muttered with a shake of his serious head. Finn and I grinned at each other.

Later on, as we were warming ourselves by the fire, Aunt Evelyn and Mr. Kirkland came and sat down and surprised us with an announcement that we would not be taking the train back as planned, but an airplane the very next day. We would then get back to New York much more quickly and could get to Fio as fast as possible. Once we got back, the airport was out in Long Island, and we'd have a driver waiting for us there to take us the hour and a half back to the city. It would cut a lot of time off the journey. I was really excited about it. I had never traveled by plane before.

An enormous yawn suddenly overtook me and my eyes watered with the effort. My yawn then traveled around the room.

"All right, everyone," declared Aunt Evelyn with a decisive clap. "We leave in the morning, so we better pack up and head to bed."

We all agreed with nodding heads and started to clean up and get ready. Mr. Kirkland and Evelyn went up the stairs while Finn and I finished neatening up the kitchen. We had so much to do, that we were a blur of activity, scurrying around doing this and that.

I ended up by the curving front window in our living room. The snow had begun to fall again, in wisps and flurries. The moon was a glowing, perfect crescent when the clouds parted. I leaned against the windowsill and put one finger to the cold glass, drawing small vines and leaves in the fog my breath created. There was a lovely pine tree across the street and I liked the lines of it, the way the snow rested in layers upon its branches. I thought through these staggering days, the tumultuous emotions, and the fact that I had definitely won a kind of victory. Things were still confusing, the mystery still being worked out, but I was on the right track. And I felt more like *me* than I had in months. Possibly ever.

I felt Finn's presence more than I heard him. He was a large man, but unbelievably stealthy. Like a cat.

"Getting one last view, Lane?"

"Yeah," I whispered. "It's been great, but I'm ready to get home."

I heard him make a sound like a satisfied smile. He came up behind me and moved my hair from my shoulder and brought his lips to my neck. My arm went up and around his neck, leaning into him.

Then the sound of bagpipes softly made their way through the crisp night air.

"I think your new friend is giving us a send-off," said Finn.

"Beautiful, isn't it?" I asked. We stood by the window and soaked it all in, the deep blue and white of the glittering nighttime, the ancient music making the moment complete somehow.

Our reverie was broken by brisk footsteps. "All right, lovebirds! Off to bed with you!" chirped a businesslike Evelyn as she energetically jogged down the steps, bringing some coffee cups into the kitchen, running by us with a swish.

In the middle of the night I awoke already deep in thought as if part of my mind had been deliberating and calculating as I slept. What else was hidden in this mysterious house? My parents were crafty and they had a funny sense of humor that left me smirking on one hand, and pulling my hair out in frustration on the other. I wanted, no, I *yearned* to trust them. I felt better knowing that the date on the bridge was most likely marking Rutherford's date of death, making it seem less likely that they were actual members of the Red Scroll.

There was no one who was perfect, who made the right choice every single time; I was under no such delusion about the imperfection of my beloved and absent parents. The work they used to do was the work of visionaries who wanted to do something to make the world a better place. But espionage, no matter how well intended, required deception and a large dose of darkness for the ultimate greater good.

What I wrestled with was how dark was too dark? How far would *I* be willing to go? The war took on greater proportions than the world had yet seen. And the excruciating, exhausting, never-ending saga of trench warfare was horrifying. In the light of such evil, I would be quite willing to do evil myself if it brought about a greater good for many. An entire generation of young men was almost wiped out. My parents found each other before the war, and they both made it out alive. Most were not so lucky.

The fire crackled and I looked down at Finn, now sleeping with both arms behind his head, his long, muscled legs stretched out. In his sleep he had shuffled off a part of his blanket. The firelight glinted off the harsh scars covering his leg. His left knee was especially bad, and he'd told me it ached from time to time. I'd catch him massaging it once in a while when he thought I wasn't looking. It made me want to help him; I wished I could heal those wounds. I knew it had to do with something his brother had engineered. And he'd had to work hard for years to build up those muscles and overcome the injuries.

I slunk down to him. In the dark with the firelight tossing our shadows about, I pulled my nightgown over my head, and gently came close. I kissed my fingertips, then touched the deepest scar by his knee and then lay down next to him. I softly opened his nightshirt to caress his chest. Then I brought my lips to his chest and neck. He softly groaned as his arms came around me, pulling me on top of him. He definitely liked being woken up that way.

Chapter 41

Back once again in my blue and white room in the heart of New York City, I held the book in my hands. I turned it over and over, still enthralled with the strange beauty of the navy blue binding and the creamy pages. I loved that book; it was a mysterious thing, creepy and provocative. Even the cover made you think of the possibility of great beauty, but intertwined with it, a twisted darkness. The tale was one of seeking freedom and adventure, but also a sinister evil that lurked at the edges. The terror and mystery wasn't from a killer like Jack the Ripper, but an evil from the inside that proved even more fearsome. The impetus that *made* a murderer.

As I looked at the volume, I noticed it had come down in stature, no longer having the capital *B* in my mind. It was no longer the Book. I scrawled a quick note on a page, smiling thoughtfully to myself. I was finished with it. I set it carefully down on my nightstand, keeping my hand on it a moment longer in a silent benediction.

I stood up and brushed my hair in front of the mirror on my dresser, thinking of the flight back to New York. I laughed to myself at the gymnastics my stomach went through when the plane took off. I had never felt those sensations of speed and liftoff other than on the Cyclone at Coney Island and I could hardly contain myself. It was so freeing. All three of the seasoned travelers with me were very smirky as they watched my obvious delight.

Just getting ready to go on the flight was a pleasure, all of us

decked out in our best clothes. It was quite a sophisticated and important *event* to travel by plane. It felt so exhilarating as I walked
through the airport with Finn looking dashing in his dark gray suit
and hat. I wore a favorite ice blue skirt suit with matching pillbox
hat and my white kid gloves. I drank in every detail, not wanting to
miss out on anything.

Right when we arrived home, we had a council of war with Fio
and Roarke. Both looked at me with wary eyes as they joined us
in the comfy little back room off the kitchen, reminding me of the
first visit I had to Rochester and the dramatic effect it had on me.
I reassured them that I was all right and told them about our high
adventures and new friends. They both looked rather wistful that
they'd missed out on the fun. I couldn't wait to get Father Mac-
Queen and Fio together. Roarke had heard all about him from the
Baldy Benson crew, but hadn't had the opportunity to meet him. I
felt sure he would be working on making Father MacQueen's acquaintance soon.

I could tell Fio had been more affected by the Hambro mystery
than he let on; he had lines of strain around his mouth and eyes, and
his countenance was like a tight wire. He had convinced himself
that the cryptic red envelope with its "We are watching" message
had been a prank. We all knew it wasn't. At least on the outside, it
looked exactly like the one Mr. Hambro received both at his home
and at the bank.

The one thing that no one had spoken of, but I was certain we
were all considering, was the whereabouts of Tucker. He had managed to escape from Rochester and he most certainly was capable
of disappearing and eluding the police. My question was whether
he was working on his own or in cahoots with Donagan and Eliza?
And what had he been looking for? The pawn? The silver gun? The
artwork? A can of soup?

And damn it! I was still mad at myself; I should have seen it
coming! It had been Tucker all along. In fiction, the villain was *always* someone you knew. I had thought Tucker's acquaintance was
a random one; I hadn't seen through his deception at all. And then
I committed the error I judge the most harshly with the characters
within a good movie or novel: *declaring to the bad guy that you know*

he's the bad guy. What was I thinking? I blurted out right to him, "You're the new Rex Ruby." Like a dummy.

I rolled my eyes and slipped into my warm, soft bed pulling the comforter up around my chin, cozying down into the pillow. It had been a long day, a long week.

Tucker. Where was that man and what was he up to? I would never get over the shock of seeing that transformation, like a mask dropping from his face. Where I hadn't seen it before, he instantly looked like Eliza and their deranged mother, Daphne. Her long mane of white blond hair and her maniacal laugh. Yet, I felt sorry for him, too. His eyes—they looked tormented and tired. Had it all really been an act? Or not? Which Tucker, or which parts, were real? Any? I'm not usually so taken in and I was not pleased that he had duped me. I felt foolish. And what actions would he take now? What would motivate him? Anger? Despair? Revenge.

I shuddered as I closed my eyes, but then heard Ripley nose the door open and come over to lie down by the side of my bed with a huff. I reached an arm out of my cozy cocoon and laid my hand on his sturdy back.

I yawned. "Good night, Rip."

CHAPTER 42

"Damn it!" she said with so much vehemence as she slammed the telegram down that she knocked her glass of brandy off the table with a tinkling crash.

"Bad news?" drawled Donagan without taking his eyes off his newspaper.

"No, I broke a nail. Whaddaya think?" she said waspishly.

A dead pause. "Eliza. What did you say . . . my dear?" he said quietly but with wicked precision, still not taking his eyes of his paper.

"Oh, uh . . ." she said with wild eyes shifting around. "Donagan. I'm sorry. I'm just so fed up with Lane and now . . . my *brother*," she said with exaggerated repugnance. She soothingly said her apologies to Donagan as she slunk around behind him, taking her slender fingers and bringing them slowly down the back of his head, along his neck, and massaging his muscular shoulders. What her words might have lacked in calming influence, her actions were well suited to do. He felt himself relax and a small part of his irritation with her petulance started to dissipate.

She purred close to his ear, "The telegram just said that he was not able to locate the pawn and that they know who he is. His cover has been blown." In her aggravation, she started to massage his shoulders with more enthusiasm. If he had been a smaller person it might have actually been painful, but his muscles enjoyed the workout.

He murmured with disdain, "Disappointing. As usual."

Her hands faltered a little, hearing a dangerous edge to his voice. His animosity toward her brother was no secret, but still . . . he was her brother.

"Well," she said, resuming her massage, "we'll see. I'm sure he has some surprises up his sleeve. He always does."

"Hmph. Yes, we'll see." She decided to distract him as she was quite capable of doing. She ran her hands down his chest, massaging and circling. She bent down and kissed his neck, licked his ear. He groaned softly and pulled her around on his lap.

Much later they were asleep on the bed in the enormous and extravagantly appointed room. Donagan rolled over and got up, pulling his black velvet robe around his naked body. He walked out and down the hall to his study, knowing each step of the way in the darkness. He opened the door and turned on the brass lamp on his desk. He reached into the ebony cigar case and pulled out a thick brown Cuban cigar from Nat Sherman's. He clipped off the end with the sharp cigar guillotine and lit it.

He puffed thoughtfully, tasting the rich tobacco of his favorite blend. He pondered and considered an idea that had been taking shape over the last week or so. Tucker was getting in the way, that was for sure, had been a real pain in the ass for *years*. Something had to be done.

Donagan was alone, yet he looked around like someone might be watching him. Under his desk, his fingers found the hidden latch and pressed it. On one side was a sawed-off shotgun that could blow out the knees of anyone audacious enough to threaten him at his desk. The other side held a small box. He retrieved it and set it on top of his desk. He opened the slim blue box and took out the letter, written in Rex's own hand. Rex Ruby. A man he had grown to love like a father. He looked at the spidery script of an elderly gentleman.

> *Take this to Putnam and Raulson's with the proof. I want you to have it all. Don't fail me, Donagan.*

He knew he had to get his hands on that final piece to achieve everything he had ever hoped and dreamed for, what he had labored on for years with Rex. It was all his, he just needed this one thing, that damn proof. And he would be *it*. He would be The One: heir apparent to the world's greatest legacy. He would be the new Rex Ruby. He could almost feel the riches and fame clasped in his groping, avaricious fingers.

But there were people constantly in his way. And a great, dirty trick oozed into his mind. The idea filled him with a devious satisfaction. He laughed as he thought through the details, relishing the idea. He reached over to the black phone and rang up a number.

A gravelly, curt voice answered on the second ring.

"I have a plan."

CHAPTER 43

I was back to work again before I scarcely knew what happened. *What a week*, I thought for the hundredth time.

I crossed my ankles under the seat as I sat squished between two very hippy ladies on either side of me. Despite the chilly December weather, the subway car was toasty. Too toasty. I found myself longing for some breathing room as both of my elbows were pinned against my stomach, clutching at my purse on my lap.

Even though I felt marginally grumpy with the tight fit of the commute, I was actually grateful for the extra people around. I hadn't forgotten what had precipitated my departure just after Thanksgiving: Donagan had come after me. He knew where to find me and he surely knew I had returned to New York. The good thing was that we all determined we have something he wants, so there was a tiny scrap of security in that. And well, you just can't stay hidden forever.

On the way to the train, I noticed a couple of familiar forms following me: Peter and one of his buddies, Scott, whom I had bumped into at the Central Park police station and danced with the night Donagan tried to kidnap me and Valerie. I pretended that I hadn't seen them, but Pete's six-foot-five-inch frame wasn't exactly invisible. I had no problem *at all* with a couple of good guys following me around. One run-in with Donagan was enough. I didn't see my tail on the train, but that wasn't shocking given the state of my cramped posture. If I had been standing, it was one of those mornings where you were so tightly packed in that you needn't have a hold for your hands; the mere pressure of the people standing around you was enough to keep you upright through all the jolts, stops, and turns of the train.

We finally arrived at the City Hall stop where I dislodged myself with a heave and made my way out to the refreshing cold air. I already felt like I had worked a few hours and I hadn't even begun the day. I started mentally ticking off the things I needed to attend to when I got to my office. I spotted a vendor selling coffee and tea and I stopped. He was a tall, thin gentleman with a great gray and black handlebar mustache. He spoke loudly with an Eastern European accent, greeting everyone who stopped as if he knew them all by name—he probably did. And there were several children standing about, one really cute freckled boy with one tooth missing. I wondered vaguely if the vendor might be the sort of kind man who gave away the older cups of coffee once the good stuff was bought.

I stepped up and ordered a tea, having developed quite a thirst on my commute. I leaned in toward the man and whispered something to him, then handed him my money. He chuckled and I bid him a good morning. I walked a bit farther, then stopped by the lamppost to take a sip and I turned back to watch the vendor. I saw Pete's form go right by him. The vendor hailed him and handed him two coffees. With a funny look, Peter looked around. I waved when he saw me.

I yelled, "Morning! You're welcome!" then turned around and went up the stairs.

Valerie and Roxy were a sight for sore eyes and I promised to fill them in on everything at lunch. The rest of the day was full, getting acclimated to the pulsing energy of the mayor's office once again. I loved it. The sleepiness of Rochester was nice to visit, but *this* is where I felt alive and well. I was in my element and with my newfound insight about my past, I felt ready to tackle more.

Which was a good thing, because Fio came bouncing into the office. "Good morning, Laney Lane, my girl!"

"Grrrrr," I replied.

"Lane! The police commissioner himself called."

"Really? What about?" I asked.

"They found fingerprints on Hambro's knife. They are over at his house right now gathering copies of his prints to see if there are any alien prints on it."

"Great! He can't have killed Marty."

Just then, Roarke came into the office, too. He rushed in, obviously excited to relay important information. "Mr. La Guardia, Lane, I found out something about Hambro." He didn't wait for us to respond, just took a quick seat in the chair by my desk and carried on. "When the stabbing incident occurred, I had a few contacts go around to some nearby hospitals just to see if they could unearth some information. They didn't find anything. However, one guy was sick the night of the stabbing and ended up at Lenox Hill Hospital, much farther uptown than I'd thought to look. While he was waiting, he saw a man who had a knife wound in the shoulder, definitely not a bullet. If it had been a bullet wound or a lethal hit, he would've been getting a very different kind of attention. My guy didn't know I was looking for information until yesterday when it came up in conversation with a different informant. And get this, the reason the guy in the hospital stood out to my contact was that he was so nice."

"*Nice?*" I asked.

He nodded, and said, "Yeah. Nice. The man was dressed like a working-class man. Not too dirty, not too rich, not too anything. He'd had a wad of cloth held to his shoulder, but there'd been enough blood to get attention pretty quick. He'd been nice to the others waiting around. A kind word here 'n' there, he even had a few little blue candies in his pocket that he gave to a little girl who had burned her hand."

"Okay then! We have a nice man, with a bloody wound, who happened to have little blue mints on hand, just like Hambro always does," I summed up.

"Yep. Has to be Hambro," said Fio.

"And if that was Hambro, he was the victim, the guy dressed as a hobo. Someone wanted Marty out of the way and used Hambro's own knife against him. But why? What's the motive?" I asked.

Roarke shook his head. "I don't know. But Hambro is definitely running in some dangerous circles."

"Agreed," declared Fio. "Good work, Roarke. All right. I have to get to my meeting. I'm going in." He never really liked meetings, but it was a necessary evil.

A group of commissioners and various city representatives were waiting for him in the conference room. Fio's meetings tended to have a clamorous volume on the whole, as if everyone was in trouble and getting a helluva talking-to. But there were obvious differences and I'd learned to classify them much as storms and hurricanes are categorized. A C1 was your everyday typical, loud, yelling, getting-business-done meeting. A C2 held a more ominous note, maybe a pen being flung at the door out of frustration, some yelling . . . and then capped off with the entire office running around all day putting out the fires that someone's incompetence started. But a C3 . . . now, that was surprisingly rare and, even to me, quite frightening.

When a C3 occurred, there wasn't a lot of bellowing and you'd think that would be a good thing, but the office had gotten used to the intense volume and passion of Fio. The only sound of a C3 was serious, quiet, and stern talking from behind Fio's door. It would send chills down our spines. At the first thump of a fist against his desk, I knew what we were in for.

Roarke looked at me and quipped, "Just a C2, probably. Right?"

"Yeah! Maybe just a C1, in fact," I said. With a quick farewell to Roarke, I handed him a "C1/C2" note to hand to Val when he left, notifying the rest of the office of Storm Fio. Then I dove into my own long list of things to get done.

When the commissioners took a break, we had a special event. The mayor and I headed down the stairs to the lobby with the great rotunda looking down on us. A large group of school students and teachers had assembled. A special award ceremony was to take place for the winners of an essay contest on "Safeguarding the Home Against Fire." I talked with a group of boys and girls to get them ready for the presentation. One skinny girl stood next to me and we struck up a conversation before things got started.

"Hi, you're Ann, right?" I asked, remembering her short brown hair, green eyes and impish grin.

"Yes, nice to meet you. It's actually Anna. Anna Theresa Higgins. But I don't like Anna. I asked the Sisters to take off the *A* in my name, so they did. I'm Ann now. And when I feel super saucy, I say my name is Ann Terese," she said with a regal air of importance. This girl would go far.

"You don't know a gal named Morgan, do you?"

She shook her head. "No, but I like her name."

"Yeah, you two would get along swimmingly."

The presentation went perfectly. Fiorello and the fire commissioner bestowed medals to each of the winners. Fio loved reaching out to the city kids. It's why he read the funny papers over the radio. A lot of families couldn't afford a paper, but a big family could gather around a single radio and have a little fun. It was important in these times. Fio fought for the little guy. He was a good mayor, but it was those little things he did that made him great.

Later on, Roxy and another secretary had been arranging the coffee and bringing in some materials for the second half of the commissioners' meeting. Fiorello had run back into his office, retrieving some notes when Roxy stalked out of the conference room, her face red as a beet and her eyes moist with indignation.

"What happened?" I asked as I rose to meet her.

"Just the usual," she growled as she slammed some books down and kicked the leg of the chair.

"What?" I asked.

"Just that one commissioner, the one with the big grin and eight hands."

"Yeah, I always have to walk way around him," I said. "Look, I'll take your place. I have a plan."

"Really, Lane? I know some of the women think it's just cute. But I don't. I hate it. I'd really appreciate it. I just . . . don't have the patience for him today."

"You shouldn't have to have the patience. Sheesh!" I said, slamming down my own pile of papers in righteous indignation. "Here, hand me the notebooks that need to be taken in."

I got the notebooks and peeked in the meeting room to get the lay of the land. The men were not quite ready to begin and some were getting up and down, filling their coffee cups or chatting in small groups around the room. Perfect. The grinning schmuck was in the corner.

I walked in and started placing the notebooks around the large table, slowly making my way closer to the smirking target. I heard him mucking it up with another cohort. The other guy, to his credit, looked a little awkward as if the guy was being too loud. *He's such an ass.* I was going to use the plan that I made in case I got groped in the subway. I only had to use it once before. Worked like a charm.

Just as I got near him, I felt him pat my fanny as he said, "Thanks, doll. Can you get me more—"

But his sentence was cut off nice and sharp. When he patted my posterior, I straightened up in mock surprise, yelling, "Hey!" and took a big step backward. Right into his insole. As if by accident. With my nice, pointy high heels.

He yelped and bent over in pain, holding his foot.

"Oh. Are you all right?"

"No! You stepped right on my foot!"

I looked around at all the men now gawking at both of us. "I did? So sorry," I said, deadpan.

He straightened up. I smiled nicely and said, "That won't happen again." Then added, "Will it?"

He didn't know what to do with that. He seemed a little dim; I hoped he realized that every time he touched my ass, I'd be stepping on him. The others were watching us with eagle eyes. The only other guy I stepped on happened to be in the room. I looked at him and he winced, obviously remembering. Two others fought a smile, taking big gulps of coffee, eyeing us over their cups.

Commissioner Eight Hands's face turned even redder, his anger boiling over. "Look here, I don't know who you think you are . . ."

Fio erupted into the room. Everyone snapped their attention to him.

"She's my trusted aide, is who she is. Lane, give this message to Morris, this one to Carter—tell him to go to hell—and then see what he says, and I want you to write up a press release on that health care idea that we talked about yesterday. And I want that Pickering guy for the inspector of Hell's Kitchen," he declared, as he sat down at the head of the table.

My opponent had lost his grin as Fio had given me more responsibility than he was used to seeing given to a woman. Then, as Fio mentioned Pickering, the grinning, eight-handed commissioner made a fatal error.

"Pickering won't do for that tough neighborhood. He's too small," he blurted out.

The room collectively took an audible gasp. Fiorello was only five-foot-two. But his manner made him feel like he towered over everyone. His size—not to mention Fiorello means "Little Flower" in Italian—was a thorn in his side. He had a bust of Napoleon in his office.

Fiorello leaped up, quickly gathering a head of steam. "What's the matter with the little guy? What's . . . THE MATTER . . . WITH . . . THE LITTLE GUY?"

Holy crap.

Later in the day, as all the ruckus died down, and I was certain the office women would not be having any more difficulties with our octopod commissioner, we got down to business. I finished my press release. I sent the messages and noted that when I told Carter that Fio said to go to hell, he laughed appreciably and said, "Okay. Okay. I'll work on my proposal and resubmit it." Fio had been delighted. He often tested his favorites. He liked to see what they were made of, and if they'd just quit or if they'd grow.

Fio peeked his head out of his office, and I noticed the tiger grinning at us. Fio yelled, "Come on! In my office, Lane. Get Roxy and Val, too. I have a plan."

"Oh dear."

"What was that?" he screeched.

"On my way! I'll go get them."

I went out to retrieve Val and Roxy and said, "Come on. Your presence has been requested with Hizzonner. He has a plan, he says."

"Oh dear," said Val.

"I know."

We all trooped in, Roxy giving quizzical glances at my chair that I brought in with me.

We sat down and waited for Fio as he shuffled around papers and got himself together. Roxy and Val were crossing and uncrossing their legs trying to find a comfortable position that wouldn't have them sliding off their chairs. I smiled serenely.

"First of all, the police confirmed that the prints on Hambro's knife are *not* his. They had some smudges on them that were most likely his, but two clear prints that most certainly were not."

"Great! Is that enough to clear him?" I asked.

"Well, let's just say he's pretty clear."

I parried with a raised eyebrow and, "Is that the technical term?"

"Heh heh. Yeah, he's still in the middle of suspicious circumstances, so they're still of course looking for him. But between no motive, the fact that there's good evidence that he was an injured party at Lenox Hill Hospital, and that there are unknown prints on the weapon . . . he's still a person of interest, but not the number one suspect."

"Now we just have to find him," said Val.

"And on that note . . . Gals? You're going to the ball Saturday."

"Saturday!" we all yelled.

Fio's horrified look belied that he had been expecting us to jump up and down with glee. But women need to *prepare* for a ball. I was excited, but I didn't have a full-length gown. With limited finances, that could take some ingenuity.

"What ball?" I asked.

"*The* Ball. Mrs. Rockefeller's."

The three of us looked at one another, quickly mentally trying to work out how we could get ball gowns and shoes immediately. The thrill of the potential of the night—the elegance, the dancing, the spectacle—started to dawn on us, making us giddy. Of course, sometimes these affairs were infinitely more attractive when you read about them in the magazines and papers. In real life, I'd heard that they could be stuffy, the journalists making the tantalizing glitz come alive. But this particular ball was a different story. It was the event of the year.

"So, Chief, what's this plan?" I asked, catching a notable gleam in his eye.

"Well," he began as we all sat forward, intent on his words. "I've heard some rumors of a meeting about to happen—an important meeting. VIPs coming into the city for a chat with movers and shakers, and none of them aboveboard movers and shakers. It's actually supposed to be over a high-stakes poker game. But I find it interesting that the red envelopes have surfaced right when this secretive game is being organized. I heard that there's some sort of ultimate gamble. It has to be connected to this case. I don't believe in coincidences.

"I figure this ball will be a highway of information: lots of people, security going in, but once you're there no one will be watching, people will be pairing up while dancing and mingling . . . I think it can't hurt to have several of us there listening in on the goings-on. Are you three game? I trust you implicitly and because of the enormous publicity, it should be plenty safe."

I'd heard that before. But this was a fantastic opportunity on several levels. Fio's logic made sense and it sure couldn't hurt to be picking up more information. Plus, I just wanted to go.

"I'm in," said Roxy with a smirk.

"Me too!" said Val.

They looked at me. "Of course."

Over lunch we talked about the ball; Roxy and I didn't have a ball gown. Val surprisingly did, but was quiet about where she had gotten it. Other than that tiny respite, we worked hard and fast as we always did. With the president's reelection complete, we now were focusing on Fiorello's campaign for his election next fall. He had a sublime ally in FDR, but Fio's Republican supporters weren't as thrilled with that as he would have hoped. So, as he was accustomed, he walked a political tightrope.

Later in the day I received a call from Finn, asking me to meet him in Bryant Park after work. I couldn't tell if we were going there on business or on a date. Either way, though, I was pleased to meet up with him. We walked through these funny worlds together. It was so strange to have something fantastic happen, like all the incredible events in Rochester, then go right back to every-day life.

Then again, my everyday life tended toward the spectacular these days. Things were really starting to pick up with the case. We needed to find Mr. Hambro *and* Marty's killer, and we still had a lot of loose ends to tie up with this heir of Rex Ruby's. It had to be Tucker or Donagan. I hoped Fio's plan would dig up the information we needed before this high-stakes poker game happened— before anyone else got hurt. Or worse.

CHAPTER 44

That evening, I decided to head to Bryant Park right from the office. I still had a tail, and I was still quite happy to have one. I waved at Scott, the policeman, as I walked down the steps of City Hall. I took my usual subway route, but as frequently happens, I must have taken an exit and stairway that I never used before and I popped out of the subway at a completely different block than I usually did. It was along 42nd behind the monumental public library overlooking Bryant Park like a gentle giant.

The scene before me was absolutely breathtaking. I stood there for quite some time, looking up and around in complete awe. It was an incredible moment that I happened to stumble upon. In New York there could be magic and mystery just around the corner at any given moment, and I loved the possibility. I looked around and wondered who else felt this way. Did they see, really *see* it? I paused to enjoy it and soak it in.

The trees in the park had surprisingly kept their leaves much longer than the rest of the trees in the city. And the ice skating rink had begun its open season. The white light that reflected off the rink illuminated the surprisingly still-green leaves of the park from underneath, creating a lacy, delicate, light green canopy. Above and behind the trees were the tall skyscrapers encircling the park with their windows aglow like glittering mountains. Music from the rink soared into the air. The fountain remained on, surprisingly, and was even more beautiful as its spray froze around the base creating diamonds of ice. I walked over toward the outdoor restaurants that I had fully figured to be closed, but the beer garden was open. The restaurant had placed several fire pits around where people were roasting chestnuts and occasionally a marshmallow while enjoying mugs of frothy beer. Over to the right, Finn was smiling at me from a bench by a fire. He never ceased to send a thrill right through me when I caught those dark eyes searching for me.

I walked over and sat down next to him on the bench, still looking around, spotting the quaint carousel lit up with its own twinkling lights and colors.

"Hi, love, you look rather stunned."

"I am. I guess I've never been here at night in December."

"It's incredible, isn't it?"

"You could say that again."

"Here you go." He handed me a foamy beer and despite the chilly air, it tasted perfect.

"Thanks, Finn, wonderful. So, what made you pick this enchanting spot?"

"Oh, I was walking around town last night and happened upon it. Couldn't believe my eyes. I figured you'd like it."

I smiled and said, "I do."

We talked a little about the ball coming up. He told me that he had Miles working on the case, too, and that he was going to arrive in New York by the weekend. Finn had him trying a different approach than we could at the ball, another avenue to find the necessary information about this high-stakes game.

"So what's he doing exactly?"

"Oh, it's too good to tell. I'll let him reveal it to you himself when he gets here."

I happily took a drink of the frothy beer. The firelight was glowing, the fairy lights strung about were shimmering, the general noise of people meeting, talking, and laughing made it all very festive.

I took a close look at Finn. It looked like something was on his mind, probably many things . . . "Got a lot on your mind, Finn?"

He breathed out a sigh. "Oh yeah, I do. You know, I loved having you all to myself in Rochester."

"Those were the best nights of my life, Finn. So far," I said with a grin.

He put his beer down on the table next to him, the firelight flickering on his earnest features. I looked at his neck, his jawline, his lips. He took his fingertips and touched my cheek and chin, then twirled a curl of my hair around his middle finger. I leaned into his kiss. Then we chatted about the day, about being tossed right back into our regular routine. He'd heard about the findings concerning Hambro and the prints. I also told him about my interaction with the handsy commissioner and it had him chuckling. Before long we were interrupted.

"*Heh hem*," came a voice from directly behind Finn.

Finn looked up at a deliveryman holding a large package, his face hidden from mine between his hat coming down on his face and the box in his arms. He whispered urgently, "You two better get going. You're being followed." Then he left rapidly, melting quickly into the crowd.

Finn and I darted our eyes to each other, clasped our hands, and got up to walk away. We tried to look natural while making quick progress to one of the exits of the park, near the Bryant Park Hotel. We passed the carousel and walked around it, its tinkling circus music a contradictory tone to our distressing predicament. We got to 40th and turned east toward busy Fifth Avenue and picked up the pace.

I took a quick look behind and saw two men most certainly in pursuit. They weren't running, but they had the piercing look in their eyes of predators on the hunt. I fought the urge to flee, knowing that if we decided to run, they would, too.

"Two behind us," I said quietly.

"Yep. Here, follow me closely," he said in a low voice, hardening the grip he had on my hand.

Just as we got to the very front edge of the library, he pulled me quickly to the left and shockingly boosted me up and on top of the four-foot cement step that led along the front of the library. He jumped up and we ran between the bushes and the building itself. It was dark and hidden, the two men surely saw us go left, but it would be hard to distinguish our forms. We walked stealthily, trying not to brush the bushes and making them rustle, giving us away. We got to the front steps and slid ourselves up onto them, staying close to the ground. In a dress, this wasn't the easiest thing in the world, but manageable. We stood up slowly in the shadows, moving backward into the even darker recesses of the front entrance, closed up for the night.

We stood silently side by side. And then we heard them. They found us.

The two men came up the steps, the clip of their heels bouncing around and echoing in the vaulted entry.

A deep, stern voice said, "We know you're there. Come out."

I felt Finn move his arm back behind him in an automatic check to see if his gun was in place. The two men came into the dim light of one of the lamps. I looked at Finn and was shocked to see his smiling countenance.

"Gentlemen," he said affably. "I don't think you want to take another step closer."

"Oh really? I think we do," said the slightly taller one on the left. I couldn't make out his face too well, and I hadn't recognized his voice. "You, Missy, have something we want and we aim to get it."

"Who do you work for?" I asked. "Tucker?"

The shorter one's head pulled back a bit and he said, "Who's Tucker?" He didn't seem bright enough to fabricate that kind of genuine response. Okay. Not Tucker. Was that good or bad?

I stole another look at the smiling Finn and said exasperatedly, "What? You're *enjoying this?*"

"Oh yeah." Oh brother.

From the fact that Finn was obviously taking pleasure in this and from his confident remark, both men took a step backward, having bet on a much more compliant prey.

The taller one braced himself and the shorter one decided to just plain take off running. My head was spinning at the quick turn of events. The big guy took a swing at Finn and was so slow that Finn had time to duck and get in two punches before the guy had a chance to reevaluate. He swung around and landed one punch to Finn, which made my stomach clench, but Finn took it and gave it back. Then suddenly he was behind the guy, shoving him to the ground with the guy's arm pinned behind his back.

Finn was slightly panting with the exertion and the look of having fun was still etched on his face. I rolled my eyes.

"How 'bout you tell us what you're after?" said Finn, his Irish brogue nice and clear.

With some "convincing," the guy said with a muffled voice close to the ground, "I don't really know what it means. They just said that you would have it with you, that it was some kind of chess piece, and that it was valuable to them."

"Them?" asked Finn.

"Well, really it's a *her*. But I know she doesn't work alone."

"Who is she?" I asked with disgust, already knowing.

"Lady Red."

"Eliza?"

"Yeah."

CHAPTER 45

"... but in the law of God, there is no statute of limitations. Ay, it must be that; the ghost of some old sin, the cancer of some concealed disgrace: punishment coming, years after memory has forgotten and self-love condoned the fault."

The darkness of the night cloaked his approach. With everyone gone for the evening, his only trick was how to be quiet enough not to rouse their dog. He had taken precautions to wear dark clothes, to wear his tennis shoes for the climbing he'd have to do and, just in case, he'd brought along a few hot dogs in his pocket, hoping they would stall the dog long enough for him to make a getaway should it become necessary.

Tucker's emotions had taken him off guard the last week. Sleep was evasive and he found himself mulling over strange and new thoughts. Darkness and light seemed to pull back and forth at his mind. Things he had known forever seemed less substantial and confusing. On one hand, he was amused by these lesser emotions that he used to mock others for exhibiting. Then again, on the other hand, there was something deep, deep down, like the tiniest sliver that had dug deep into the skin, unable to be extracted, deep enough that it was almost impossible to feel at times. Then out of the blue: penetrating and obvious. *What does it mean?*

Tucker climbed up the gutters and along the window frames to the top story. It was tricky, but doable. The small window was just big enough for him to squeeze through. He slowly looked around, taking in the scent of oil paints heavy in the air, canvases scattered about, a particularly large canvas with wild colors that strangely moved him to walk up to it and touch it. He wondered what the colors and swirls meant; even in the dimness of twilight, he could see the fingerprints of color at the top and the passionate swirls and wide strokes in the midsection and at the bottom.

Tucker had done his homework and knew where he needed to go. He did a cursory look around a few nooks and crannies in the loft, but it was the room just below that he zeroed in on. He took off his shoes, laying them carefully by the window where he'd have to climb back out. He slowly, slowly crept to the stairs.

Toe, heel, toe, heel. He kept to the far sides of each step. Sweat began to dampen his forehead and his shirt. He made it to the bottom of the flight without a single creak. Lane's room was directly on his right. He felt a passion rise in his chest, wanting to devour the place looking for what he sought. Something else pulled at him as well, a desire to see *her* room. Where she slept, where she thought, where she lived.

He went in and it looked just as he imagined it. Soft, but not silly or frivolous. Warm with inviting smoky blue walls. A white chair in the corner by the window where he could easily imagine Lane with her hand holding her chin deep in thought as she read a good book.

Tucker focused on the dresser and walked toward it with his hand out, ready to pull open a drawer. Something held him back. *Why?* Why should he hold back from this particular indiscretion? He was reminded of that moment of indecision with his complicated plan involving her maple tree.

He was a thorough planner and he had used Tabitha quite easily. She was young and impressionable, especially because of his good looks and sophisticated style, something a teenager in a rural area always longed for. It had been her idea to cut the limb off that tree. She'd known from her parents that the tree meant something to Lane. He'd just needed to give Lane a little push. Something that might draw her toward him, and his open arms.

But it had been more than he'd bargained for. He had watched as Lane first glimpsed her beloved tree. She walked slowly over toward it, stumbling once over something. He lurched to catch her, but something stopped him. He'd stood there, stunned by an unfamiliar feeling, something uncomfortable and agitating.

She had turned in his direction and his heart sank. He saw her face and in it was something he had never seen in her before: deep resentment and pain. He saw the remains of a single tear that had made a track down her cheek. He had felt odd sensations at seeing all this, completely alien to him. He felt sadness, anger, and a kind of fear. At that thought, a feeling of dread started to seep into him as he looked at his hand, touching the handle on the dresser. The intensity of those memories made him shake his head, trying to clear his mind that fought against that alien indecision and insecurity.

He pulled his hand back and turned away from the dresser. He glanced over at Lane's nightstand stacked with a couple candles, a brass clock, and several books. One book had been selected and stood alone by itself, closest to her bedside. He walked over and stroked the cover of the book, curious as to what had been piquing her interest. He picked it up to have a closer look, not wanting to turn on any lights nor strike a match. The cover was exquisite, a deep blue with artistic swirls like an artist's brush, embossed with gilt. It was beautiful, but somehow . . . off. And then he saw it. The title had been cunningly secreted within the swirls, but then once seen in its entirety, suddenly leaped off the page. The spacing was meant to make you feel the abnormality that was right in the middle of the beauty. He gasped as he recognized the title and almost dropped the book.

He didn't fear much. Pain could be overcome. Death was just an end. He had always—only—feared one single thing. Tucker had read this book one time in his life and within the peculiar story, there was one idea, one thought, that made him wake up in a cold sweat on more than one occasion.

His hand went to his forehead, wiping away the prickly heat. He walked to the window where it was just the smallest bit lighter. He opened the book and it naturally fell to a certain page. He read the main passage and then flipped to another page. To the words that gave him nightmares. A moan almost escaped his lips as he read it, and he hastily put the book back in its place, instantly pulling away his hand as if the leather cover might burn him.

He left.

Outside, the twilight had grown a heavier mantle of darkness, in exact imitation of his mind.

"Did you find it, Tucker?"

"No," he snapped.

"You weren't in there very long, did you do a thorough search?" Eliza demanded, scorn dripping from her voice.

They had been walking down the block at a quick clip, her shoes echoing off the cold, harsh sidewalks. At her disrespectful tone, he stopped dead in his tracks and turned slowly toward her, his hands deep in the pockets of his black trench coat. He just stared at Eliza, the street lamps glistening off her bright red head, an impudent look radiating from her face, which was pinched with disgust.

He was surprised at her disrespect, but ever since her relationship with Donagan, she had accrued more and more ability to disdain his charms and power that had always wrapped her around his little finger.

His mind retraced over fragmented memories of their irregular childhood years. The father who had in the early years been kind, but absent most of the time, consumed with his business. Then something drastic had changed when they moved abruptly to Michigan. Ties with his grandfather had been broken, a quick move in the middle of the night, leaving behind a great number of treasured things due to their hasty retreat, their father leading the way. And Eliza. She was so little then. So fragile.

He hadn't liked her back then either, a baby sister was mostly a hindrance to his boyhood desires. Then as she grew and matured, he disliked her even more. She had a propensity to be at once clinging and boisterously independent, demanding her own way. Of course, their alcoholic mother with already surfacing mental problems had a great deal to do with this, giving them a difficult and unnatural home life.

But his father had been around more after that. He had liked that. For a while. Until his grandfather secretly found Tucker and set up clandestine meetings. That's when it had been revealed that his own father had been *weak*. A loathsome trait that repulsed him, especially in the eyes of a teenager who craved a hero. His grandfather became that hero. Rex's strength and cunning mind flamed his own desires and ambitions; and lit a fuse that led him on a path of passion, progress, and cruelty. He devoured it, having opened his heart and mind to things he had never before hoped or dreamed. His own hatred of his feckless father grew and blossomed.

Then it transferred to the *real* culprits; the ones whom his father actually turned to for help. The ones who clinched the altering of his father's once proud countenance and profession to a new cowardly and useless personage. The Lorians. *That* was something he shared with his sister: hatred of the Lorians.

Eliza. His eyes flickered down to look at her hands, still small and slender. It was a shock to realize he never truly liked his own sister. Yet there was something about one solitary memory of his, that night they ran away to Michigan. A small, weary, and frightened hand that had found his in the back of the cold car, traveling to God-knows-where, taking them to who-knew-what kind of home . . . And it was that one single memory that he realized he *did* like. If not the person before him, then that one night.

All this happened in a moment, but Eliza saw emotions flash across his face in a most unusual pattern for him. She could always sense his masterful mask of deception and though the diabolical nature of it annoyed her, she admired it deeply. But here . . . his face showed an honesty that she wondered if she had ever beheld in her entire life. At most, she had been but a tool to him. Her eyes dashed from side to side, completely unsure of what to make of it. Something happened. Something had transpired between them.

"No. I didn't find the gold pawn," said Tucker. "I did do a thorough search. Thorough enough to know that she most likely has it on her person. We need to find it before . . . anyone else does," he said, catching himself before he uttered Donagan's name, certain that her loyalty was now with Donagan. Not him.

"Tucker," she sighed, with the first sign of genuine interest not marred by disdain, disapproval, nor her particular brand of mockery. "What exactly happened in Michigan?"

CHAPTER 46

Finn couldn't get much more information from the guy on the library porch (not because of any lack of prowess on Finn's part, but from a lack of cranial capacity of the miscreant). We walked him to Fifth and 42nd. Finn knew that we'd find a couple of cops walking their beat. Finn and I, not to mention Fiorello, had become somewhat of a spectacle within the police force in the last few months, so the two young policemen were delighted to be able to share in a Finn and Lane caper.

They relieved us of our burden and we were left on the sidewalk looking rather despondently at each other. Finn looked a bit crestfallen as I took a good look at him. I thought about those last few sentences we shared at the beer garden about wanting that time alone. Time with no one chasing us, for starters. I suddenly had an inkling of what was seeming to worry him.

He raised a hand and ran it through his hair. "Well, Lane. That was exhilarating."

"Oh definitely. Just another ordinary date." He smiled. I took a step closer, putting a hand on his chest, and said, "But you know by now I don't want a humdrum life anyway, right? I want the adventure. With you." I stepped in to him, putting my hands behind his neck and the back of his head and brought his lips down to mine, my mouth open, finding his and melting into him. And for those long minutes, smack in the middle of the busiest city on earth, the tall sparkling buildings looking down on us, hundreds of people milling around us like a river effortlessly slipping around the rocks and branches in its path, horns honking and the din of traffic, the music floating up and over the library toward the velvety sky . . . we were alone.

Finn dropped me off at home and I walked up the steps to find Aunt Evelyn in her studio. I quickly relayed the events of the evening to her, both of us curious in the extreme about the ridiculous number of people wanting to get their hands on one of those gold pawns.

"Hmmm," I ruminated out loud. "Do you think they know there's more than one gold pawn?"

"What makes you say that, Lane dear?" she answered while dabbing a deep fuchsia into the middle of a square shape in the bottom left of the canvas.

"Well, they seem to think that I have it. I haven't heard of any other approaches made to other people," I said.

"Huh. You're right. You have your father's pawn, Kirkland has his. I wonder if there are even *more*," she pondered.

"I guess that remains to be seen," I said. "But I have an even bigger quandary, Aunt Evelyn."

She pursed her lips and her brow and looked up at me with her piercing gaze. "What could that possibly be?"

"I need a dress for the ball."

"Hah!" she laughed. "Well, don't you worry about a thing. I have something perfect for you."

Just then the doorbell rang, which was a strange hour for visitors, but not absurdly late. I went downstairs and opened the door to a surly looking Roxy.

I smirked a little at her disgruntled look. "Hi, Roxy. What's wrong with you?" I said with a laugh.

"I can't go," she stated obstinately.

"Go where?"

"To the stupid ball," she said with the exact and exasperating voice of a teenager who can't find a date to the highly anticipated prom.

"Ah," I said, nodding sagely. "You didn't find a dress to borrow?"

She shook her head, scowling.

"I think I can help." I took her by the hand and was happy to see a tiny look of hope dart across her furrowed brow.

"First things first." I took her to the kitchen, gave her a bottle of white wine to carry, and I took three glasses. Then I led her upstairs, past the now reclining Ripley, who was keeping watch over the front door.

"Wondering where I'm taking you?" I asked as we started up the second flight.

"Nope. Now that wine is involved, I'm happy to follow you anywhere," she said.

We rounded the last flight and trooped up to the attic.

"Hello, Aunt Evelyn!" I greeted, slightly out of breath.

"Why, hello, girls. What do we have here?" she asked, wiping the paint from her hands, preparing for what was obviously going to end up as a party.

"We have a Cinderella situation, Aunt Evelyn. But there are two of us. Two beautiful girls in need of ball gowns. Is there any way you could step in to be our fairy godmother?" I asked, pouring three generous glasses.

"Oooh . . ." she said, as if anticipating a gratifying challenge. "All right. Now. Let's see, stand there, please. Let me get a good look at you both." Roxy and I eyed each other, smirking at the close attention Aunt Evelyn was paying to our faces and our anatomy. "You're both very different, yes, hmmm . . ." she muttered. "I like it. I like your differences. And I think I know what I am looking for. It might take a little tailoring, but I have just the thing for you both."

She left the room, running down to her capacious and wondrous closet. Roxy and I clinked our glasses and both wondered what she would find for us. I felt confident she would find something good. Roxy looked a little dubious, probably given the fact that Aunt Evelyn was currently dressed like a gypsy with a long skirt and peasant blouse (her favorite outfit for painting). We sipped our wine, both lost in our thoughts for a few quiet moments. Then we heard Evelyn from downstairs, directing me to go to my room, Roxy to

Evelyn's bedroom. We both whisked down the steps in a clatter of anticipation, feeling the excitement Cinderella and all fairy-tale princesses must have felt.

The dress was . . . incredible. And judging by the dreamy look in Roxy's eyes when she came back up to the loft to finish her wine, she felt the same about hers. Our dresses would both need a little tailoring, but only small touches here and there. The dresses themselves were perfection.

We had a truly enjoyable evening laughing, telling funny stories, talking about the ball and where exactly Aunt Evelyn got such glamorous ball gowns. After Roxy left for the night, with her gown folded carefully over her arm and a smile of thanks adorning her little round face, I said good night to Aunt Evelyn and headed up to bed.

As I did all my nighttime ablutions, a funny feeling crept over me. While I brushed my teeth, something made me think of Tucker. Rochester seemed more and more distant, like another life, and in some ways it was. But I *wanted* to remember what I faced. What I had learned. Where *was* Tucker? What was he doing? What was he thinking?

I walked over to my bed and immediately my eye was caught by the strange angle of the book on my nightstand. It was off-kilter from how I remembered leaving it, one corner off the edge of the table. I froze.

My eyes shifted around to the other elements of my room. My dresser, my jewelry boxes, drawers. All were in place, nothing odd. *Could he have?* No. That was ridiculous. My imagination was getting the best of me. I certainly could have hit the book with my elbow or my purse and made it move to that unnatural angle. Or Ripley could have bumped it. It was just a funny set of circumstances: my thoughts focusing on Tucker at the same instant that I noticed something out of place. Nothing was missing. I double-checked my dresser, just in case.

But as I slipped into bed, those thoughts of Tucker and the out-of-place book engendered a feeling of impending urgency. Hopefully, the ball would bring us new information. I was getting more and more concerned for Mr. Hambro and it now seemed that he was wrapped up in all this cloak and dagger business of the red envelope, the gold pawn, and whatever my parents had been involved with. If we couldn't get more information at the ball, perhaps Finn's contact Miles would be able to help. Whatever he was doing, it sounded intriguing. I couldn't wait to meet him.

CHAPTER 47

Miles felt so completely out of place that it took every ounce of his effort to remember his training and stay in character. Given the past several years of obscurity, he was out of his league. However, he used to be a top agent and that kind of intense lifestyle was something that could never really become obliterated. It was in his blood, in his genes for better or worse.

He had received Finn's telegram and followed the directions to the hidden compartment in his boarding room where he found money, papers, and everything he needed. When Miles saw what he was to try to accomplish and *how*, he laughed. It was absolutely absurd! But the absurdity itself had a certain allure to him and he knew the information was crucial to the case, not to mention crucial to the safety of a couple of people he had an affection for, as well as a cause that was ingrained in his heart.

He stood erect, took a deep breath feeling the trim and elegant clothing on his body. His hat dipped down over one eye, he clasped a beautifully crafted bag in one hand, a *London Daily* in the other. He nodded smartly to the others around him, sensing the tension of excitement in the air as he prepared to board the behemoth aircraft in front of him.

For a few moments, all thoughts of the case blew out of his mind just as the wind blew the flags and ropes around. It would take only fifty hours, give or take ten hours depending on the wind, to cross the Atlantic, a marvel of time and technology. It made his head spin that they could do it that quickly. But that meant that those brief hours were all he had to collect the information that he needed. And once he boarded this craft, he was bound to it until they docked in Lakehurst, New Jersey. His approach would have to be stealthy and cunning, because there was virtually no escape if he was discovered.

He looked around at the other high-end travelers surrounding him, giddy with expectation. Millionaires, mostly. Across the smoky room where everyone was getting their last easily smoked cigarette for two days, he spotted the two men he would slowly approach. He kept a smug stance and hoped that his carefully placed statements would make their way over to those two, getting him the meeting he craved.

The boarding call came over the loudspeakers of the waiting area. He made his way across the field and deliberately, confidently, walked toward the cavernous hangar that held his transportation to America: the *Hindenburg*.

CHAPTER 48

Time flew up until the ball. I found a pair of shoes that *needed* to be worn with the dress. Work was busy and frenzied as we were coming up to the holidays. I saw Finn only once that week for a quick lunch as he'd been just as busy with his work. There hadn't been any activity from our other sources of concern: Venetti was utterly silent, Hambro remained missing, Donagan and Eliza hadn't made a peep, even the guy Finn took into custody at the library was completely quiet not wanting to say one word in obvious fear for his life. We were all getting a little edgy, feeling like there was a buildup to something coming down the pike.

The morning of the Rockefeller ball finally dawned. And I was grouchy. Annoyed in the extreme. I made my way down the stairs and to the kitchen counter, still grumping to myself as I dumped a load of sugar into my tea along with the milk.

"Good morning, Lane. Why all the grousing?" rasped Mr. Kirkland with a sardonic look on his face, turning to lean casually up against the counter.

"Oh, just my *book*," I replied, with a great, loathing, despicable emphasis on the word *book*.

"What terrible wrong did this novel commit?" he inquired, while taking a big swig of his strong coffee, his other hand absently patting Ripley's head.

"Thwarted love. Bah!"

He was still chuckling as I left the kitchen, toast in hand.

I got ready for the day and went about doing my errands. I picked up my tailored dress, bought a new lipstick, and took a little breather by taking a walk out by the river despite the freezing temperature. I needed some space to collect my thoughts and consider different pieces of the mystery. I went over the elements to the evening that Fio and the girls and I had discussed yesterday in Fio's office.

The goal of the ball was not to get close to the bigwigs of this supposed meeting or poker game happening sometime soon, but to the ones slightly below them, the ones who might know of the meeting, but perhaps not directly involved themselves. Just to overhear what was going on, maybe get a feel of what was happening. Finn, Pete, and several of their trusted undercover cops would also be in attendance and would help direct any of us toward possible targets while keeping an eye on all of us. Fio would have to maintain his own mayoral role, which bothered him to no end. Being a romantic, he wanted desperately to be able to go undercover. But it was a virtual impossibility. He was too famous and his physical characteristics would be inconceivable to disguise, which brought a smile to my face.

In order to have more freedom to mill about at the ball Valerie, Roxy, and I would go along with Fiorello and a few other office staff. We would go as a group so that each of us could meet, mingle, and dance without looking like we were already a couple with a particular person. Although I approved of this approach in theory, and had no problem dancing with other people, I wasn't fond of seeing *Finn* dance with anyone else. I knew just how good he looked in a suit, not to mention a tuxedo. Girls would be practically swooning over him. *Thwarted love. Bah!*

CHAPTER 49

Finn had been working endlessly this week to set up undercover agents for the ball and to get Miles all set on the *Hindenburg* flight. He'd gotten that idea after his military friends got him a ride on a dirigible from Europe when he had been frantically racing to Michigan. He hoped against hope that Miles would find out more information about the gold pawns and the impending poker game. They were all pretty sure at this point that the game was some kind of major move on either Donagan's or Tucker's part. Finn also had one final backup plan for the ball that he set up just that morning. He had a chance meeting with someone he hadn't seen in quite a while, someone he bumped into.

A slow, easy smile had spread across his face when he had come up with the idea of that one last precaution. It was a long shot, but he had a feeling it was a stroke of genius. Hopefully, it wouldn't come to that, but given Fio, Lane, Kirkland . . . *Jesus*, he had never known a group of people more inclined to get into trouble. He was going to need an army just to keep watch over them all.

Finn was dressed in his tux and already at the bar getting a martini—light on the vermouth, two olives—before most people arrived for the ball. He was feeling antsy. He hadn't had near enough time with Lane the past week, which always made him feel less like himself. It was a strange and surprisingly welcome emotion to him. The ballroom at the Plaza was massive and glittering in silver and black with elegant, understated touches of red, green, and blue holiday colors. He prepared himself for what he needed to accomplish that night, running through the people he knew would be there, the ones the girls were going to try to target.

Just then, a few friendly hellos made their way through his deep concentration.

"Hey there, Roarke. Scott. Pete."

"Hiya, Finn."

"Hey, Finn. Everything all set?" asked Roarke with his dimples showing, but no smile emanating from his mouth. Finn guessed he was feeling just as apprehensive.

"Yes. As good as we can do," replied Finn, finishing off the last swig of briny gin. They had made as many proactive plans as possible, securing the area, talking with everyone about who was coming to the event, and what kind of information to go after. Now? It was in Fate's hands. He felt that this was their only avenue to get ahead on information. With all the unwanted interest in Lane lately, people obviously wanted to get their hands on that gold pawn or possibly the silver gun. Whatever it was, Lane was involved yet again. And, as much as he hated it, they needed her involvement to have any hope of getting her out of harm's way. Plus, he figured, it was just safer having her close by. Luckily, this scheme wasn't as dangerous as the one in August that involved him shooting her. He shuddered as he remembered pulling that goddamn trigger.

Just as he was going over in his mind, one last time, how the events of the evening would go down, she walked in.

There was a hubbub in the main doorway as a large number of people arrived at once: Fiorello's entourage. They were a stunning group. Of course, Fio was bellowing hearty hellos already and he vaguely saw a smashing blue dress on Valerie and a silvery black dress on Roxy. But Lane . . . She took his breath away. Her dress was cranberry red, sleeveless with a deep square neckline, long and flowing with a low back. Her dark hair was pulled up with one long, curling strand coming down along the side of her lovely face. She had on a black choker with a brilliant Art Deco diamond brooch on the front and a simple diamond bracelet over her elbow-length gloves. She caught his eye and her smile lit up her face even more. Sure, the others looked amazing, too. But *Lane* . . . She was his. And he was *all hers*. No doubt about it.

The girls were whisked away and began their mingling. He heard a chuckle coming from behind him. He turned and Roarke was snickering at his obviously besotted expression.

"Shut up, Roarke," said Finn with a deep grin. More chuckles all around.

The rest of the evening went as planned, everyone dancing and talking with a lot of people. He had a hard time concentrating on his own role as he made sure to keep an eye on Lane. For professional purposes, of course. The most humorous moment, and his most favorite, was when he had been dancing with a buxom blond gal. He couldn't even remember her name, but at one point he looked down at her and she was stroking his chest as they danced, saying how much she loved his tux. He felt flattered that she liked his tux. Then he looked up and over and caught Lane's eye. Her glittering orbs were absolutely brimming over with jealous anger. He almost laughed at the look on her face that truly was shooting him daggers. Of course, she was dancing with her own handsome beau, but that didn't seem to count.

It wasn't supposed to be part of the plan, but screw the plan. He finished the dance with the blonde and made his way over to Lane.

"May I have this dance?" he asked with a large grin.

"Of course," she replied with a quick smile of pleasure.

He took her into his arms, something he had been envisioning all evening. He held her much closer than the other gals. The silkiness of her dress against her lithe body was sexy and just as sweet as he had thought it would be.

She looked up into his face with a wide smile, almost laughing. "So," she said with a cocked eyebrow, "Blondie seemed to enjoy you quite thoroughly."

"She liked my tux," said Finn happily.

"Hah! She didn't like your tux. She liked what was *underneath* the tux," she said with a droll smirk.

"Love, you look . . . incredible."

"You clean up pretty nice yourself, Finn."

He smiled down at her, listening to the music, feeling her body against his. He wanted to take that gorgeous dress off, one little bit at a time, and he imagined her lying down on his bed, naked and beautiful and all his.

"What are you thinking about, Finn?"

"Oh, ah . . ."

She took a deep breath, smiled, and put her head on his shoulder. "Mm hm . . ."

CHAPTER 50

Miles was fully ensconced on board the *Hindenburg*, slightly apprehensive, well, actually, *quite* apprehensive about traveling over the ocean in an oversize balloon. A balloon full of flammable gas, for Christ's sake. Before boarding from the zeppelin hangar, they had been instructed and warned about the dangers of carrying matches aboard. Then they climbed a retractable stairway into the bottom of the craft. Hundreds of citizens of Frankfurt crowded around the ship shouting farewells, enthusiastically waving flags while a band played patriotic German music. When ready to launch, two hundred men from the ground crew firmly grasped the cables as if they were merely holding a Thanksgiving Parade balloon, and walked the floating giant out to the field. At the captain's command, the cables were thrown off and the ship that was as tall as a thirteen-story building and about four city blocks long, gently, peacefully, silently, lifted off.

Miles made the most of the short amount of time eating in the grand dining room, listening to the piano at night, and talking into the wee hours with the other passengers. Word had indeed gotten around about who he was and his desire for a high-stakes game in New York. Being a "reclusive, eccentric millionaire," just *any* game would not do. After years of being off duty, slightly out of his mind to boot, Miles was more than a little excited to see the ease of assuming an identity and a mission coming back so quickly. It was gratifying to mold and create in this way. Like an actor, but with an intense goal and deadly consequences.

Some passengers never slept, but he got a few hours of shut-eye in his own modest room, just like all the others, that held a small bed, a washbasin with hot and cold water, a tiny desk, a closet, and an electric light. The room on board that most intrigued him in a ghastly way was the smoking room. He understood that everyone smoked, but he was dubious in the extreme, flying half a mile over the ocean in the midst of sixteen enormous hydrogen gasbags that were highly inflammable . . . that perhaps one could do without a smoke in light of the extraordinary risk? Apparently not. So, the smoking room was specially crafted. You walked through an air-locked entrance, kind of like a revolving door, where the pressure was higher inside than outside to prevent gas from entering. The ash receivers were automatically closed airtight to extinguish lighted butts. He went ahead and smoked his own cigarette or two, albeit with great unease and positively no enjoyment.

At one moment, alone on deck where he looked out the slanted windows, he felt the great romance of this ship in flight. But juxtaposed against that notion was another that was the exact opposite. Not that long ago, zeppelins just like this were sitting over London dropping bombs. And he was underneath, dodging those goddamn bombs. It was a terrible and surreal feeling. It was a long time ago . . . *No, actually.* It wasn't that long ago at all.

In the final hours of the flight, he at last got word of someone desiring a meeting with him over drinks. He had known that it would require great patience and a nonchalance that bespoke an intended indifference to the game to acquire the needed information. He let it be known with elegant subtlety that his presence would be greatly desired at any important game and if they didn't care for his money, somebody else more important *would*.

He walked over to the gentlemen at the bar and ordered a bourbon, straight up. "Hello, gentlemen. Miles Havalaar, at your service."

His patience, tact, and timing paid off. After only a few minutes, he secured the time and place of the big game.

CHAPTER 51

Despite the working nature of the night, the ball was just plain enchanting. My red dress was a dream, fitting perfectly after the tailor took it in around the waist (and of course the bosom, darn it). It was a timeless piece that felt sumptuous. My dance with Finn was sweet and unexpected as I had thought we were going to have to stay away from each other. He looked sensational. I noticed more than one girl completely unable to keep their eyes off him. One blonde in particular. I had to fight off the urge to trip her whenever I happened to be in her vicinity.

We slowly gathered names of people who were most likely in town for the big game. I kept getting the feeling that the main event was soon, maybe even tomorrow. But nothing concrete surfaced. Around eleven, I was just starting to get a little tired when I thought I'd hit the ladies' room to freshen up. I left the dance floor, admiring the majestic room and the beautiful forms of my friends. Roxy looked wonderful in her sleek silvery black with her shining head of short blond waves and Val was a delight in her silky, watery blue dress. I noticed with a smile that there were several men who were keeping their eyes on them. And *not* just for professional purposes.

Just as I was coming out of the powder room, I glimpsed Fio racing toward the door with the childlike look of glee on his face, which could only mean one thing: He had heard of a fire happening and he wanted desperately to go and "help out."

"Fio!" I yelled. "Where do you think you're going?"

"Oh hey, Lane. I just got word that there's a big fire in one of the abandoned factories. I thought I'd go check it out on my way home." He said all this in top speed while bouncing on his toes in great anticipation. He was mumbling under his breath about the fact that he was vexed that he didn't have his fireman's coat with him.

"Have fun!" I yelled to him as he raced out the door. Then I had second thoughts about him running around unchaperoned and went out the door after him.

"Hey, Fio! Wait a minute!" I yelled to him. He was jogging down the block, looking for a taxi. I started to laugh and called out to him again, taking a few quick steps after him.

Just then a van pulled up to a screeching halt right next to Fio.

"Fio!" I screamed. Men in black pulled his stunned form into the back of the van. I looked wildly about, and just opened my mouth to scream for help when a hard hand wrapped around my mouth and a harder arm wrapped around my body.

"Well," purred a deep voice right in my ear, his hot breath scalding my face. "This is an unexpected pleasure. And don't you look *and feel* ravishing. I think you'll just have to come with me."

I fought the nausea rising in my throat, keeping my eyes wide open, taking in any piece of helpful information I could. No one saw me. No one knew we had gone outside. I felt a tear of fear and desperation come to my eyes. Donagan had me completely and utterly bound up in his arms. Struggle was vain and useless, but I still tried. It only made him laugh harder, giving him more opportunity to enjoy the moment and grope me further.

I finally stopped at the point where he cheerily threatened to strike me. He took me to a different car, one where another big goon was waiting in the back, ready to keep me still by the persuasive revolver in his hand.

I kept my eye on the van where they had Fio. We followed it. I tried to look like I was crying and *not* keeping track of where we were in hopes that they wouldn't put a hood over my head. We were staying in Manhattan. I had wondered if we would go out to the establishment that had been Eliza's in Queens. But no. We pulled up to a factory-like building downtown on the west side. It was a lonely spot. I caught out of the corner of my eye that they were pulling Fio

out of the van, and he was alive and well, walking on his own accord. They had gagged him—no surprise there.

At this point, Donagan was fully occupied. Eliza had met him
as he got out of the car. She was gesticulating wildly, obviously not
pleased with something. Then he grabbed her and kissed her with
something near aggression. But her own violent nature seemed to
take that in stride like it was an ugly kind of foreplay.

My gunman ushered me out of the car on the opposite side to
where Donagan and Eliza were still talking earnestly. It ended up
giving me the perfect opportunity to overhear part of their conversation, so I stayed quiet and compliant.

"Eliza, my beauty." *God, he makes me want to gag.* "Trust me. You
need to decide where your loyalties lie. I love you and I know the
best for you. We can do this together. *Now* we have quite a prize
for our big poker game. That will give us what we need to flush
the pawn out, darling. And *that* will provide us with more money
and grandeur greater than even you can imagine. Besides, he keeps
drawing blanks. I'm beginning to suspect he's off his game and that
he can't be trusted any longer."

Eliza had been looking at Donagan like a puppy looks at a masterful owner. But a flash of uncertainty and confusion raced across
her face in just one instant, to be then quickly secured back in
place. *Hmm. Loyalties. Does he mean Tucker?* Donagan kept going, relentlessly backing up his argument, and her face and heart seemed
to be devoured before me.

Lucky for me, by that point, my gunman had tired of the conversation and had already started to take me off toward the building, so
I didn't attract Donagan's or Eliza's attention at the moment. There
was no way in hell I wanted it known that I had overheard them. I
looked about, searching, newly desperate for my own grave situation. How was I going to get out of this mess?

Inside, I lost track of Fio completely, not hearing a sound nor
hearing a single thing that could help. I was taken to a room where
there was a mat on the floor and one small light on a table. It wasn't
filthy, just dusty. But before I was left alone and locked in, I got the
meeting I had been dearly hoping would be overlooked.

"Mmmm," came the oily voice of Donagan from behind me. I

whipped around to face him. "You just look . . . good enough to eat, Lane, my dear." I backed up as my heart raced. My fear seemed to fuel his desire for me as he stepped closer. I suddenly remembered that in a ridiculous moment of a swashbuckling nature when I was getting ready that night, I had strapped my dagger to my thigh. Something about my red dress had engendered romantic visions of pirates and swordplay. That one, clear, funny memory brought me to myself and helped assuage my fear. Plus, I had a weapon; I was by no means helpless. I controlled my breathing.

Donagan drew near. His pale face, rust-colored hair, and scarred mouth that had been covered over by makeup repulsed me. He started to stick out his tongue like he was going to lick my face. I was prepared to rip that smug look right off him, my anger got such a strong hold of me. But before either of us could react, a loud blast with glass breaking and screams exploded from another part of the building not too far away.

Donagan shoved me and I fell backward onto the floor, banging the back of my head on a table. I heard a bolt slide across from the outside of the windowless room. Despite a possible fire and the fact that I had no escape, I was deliriously excited to be away from him.

I stood up and straightened my dress. My hair was coming out of its neat updo, so I took it down, smoothing it out around my face and over my shoulders. I retrieved my dagger and held it in my hand, the cool ebony and the weight of the handle a pleasing sensation. Having prepared myself, I felt much better. I could hear a lot going on in the factory: shouts, orders given and received. I smelled smoke . . . I started to think of options for the moment when someone came to my door. *If* someone came to my door. But before I could get any farther, I heard the bolt thrown. I got to the other side of the door, ready to pounce.

The door swung quickly open, but I stayed stock-still, frozen in place by surprise.

"Lane? Come on! We gotta get outta here!" she commanded.

Holy shit. It was Morgan.

CHAPTER 52

We slunk our way out of the factory completely unnoticed. She had taken me by the hand as I had been absolutely gobsmacked into immobility. She pulled me along, murmuring angrily that I had those ridiculous high heels to contend with and that great big, swishy red dress, could I possibly be more conspicuous, et cetera.

We got outside and ran to the back of the factory. We met up with three of her urchin buddies and I started to get an idea of what was going on.

I sputtered, "You mean to tell me . . ." But Morgan cut me off, telling me efficiently that it was not the time for loud voices and everything would be explained later. I shut up with a hand brought quickly to my mouth to stifle the absurd laughter, making two of the boys snicker at me. They all gawked incredulously at my bigger-than-life attire. We walked even farther west, being a less conspicuous area where Donagan was unlikely to follow, but a much more difficult location to find a cab. However, Providence gave us a kind, if not humorous, hand and we found a huge junk cart whose driver was willing to haul us all uptown. I gave him one of my tiny diamond earrings as collateral and told him to go *fast*. We directed him to take us to the main police station.

Morgan and I sat side by side, but with the loud ruckus of the horse-drawn, clanking junk-mobile, it was impossible to carry on a conversation. Plus, I had to hold on for dear life.

The junk cart was loaded in hillbilly style with mounds of junk teetering precariously on all sides. We made a mighty clinking and clunking noise rolling at breakneck speed down the streets. The kids thought this was the most fun they had ever had, far better than any parade or police chase they had ever witnessed. I, in my glorious, full-length red dress, sat on the back of the truck, clutching to the side as we careened around corners, my legs dangling carelessly off the back, high heels held in one hand, dagger in the other, red-painted toes dancing around in the considerable breeze.

We at last slowed down as we pulled up in front of the solemn, stern police station. After a wind-blown drive, with ears ringing, we arrived.

Words fail me as I try to fathom what we must have looked like pulling up to the police station. It seemed that the entire department came flooding out of the precinct to witness our arrival. We stuttered to a stop, the horses loudly panting and shuffling, as a large metal pot lost its precarious grip and clattered to the ground, noisily bouncing along down the street. The stunned police force sort of melted apart in front of me on my perch, revealing Finn, hands on his hips, eyes burning like fire, searching. For me.

A wildly awkward silence ensued. I stammered, "Hi. Um . . ."

Then my police buddy Scott, the one who seemed to *always* be there right at my most stunning moments, was standing next to Finn and sputtered into the dead quiet, "Her dress . . . the wild hair . . . a dagger . . . ? She looks like a pirate." And then completely lost it. He started laughing so hard he threw his arms around his waist as he bent over from the loud guffaws that were emanating from his shaking body. Then of course my urchin friends, who were just dying to see how this would all pan out, started laughing and giggling, and then it spread to everyone else.

Finn walked over to me, pulling me off the back of the truck and crushing me to himself. He set me down and took my face into his hands. "What am I going to do with you?"

I shook my head, just as dismayed. "I have no idea. Good luck." Then he laughed and kissed me soundly.

Morgan came sauntering over with a smug look on her smiling face. Finn gave her a knowing look and smacked her on the arm with his fist, like he would a buddy. "Nice job, Morgan."

"Thanks."

"What?" I exclaimed. "No. You did *not* hire her to keep an eye on me. You did! You dogs!"

She came over to me and laid a small, motherly hand on my shoulder (even though I was taller than her). "Well, someone has to watch out for you."

"Yeah!" squeaked a tiny miscreant hopping off the truck. "And that ain't easy, lady!"

I gasped, "You! You?" I went over to him, grabbed him under the armpits, and brought him to my eye level. His grubby little face was looking right back at me, his small hat off-kilter on his dirty head, his freckled face smiling for all it was worth minus its one tooth.

"I remember you from the coffee cart outside City Hall! Have you all been tailing me?"

"I'll explain later," said Finn, totally enjoying himself, but then turned determinedly solemn as he addressed the kids. "But for now, did you find out anything about Mr. La Guardia?" he asked.

They told him they couldn't find him in the factory, and that from what they overheard, they figured he had been moved before they had thrown their homemade bombs into the building for a diversion. I looked at our band of Irregulars with a cocked eyebrow and more than a little concern at their wily ways.

"All right," said Finn. "Miles arrives tomorrow and hopefully he will have been invited to the game by then. He should have the where and when. Now we just have to decide how to handle it."

I told him what I'd learned. "I overheard Donagan and Eliza talking. I think he's trying to get her to side with him and ditch Tucker; he kept talking about her loyalties. And he mentioned that they have a nice prize for the poker game that should give them enough funds to get their hands on the pawn and that the pawn will deliver them treasure beyond their wildest dreams. Finn, I think Fiorello is the prize. It's a high-end poker game with all of Fio's enemies. The ultimate game."

"Hmm . . ." muttered Finn, with his hand on his chin, pondering the problem. "I'm certain Miles will have our information. Now we have to come up with a plan on what to do with the game."

I looked at him and smiled. "Let's go talk. I think between you and me, we can come up with a plan. I have an idea."

The freckled little boy right next to me smacked his forehead in disbelief.

Finn said, "Bloody hell."

That night we met with our friends at our place for a council of war with Kirkland and Evelyn. As we all sat around the parlor, still dressed in our glittering garb from the ball, the plan solidified in my mind. I had talked with Finn about the general gist of what I was thinking. As we sat together on the couch, I took a good look at the tuxedos on Roarke and Pete, the fancy and sophisticated dresses on Val and Roxy . . . I looked at Finn and nodded at the circle. A slow grin spread across his face and he nodded.

"Yeah. This could work, Lane. All right everyone. We have a plan. It's going to take a lot to pull it together and it's quite dramatic. But given the, uh, *talents* of this circle of friends, I think we can handle it."

It was already well after two in the morning, but we finished up in about an hour. We all departed, hopefully to get a few winks. Depending on what Miles told us, we would have to be ready as early as the next afternoon. I prayed that Miles really did have what we needed. Everything hinged on knowing the exact time and place of the big game, and getting out a few well-placed messages. It would take a miracle to do it. But Team Fio *had* to do it. And if there ever was a group able to pull off a miracle, it was this one.

CHAPTER 53

Fiorello had been in their custody for only one night and one long day, but it seemed like weeks. He knew his team of capable friends would figure out a way to help him, but the waiting was killing him. That goddamn gag had been just too much. He knew he had to keep his mouth shut, but the last time they took it off he just couldn't help himself. His outrage knew no bounds and he started bellowing and ranting. Back came the gag. The next time they took it off, he kept quiet. At least for the time being.

He couldn't tell where they had taken him after the factory, someplace still within Manhattan. And it was some place fancy. The bed and room were furnished with a gaudy, expensive taste. Despite the ridiculous amount of furniture in the small room, there wasn't anything that could be used as a weapon. He'd done a good scouring of the drawers and under the bed, but came up with nothing. Even the lamp was too bulky to wield. He hadn't seen anything of the main part of the building; they had kept a hood on him the entire way. But this room, covered in reds, greens, and gilt furnishings, had something familiar about it, like he had seen it before but just couldn't place it. None of the hotels he had stayed in had been anything like this, though.

He never saw anyone who seemed to be the one in charge. He figured it had to be Donagan or Tucker behind his kidnapping. But then again, it could be Venetti or another unknown criminal. God knows he had angered many, many people. He smiled to himself. He loved it that he had done enough good to make the bad guys angry. Loved it. Never got tired of it.

He had been provided with bread and water, and he had actually slept a little on the lavish bed. He worried about Lane; he saw them grab her when he had made his foolish run out to see about the fire. *Dumb dumb dumb*, he berated himself. He couldn't *believe* how stupid he'd been to get caught in an ambush like that.

He stood up to the mirror over the dresser and tried to smooth out the wrinkles in his tux that he still wore from the night before. Something was going to happen soon, he felt a sort of tension in the air, and he wanted to be ready. He used a little of the water to wash his face. He ran his wet fingers through his black, wild hair and made it more presentable.

Finally, the door opened. He thought about shouting for help, but the gun pointing at him checked that desire. At last, the guy in charge sauntered in. He knew that large frame, rusty head, and scarred mouth anywhere.

"Hello, Donagan. Are we ready?"

Donagan smiled at Fio's forthright attitude, liking his aplomb, but also wanting to dig at him.

"Hello, *Little Flower*. Yes. I'm ready. I've been waiting for this game for a long time. But you should enjoy it, it will be the last game you're a part of, I can assure you of that. Poor, poor *Marie*, she'll never really know what happened to you. Such a shame. Perhaps I'll just make a little visit to her."

At Marie's name, Fio's wrath boiled up and over and in agony he lurched forward, ready to pound the hell out of that bastard. But Donagan leveled the gun at his head. "Ah, ah, ahh . . ." he crooned, like a mother warns an errant child. "I wouldn't do that. We don't want to make a premature exit, now do we?"

Donagan's singsong, oily voice grated on Fio like nothing else. But he knew he had to keep his head. As long as he was alive, there was still a chance. It may have been a slim chance, but a chance nonetheless.

"All right. That's better. Now, let's go." Donagan pointed out the door. Another guy bound Fio's hands behind his back, then led the way with Donagan behind him, the barrel of the gun digging into his spine.

They marched down a few hallways. The lush carpeting soaked up the sound of footfalls, gilt-framed pictures lined the walls, and there were a couple of tables placed along the way with a profusion of flowers overflowing gold vases. The red, green, and gold reminded Fio of the Russian Tea Room.

They turned down another, much narrower hallway, then up a flight of stairs and then down yet another hall that was darker and narrower. They had to walk closely, single file. He could feel Donagan's breath on the top of his hair. They passed three, four, five doors. Turned one more corner, then stopped. The corner made it an even tighter fit. The door in front of them was number 607. The dark green door had the numbers in gold upon it, and he could hear the unmistakable clink of poker chips on a table on the other side along with a murmuring of low voices.

The lead guy knocked on the door once. Then three times. The sounds within stopped. Fio could tell Donagan was holding his breath. Footsteps made their way over to the door. The lead guy stepped in and then moved to the side. Donagan pushed his gun farther into Fio's back, nudging him through the doorway, making his grand entrance.

Fio blinked hard. Arranged around the table were three men of obvious mobster glory and two richly if not outrageously dressed women, clearly top-notch mobster women. And then . . . then . . . He blinked harder, the breath whooshing right out of him.

Donagan edged into the doorway, still behind Fio. He started in on a pompous announcement that sounded like he had rehearsed it in front of a mirror. "Ladies and gentleman. I have before you the Mayor of New York City!"

And then it hit him. A catch in his throat cut off the next arrogant declaration just as he was opening his mouth. Donagan stuttered, "Wh-what?"

Fio looked around the table. Dressed in incredible getups that *almost* obscured their real identities were the most welcome, warm, strong, determined group of people he had dearly wished to see more than anything in his life. His starving eyes hungrily ate up each of their faces: Finn. Lane. Mr. Kirkland. Evelyn. Roarke. Peter.

Mr. Kirkland, Finn, and Peter simultaneously leveled their guns at Donagan and the other guy.

Donagan was flabbergasted, but still in control. He cleared his throat, then said, "Well. I guess we have a change of plans. But don't forget that I still have a gun right in our dear Little Flower's back. Don't move. In fact, you better put your guns down unless you want my little shield here to get blown apart."

Fio, caught in the euphoric ecstasy of being saved, was suddenly crushed by the fact that he couldn't see a way out of this. His friends carefully placed their guns on the table. No. No. It *had* to end. He couldn't still be held captive. He had work to do! But then two things happened at once.

A voice he knew well came from behind him, surprising them all.

"Donagan! Did you do it? Did we get it?" It was Eliza coming down the hall, completely unaware of who was in the room.

Then, as Donagan had been distracted but still easily keeping his gun right in Fio's back, Lane pulled something out of the front of her dress. "Donagan! Here! You want *this?* Take it!" And she threw something gold and shiny right into the left hand of Donagan. As he caught it, he shoved Fio into the room with a mighty heave.

Fio was launched forward, falling against the table. Everyone grabbed their guns at once and Finn and Pete leaped around the table to go after Donagan. Roarke and Mr. Kirkland helped Fio up, making sure that he was all right and unbound his wrists. He could barely control his thoughts and all his questions and grateful things to say all came tumbling out at once.

"My God, you're a sight for sore eyes! How did you—? Lane, your hat is enormous! Roarke, you have a mustache! Kirkland, your hair is *black!* Good God, Evelyn, look at your cleavage. I mean, no—don't look. I'm not looking. Oh, my God, I better sit down."

Lane was cracking up, Evelyn made a squeak as she ran to get a little shawl for a cover-up. Lane took off her enormous purple hat and fanned herself in complete satisfaction as she sank into a chair. Roarke sat, too, right next to Fio. He was scratching his fluffy blond mustache, obviously itchy from the glue. He put a hand on Fio's shoulder.

"You really all right, Fio?" he asked earnestly with a relieved smile, his dimples showing around the mustache.

Fio exhaled in a great poof. "Well! Yes, I think so."

Finn came jogging back into the room. "Everyone all right?" he asked, looking at Fio with a worried frown.

Lane went over to him. "Yeah, everything's okay. Did you catch him?"

"No. These hallways are too twisting, there's about a hundred ways out of the building. Pete went ahead to notify the force. The guys we have surrounding the building are keeping watch, but we couldn't have too many, otherwise it might have given us all away. Hey, nice thinking about throwing the pawn to him."

Lane replied, "I figured the top priority was getting Fio back in one piece. We can deal with the pawn later. Besides, we have an extra," she said with a big grin.

Fiorello looked around at these dear friends and a gratifying peace stole over him. He could finally relax. The tension of the last day started to ease off his shoulders. Evelyn, sufficiently covered up now, came over behind him and patted his shoulder.

Evelyn quickly and calmly explained how Lane escaped the night before and had overheard Donagan and Eliza speaking. "She heard that you—their big prize—were going to be gambled to fetch a price that would enable them to get their hands on the pawn. But they didn't know the time and place of the big poker game. That was where Finn's contact, Miles, came into play and he had indeed weaseled an invitation to said game, on the millionaires' trip on the *Hindenburg*. They landed early this afternoon, finally getting us the location for tonight's game. A few choice, clever messages about a possible raid on the game had kept the cautious high rollers away, so we could take their place without giving it away to Donagan." Her flinty eyes sparked with enjoyment as she regaled him with their story.

"Well, you sure don't lack in imagination," he declared.

Evelyn said, "You can say that again." Then she went over to the bar and began pouring restorative beverages for everyone.

Fio sat back in the chair and took a deep breath. The shrewd and crafty way this group handled themselves, not to mention their devotion and courage, made him feel proud and humbled at the same time. He was pretty darn sure this crazy scheme had been Lane's. He'd seen those characteristics in Lane the day he'd hired her. Courage, imagination, devotion . . . He had asked her a few carefully considered questions that day. She'd picked up on nuances that no else had. He lacked sensitivity like that. That's why he needed her.

And she knew the profound lesson of loss. When his first wife died, along with their one-year-old daughter, Fio thought he might not make it. *But he did.* There was something special about people who could overcome. He saw that in Lane.

He looked at her sitting on a nearby couch and laughed to himself as he overheard Finn talking with her, his arm around her shoulders. Finn was smiling widely as he said, "Lane, you can stop speaking with a Southern accent now. Besides, you were supposed to be a mobster. They don't have Southern accents, love."

CHAPTER 54

What entered my life now was a delightful time of enjoying simple pleasures. It was abrupt and pleasant like rushing and running all week, then suddenly having the satisfaction of plopping down at a favorite movie theater on a Friday night with the delight of nothing but a lovely weekend ahead. The police were still working on locating the whereabouts of Mr. Hambro and rounding up Donagan. For me, although my job was busy, it seemed as if a lull had at last arrived. I finally wasn't the center of attention, perhaps from the fact that Donagan had his hands on that precious gold pawn. I wondered where that would lead. Would retrieving whatever treasure the pawn promised create new problems? Did Rex leave a legacy that would usher in more drama? Or was it simply about money and Donagan would run off to an island paradise? One could hope, but only time would tell.

Valerie and I went to see *Romeo and Juliet* at the movies. It was incredible. The only thing that struck me as odd was that the teenage Romeo was played by Leslie Howard, who I swore was almost fifty. But he played the role so well that I soon got over the age discrepancy. And Finn and I thoroughly enjoyed *The Petrified Forest*. Even though we personally lived a real story of dealing with gangsters, the mix of the up-and-coming actor Humphrey Bogart with his role of vicious gangster and the enormous, remarkable eyes of the waitress and poet Bette Davis, who falls in love with him, captivated us completely. Then a big group of us from work saw *Mr.*

Deeds Goes to Town. It was so fun, I'll never forget Gary Cooper's performance.

We also went to the annual lighting of the Rockefeller Christmas tree. The ritual started just a few years ago in '33 when 30 Rockefeller Plaza opened. Actually, unofficially, the first tree was in '31 when the construction workers brought in a twenty-foot tree and decorated it with strings of cranberries, paper garlands, some tin cans, and even some blasting caps. Also at Rockefeller Center, they'd just opened a temporary ice skating rink in the Sunken Plaza.

December 12th, the day after Fio's actual birthday, Robert Moses, New York's famous parks commissioner, threw a big shindig to celebrate the opening of the Henry Hudson Bridge and Fio's fifty-fourth birthday. But two things interfered: a rainstorm sent everyone running from the bridge dedication and then more interestingly, England's King Edward VIII announced that he abdicated the throne the day before to marry the American divorcée Wallis Simpson. Fiorello had stopped everything in the middle of the festivities and made someone turn on the radio so he could listen to the historic broadcast. It had been an ongoing scandal as the king and Wallis would travel together—with her husband in tow—as she didn't get a divorce from this second husband of hers for quite some time. No one could believe Edward actually abdicated. He'd be succeeded by his younger brother Albert, now called King George VI. I personally liked Albert better anyway.

One night, I was dancing the Balboa with Roarke, a dance that you just sort of shuffled to, especially good in small, crowded spaces. He'd been in and out of town as usual on assignments. I loved a new song that just came out by a new singer, Nat King Cole. I could listen to him all day. I was singing softly as I danced with Roarke, *"You gotta S-M-I-L-E to be H-A-P-P-Y . . ."*

"Hey! You got it right!" he quipped, dimples showing.

"Yeah, it helps when they actually spell it out," I said, firmly acknowledging my deficiency in getting lyrics right.

The song came to an end and Finn came over to pick me up for the next one. My feet were just starting to notice the long hours of standing, but I would never say no to a dance with Finn.

"Having fun, Lane?" he asked with a smile.

"I am! And I just got the lyrics right to the last song. Impressive, I know."

"Mm hmm . . . It helps when they spell them out."

I slapped him on the chest with a laugh. "Cut it out."

"I really like your dress, love," he said, taking an appreciative look up and down.

It was dark red, my favorite color, and especially nice coming up to the holidays. It had elbow length sleeves, a deep V in front and back, and a swishy skirt. Of course, I had delightful deep red high heels on as well. Oh wait, swishy skirt . . .

"Are you thinking of my red dress the night of the ball?" I asked.

"Oh yeah. That's my favorite."

I bet it was. "I heard Scotty say I looked like a pirate."

Finn started laughing in earnest. "I'll never—ever—forget the sight of you rolling up on the back of that junk cart." He drew me closer and I put my head on his shoulder, my face in the crook of his neck. He smelled delicious.

After a while of dancing slowly, he said, "You know, Lane, we've had some time off from this case lately. God knows we needed it . . ."

"Mm hmm," I agreed.

"But we need to figure out what's been going on with Donagan and why he wanted that pawn. And Mr. Hambro—he's smack in the middle of it all—and Venetti has been all but silent lately . . ."

"Which is scary in and of itself," I cut in.

"Oh yeah. Despite the ongoing investigation, it's like they fell off the face of the earth. Well, I have a meeting set up with Miles tomorrow and I thought maybe you should come with me. We could talk through everything, see if it triggers any ideas. Would you be up for that?"

I'd been dying to meet this character. After he took the big ride on the famous, exorbitant *Hindenburg*, for crying out loud, he was laying low here. "I'd love to meet him, Finn. What time?"

"Let's meet tomorrow after the morning meeting where the detectives all gather to look at all the accused felons we've brought in to see if we'll book 'em and what to charge them with . . ."

"What, like a show?" I asked.

Out of the corner of his mouth he said, "Kinda. After that, I set up a lunch meeting at that little pub on 37th between Madison and Fifth. Miles is really missing London, feels like a fish out of water. It's the best place to get fish 'n' chips, so he eats there pretty much every day. You want to meet us there at noon?"

"Sure, sounds great." We kept dancing and I had one of those moments of complete awareness and wakefulness. Where time stands still for just a minute, and you make yourself soak up the sounds, textures, and the feeling of the moment, cementing it in your mind, becoming fully aware of life happening right that second. The dance hall was packed, and the extra fairy lights strung around the place were the main holiday decorations.

"Hey, Finn, you feel like taking off?"

He looked at me with a smile pulling at one corner of his lips. "Sure. You have an idea, don't you?"

"Yep. Come on."

I took him by the hand and we made our way across the floor, saying quick good-byes to our buddies. We retrieved our coats and bundled ourselves out the door as about fifty more people tried to get in.

We took the subway uptown to the Upper East Side. Finn's place was in midtown, a small upper-floor apartment of a townhouse. It dawned on me that I'd never been to his place.

"I'd like to see your place sometime, Finn."

"I'd love to take you there, Lane. But if I did that, I don't think I'd ever let you leave."

"You have a point," I laughed.

It had snowed just a little bit, our shoes making crunching noises on the icy sidewalk. The air was frosty and the city at night held its usual charm. The tall mountains of skyscrapers with their glowing windows, the ever-present energy of people milling about, the air itself full of something lively and transcendent, all came together and made you feel lucky to get to be a part of it. I could smell my intended destination before I could see it.

The Christmas tree stands started coming into the city the first week of December. Many people got their trees on Christmas Eve as a tradition. There was no possible way I could *ever* wait that long.

The whole lead time to the holidays was my favorite time. The scent of pine was one of the best aromas in the world and when the trees came in, although they make the sidewalks more cramped, it brought a divine scent to the everyday experience of just walking around.

Every little shop, bar, bakery, and storefront was decorated in some way for Christmas or Hanukkah. We walked by a favorite neighborhood pub and I peeked inside. I loved the look of bars at Christmas. Not the outside of the building, but the actual bar where all the shiny bottles were lined up, the flashy colors of the liquors, the social aspect bringing people to one place all together, and then some twinkly lights thrown in with greenery. It was a rather sacrilegious pleasure, but I loved it nonetheless.

"Here we go," I said as we pulled over to the stand. The trees came from tree farms upstate and even in Canada. I went to this stand every year, from a farm in Quebec. My favorite saleswoman remembered me from year to year.

"Hi, Annie! Welcome back!" I greeted her.

"Bonjour, Lane! Wonderful to see you. And who is *this?*" Her Quebec accent was instantly accentuated from her very French zeal for love affairs, making it sound like *Who izziss?* With my eyebrow cocked, I half-expected her to shout out *Ooh la la!*

"Annie, this is Finn Brodie."

"Hello, Annie, nice to meet you," said Finn as he shook her hand.

Annie returned the handshake with a silly smile, making me feel like an awkward ten-year-old who accidentally let it slip that she liked the cute boy at school. In a now even more pronounced French accent—the language of lovers—she said, "Ooh, Lane, you are getting a little tree for your little love nest, yes?"

I blushed immediately and furiously. I countered with a witty, "Er—"

Looking at me with unbridled amusement, Finn replied, "Yes."

Annie was delighted; clapping a little and bouncing, her winter hat with tassels dangling with glee as she bobbed up and down.

I gave up. "We'll take that one," I said as I pointed to a large blue spruce.

Annie handily tied it up and I paid her. Finn picked up the trunk end, I grabbed the top end, and we trooped off toward 80th Street. I could hear him laughing and mumbling, "Love nest, hmmm."

Since I hadn't really planned on this from the beginning of the night, I found myself carrying this large burden with high heels on instead of a stout pair of boots. We did just fine until we were going up our steep set of stairs to the front door of the townhouse. We turned the tree around so we could take it in trunk first. I set down my end near the bottom of the stairs, ran up and opened the front door, told Ripley to stay, and turned on a light in the foyer. I went back down to the bottom and lifted the tree again.

"Okay, here we go!" I said, and Finn started taking the tree in the front door.

The tree was *much* too wide. It was a very large fir tree.

Fingering his chin, Finn said, "Why don't we switch places? You go in first and direct it, I'll push from behind. I think we can make it."

So we switched places and I held the trunk. It got stuck about a foot or so into the doorway. Finn got a good grip of the trunk at the top and middle of the tree, and said, "One, two, three!"

Finn may have been stealthy like a cat, but when he decided to do something, he did it with great vigor. He shoved that tree in the door, and in it came like a freight train. I was barreled completely over, the tree rocketing over me, with Finn racing in the door utterly shocked that the tree had bust through so effortlessly.

I'll never forget the look of shock on his face and the loud, "Whoa!" that escaped his astonished lips. The tree shot past me, knocked over the table with the vase on it, and Finn landed with about as much grace as I did when I went plummeting down that sledding hill in Michigan. He landed with a couple of audible cracks of the branches, and then all was silent.

"Anything else I can help you with?" he asked from the floor.

That night we brought up several boxes from the basement that held our Christmas tree decorations. I opted for my slippers instead of the high heels. Once we got it into the stand, the tree was almost too much for the parlor, the tip just touching the ceiling.

Mr. Kirkland and Aunt Evelyn came home just in time, but I would have waited for them had they not. It's tradition. We first put up the lights and then set about hanging the ornaments. We had all sorts of ornaments from when I was a kid, mementos from little trips, to frames that held little pictures. We even had a few ornaments from my house in Rochester.

The fire was crackling, Christmas music was playing, and I sat on the couch for a minute just looking at the three of them while I sipped my coffee. It wasn't a spectacular moment, just normal and lovely, which made it even more divine. I looked at Finn, smiling and joking with Mr. Kirkland and Aunt Evelyn giving him a friendly clap on the back as he reached up high to place an ornament on a sparse section.

Finn must have felt my gaze because he looked over at me right at that second. His face broke out into that bright smile that I loved so much.

"What are you thinking, Lane?" he asked.

"Actually, I was thinking that we have a little problem."

"What's that?" he asked.

"Well, the tree fits in the room, just barely. And we haven't put the star on top yet."

"I can take care of that!" yelled Mr. Kirkland, which made us all jump. He darted out of the room, making Ripley bark in enthusiasm and run after him with a clatter of paws.

Aunt Evelyn, Finn and I all exchanged dubious glances. He came back in jauntily carrying a saw. But not just any saw, a powered circular saw.

"Uhh . . ." I said. "Are you sure about that?"

"Of course! Don't be silly, Lane. This is a piece of cake."

Aunt Evelyn just shrugged her shoulders. She *looked* unconcerned, but she *did* go over to the drinks cabinet and got a little restorative tot.

My feet were rooted to the spot as I watched Mr. Kirkland get the step stool, put it next to the tree, plug in the circular saw, and climb up the steps, saw in hand.

I tried again. "Uhh . . . I don't know about that—"

Finn said at the same time, "Hang on, how about—"

But as we both tried to voice our objections, the saw burst into action. Mr. Kirkland put the blade to the top about eight inches below the ceiling, and as it was only one little branch that was about three quarters of an inch thick, the saw went *ZIP* and the eight inches of branch went *ZING*. All the way across the room about twenty feet, smacking the wall with such force that there was a visible notch left in the plaster.

All our eyes had watched in fascination, our heads turning with a jerk to see the branch go zipping across the room and banging into the wall, and now they all slowly swiveled back to the satisfied and grinning Mr. Kirkland.

"See? Piece of cake!"

CHAPTER 55

About nine in the morning every Friday, the detectives from the NYPD gathered. Finn told me all about it, as I'd asked him all sorts of questions. All the arrested people had a chance to voice their opinion about their arrest. Then the surrounding detectives would decide if they would book 'em. It was a day that partly saddened Finn. Some people were so frustrated with their lot in life, the lost potential stark in their haunted eyes. Then there was the plain old fucked-up luck of others. And yet, there were moments that were hilarious. The smarter felons knew that with this audience, if they were a little witty, they might get a friendlier result as the detectives clarified the exact charges. The idea that this was a show, like I'd commented, was highlighted by the fact that there was a little stage and a microphone for the accused to speak into.

Finn would make his way over to the pub after this ritual. When I arrived, he and Miles were already seated. The smell of beer and peanuts permeated the air as my footsteps crunched through the hay on the old floorboards.

"Hi, Finn."

"Lane, I'd like you to meet Miles Havalaar."

"Miles, wonderful to finally meet you," I said as I held out my hand. I was a little worried that I might overwhelm the rather shy-looking Miles. He seemed to be a thoughtful man, who took his time and made careful, deliberate decisions. As he took a contemplative breath, his eyes smiled with a certain kind of glimmer. I was betting that he was quite a witty raconteur.

We chatted and I told them about some funny little events that happened at the office as the waitress brought over three baskets of crispy fried fish and heaping servings of French fries.

Over lunch, with the ice plenty broken, we started in on business. Miles first filled me in on his trip on the *Hindenburg*. Then Finn asked his questions. "So Miles, as you've been digging around both as yourself and as the millionaire within . . ." said Finn with a smirk. "Have you found out anything about that pawn piece and what it means exactly?"

With a grudging smile at the *millionaire within* comment, and because he was obviously pleased that he'd been able to pull it off, he replied, "Yeah, that little game piece is very interesting indeed."

I sat up straighter.

Miles continued in his slightly Cockney accent, "We all know that Rex used those as a kind of lethal calling card, but he was tied to his symbols in a deeper way than that. I think that's why he used the scroll design on that railing in the bridge in Central Park. And he loved the pawn. Everyone was a pawn to him. In fact, I've been wondering if we should not be asking *what* the pawn is, but *who*?"

Finn and I exchanged a glance, then Miles continued. "Anyway, Rex never had many pawns made at once. So, he had two on him when he was killed. Kirkland took one and your dad took the other, Lane, right? At that time, no one figured they meant anything but a tool to manipulate and bring fear to people. I don't know if he had any others. My guess is at most one more. But Rex was all about being bigger than just himself. I mean, he saw himself as the center of the universe, but he wanted this organization to be more than just a moneymaker. He wanted the Red Scroll Network to be something more than just another gang. He wanted his impact to last. Did you know he made everyone involved get a red scroll tattooed on them?"

I interjected, "I bet that's why they call Eliza Lady Red; it's not just her hair . . ." I had heard things about that little tattoo, and it was on a part of her anatomy that was rather unmentionable. I felt Finn looking at me closely right at that moment.

"Oh, I know where it's located," I chortled, completely unabashed.

Finn, trying unsuccessfully not to blush, asked another business question. "So, do you know why anyone would want those pawns now?"

Choosing not to pay any attention to our playful little interaction about the tattoo, Miles blithely went on, "I haven't found anything conclusive, but I have an educated guess that I'd be willing to bet big money on. Yeah, I think the pawn is a kind of an icon or symbol of Rex. I bet, that before he died, he set up something to ensure that his legacy would not only live beyond his mortal body, but that it would go to whomever he wished. Yeah, controlling things from the grave, like."

Finn said, "So you think the pawn is some sort of key to receiving the Rex Ruby legacy or inheritance?"

"Yes. Exactly."

"Makes sense," I said, as I bit off another bite of French fry with a snap of my teeth.

Miles said casually, almost to himself, "Yeah, and since the two silver guns have been missing . . . it has to be the pawns."

"What?" exclaimed Finn and I at the same time, both of our eyes snapping toward him. "What about those guns?" asked Finn.

Miles jumped at our sudden and loud response. Finn said, "Fill us in on what you know about the silver guns." We knew where they went, but we didn't know their story. Did Rex just have them made because he liked unique firearms? Or was there more purpose behind their design?

Miles shifted his eyes between the two of us and carried on where he left off. "Well . . . Rex had a silver gun with a red scroll on the handle for his own personal use. Everyone was deathly afraid of that gun; it was the one he used to execute people. Especially his own people who had failed him or particularly personal enemies. But the gun was actually a twin. There were two made." Finn and I both nodded. "He used one, and the word on the street was that he kept one at home. Unused. But like a treasure to him. They say he slept with it under his pillow. Might be that it's all just stories, but that's what I know."

I said, "Well, my dad got the one off him when he was killed. I have it now."

"*You* have one?" Miles exclaimed. "Can I see it sometime?" he asked with ghoulish interest.

"Uh . . ." I replied, with a look of uncertainty at Finn. "Sure."

Finn asked, "But no one knew where the second gun was?"

"Nope. Never heard of it after Rex was killed. Some say he was probably buried with it. And since I had never heard of Rex's own everyday gun being found by the Lorians, I figured no one else probably knew if it survived either."

I filled in some of the gaps of the story that we knew. "Well, we know where it was, at least. Somehow, Eliza had gotten her hands on the gun. We don't really know how, but now that we know her grandfather was Rex, the degrees of separation between her and that gun are fewer. But she lost it over the Queensboro Bridge a few months ago. It's possible it's still out there, I *feel* like it is, but there's no proof. For all intents and purposes, I think people would consider that one out of the picture. So, if no one heard about the silver gun my dad had, then I think we can safely assume that Donagan and Tucker were looking for the pawn. And now . . . Donagan has it."

Finn said, "What's puzzling is that it's been so quiet. If Donagan was able to get the inheritance with that pawn, I feel like he would have made that very known. It would be a monumental victory for him."

"Unless he's waiting for the perfect timing. Something is holding him back," I said.

While thoughtfully stroking his chin, Finn asked, "Say, Miles, have you heard of a Mr. Hambro working for or against the Red Scroll Network?"

Miles gave it some thought as he finished his pint. "No, doesn't ring a bell."

"Hmm," I said. "You're right, Finn. Hambro's wrapped up in this for sure. It shouldn't have surprised us, since he received that envelope. That picture my parents left in the safe just confirms that he's involved. Plus, don't forget Venetti. Miles, what about Louie Venetti? Do you know much about his connections?" I made sure to keep my voice nice and low while saying Venetti's name. Nothing brought terror to a place more than that man's name.

I considered the fact that Venetti had been awfully quiet and unusually absent for a quite a while now. Only surfacing that one time to extricate Val and me from a sticky situation. I was grateful Venetti had kept an eye on us, but then again . . . It was Uncle Louie. *The* Uncle Louie. *Strange kind of benefactor.*

Miles finished his pint, then said, "No, I really don't. I mean, I've been in this business for a long time. However, most of my work was in Europe."

I was making figure eights on the wooden tabletop with my middle finger as I thought about the many players and motives in this mystery. "Business, huh?" I said to mostly to myself. Then louder, I said, "Well, try this on for size. Venetti has always been about business. What if that's what's linking them all together? What if Venetti isn't really an ally, but let's just say that we all fall on the same side right now. The Red Scroll Network would have threatened his business, so with an eye out for remaining the big guy in town, what if he worked with my parents against Rex?"

The men both nodded as they thought that through. "Still doesn't explain why he's had an eye on *me*," I continued, "but it might explain some of his involvement."

Finn added, "And Hambro has been a powerful businessman for quite a while. I highly doubt he was an agent like Kirkland and your parents, but what if he just gave information to the authorities whenever he heard of dubious things going on in the high-roller world?"

"That's definitely a possibility," I said.

We all finished our lunch, a little more thoughtful and less talkative than when we started out. We had come up with some good theories and now we needed to think about where to take it from here.

CHAPTER 56

After that most intriguing lunch with Miles, I was back at City Hall trying hard to concentrate on the work at hand. I started to put some press packets together, hoping that while I worked on that menial task I could think through a few things.

I made my way down the assembly line of stacks of papers to be included, collating the materials over and over again. My mind then drifted with a wry smile to my morning meeting. My weekly standing appointment with Miss Morgan, spy kid extraordinaire. Apparently. We'd had a most interesting conversation.

I had found her waiting outside, leaning up against the soda shop, wearing a smug, impish grin.

"Don't rub it in, Morgan," I said in greeting.

"Oh, I'll be rubbing it in for *quite* a while," she said, enjoying every moment of being my rescuer the night of the ball.

"Okay, in you go. Let's get your morning ice cream."

Over the turkey sandwich that I made her consume before the ice cream that she desired above all else, she let me in on how that plan had come about. She told me that Finn had run into her right before the ball. He had heartily laughed when he found out that Morgan had taken upon herself the role of daytime body-guard for me. Word on the street had been that Donagan was out to get me. Given her own past with that crew, she was honestly worried about me, at which she blushed and I grinned. So, she and her band of little urchins took shifts in watching me go to work and come home at night. I couldn't believe that I hadn't spotted her.

She'd said, "Oh I was careful to stay out of eyesight, knowing you'd spot me. But you didn't know some of my friends, yet. And I have to say, I was mighty glad to run into Finn when I did. I was starting to get the feeling that *even I* was getting out of my depth."

"Even you . . . hard to imagine," I'd responded with a roll to my eyes.

"Yeah," she'd said, completely missing my sarcasm. "I know. So, I told him everything and he came up with the plan for watching the perimeter around the ball." I had almost laughed outright when she used the word *perimeter*, sounding like a military guard. I put my napkin up to my mouth to hide my smile.

"Well, I can't thank you enough for helping me out, Morgan. Really." At which her chest puffed up proudly, as a shy look simultaneously crossed her face. I wondered if anyone had ever told her "thank you" and "job well done."

"So, you know how to make a petrol bomb, huh?" I was snickering, thinking that Finn must have helped out with that.

But no. She'd prattled on most frighteningly, "Yes. I read about petrol bombs this summer in an article about the Spanish Civil War. They used 'em against the Soviet tanks. Actually, if you want a bigger explosion, the fumes of gasoline are the best over the whiskey bottles we used. You fill a tank only about an inch or so. It's the fumes that make a good explosion, y'know. If you want a longer burn, you use more gasoline so it gets all over everything. But if you're not careful, the fire can go up real fast; gasoline is so volatile. If you want a really good burn, you have to use fuel from a smoker. You know, the gas for one of those diesel trucks. Not as flammable, but burns real long." At that point I'd started choking so hard, she'd pulled an Aunt Evelyn and started smacking me on the back.

I laughed quietly to myself as I finished up my last packet. Happily tamping them all together and stacking them on my desk, I turned to see Fiorello walking past.

"You busy, Chief?" I asked.

"Always. But come on in," he replied and I brought my chair into his office. I filled him in on everything that Miles had discussed with us and the resulting theories. But I had a lot of questions. "Fio, it still doesn't explain anything about Hambro. I mean, I can't see a motive anywhere. And Marty's death was deliberate, not just a mugging gone wrong, or something. What do you think?"

Fio rubbed his forehead. "You ask a lot of questions."

I gave him a disgruntled look and said, "You make that sound like it's a nuisance . . ." My sentence died on my lips as I thought of something.

"What, Lane?"

"You know, the last time Roarke and I saw Marty alive, he said that he was determined. That he'd be asking a lot more questions. What if he made a nuisance of himself? What if he got in the way of some business deal going down?"

"Now that's a possibility, Lane."

I also offered one last tasty tidbit to see what he would do with it—to test a funny little hunch I had about Hambro. My mind kept going back to those photographs of him and Mrs. Hambro and I wondered if he hadn't really vanished, but was just *hiding*, let's say. In the best place to hide: plain sight. I thought I'd say something to Fio, to see if he'd take the bait. If he did, I'd follow him and see what happened. I just felt that he knew more than he was letting on. "You know, Fio, I was thinking that I might have a theory about Mr. Hambro. He may be closer than we think. I need to digest it a little more, but I'll get back with you as soon as I develop it a little bit." He tried to finagle more details out of me, but I would not say another word.

Later that day I followed Fio on his way home. *He took the bait.* I found Fio talking on the sly to someone who looked very intriguing indeed.

CHAPTER 57

Tucker was alone at the side of a brazier, warming his hands for a moment's respite on his way home. There was no one left to talk to. Fate had run its course and he was left alone. It had never bothered him before. But now, well . . . He had emotions he didn't—couldn't—understand. He continued his job on Wall Street, needing to do something constructive. He wasn't safe in the apartment he used to call home, so he moved to a small, insignificant motel. He needed to be quick and agile.

He had started to feel like a cornered animal. Eliza had clearly taken sides with Donagan and if what he heard on the street was right, Donagan had beat him to the gold pawn. All his dreams of attaining Rex's legacy were going down the drain. With a sudden burst of anger, he turned and savagely punched the wooden side of a cart that had stopped right next to him on the street. The pain in his hand cleared his head and he actually liked the ache it left behind. It was real. He understood it. He could do something about it and it just plain felt good to take his anger out on something.

If only Lane hadn't turned away from him. *God*, he was livid about it. He wanted her like no one else. And she was *this close*, he thought, feeling the anger rising. And she slipped away. *Damn it.* He turned and with the other fist, struck the cart yet again, making its horse shimmy at the bump. Both fists now bloody, he rubbed his hands over the fire, unaware of the drips of blood that dropped into the flames with a small hiss.

She had turned so easily from him. Yet he had seen inside her, and it was not all sunshine and roses. There was darkness in there. *Just like me.* But somehow, she turned from it. From him. He hated this feeling of impotence. He wanted revenge. He wanted to do something. And if he couldn't have her, no one could.

Just then, the hackles on his neck rose and a presence made itself known. He felt it before he heard him. "Hello, Donagan," he said with a curl to his lip, unable or unwilling to mask his distaste.

"Hello, Tucker," Donagan said with a lick to his lips.

"What can I do for you, Connell?"

"Actually, it's what I can do for you."

"Yeah, right."

"Hear me out, don't hear me out. I don't fucking care. I have what I want, but since a certain *someone* who loves red shoes has been such an irritation to me, I thought I'd have a little fun with her. And I thought you might want in on that action."

Tucker's ears perked up at that. Donagan got the pawn he so desperately wanted, what should have been his. And maybe being in league with him on something would draw him just a bit closer to connive a way to get it back. And have Lane get her just desserts? Yeah, he'd be interested in that.

Donagan could see Tucker's interest before Tucker even understood it. A sneer tugged at his marred lips. He pulled at his hat, bringing it down slightly more on his right side. He puffed up his chest, knowing they were all going to fall quite nicely into his little trap. The power of it was intoxicating. He deserved the Rex Ruby legacy. He *was* the legacy. He just needed to get the others out of the way. *All* the others.

"All right, Tucker, here's the plan. I have this little shack of a house, got it just for this meeting to take place . . ." Tucker listened to the cunning plan, the plan where he could get rid of Finn Brodie and put Lane in her place. But in such a way that opened a small window of opportunity to have her to himself one day. One day . . .

CHAPTER 58

Over dinner that night with Aunt Evelyn, Mr. Kirkland, and Roarke, who had stopped over, I filled them in on the hypothesis about the pawn from what Miles told us, and the theory that Venetti and Hambro were perhaps involved with the Red Scroll Network with business as their motivation.

After taking a bite of the pork chops covered in sautéed onions and apples, Roarke said, "I think that all sounds pretty reasonable. What next? How do we find Donagan?"

Mr. Kirkland replied, "Well, I don't know that we'll need to do anything."

Aunt Evelyn added in, "What he means to say is, *Lane*, don't do anything."

"Hey!" I exclaimed indignantly. But I didn't defend that position, I had already begun to think of ways that would drum up some action.

Roarke replied, "Yeah, I also believe that with Mr. Hambro, no news is actually good news. Whatever Mrs. Hambro says, I think she knows more than she thinks she knows or thinks she can reveal. Either way, I don't get the feeling he's in imminent danger. As far as Donagan is concerned, he's been awfully quiet, but that's going to end soon. It has to. He'll act on it."

Right then, the clamor that is Fiorello came bursting into the house. Ripley greeted him and ushered him into the kitchen. He looked longingly at the last remaining pork chop on the platter, but

Mr. Kirkland had already popped up and retrieved a piping hot plate from the oven (he often did that, *someone* was bound to drop in unexpectedly). He set it before Fio's place and received a wide grin of appreciation from that party.

Fio dug into the delectable meal, stopping only to say a quick, "What'd I miss?"

Roarke quickly filled him in on what we'd been discussing. I put my chin in my hand and looked at Fio closely, trying to discern anything that his face might give away, ready to pounce.

Fio took a big swig of his wine and said, "I agree. I don't think we need to do much, something is about to turn up. I think we should all be on our guard, though. I highly doubt that Donagan is just going to take whatever he finds from the pawn and go retire to Monaco. Although one can always hope."

Later that night after everyone went home, I was reading by the fireplace in the parlor when the doorbell rang. I got to the door just as quick as Ripley, who looked at me in annoyance as if I had taken his pivotal moment in the spotlight.

I opened the door to a frigid blast of winter wind. "Hey, Finn, come on in."

"Hi, love. Thanks." I gave him a quick kiss; his cheek was freezing and he smelled like winter. I took his coat and even though he hadn't been wearing gloves, his hands were as warm as if he'd been sitting with me by the fire.

I took him to the parlor and we sat down on the floor right in front of the fireplace, next to the colorful Christmas tree. Mr. Kirkland hollered from the kitchen if we'd like a cup of coffee and I yelled back that yes, we would.

"Did you get something to eat, Finn?"

"No, didn't have time."

"Okay, hold that thought." I left him and ran to the kitchen to make him a plate. I put the plate and the two coffees on a tray and made my way back. Finn's eyes were drawn to the heavily laden tray and he jumped up to help.

He started eating as I fixed my coffee with cream and sugar. As I stirred it, I thought about my confirmed hunch, with that interesting person I'd seen Fio talking with. I went back and forth in my mind deciding if I'd let Finn in on what I learned. I did like a good reveal. But I decided to tell him all about it, his eyebrows almost shooting off his amused face.

After a good chuckle, he said, "Hey, Lane, I wanted to tell you, I have a new case at work and I might be out of touch a little bit the next week."

"Oh yeah? Anything to do with *our* case?" I asked with a tilt to my head.

"Surprisingly, no," he chuckled. He told me of a particularly intriguing bank heist and how he needed to go undercover, not deep cover or anything too dicey, but to talk with some of his informants to get the word on the street about this gang that seemed a little more intelligent and patient than most bank robbers. It sounded kind of fun, pretending to be someone you weren't. Living in a world that wasn't real. For a while.

"Can I get word to you if I need you?" I asked.

His eyes met mine, a deeper connection happening than I had actually intended. "You need me, Lane?" he asked in his accent that was all his own.

And in that instant, it hit home just how much I needed and wanted him. I looked in his dark eyes, and saw reflected there the same awareness. He put down his coffee cup and shifted over next to me where I had been leaning back on my hands, my legs stretched out in front of me, ankles crossed. He put his arm around the small of my back and pulled me over so that I was sitting next to him on the other side, my legs draped across his lap. His other arm came around me and enveloped me in the warmest, most content embrace. Completely intertwined with each other, his lips naturally came down to mine.

When we pulled apart, just a little, I whispered, "Yeah. I need you, Finn."

"I need you, too," he whispered with a smile. "And you will *always* be able to get a hold of me. I might not be around in my usual sense, but I'll be keeping an eye on you."

CHAPTER 59

I lay in bed that night thinking. Deliberating and tossing around in the sheets. Some things had come together, but back in Michigan, why were my mother and father in a photograph with Rutherford Franco, a man who was supposed to be an enemy? And how could I figure it out?

The only other person who might know more was Uncle Louie. Who *also* was in that wretched picture with my parents. They were all in this together for some reason. And what exactly was Venetti's role? If I was normal, I would stay away from him. But I wasn't normal. Well, let's say average. Average sounded better. A well-known banker, a gangster, a master villain's son, and my parents. What did they all have in common?

At work the next day I had lunch with Valerie and Roxy, to try to sort out everything. It was complex to say the least, with mixed motivations and agendas all over the place.

"I think you should talk with Venetti," blurted out Roxy.

Valerie almost spit out the soda she had just gulped, and I almost tipped over in my chair as I had been leaning back while deep in thought.

After Val stopped choking, she said, "No. Absolutely not."

"Says the girl who stomped into his *home office* a couple months ago to have a little chat," I said sarcastically.

Roxy chuckled. Val said, "That was different. You were nowhere to be found and he was my last resort. It was life and death, Lane!"

"I know, I know," I said in a placating tone. "Don't worry, I'm not that desperate yet. But can you think of anyone or any way to help me figure out Rutherford's role?"

"What about Daphne?" asked Roxy.

"No." I was never—ever—going back to Metropolitan Hospital to visit the horrible creature that was Tucker and Eliza's mother, and Rutherford's wife. She scared the hell out of me, tried to kill me as a child, and hated me with a cutting bitterness. Roarke and I went to try to get some information from her only once, but I'd never forget her long white-blond hair, and the way her face was a mask of hateful rage. "Not a possibility. Besides, in her mental capacity, you'd never know what was truth and what wasn't."

"How about that Miles character?" asked Val.

"Yeah, that's a possibility. He's on his way back to London now, but there are some roots of the Red Scroll people there. Maybe I could ask him to dig around. He's already retrieved a good amount of information, but I don't know if he's exhausted all his resources. I'll send him a telegram today," I said. Sure couldn't hurt. Only when all my resources were taxed would I consider a meeting with Venetti.

It was not only possible, but quite likely that he might have had a hand in the hit on my parents. I was able to look at the details of the case with a logical mind when I was keeping busy, but if I left my mind to drift . . . a savage hatred of the person behind their deaths was lurking right beneath the surface.

When I was honest with myself, I hated Venetti. I hated him if he put out the hit. But I also hated that he had come to my rescue enough, why couldn't he have done something about my parents? If he was so high and mighty, and they were in league with him to some extent, then he must have known what was going on. And either was incapable of helping, or uncaring. I despised both.

Ralph interrupted my thoughts as he came bopping into the conference room where we had decided to eat our lunch.

"Hey, girls!" he chirped. I nodded to Roxy.

She dove in, "Ralph, how are ya? What are y—"

"Well, gals, I got a lot goin' on this weekend. Whattaya say we all meet up for the Rockettes' show, then maybe some dancing at the Ricochet Club? They fixed up the place after that big shooting a few months ago. All the guys are in jail, and well . . . that's where the name Ricochet came from anyway, that's hilarious, right?"

As he took a breath I quickly burst out at top speed, "Sounds great, Ralph! I think we should meet up ahead of time for a bite to eat and then head to the Rockettes, should be—"

"Yeah! That's great, let's plan it. See you all later!" he said, and raced out the door.

Val looked at us with a smirk.

Roxy and I were simultaneously counting on our fingertips the number of words we each spoke.

"You win, Lane! Nice one." She delicately reached into her purse—I was glad it wasn't in her bosom—and took out a dollar. We clinked our soda bottles to seal the deal.

CHAPTER 60

"Are the messages all ready?" asked Donagan.

"Yes. I have it all arranged. This is the week, Donny," said Eliza as she slithered behind him, rubbing his shoulders in that way he enjoyed most. "Lane and Finn won't expect a thing. And if Fiorello happens to get in the way, even better."

"Excellent. We will have everything we've ever wanted *soon*." He could barely contain his excitement. It was gloriously eating him alive. And he let it. The control, the power, the lust. It was delectable.

And none of them knew what was coming for them.

CHAPTER 61

The following day, late in the afternoon, a message came from Finn. He said he had a break in his case and asked to meet me in the evening at a small house on the Lower East Side. I was excited to see him so unexpectedly. And I wanted to run by him the thoughts I had about Venetti and trying to find out more about Rutherford from Miles. I was disappointed that I hadn't heard back from Miles already. It felt like the clock was ticking down and we needed that information before Donagan got his legacy and began, what? A whole new era of a gangster more powerful than any other?

And I'd get a few minutes with Finn. Because of that, it was hard to concentrate on work. Fio was in a funny mood. He kept winking at me knowingly. He had such an affinity for the dramatic! Honestly, he should have been in Hollywood. If he didn't have such a deep passion for government, he would have been a splendid actor.

The time finally trickled to the appointed seven o'clock. I took the elevated train downtown, then walked toward the house on the Lower East Side. I knew most of the city like the back of my hand, but I wasn't too sure about this particular area; not only unsure of where I was going, but also not liking the look of the place. Or maybe it was just the night.

It was cold and damp, the penetrating bitterness of the sidewalk seeping right through the soles of my shoes into my bones. There was no moon, no sense of cheeriness in looking up to see that pure white crescent peering down. The city was always bright, unlike the countryside, so at least I could still see quite well. But the atmosphere was dank and raw.

I finally saw the little house that was slightly more than a shack up ahead.

I was only a block away and I could see Finn's shadow in the house, moving around in the low light. His silhouette looking around, probably making sure the house was clear like the good detective he was. But then a woman stepped out of a car parked next to the house. She had long red hair. It was Eliza. She held a machine gun in her hands. Then she leveled it right at the house. At Finn.

Eliza put her finger on the trigger of the machine gun and the world completely stopped. I was too far away, too helpless, too slow. Finn was going to die. Right in front of my eyes. She lifted her chin, her very stance godlike. The ability with the flick of her wrist to give life—and to take it away. She slowly pulled the trigger.

"Nooooo!" I screamed. I started to run, hardly able to keep from stumbling and falling in rage and utter fear, the bullets ripping into the building.

Something suddenly bowled into me, shoving me to the ground. Then another great thump landed on me, bringing tears to my eyes as I felt a crack in my ribs. After an eternity came silence. Everything was black, a pain shooting in my side, I could barely breathe. Then everything slowly lifted.

I smelled him, felt him before I could really see him.

"Oh God, Finn. You're okay."

"Are you all right, Lane?" he asked with a desperate voice.

"Yes, I'm okay."

"Fio, you can get up now," said Finn.

In the semidarkness, Valerie and Roarke came running up to us.

Valerie yelled breathlessly, "I knew it! I knew something wasn't right. Are you guys okay? I saw the house, you told me about your rendezvous. Then the gun went off . . ."

We all slowly swiveled our eyes over to the ruined house. Eliza's ammunition was completely spent, the gun tossed aside. I just glimpsed the back of Eliza's coat as she entered the house, when a savage scream tore into the silent night. Whoever was in there, it wasn't who she thought it would be. Could it be . . . ? No. That wasn't possible. Was it?

I started to say, "I think it's—" but was cut off as we saw two forms stagger to the front of the door, holding each other up.

It was Eliza and Tucker. *My God.* She had gunned down her own brother.

As they started to drag themselves toward her car, we slowly made our way nearer. Then a huge ruckus attacked us from the left.

"Get down! Get down! Lady! Get down!"

We all stopped and a small posse of ragtag urchins was running toward us, all yelling at the top of their lungs. I saw one head above all the rest: Morgan.

She yelled a commanding, "Get down NOW!"

All of us instantly dropped to the ground as an earsplitting explosion roared over us. Intense heat roiling through the air, the thunder almost unbearable even as I'd covered my head. Then a silence that was heavy and muffled, things sprinkling down on top of us like hot, hard rain. Then everything went black.

CHAPTER 62

I felt someone lift me up off the ground. I took a deep breath and enjoyed the comfort of his chest. I felt a sharp pain in my side, but it wasn't too bad. My ears were ringing. Then he set me down, leaning me up against something sturdy.

"I'm okay, Finn. Thanks," I said rather dreamily. I could see him, he was talking to me, but it was hard to hear him. There was smoke everywhere, people running. I quickly scanned the area for my friends. All of us at this one spot. All of us in terrible danger. A hand turned my chin to look into his eyes. My hearing started to come back slowly.

His muffled voice said, "They're all okay."

But off to the side I caught a glimpse of Morgan as she staggered, then fell to the ground. Roarke had been coming over toward us and saw her, too. He yelled to Finn and me, "I got her!" while running over to her and dropping to a knee. His hand gently pushed the hair from her forehead and I could see him trying to talk to her. I let out a breath as I saw her nod. He gently picked her up and carried her as if she weighed nothing at all. He set her down on the curb and sat down next to her, giving us the *okay* sign.

I smiled, then touched that pain in my side. My fingers came up. They had blood on them. "Oh, bugger," I said.

Finn carefully lifted my blouse on the side where the blood came from. "Something jabbed me when I landed on the ground. I don't think it's bad. You knocked me to the ground when Eliza shot up the building, but then what happened?"

"Fio," was all he said.

"Ah. Got it."

"It looks okay. There's a small puncture, probably from a stick or something on the ground. You had about four hundred pounds of man land on top of you. I guess you're lucky that's all that's wrong with you. How many fingers am I holding up?" he asked. I counted carefully just to be sure.

"Three."

"Good," he said softly, and exhaled, relieved. Then he looked at me. Really looked at me.

"I have to say, I think I'm actually a little tired of adventure at the moment," I said. He softly laughed, which made me laugh, then wince in pain.

"Come here." He pulled me gently toward him, wrapping his arms around me, my head resting on his chest and his shoulder. We sat there for a long time, letting everyone else handle everything.

I looked over at the front of the shabby little house, torn apart, hundreds of shiny casings sprinkled on the ground in a macabre shine of glitter. Tucker and Eliza were nowhere to be seen.

CHAPTER 63

After a lot of rigmarole, we were able to usher everyone back to headquarters. That is . . . my house. Shortly after the explosion, Mr. Kirkland and Evelyn had shown up at the scene along with the police and fire department. Shockingly, none of us had been hurt more than surface scratches and bruises. The medics looked at my puncture and cleaned it up. I didn't need any stitches, it was just uncomfortable. We had them take a look at Morgan, too, much to her chagrin. But she was fine, just a bit disoriented from the explosion.

Evelyn and Kirkland took charge of us and the Irregulars who had been our warning about the car bomb. I watched as they corralled the little rascals and coaxed them to come back to our place. Once they started calling our home "headquarters," the little adventure-seeking devils were more than willing to accompany us. Of course, it was also under the assumption that there would be food and treats aplenty.

After a great number of miracles in organization, we all made it back, cleaned up, filled our plates with food that seemed to magically appear, filled up coffee cups and glasses with more medicinal beverages, and all of us sat down in our parlor. We squashed ourselves in, making an outer ring of adults with an inner circle of kids sitting cross-legged on the floor.

The kids, about eight in number, ranged in all manner of sizes, ethnicities, and ages. Although with their general griminess they all looked a lot alike. I noticed with a grin hidden behind my hand that Captain Morgan sat in the outer ring with the other adults. The urchins had been reluctant to enter our house. But once they made it to the top of the stairs and the delicious scents of hot hamburgers, sugary baked beans, and warm brownies in the oven wafted over, they made no bones about it.

After an exceedingly long period of disorganized and excited yelling from the children and Fio, Morgan gave us the lowdown. While holding a coffee cup in her hand, she began a thorough account. "Well, we were still on assignment from Finn. We had been following you, Lane. We are very familiar with the Lower East Side, and we had known about that particular shack. In fact, several of our group had used it for a place to sleep on more than one occasion. Once you made your way to Cherry and Clinton Streets, we had an inkling of where you were headed. There had been some rumors of some big gangsters scoping it out. You know I don't believe in coincidences . . . So we split up, one team staying with you, Lane, and the others going ahead to the shack. They had seen a man, who turned out to be Tucker, enter the building first, a good ten minutes before you got near the place."

She nodded to the other tall kid, her lieutenant, I supposed, and said, "Spry, I mean Eric, was in charge of the team that went to the shack."

The tall, good-looking kid with serious eyes sat opposite Morgan, the only other of the Irregulars to sit with the grown-ups. He had his elbows resting on bent knees, taking in every detail of our meeting. I watched Eric look around the room, scrutinizing each one of us. He'd finished his entire plate and as Morgan nodded to him he spoke up. "One of our best scouts, Connor there, had split off from the group by the house and had gone far off to the side to keep watch."

Connor was the freckled rascal with a big grin, showing one tooth missing. He looked like he'd be the class clown. But as soon as Eric mentioned him, he got down to business. He looked like a playful spaniel, cute and goofy until the moment his master had him on the hunt. Then he was on point, competent and professional. His big brown eyes looked up at Eric. "Connor was the one that noticed

Eliza's car there. She had driven up slowly and quietly just after Tucker had arrived at the house."

Connor chimed in, "Yeah! I was just about to report back that a suspicious car was there, but just as I was about to leave, I spotted a shadowy guy creeping over to the car, staying close to the ground. The man reached up under the side of the car with something bulky in his hand and when he pulled back his hand, the box or whatever it was, was gone. I knew it was a bomb. As soon as the guy left, I booked it over to Morgan."

My eyes shifted to her and I saw a look of fear slide across her face as she remembered that message being delivered. She cleared her throat. "But before I could run to intercept you, Lane, Eliza blasted the house. There was so much going on at once—it was crazy! I saw Finn tackle Lane, then Fio jumped on to the pile. Afterward, I watched Eliza enter the house, heard the scream, and then saw Roarke and Val running to you. Then I remembered the car bomb. And you guys had started to walk *toward the house* where the car was parked. Toward the bomb!" She shook her head like she couldn't believe our ineptitude.

Having told their story in full, they started happily cramming their mouths with more food. I looked around the room and every one of us adults had the same shocked look of disbelief on our faces.

After we all ate our fill of good, honest, homey food, we asked the kids if they wanted to stay the night; they could camp out in the little room off the kitchen. They politely declined saying that they already had plans. When I cocked an eyebrow at Morgan, she smiled slyly at me. I gave her a hug, said thank you, and we set up our next appointment for our morning ice cream.

After the Irregulars departed, we adults arranged ourselves in a circle around the fire, all holding our cups of hot coffee. I sat on the floor in front of Finn, Ripley lying next to me as I rubbed his sides and soft head, playing with his pointy ears. Finn occasionally stroked my hair, letting it slip through his fingers. It felt sweet and comforting.

Roarke started the conversation we were dying to get to. "So, how did we all end up at the house?"

I spoke up first. "I got a message from Finn asking to meet me down there."

Finn said, "I got a message from Lane asking me to meet there."

Evelyn asked, "But you didn't write them? Do you think Eliza could copy your handwriting?"

I nodded. "She knows what my writing looks like and she copied Roxy's perfectly once. There's no doubt that she was capable. I'm sure Finn's wasn't exact, but she was careful to keep the note very short, so I didn't think for a second that it wasn't from him. With him being undercover at the moment, I was just happy to have a time to meet."

"Same here," said Finn. "But how did you and Roarke get there?" he asked Val.

"I called him," replied Val. "Something just didn't seem right. And here we'd been waiting for something to happen—it just seemed fishy. So I thought we should try to follow you. I would have just said something right to you, Lane, but you had gone already by the time I decided that we needed to do something. I knew where you were going because you told me earlier."

"Fio, what about you?" I asked.

"I got a message from you, Lane, that asked me to meet you there, too," he said. No wonder he'd been winking at me conspiratorially all day.

I summed it up as I thought out loud, "So other than Roarke and Val, who were smarter than the rest of us . . . we were all supposed to be there. It looks like Eliza was going to take out whoever was supposed to be in the shack; certainly, she supposed that was going to be me and Finn. But someone else obviously put the car bomb in place, I'm thinking to take out as many of us as possible. But it was also meant for Eliza. It was *mostly* meant for Eliza. And she definitely didn't know Tucker was there."

Mr. Kirkland gruffly spoke up for the first time, "Seems to me . . . Donagan was getting his competition out of the way."

Roarke added, "And now he can do whatever he needs to do, using that pawn he's been working so hard to get his hands on."

"But he didn't really get Tucker and Eliza out of his way, now did he?" I said.

"He might not know that," said Evelyn, her chin resting in her hand.

"Well, he certainly made two vicious enemies. A woman scorned . . ." I said with an appreciative whistle.

"Tucker might not make it, by the looks of how she shredded that house," said Finn.

"He was well enough to stagger outside," said Kirkland. "That crew doesn't go down easy."

"Hmph," said Evelyn and Finn at the same time.

After a long pause where I imagine we were all reflecting on the spectacular events, Aunt Evelyn started making sounds of the evening coming to an end.

"Uh, well, Aunt Evelyn, I think we need to talk about one more thing. Seeing that Donagan is going to be making some sort of move, there are a few loose ends that need tying up."

"Well, dear, I don't know that we have anything new . . ." said Aunt Evelyn with a yawn.

I turned back to Finn and tapped him on the knee. "You ready?"

"Yup," he said, getting up and gingerly helping me to my feet.

"We'll be right back," I said. Fio started to splutter and wave his arms about. I winked at him and said, "Relax, we'll be just a minute."

Finn and I got our coats on and went outside walking hand in hand to the end of the street where Lexington picked up.

"You really feeling all right, Lane? How's your side?" asked Finn, putting his arm around my shoulders.

"Oh yes, merely a scratch," I said, chuckling, then wincing. "Well, it's a bit more than a scratch, actually," I murmured, carefully touching my side. "I wonder what Donagan's going to do now. And if it will have ramifications for us."

"Well, I think he really couldn't care less about us as far as his business and his money are concerned. We never had a stake in his legacy. I think we were thrown into the scene tonight to draw Eliza in and hey, if we got killed along with them, the more the merrier," he said darkly.

"True. But I can't help wanting him to get his just desserts. He makes my skin crawl. When he came at me—"

"He came at you?" he asked sharply.

"That night when they grabbed me and Fio. But Morgan and her friends disrupted his plans. He is an evil man, Finn."

"Yeah, he is." He stopped and turned toward me. "We'll take care of him. Somehow." He kissed my forehead. I saw the vendor for roasted peanuts and hot coffee up ahead on the corner.

I smiled up at Finn and nodded. "Wanna get a cup of coffee?"

"Yes. Yes, I do."

We went up to the smiling vendor, chattering away with a young couple who had been heading down Lexington. He handed them their bag of peanuts and then turned to us as the couple walked away.

In a heavy Cockney accent he asked, "Now, what can oy get you loverly folks tonoyt?"

Finn took out his gun, leveled it at him, and said, "You're going to come with us. Right now."

CHAPTER 64

We entered our house with me leading the way, then the vendor, then Finn bringing up the rear, gun still drawn. We trooped into the parlor and as our group took in our grand entrance, I got the pleasure of seeing their shocked faces all at once. They scrambled to their feet, Kirkland and Roarke bracing themselves.

Even Fio was shocked into silence. For once. It was so gratifying.

I cleared my throat and said, "We found someone we think can help us answer questions. A lot of questions." I turned to the vendor, who had turned a deep shade of crimson. "You can put your hands down now." Finn put his gun away as he laughed to himself. I turned to the group and said, "I'd like you all to meet . . . Mr. Hambro."

They all sat down with an exhausted *whoosh*. Evelyn said an appropriate, "Good Lord."

Fio finally found his voice. "Finn! What was the gun all about?"

Finn, taking a rare pleasure, said, "Oh, I was just messing with him. And you." At that Kirkland emitted a growl of a laugh, startling Ripley from his spot where he had just hunkered down.

I looked at Mr. Hambro and decided to have mercy on him. I got up and poured him a good tumbler of whiskey, took him by the arm, and led him over to a chair by the fire. "Come on, Man of a Thousand Faces . . ." I said with a soft laugh. "Take a load off." At which he did. He sat down with a grateful glance at the deep amber liquid I had handed him. He had such a weary look of a burdensome weight being finally lifted off his shoulders, that I felt a little sheepish that Finn and I had scared him so soundly.

I smiled kindly at him. "Mr. Hambro, we want to hear your whole story, but I, uh . . . I'm sorry if Finn and I . . ."

He looked up at me then, eyes bright and mouth twitching. "Are you kidding me? You scared the shit out of me! Oops, sorry for the language, Evelyn. But that was the biggest surprise I've had in years!" He started to laugh long and hard and I was a tiny bit concerned that he had gone off the deep end. I looked over at Fio, who had by now fully recovered, and *he* was laughing and shaking so hard that he was wiping the tears from his eyes.

When Fio managed to stop laughing, he said, "I've never seen you so scared, Hambro. That look on your face was priceless!"

"All right, you two," said Aunt Evelyn, with a shake of her head like a half-amused, half-disgusted parent at finding her two little boys had been up to no good. "Get on with it."

The mayor of New York City and the president of one of the most distinguished banks in the country finally collected themselves enough, after much wiping of eyes and nudging of elbows at each other, to tell us the story.

Mr. Hambro now sat upright and cleared his throat, looking all of a sudden like the formidable businessman that he was despite his pauper's clothing. He took a deep breath and a drink, preparing his thoughts for a moment. "Well, as you know, this all started when I received one red envelope at home, then another at the bank just before I disappeared. Those envelopes had a threatening message in it, telling me that the Red Scroll was back, that they were watching. Back in the day, Rex Ruby used to send those out to a variety of people and they only conveyed one of two messages: Either he wanted your cooperation in a business matter, or it was probably your last day on earth."

Kirkland spoke up, "Yeah, and I hadn't seen one since we were working in the war."

"I know. Me too," said Hambro. "That's why I felt the need to disappear and discover what was really going on. I knew Rex had been killed, and I also felt that the message didn't have the same . . . *feel* that his had. I figured something was going on with someone trying to take his place. But I was also worried about my wife. I figured if he thought I was gone, he might leave her alone. At least it would give me time to figure out what was going on."

"Did your wife know?" I asked.

"No, I didn't tell her. But I decided to leave her a message of sorts. I didn't want to tell her outright where I was, I didn't want to make her more of a target, but I needed her to know I was all right. I put a bag of chestnuts and a hot chocolate on her doorstep two days in a row. She knows I hate chestnuts and we have this ongoing joke about it . . . I try them every year, thinking that maybe one day I'll like them. I never do. I hoped it would work." A look of pained frustration raced across his face. Their relationship was a deep, sweet friendship. You didn't see that kind of marriage often enough.

"She did know you were all right. It worked," I said encouragingly. "When Roarke and I visited her a second time, she didn't know where you were, but there was something different about her. I knew something had happened; she knew something. But at the same time, it also seemed like she wasn't lying: she hadn't *really* heard from you or seen you. But she was . . . hopeful," I said, groping for words.

He smiled and took a deep breath. To get back on track I asked, "So who do you think sent the red envelopes?"

"I thought it had to be someone who used to be involved with the Red Scroll Network. But those people were few and far between. With Rex's death, then Rutherford's . . . not to mention I'd never really known who this heir was supposed to be . . ."

"Hold on, did you know Rutherford Franco?" asked a perplexed Kirkland.

Mr. Hambro took a thoughtful, slow swig of his whiskey. He tilted his head as he considered. Then he slowly brought a hand up to his face and began peeling away a small sliver of extra eyebrow hair, first the left, then the right. "Well . . . let me tell you what I know."

I looked at Mr. Kirkland, who looked surprised and maybe miffed. I had been wondering about what he knew and what he wasn't telling me. He and my father had been thick as thieves, but it seemed my dad had kept some things back from him.

As Hambro's story slowly played out, he meticulously removed different parts of his disguise. The remarkable thing was that each little piece was hardly anything in and of itself, just a sliver of hair or an edging of skin-toned putty. But when applied to the right part of the face, at the precise angle that would hinder recognition of a particularly identifiable expression, it was like a new person was emerging to sit with us in our circle, a person familiar and warm with remembered friendship. His hands were slow, careful, and pleasing to watch.

His resonant, calm voice filled the room. "Yes, I knew Rutherford. Lane, your father and I had a . . . business relationship. One that turned into a friendship. Of sorts."

Mr. Kirkland emitted a soft, "Grrr."

"Hey, that's my line," I said quietly, encouraging him with a sympathetic smile.

Mr. Hambro continued, "Back in the Twenties, after the war and after he and Charlotte moved to Michigan, a few of those red envelopes turned up. I hadn't known about the Red Scroll group, but I had heard rumors of a gang rising in the ranks here in New York. I got an envelope from Rex offering to make a business alliance. I don't mind saying that scared the shit out of me. Er . . . sorry again." Evelyn rolled her eyes. "Anyway, I didn't know what to do. It seemed like every way I turned there was another corrupt official. I had hardly been sleeping at all for days on end, there just wasn't anyone I could trust. Then one day I had an appointment at the bank, someone who asked for a personal conference with me. It was your father, Lane, Matthew Lorian.

"I was unsure of him at first, but then I began to trust him as we talked. He had a hardness about him that showed he was quite a *capable* man, but he was also kind. I've been bamboozled before, but I would have bet everything I had that I could trust him. He told me that there had been a few red envelopes handed out to leading businessmen around the city. I couldn't believe he knew what was going on and that he'd found out about my envelope. But it was such a relief to be able to talk to somebody about it."

He paused to take another drink and consider his next words. I looked at the small ball of detritus left from his disguise, hardly bigger than a walnut. Hard to imagine that something so small could transform someone, making them unrecognizable. Well, almost.

"So, at first Matthew wouldn't tell me who else had received an envelope, but that there were a couple of others. I told him everything I could, which wasn't much. After a few days, he contacted me again and three people who received envelopes had a meeting. One of them was Rutherford."

"But he was Rex's son!" exclaimed an indignant Evelyn.

Mr. Hambro nodded solemnly. "I know. Rutherford ended up telling us everything he could. Apparently, he had turned out to be something quite opposite to his father. And his father detested it, felt that it was a shameful weakness that his son wasn't as, ah . . . *dedicated* to the cause as himself."

Finn piped in, "Miles had heard the same thing."

Mr. Kirkland spoke up, "But how did he and Matthew come into contact?"

"Matthew said that Rutherford had started up an anonymous correspondence with him, looking for someone to help him. To hide him, actually. He'd heard about Matthew from Rex, his fight in destroying the ring of thefts in the war. Rutherford turned to Matthew in utter desperation figuring that Rex's enemy was probably *his* friend. Rex had actually sent Rutherford, his son, a red envelope telling him he'd better pick a side. He and Matthew kept their friendship on the lowdown, but Rutherford gave Matthew what information he could about Rex."

Mr. Kirkland leaned forward with his elbows on his knees, hands clasped. "Matthew had told me about an informant; I wondered who it could have been. It had to be Rutherford. That information is what helped us nab Rex. We had no luck whatsoever until then."

"Yes. In fact, Matthew is the one who picked up Rutherford's entire family in the middle of the night and moved them away, out of the clutches of Rex. I hadn't realized that they moved to the same town as you and your parents, Lane. Maybe Matthew thought it was easier to keep his eye on things that way."

"Maybe," I said, reaching out to hold Finn's hand. I couldn't believe my dad was the one who had helped Tucker and Eliza's family in that way. My mind was quickly ticking away the questions I had and the corresponding answers we had just received. And a thought struck me. "But wait, you haven't told us the third person who received a red envelope. Who was it?"

At this question Hambro look flustered. He hemmed and hawed, "Well . . . Ah, that is to say . . ."

"Oh dear," said Aunt Evelyn.

"Louie Venetti. Uncle Louie also got a red envelope. And, uh . . . Well . . . He and Matthew and I worked together on a . . . solution."

CHAPTER 65

"Damn," I said, in appreciation. "So, Venetti was threatened by Rex, too?" I asked.

Hambro nodded. "Yes. It seemed that Rex's ego knew no bounds. He'd been top dog in the war, now he wanted to be top dog in the States. To do that, you have to take out the competition."

Thinking of that picture of my mom and dad outside the Central Park casino with Uncle Louie in their party, I asked, "So how did my parents become involved with Venetti?"

I was ready for it, so I caught the look that went between Kirkland and Evelyn. I pounced, "So what do *you two* know about that?"

"Well, Lane," Mr. Kirkland rasped, "I didn't know about this meeting that was happening with Rutherford, Hambro, Venetti, and your father, discussing the red envelopes. I'm not sure why he kept that quiet. But right before we nabbed Rex, Venetti, ah, well, he helped us, too. A bit."

"What?" I exclaimed. "You're buddy-buddy with Venetti and you never told me?"

"Oh, don't get me wrong," he said in all seriousness. "We were never friendly. It was like using the tiger to ward off the wolf. Either one might bite your hand off—or worse—but was a necessary evil."

"What exactly did he help you with?" asked Finn.

"He gave us information about Rex. With his information and what I take to be Rutherford's, we found Rex before he could find us," said Mr. Kirkland. "You know, Louie's bottom line has always been about business, just like you surmised, Lane. And believe me, Rex was a threat to his business."

I thought about that for a second, then asked Hambro, "So why did you get together with Venetti again after all this time? You surely have many more people you could have turned to . . . ?"

"Oh, I didn't turn to him. He showed up on my doorstep. It was a nonnegotiable," said Mr. Hambro with his eyebrows raised expressively high.

I kept going, "And if Rex is dead, who sent the envelopes this time and why?"

Aunt Evelyn took a turn. "Oh, that's obvious. It could only be one of two people. Tucker or Donagan."

Finn chimed in, "And I'm certain it was to try to force out the pawn. Both of them have been after it. I guess one of them thought that he could use the old scare tactics. They were trying to raise the Red Scroll gang from the dead anyway, why not use what worked in the past?"

Mr. Kirkland said, "I think Donagan sent the envelopes; Tucker's approach was through, uh, Lane. The question is, now that Donagan has the pawn, what will he do with it?"

"Oh, that's easy," said Mr. Hambro. "Rex was a son of a bitch— sorry again—"

"Stop saying that," Evelyn snapped.

He quickly continued, "Rex didn't leave one single penny to Rutherford. He completely disowned him. Rutherford was originally the rightful heir to not only Rex's money, but his legacy; and no one knows who got it. If my knowledge of Rex is correct, he wouldn't make it easy to collect. Remember, he loved to play games, to toy with people. The heir *he selected* would have to demonstrate loyalty and some kind of concrete evidence that the inheritance belonged to him, thus the gold pawn."

"And that must be who was behind Marty's murder," said Finn. "What happened that night?"

"God, I still can't believe that happened," said Mr. Hambro, shaking his head. "I kept in touch with a very discreet employee of mine, who helps me with cases that need a delicate touch. I wanted to see what was going on in the bank during my absence. He told me about Marty and I got very concerned when I heard that he'd started asking a lot of questions. The people at the bank were not a problem, but when he started looking around outside the bank, I figure Donagan's gang got word of it. I set up a meeting with Marty to fill him in on everything. I wanted to tell him to stop digging around, that I was on it. We met up at Union Square when suddenly a man caught us off guard from behind. I stood up and he had a gun, so I put up my hands. Before I knew what happened, he switched hands with his gun, and grabbed my own knife. My coat was open, so he could have easily seen the handle. It happened so fast, it was definitely a professional, not just a robbery. Marty didn't even get a chance to turn around when the guy suddenly stabbed me in the shoulder, then stabbed Marty in the back and ran off. I tried to help him, but he must've hit his heart, because Marty was already gone."

Fio put a hand on his friend's shoulder. "I'm so sorry, Ted."

"I feel so bad. I already set up a trust for his parents. He wasn't married, but he had a sister. I'll make sure they're taken care of."

Finn said, "Can you identify the killer?"

"Definitely. Give me a lineup or some mug shots. Has to be one of Donagan's crew, this seems like his work. He's much sloppier than Rex. Grasping at straws and running all over trying several ideas at once. Rex was patient, methodical; he'd never try something so slipshod."

"Good. Because we got prints off your knife that weren't yours. We should be able to clear this up pretty fast."

As I pondered about all this, I caught a glimpse of the Christmas tree in the parlor, the glittering shine that spoke of childlike pleasures and colorful joy. Such a good feeling strangely mixed in with our discussion of secrets, murder, and betrayal. Finn's hand stroked the back my head with lingering fingertips on my cheek.

Fio said, "Well, Hambro, I think you deserve a night off. But, my friend, you have one last job to perform before you can fully put your disguises away."

Hambro nodded. "Oh yes. That's for sure. I need to follow Donagan while I'm still invisible. Find out his next move."

Everyone started to slowly get up and took their cups and dishes to the kitchen counter, finishing up our evening. I stayed put, my eyes mesmerized by the fire in the fireplace. Thinking about the revealed information, putting the people and their motivations together, and taking them apart like a puzzle.

A grim thought stole into my mind like a slithering serpent. In the midst of finishing the current mystery, an old one had been pushed to the background. And it was like an icy drip of water splashing onto my unsuspecting head. Who called for the hit on my parents? And *who* executed it? It could be this heir we were talking about, but there was no evidence that pointed to a specific person. Not yet. But it had to be one of them. Venetti, although his relationship with my parents made that a little less likely, but not impossible. Or Donagan. Or Tucker.

I wondered if I'd ever really know.

After everyone left, I slowly went up the stairs to my bedroom, weary and ready for bed. My mind mulled over the possibilities of the weeks ahead. I found my fingers itching to play the piano, an unaccustomed feeling. It took me right back to my house in Rochester.

I walked into my soft blue room and put on a lamp, casting golden light all around. As I washed my face, brushed my teeth, and put on my pajamas, I thought about Donagan and his next move, Finn and our close call tonight, Morgan and her band of Lost Boys. I stroked the white comforter as I sat down on the edge of the bed, and the other hand gingerly felt the bandages on my side, which were beginning to itch.

I thought about seeing who I thought was Finn in the window of that house, about to be torn to shreds from that lethal machine gun. I looked over to the other side of my bed, at the slim volume on my nightstand. The one whose words I now knew by heart. I got up and slowly walked around the foot of my bed to the other side. I picked up the beautiful book and outlined the embossed swirls with my fingertip.

No. There was no longer any pull. No hold left. I smiled to myself, patted the book, walked over to my bookshelves, and put it away.

CHAPTER 66

"I became, in my own person, a creature eaten up and emptied by fever, languidly weak both in body and mind, and solely occupied by one thought: the horror of my other self."

Tucker tried to roll over, in utter agony of mind and body. They had somehow made it back to a hideout of Eliza's. The bloody journey was a blur to him; only the raw, deep pain was etched into his mind. He was told that he might not make it. Several bullets had penetrated his body and he'd lost a tremendous amount of blood. Yet he somehow knew he'd survive. There was more to do. Much more.

With a shaking hand, he stroked the cover of the slender blue volume that he'd asked Eliza to put at his side. There was a strong, magnetic pull from it and it scared him. Nothing scared him . . . except this book. Except those words. Those words that had sprung out at him as he opened the book on Lane's nightstand—the one thing bigger than death, more terrifying than pain. He had to figure it out. He'd sought out the same edition at several bookstores and at last finally found it. The same beautiful, but disturbing copy.

He loathed those lines that leaped out and burned him. They revealed to him something more potent than anything or anyone he'd ever faced. But those words were also the key to his survival. They became his bible. He carefully slipped the volume under his pillow, to safely hoard it and keep it close, keep it secret.

He came to a decision. He needed to do it. An action that would counteract the power this revelation had over him. Maybe. A last-ditch effort, a desperate move. With a trembling hand propelled forward by sheer will, he painfully took up the pen and scribbled the note. A note that would change everything.

The crunchy white snow, the red bows on the lampposts, and the fairy lights that hung here and there were a strange contrast to his thoughts. Donagan sneered at those who enjoyed such things, his own childhood devoid of such simple pleasures. He prided himself on this utter dismissal of holidays, wearing a sort of badge of honor, as it were, that he didn't need them, barely recognizing the time of year as any different from any other day.

Donagan took a quick look at the swarthy face walking along next to him. The man walked along with nothing but his suit coat for winter covering, impervious to the harsh wind and cold. He expected he had either an inner fire that warded off the winter or, perhaps, was simply cold-blooded.

"The rendezvous is just up ahead," he said, nodding to the large banklike structure a couple of blocks away.

His subordinate nodded in understanding. After a few more paces, he said to Donagan, "So you got the pawn?"

"Yes."

"Your strategy worked well."

"Yes, it did," said Donagan, smiling. "I got what I wanted. Rex's legacy is mine. I want the power, but I'll handle it my way. All his games and shenanigans, wheeling and dealing with red envelopes, gold pawns . . . It's tiresome. Childish. I couldn't care less how the diabolical maniac fucked around with his empire. I just want the empire. And it's finally *mine*," he said as his fist clamped ferociously around the gold pawn.

His comrade grunted his approval. He wasn't made for all these complicated games, either.

Fueled by his passion and the last hoop to go through within sight, Donagan said, "Rex was so high and mighty. Thought he was God. Honestly, *how* did he have time to do all that crap? For me, it's about money and power. No games. I find a good deal? I'm in, I'm out. Done." He snapped his fingers, the sound surprisingly loud as it ricocheted off the wet sidewalks and stone buildings. "It was hard enough working out the delivery of those damned red envelopes and then carrying out the deception on Eliza and Tucker. Can you imagine running your whole life like that?"

His partner shook his head in full agreement. They had both been astounded at the amount of thought and precision that was needed to pull off those events. It irked Donagan to no end that he didn't get a little more collateral damage with the car bomb. It was a Hail Mary, but he'd still hoped to kill at least one of those bastards. But at least he hit his mark. Now Tucker was out of the way and Eliza realized she was the pawn she'd always been to him, or she was dead.

With their heated discussion and heady thoughts running through their minds, they didn't notice the shadowy figure trailing along behind them.

The two men came to the ancient-looking marble building that was grand yet blended into its surroundings, making it strangely invisible. They were far downtown toward the oldest part of the city. The docks were nearby, obvious from the scent of brackish water and the dampness in the air. A freezing winter fog rolled in from the river.

They walked in the door of the impressive establishment, the golden opulence of the plush interior feeling that much more extravagant in comparison to the dank weather. They were immediately greeted by two large, somber gentlemen. They took Donagan's coat without a word, then ushered them into a room off to the side. In any other place the colors of the room would be inviting with dark woods and deep blues, but somehow there was a lack of actual warmth. Without a single piece of personal detail, not one picture frame or throw pillow, with sharp corners to all the furniture, the atmosphere spoke of cool dealings, raw business, and a conspicuous lack of humanity.

Donagan took it all in, desiring to emulate the feel of the place in the design of his future domain. His mind was reeling with the potential of what he could do. How he would become the next Rex Ruby. A better one. A more powerful and brutal leader who wouldn't get caught up in juvenile games. He licked his lips in anticipation.

A tall, bald man with cold, all-seeing eyes came into the room. He quickly and professionally shook hands with both men. He stood straighter than a pool cue. "I'll need your identification and your authentication from Mr. Ruby."

Donagan took out his passport, handed it to the man, and then looked one last time at the shining gold pawn in his hand, warm from his own grasp. It had become such a part of him these last days, never letting it out of his sight. He brought it to his lips, pressing it to them and smiling at the gentleman.

"Here you go." He placed the pawn into the man's outstretched palm. The man took it and held it up close to his eye. He took out a jeweler's loupe and scrutinized it for a full two minutes, which felt like an hour to Donagan.

"Yes. It's authentic, Mr. Connell."

Donagan smirked in acknowledgment, feeling a flush of pleasure.

The bald man said, "I will go get what Mr. Rex Ruby has left to you. I shall return." He turned on his heel and left the room, closing the double doors behind him.

Donagan took a stroll about the room, taking in its expensive furnishings, dreaming of his own palatial residence that he'd build, a symbol to everyone of his prominence. His partner took a chair and sat, still as a statue and with just as much emotion.

The man came back in and handed to Donagan, with the utmost care, a thin black briefcase.

"Here you are. Good day, Mr. Connell. You may use this room as long as you like. Our business has concluded with you. When you're finished, my associates will show you out," he said as he nodded to the two large gentlemen now standing in the doorway that led to the lobby.

Donagan smiled and replied, "Thank you. Perhaps we'll be seeing more of each other."

The bald man pressed his lips together and nodded curtly in return. Once again, he turned on his heels with military precision and exited the room.

Donagan looked at the black case, closed for years, its sole purpose for this very moment, to be opened by the new master. He walked carefully to the desk and placed it gingerly on top. His fingers gripped the outside of the case, his thumbs stroking the buttons that would unclasp the locks and his destiny. He pressed the mechanisms and with a satisfying *click*, the locks unfastened. He slowly opened the case.

From outside, the shadowy figure had crept as close to the doors as possible without giving himself away. Even from a distance, it was a serious place, not one to take for granted. A cold building that took on its own formidable air, as if what happened inside seeped into the very walls. Hambro was careful to keep his distance.

He watched Donagan and his partner enter the establishment, overhearing a smattering of words here and there. Enough to know that he was finally going to make a move with that pawn. And from the arrogant remarks he overheard, Donagan seemed certain he was about to retrieve Rex's fortune. This, he thought darkly, was the beginning of something terrible. Then he moved into the recesses of a niche in the wall, listened intently, and waited.

Just as his feet felt like they might freeze in place, after countless times of stretching and flexing his legs to keep the circulation going, he heard from within the building a horrible scream of anguish. He shrunk down deeper into the shadows, bracing himself for whatever happened next.

The door burst open and Donagan erupted from within, stumbling from the assistance that came in the form of two huge men, pushing him out. Another man came out, that partner of his, strangely steady in comparison to Donagan. His only movement was pulling his hat down farther onto his head, a little over his eyes. He didn't so much as nod in Donagan's direction, just walked off, disappearing into the darkness of the night. Donagan seemed oblivious, trapped in some kind of loathsome world of his own. One hand was plastered to his forehead in shock or disbelief, the other loosely clasping a piece of paper. He started to stumble off in the opposite direction of the other man, the piece of paper fluttering to the icy ground, left behind.

After he got far enough away, Hambro, still in the deep shadows, slowly emerged and picked up the lost piece of paper, one corner of it already iced to the frosty ground.

We are either kings or pawns of men.

Hambro took the paper, stowed it in his inner coat pocket, and quickly slipped away.

CHAPTER 67

The next night Finn and I walked hand in hand as I appreciated the glowing buildings overhead, their golden eyes peering down at us and out at the world around. The lone star that was bright enough to shine despite New York City's brilliance was out, as well as the pure white, almost full moon, lighting the streets for us. I looked at Finn, catching his eye, and smiled. He nodded up ahead to our friends we were following.

Fio was practically running alongside Hambro, who had just delivered the news to us of Donagan attempting to retrieve the fortune a mere hour before. Rex had the last word apparently, even from the grave. Delight in Donagan's mortification made me rather cheery inside. But I knew Rex would leave nothing to chance; just *who* was the heir, then?

Reading my thoughts, Finn interjected, "Maybe there never was an heir. Maybe he wanted his legacy to die with him, no one benefiting from his work."

"It would make sense. It seems like he'd rather his followers play hide 'n' seek the rest of their lives. Like Captain Flint in *Treasure Island*. A kind of torture, really."

Before we could delve into more theories, we arrived. As we came up the walk, the front door was flung open, the yellow light from within bursting out upon us like a lighthouse in the midst of the Atlantic. A blur of white and tan came running out and leaped into Hambro's waiting arms. The reunion of the Hambros was something I would long remember. Their obvious delight and joy in being together again was palpable. Fio was bouncing on his toes, smiling ear to ear.

Mrs. Hambrow squeaked, "The chestnuts?" Hambro just nodded, unable to speak as he embraced her.

Finn's arms came around me from behind and the three of us watched and then were suddenly folded into the hug as well. Mrs. Hambro and Fio were wiping their eyes as we all went into their home for a hot coffee and a little chat.

We sat in that inviting soft room of cream and rose with all the luscious textures. The strain that had been in Hambro's eyes and around his mouth loosened and he smiled his old smile. We all sat in a circle and then the door to the parlor opened again. It was Robbins, the butler.

"Hello, Robbins," said Mr. Hambro.

"Hello, sir," Robbins replied.

I was waiting for more . . . something. Something more. Anything. My eyes darted back and forth in confusion from the dignified stare of Robbins to the amused smirk of Mr. Hambro.

I blurted out, "Well? Is that all you got?"

Robbins took a deep breath in, and as he exhaled, his shoulders relaxed a fraction of an inch. A tiny speck of a movement from the left side of his mouth caught my eye. "Good to have you home, sir. I'll go get you something to eat." And he left the room.

"Oh, for cryin' out loud," I muttered.

Mr. Hambro laughed. "Not a fan of the British stiff upper lip, Lane?"

"No, not really," I replied.

Fio said, "Well, Lane, for Robbins, that ah, *smile* was an extravagant display of affection."

"Indeed it was, Fio," said Hambro. "So, Lane, we never discussed it, what made you realize I was the vendor? Well actually, *vendors*. I thought my disguises were quite thorough," he asked, amusement lining his affable face. But I could tell he was also a touch disgruntled that I had seen through his ruse.

"Well, I have to admit it took me quite a while. Mrs. Hambro, when Roarke and I came back to see you, your peaceful demeanor made me think a little differently about it all. I'm good at thinking creatively, but this was *ridiculously* imaginative. And I was fascinated by those photographs of you both in your back office. There was something about them that I kept going back to but I couldn't put my finger on it for a long time.

"Then one day it hit me. In all of the photographs, you, Mrs. Hambro, looked the same even after many years. But you, Mr. Hambro, you had different hats, different hairstyles, facial hair, even your clothes changed styles easily. Seeing them all in one place on the wall made me see your face in different lights and circumstances. Your face became familiar in a new way. When Finn and I had lunch with his contact Miles, I started thinking of how he had disguised himself as a millionaire. For some odd reason, all at once I thought of you, and I started to put together the faces of the vendor out here in Gramercy Park and the vendor outside City Hall."

"And those were just the ones you remember . . ." said Mr. Hambro provocatively.

"There were *more?*" I exclaimed.

Finn added, "The delivery man that warned us we were being followed in Bryant Park . . ."

Fio said, "I saw you in a policeman's uniform outside City Hall yesterday." Finn's head twisted to him in a flash, clearly wondering how he had managed that. "And you rang up my groceries once as the cashier at the market." That did it, we all began laughing at his outrageous sense of humor as well as his comprehensive talent in disappearing and reappearing.

"How did you learn to do that?" I asked.

"I went to the library. I like to learn," he said simply. "Then I went to a shop downtown that had the supplies I needed."

"Speaking of disappearing," said Fio as he wiped his eyes from mirth. "What do you think will happen to Donagan?"

I looked at Finn, who had considerable experience in figuring out the criminal mind. "What do you think, Finn?" I asked.

"I doubt he'll disappear. He may have been outmaneuvered by Rex, but he's built his own empire. Nothing to sneeze at, that's for sure. And now he has more motivation to become greater than Rex."

I asked, "Well, if he's not it, do you think there really is an heir? Did Rex leave his legacy to someone?"

Fiorello responded, "We can theorize, but it's basically unanswerable. Until we find more evidence, that is . . . Which is a scary thought."

I took a sip of my coffee, wondering what Donagan would do next and how I hoped it wouldn't involve me. I wished there had been a more concrete ending. It was unnerving having him out there still. And what would he do with all the pent-up rage, thwarted from his lost legacy? A shiver ran through me as I thought of that last meeting with him in the factory, what could have happened.

A knock at the front door interrupted my thoughts. After a few seconds of muffled discussion in the hallway, Robbins came in and announced that there was a policeman at the door needing to speak to Mayor La Guardia. All of us looked at one another expectantly. Fio rushed out of the room to the front door.

An hour later, Fio, Finn, and I stood on the cold pavement, the winter fog rolling in from the nearby water. I could hear the dock workers yelling to one another and working even at this late hour. My feet were instantly frozen, standing there immobile, unable to tear my eyes from the sight before me.

I got my closure.

Donagan lay on the ground, dead beyond a doubt from multiple gunshot wounds, his eyes still open and looking beyond us. His blood lay in a pool around him, grotesquely freezing to the ground. Around him, on top of him, and still fluttering in the wind were many hundred-dollar bills. Three remained on his chest, the black blood having seeped into them, gluing them into place. And on top of the bills stood a gleaming, bright gold pawn.

CHAPTER 68

Later that night, I reclined on the chaise longue near the Christmas tree looking up into the sparkling, glittering branches. The pine scent was all around me, the colors and lights making me think of far-off memories and feelings. The house was empty, Evelyn and Kirkland were out for the night. Ripley was over by the front door, waiting.

Eventually, restless, I wandered out to the dark kitchen and lit a couple of candles, wishing for a thunderstorm to keep me company. I put on some music, a deep cello playing soft Christmas jazzy tunes. I took out a bottle of wine and brought down a glass.

There was a knock at the door. *Finally.*

I opened the door to Finn, who'd had to go back to the precinct after we discovered Donagan. Snowflakes danced down from the sky, showing bright white on his dark head.

"Finn. I was waiting for you."

We went into the kitchen and I brought down another wineglass as Finn opened the bottle of dark red cabernet. The cello played its tune, the delicious tension rising between us. I wore a deep green, soft velvet dress from a work party earlier that day.

He poured our wine, we each took a glass of the deep red liquid and took a drink. I put my glass carefully down and went toward him. I raised up on my toes and brought my face toward his neck, his arm pulling me toward him as he brought his head down into the nape of my neck.

After a long, hot kiss, Finn and I sat on the floor in front of the fire talking, laughing, and making plans for Christmas in just a week. I took a good long look at him and suddenly smiled, realizing I hadn't told him something I had discovered.

"Hey, Finn. I had a thought the other day about the clues we found in Rochester. I forgot to tell you. Take a look at this." I got up and retrieved my dagger from a drawer in a small side table. He had a funny look on his face like he was still a little disconcerted at my extensive abilities in wielding that dagger. "Look familiar?"

There was nothing new about it. It was the same glossy, sharp blade. Ebony handle with inlaid mother-of-pearl curves and scrolls. Very beautiful, yet deadly, too.

"Take a look at it from afar," I said. I walked a few paces away from him and held it at a forty-five-degree angle.

"Good Lord, it's the sword from the molding in your father's study. It's the pearl dagger."

"Yes! That's what I think," I said. "I had been scrutinizing it up close, looking at every little curl in the handle. But when you take a step back it's the exact shape of what we thought was a sword carved into the woodwork."

"We'll have to ask Mr. Kirkland exactly where he got it," said Finn.

"It's very intriguing. And I finally looked up *pulchritudo ex cinere*."

"You did? What does it mean?"

"Beauty out of ashes." I held the beautiful dagger in my hand, the interplay of the black ebony mixed with the pearl swirls. Darkness and light. Beauty out of ashes. I wondered just what ashes this came from. It was the same feeling I got every time I gazed at the Chrysler Building. The beauty and the art of Right Now was so yearning and reaching and oh, so poignant. It's because it came out of ashes. Between the end of the war, the awful wounds and so many lost loved ones . . . Then the crash and resulting depression . . . This era was a soul-crushing one, to be sure. But my God, there was an unspeakable beauty that took my breath away.

After more talking and more laughing, it was quite late when another knock came at the door.

"We've really got to get working on our own place. And not tell anyone where it is," I grumbled, rolling my eyes.

"Already working on it, love," said Finn, chuckling to himself.

"Oooh. That sounds interesting."

I quickly opened the door and was surprised to see a messenger standing there. He thrust a note into my hand, saying, "Message for Lane Sanders." He immediately ran down the stairs and off into the night.

"This can't be good," I said, turning back to the parlor. "A message from someone this late at night? And the messenger didn't say anything about who sent it. Just handed it to me and raced off."

"Oh boy," said Finn.

He came to my side as I opened the cream-colored piece of paper, his hand on the small of my back. We both noticed a smudge of what looked like dried blood on the outside of the message, along with my name. We exchanged a glance and I opened the note. I read out loud,

It was on this side that my new power tempted me until I fell into slavery.

I gasped.

Finn asked, "What does that mean?"

"Well . . . That's . . . That's a quote from the book I've been reading, *The Strange Case of Dr. Jekyll and Mr. Hyde.*" I shook my head, baffled. "I'll keep reading."

Lane. It's the only thing I fear. In an effort to keep it from devouring me, here is a piece of information that I know will not exonerate me, nor do I wish it to. But God help me, more than death or pain, I am afraid of this sentiment. Rex set up the assassination on your parents. At the time, I didn't know it was an assassination. I was an arrogant teenager and pleased to get Rex's attention. I wanted to impress him. I thought it was just a scare tactic and I was certainly happy to scare my father. I set up the explosion on the lake. But Rex arranged the hits and I had no idea the whole plan would involve a child—you. I can guess that it was Donagan who had been sent to shoot them. You might still find casings near an old oak tree to the east. He was an excellent sniper, so it was farther away than anyone would think to look. If I'm honest, I'm not sorry I helped kill the Lorians. But I am sorry that they were your parents.

—Tucker

I sat down hard, almost missing the chair. "That's it, then," I gasped. "It was Rex and Donagan. They did it. They killed my parents and Rutherford."

Finn nodded. "Seems to be."

"So, do you think the Red Scroll gang is officially done? Eliza and Tucker have seen the light about Rex and Donagan, Rex has used up all his tricks, and now Donagan is dead. It would have all died with him, right?"

Finn nodded as he contemplated. "We don't know who killed Donagan yet. But it was someone who didn't take the pawn. And someone who didn't need those hundred-dollar bills, which is odd. But one thing we know beyond a doubt: Donagan's done. He's gone." Finn stroked his chin, deep in thought. "But I don't get it. What is this fear that Tucker is talking about? What does that line from *Jekyll and Hyde* mean? What is a fear that is worse than pain or death?"

I blew out a soft exhale and recited that line, *"It was on this side that my new power tempted me until I fell into slavery."* I looked intently at him. "Control. That line is the pivotal point of the whole book. As life plays out, the good and the bad commingling, both making their mark . . . His fear, I think, is losing control, becoming a slave to something uncontrollable. One side conquering the other without the ability to restrain it. You see, Jekyll had to choose. He continued to give in to that dark power that made him a brutal killer, made him Mr. Hyde. Eventually, there came a time when he was no longer able to choose. The choice was gone, because it consumed him. He became a slave to it."

That night as we talked into the small hours of the morning, a great revelation dawned on me. I too had made a choice back in Rochester. But in that choice was something else profound. It wasn't just about finally dealing with my past, it was more than that. I had felt what Tucker was talking about. The lack of control that was half-seductive and half-terrifying. I understood that fear. And I, too, made my choice.

The hair rose upon my neck as I wondered what would it look like for someone who continued to choose that evil? Someone who didn't care if they were utterly controlled by darkness even to the point of becoming enslaved? I had a feeling we would find out.

Well, now. The silver gun and the gold pawn did indeed have a destiny of their own.

So did I. And I'd be damn sure to make it a good one.

EPILOGUE

In a burst of rage fueled by the ultimate betrayal, Donagan shoved his way out of the building into the frigid, damp night. The lights were a blur to him, his seething anger making his vision go red. The small piece of damnable paper slipped from his fingertips, floating along. Donagan turned his head toward the river as he stumbled on a cobblestone, oblivious of his subordinate who crept away into the darkness, nor the shadowy figure who had been tailing them.

He cleared his throat, just barely getting a grip on himself. He shook his head, wishing to clear away the sting of duplicity. He forced himself to just keep walking, stumbling along farther into the deep night. Maybe there was more to this . . . Maybe Rex was sending him on another mission of sorts. It just wasn't possible. It was unthinkable. He had to be the heir! That fortune was *his*.

Out of the deep fog, far up ahead, a hooded form was standing very still. At first, he thought it was a figment of his imagination, but then the form started to walk toward him. Very slowly, almost floating. He staggered slightly as he was still reeling from the shock of what had just happened. But he was still Donagan Connell, for Christ's sake! Men cowered before him. They obeyed him. Yes, he was still king. He could shake this off. He'd worked hard to build up his formidable empire, hadn't he? Yes. He was all right.

The figure walked slowly toward him, probably a prostitute looking for some action. He tugged his hat down over the side of his brow, pulling himself back together. Back in control.

Just as he was about to make a crude comment telling the prostitute that he'd be a more than willing customer, he saw her hand reach into her robes. He grabbed for his gun—a mere second too late. With lightning speed, she shot him in the shoulder, just above his heart. His gun skittered across the stones and pavement. He grabbed at his shoulder in total disbelief. He reeled back, lurching to the side, then fell to the hard, frozen ground. He couldn't move, the blood flowing out of his body, shock moving in fast.

He awkwardly rolled his head to the side, the pain shooting down his shoulder, throbbing and deadly. The hooded figure came over toward him. It stopped only a couple of feet away; he could almost touch the edge of the robe. He looked up at the hood.

White, ghostly hands came up with calculated deliberation, placed them on either side of the hood, and carefully pulled it down, revealing a white-blond mane of hair.

He uttered, "Daphne?"

She walked a step closer and gracefully sunk down to her haunches, like she was going to whisper a secret to him. Her eyes were wide and vacant. She held out her hand, a shiny gold pawn perched there, glistening and solid.

She whispered to him, "You really thought he left it all to *you*? Sorry, but no. *This* is the last of the gold pawns." And to his horror she quoted the very line from the slip of paper in the briefcase that Rex had left to him. The famous quote from Napoleon Bonaparte. "We are either kings or pawns of men, Donagan. And *you* were the final pawn. Now listen. Listen closely, sweetheart." She looked around for a moment, her face lighting up from some strange fire within, then raised the gun so Donagan would get a good look at it. It was shiny, it was silver, it was Rex's gun. The deep red scroll looked even more bloody than usual. She looked closely at that handle, then took a deep breath, her eyes closing for a moment. Then they flashed open, focusing on him. "I showed Rex the ultimate loyalty. From the beginning. *I'm* the heir."

She stood up and grunted a soft, calculated laugh, the echoes eerily bouncing off the nearby buildings. "But I didn't forget you. Here's your share, Donagan." She took out a large wad of hundred-dollar bills and slowly, slowly sprinkled them onto him.

He grasped one bill in his clenched fist, fear and loathing oozing out of him along with his lifeblood. She looked at him, lucid and clear-minded. But then smiled a wicked grin, a weird vestige of insanity. He wondered dimly if she could summon it at will.

He called up the last ounce of strength he had and croaked out his final words, "It *can't* be you!"

She pulled up the hood again, covering her long pale hair. She said in a calm, cold voice, "Yes. It can. And now for you, Donagan. As stupid and worthless as they are, you're going to pay for going after *my children*."

She aimed the silver gun, kissed the air toward him, and pulled the trigger five times.

Daphne cocked her head to one side as she looked closely at his lifeless form. A few of the bills were turning dark red in the moonlight. She took Rex's last remaining pawn, tossed it in the air, and caught it without looking at it. With a flourish, she placed it on the blood-soaked hundred-dollar bills on Donagan's unmoving chest. With a smile, she carefully put the silver gun back into the folds of her cape.

From the shadows, Morgan watched this scene with dread as she had tailed Mr. Hambro and watched him slink off once it became quite clear that Donagan did not collect anything from Rex after all. She had decided to follow Donagan, keeping her watchful eye on that dangerous man. Heir or not, Donagan was a deadly force.

She barely trusted herself to breathe, her lungs aching from the effort. She couldn't believe her eyes. She'd heard of Daphne, supposedly locked away in the lunatic asylum, mother of Tucker and Eliza. She'd been part of Rex's ultimate plan all along. Despite the relief of knowing that Donagan would now be incapable of going after any of her loved ones, a hot tear trickled down her cheek at the brutality of what she just witnessed. And she wondered what this ghastly woman would mean for their future.

Morgan didn't move a muscle, determined to be smart and safe before she ran off. She needed to get with Lane and the whole gang right away. She barely breathed as Daphne stood up, nodded her head in farewell to the dead man, and turned on her heels. With her hands clasped casually behind her back, she slowly entered the fog that almost instantly enveloped her figure. She whistled an eerie tune, making Morgan's stomach clench in fear and disgust. For much longer than she was visible, the lonesome tune echoed off the pavement as she walked back to wherever she came from.

> *"If this were much prolonged, the balance of my nature might be permanently overthrown, the power of voluntary change forfeited . . . I had gone to bed Jekyll, I had awakened Edward Hyde."*

A NOTE FROM THE AUTHOR

This is a work of fiction with real history woven in. None of the character dialogs nor mysteries are real. Of the main characters, only Fiorello was an actual person in history. I included a lot of real history with him, but the storyline with the other characters of the book are entirely fictional.

All the epigraphs were taken from *The Strange Case of Dr. Jekyll and Mr. Hyde* by Robert Louis Stevenson. I've always been enamored of the conceptual idea of Jekyll and Hyde. But I think most of us get our first ideas about it from cartoons like Bugs Bunny where the concept of morphing into another personality—one side good, one not so good—is merely a Halloween caricature of the original work. But one day, I picked up the small tome and was astounded at the depth. And the creepy, edgy nature of it.

Although this is a work of fiction, here are some fun real-life tidbits. Penn Station was not the ugly monstrosity it is today. In fact, when it was torn down in 1963, it had been considered the most beautiful train station in the world. And it was only fifty-three years old when it was demolished—all in the name of progress. It hurts my heart. Bryant Park as described in *The Gold Pawn* is more indicative of what it is today. In 1936, they didn't have the carousel yet nor the restaurants. The park was redesigned in 1933 as part of the Great Depression public works and it received its great lawn and surrounding iron fence. But I wanted to bring in some elements of the magic of the current New York City to help readers experience the city's timelessness. The city has this way of always changing, yet always staying the same.

Fiorello did not have the C3 storm categories, yet it is hilarious how often storm imagery was attributed to him. He did indeed have a Tammany tiger skin in his office and he most certainly "enhanced" his office chairs. He vehemently opposed Hitler before others barely knew his name. And the scene where he is angered about the little guy not being a suitable inspector happened, but the rest of that scene is fictional. Fiorello was indeed at most car accidents, crime scenes, and fires in the city. He was known for being everywhere at once, and often a first responder.

The *Hindenburg* was often traveling back and forth across the Atlantic. I think most of us just think of its infamous crash, but it had been tooling around for quite a while. Miles's journey was reminiscent of a special trip on October 9, 1936, the Millionaire's Flight. The only fictional part of the journey, besides Miles himself, was that in December the dirigible wasn't traveling to the States due to the weather turning toward winter.

The guests at Thanksgiving were Albert Einstein and his wife, Elsa. He did always travel with his violin, Lina, and Mozart was his inspiration. Another notable guest was first known as Leslie Hope. He became known as Bob Hope. He was popular in films and on the radio beginning in 1934. Both Albert and Bob were often in New York at that time. Big Sam is Samuel J. Battle, and he did indeed become the first black officer in the NYPD on June 28, 1911. There had been other black officers in Brooklyn (including his brother-in-law Moses Cobb), before the Brooklyn police joined together with Manhattan as the official NYPD in 1898. But after the union, Battle is noted as the first black officer appointed. He personally stopped a riot in 1935 and he saved the life of a fellow white officer in 1918. In 1926, he became the first black sergeant, in 1935 the first black lieutenant, and in 1941 he was appointed the city's first black parole commissioner by Fiorello La Guardia himself.

Meadow Brook Hall is open to the public. Go take a tour! They have some really great parties, too. It is part of Oakland University, in Rochester Hills, Michigan. The main big house was closed at the beginning of the Depression, but Matilda opened it up again in 1937. The pieces of art mentioned were taken directly from their guidebook and my many tours there. I tried to be true to my own impressions of the place—I love it—and my impressions of both Matilda and her husband, Alfred Wilson. I always admired Matilda and her abilities. The hall *does* have a hidden staircase, game room, ballroom, fountain, and a vault. The other specific places mentioned in Rochester and Detroit were around in the 1930s and I'd like to thank Judy Freeland, Carol Thorson, and Terri Miller for their memories and help with historic Detroit. And the Hilty Dilty cocktail mention! Michigan Central Station (which had the same architectural and engineering firm as New York City's Grand Central, WASA Studio, founded in 1891 as Reed and Stem) is still around and has recently been reclaimed as it had been abandoned for decades. I hope they bring it back to life.

The NYPD detective scene, where they have a "show" of all the arrested felons for the week, was true and taken from Hulbert Footner's absolutely delicious 1937 tour book called *New York: City of Cities*. Annie, the Christmas tree saleswoman from Quebec, is based on a sweet friend who currently does sell the trees annually and I look for her every year. She is indeed from Quebec and wears a cute hat, but *The Gold Pawn* version of her is much sillier. I love them both.

The amazing cars I mention were in fact real. And spectacular! Worth the Google. Especially Tucker's car he gets for his date with Lane. Also, the cranberry red Duesenberg J was indeed *super fast* and it had been created for Mae West. She turned it down. She must've been out of her mind.

Acknowledgments

Thank you to my biggest supporter, my husband, Bryan. You are the kindest man alive. I still can't believe you found me an edition of *Jekyll and Hyde* that was around when Lane was living in New York! You've helped me so much with tech issues and marketing, but most of all, you've helped me enjoy this whole journey. My favorite thing about Lane is that she soaks up life, and wants to take it all in. That's the kind of thing you have inspired in me. I'll love you forever.

Jack and Logan, you're the best kids a mom could ever have. I thank God all the time that I get to be your mom. You inspire me to live life well. You've been a huge help at signings, given me giant hugs of support, did extra chores when I was working late, and you've shown me the biggest support a teenager can show . . . you told your friends about my books. Wow! I'll love you forever, too.

Many, many thanks to my dear friends and family, who are a great source of encouragement and inspiration. You attended signings, put up with the faraway look in my eyes when I was distracted with a scene, encouraged me when I was down, celebrated my wins, shared this dream of mine with me, which made it better than I could have imagined, told your friends about my books, and overall made me feel like the luckiest woman. I truly hope you know, new friends and old, that even the smallest words and gestures have meant the world to me.

Thank you to Joe Karlya who introduced me to his mother, Ann Theresa Higgins. Thank you, Ann, for your wonderful insights and fun stories about winning that medal from Fiorello La Guardia for your most excellent essay on fire prevention.

Thank you to my cousin Jeffrey Claphan, for the fantastic books on the history of Detroit. They were amazing, and so are you.

Thank you to Bruce Miller's alter ego, Miles Havalaar, Nina

Mittman, Eric Spry, and Cindy Hambro for letting me use your names. They were perfection.

Thank you so much, Esi Sogah, my editor extraordinaire, of Kensington Publishing. Your enthusiasm for life and good story-telling is contagious. I've learned so much from you. Many thanks to my Kensington Crew: Lauren Vassallo, Paula Reedy, Carly Sommerstein, and Gary Sunshine. Your excellent work is very appreciated. And to my agent, Jill Grosjean, I hope you caught a few of my Amelia references and that they made you smile. Thank you so much for your hard work and encouragement.

Lastly, thank you to you, dear Reader. Thank you for coming along on the journey with me. I hope that I gave you a glimpse of the beauty, the art, and the indomitable spirit that came out of the difficulties of the 1930s. And that the friends, humor, love, and cocktails of *The Gold Pawn* will have increased your own delight in life.

Selected Bibliography

Abbott, Berenice, and Elizabeth McCausland. *New York in the Thirties*. New York: Dover Publications, 1939.

Brodsky, Alyn. *The Great Mayor*. New York: St. Martin's Press, 2003.

Detroit Free Press. *Detroit Memories*. Detroit: Pediment Publishing, 2017.

Footner, Hulbert. *New York: City of Cities*. Philadelphia: J. B. Lippencott, 1937.

Jackson, Kenneth T. *The Encyclopedia of New York City*. New Haven and London: Yale University Press, 1995.

Jeffers, H. Paul. *The Napoleon of New York*. New York: John Wiley & Sons, Inc., 2002.

Jennings, Peter, and Todd Brewster. *The Century*. New York: Doubleday, 1998.

Long, Meredith, and Madelyn Rzadkowolski. *Images of America: Rochester and Rochester Hills*, South Carolina: Arcadia Publishing, 2011.

Lowe, David Garrard. *Art Deco New York*. New York: Watson-Guptill Publications, a Division of VNU Business Media, Inc., 2004.

Poremba, David Lee. *Detroit: A Motor City History*. Charleston, South Carolina: Arcadia Publishing, 2001.

Stevenson, Robert Louis. *The Strange Case of Dr. Jekyll and Mr. Hyde*. New York: Grosset & Dunlap, 1932.

Stolley, Richard B. *LIFE: Our Century in Pictures*. Boston, New York, London: Bulfinch Press, 1999.

Tauranac, John. *The Empire State Building: The Making of a Landmark*. New York: Scribner, 1995.

Wilson, Matilda Rausch Dodge. *A Place in the Country: Matilda Wilson's Guidebook to Meadow Brook Hall*. Michigan: Oakland University Press, 1998.

THE GOLD PAWN

L. A. Chandlar

ABOUT THIS GUIDE

The suggested questions are included
to enhance your group's reading of
L. A. Chandlar's *The Gold Pawn*.

DISCUSSION QUESTIONS

1. What were your favorite overall themes? Identify and talk about them, then take a look at mine. I have a few in this book. Of course, one of the overall themes is of good and bad commingling in all of us. What do you think about that? Are people all good or all bad? Why or why not? Do you think, like Robert Louis Stevenson, that there is a point of no return, where choice becomes forfeited?

2. My favorite theme of this book, which will overarch into all of the books in this series, is from the Latin phrase that Lane discovers in her father's study: *pulchritudo ex cinere*, "beauty out of ashes." I think it sums up this era and the beauty that I wanted to highlight. What are examples of beauty coming out of ashes in *The Gold Pawn*? There are many!

3. The other theme I enjoyed that stems from the two themes above: choices. What are examples of pivotal choices that were made by the characters? What impact did they have on the story?

4. Had you read *Jekyll and Hyde* before? I didn't want to reveal the title early on because of all my own prejudices I'd had before I actually read the book. From movies like *The League of Extraordinary Gentlemen* and cartoons like Bugs Bunny, we get a more lighthearted and Halloween-y feel than the book merits. It's much darker and grittier than that. What were your thoughts about the choice of that piece of highlighted art for this book?

5. The scene where the limb is cut from Lane's tree actually happened to me, just not with such a nefarious intent. Much of Lane's house is taken from memories of my grandparents' home. The dream Lane has that was almost

real to her, of walking up the stairs and experiencing that home once again, was one that I had, many years after my grandparents were long gone. When I drove by their old home one day, I parked and just walked around the block. I came to their house, and the owners had cut off that limb from the purple maple. It honestly felt like I'd been sucker punched. I couldn't believe it. It was certainly because it had become overgrown and just needed pruning, but I felt like I'd lost a friend. For you, what memories of your own childhood are your favorites? Do you have anything that was iconic for you, like my tree was for me? What place and time would you go back to if you could for just one day?

Connect with  U s

Visit us online at
KensingtonBooks.com
to read more from your favorite authors, see books
by series, view reading group guides, and more.

Join us on social media

for sneak peeks, chances to win books and prize packs,
and to share your thoughts with other readers.

facebook.com/kensingtonpublishing
twitter.com/kensingtonbooks

Tell us what you think!

To share your thoughts, submit a review,
or sign up for our eNewsletters, please visit:
KensingtonBooks.com/TellUs.